The Golden Lily

A *Bloodlines* NOVEL

RICHELLE MEAD

razOr bill

An Imprint of Penguin Group (USA) Inc.

The Golden Lily

RAZORBILL

Published by the Penguin Group
Penguin Young Readers Group
345 Hudson Street, New York, New York 10014, U.S.A.
Penguin Group (USA) Inc., 375 Hudson Street, New York, New York 10014,
U.S.A.
Penguin Group (Canada), 90 Eglinton Avenue East, Suite 700, Toronto, Ontario,
Canada M4P 2Y3 (a division of Pearson Penguin Canada Inc.)
Penguin Books Ltd, 80 Strand, London WC2R 0RL, England
Penguin Ireland, 25 St Stephen's Green, Dublin 2, Ireland
(a division of Penguin Books Ltd)
Penguin Group (Australia), 250 Camberwell Road, Camberwell, Victoria 3124,
Australia (a division of Pearson Australia Group Pty Ltd)
Penguin Books India Pvt Ltd, 11 Community Centre,
Panchsheel Park, New Delhi – 110 017, India
Penguin Group (NZ), 67 Apollo Drive, Rosedale, Auckland 0632, New Zealand
(a division of Pearson New Zealand Ltd)
Penguin Books (South Africa) (Pty) Ltd, 24 Sturdee Avenue, Rosebank,
Johannesburg 2196, South Africa

Penguin Books Ltd, Registered Offices: 80 Strand, London WC2R 0RL, England

10 9 8 7 6 5 4 3 2 1

Copyright © 2012 Richelle Mead

ISBN 978-1-59514-318-1

Library of Congress Cataloging-in-Publication Data is available

Printed in the United States of America

For my beautiful son,
who was born the day I finished this.

CHAPTER 1

MOST PEOPLE WOULD FIND being led into an underground bunker on a stormy night scary. Not me.

Things I could explain away and define with data didn't frighten me. That was why I kept silently reciting facts to myself as I descended deeper and deeper below street level. The bunker was a relic of the Cold War, built as protection in a time when people thought nuclear missiles were around every corner. On the surface, the building claimed to house an optical supply store. That was a front. Not scary at all. And the storm? Simply a natural phenomenon of atmospheric fronts clashing. And really, if you were going to worry about getting hurt in a storm, then going underground was actually pretty smart.

So, no. This seemingly ominous journey didn't frighten me in the least. Everything was built on reasonable facts and logic. I could deal with that. It was the *rest* of my job I had a problem with.

And really, maybe that was why stormy underground trips

didn't faze me. When you spent most of your days living among vampires and half vampires, ferrying them to get blood, and keeping their existence secret from the rest of the world . . . well, it kind of gave you a unique perspective on life. I'd witnessed bloody vampire battles and seen magical feats that defied every law of physics I knew. My life was a constant struggle to hold back my terror of the unexplainable and try desperately to find a way to explain it.

"Watch your step," my guide told me as we went down yet another flight of concrete stairs. Everything I'd seen so far was concrete—the walls, floor, and ceiling. The gray, rough surface absorbed the fluorescent light that attempted to illuminate our way. It was dreary and cold, eerie in its stillness. The guide seemed to guess my thoughts. "We've made modifications and expansions since this was originally built. You'll see once we reach the main section."

Sure enough. The stairs finally opened up to a corridor with several closed doors lining the sides. The decor was still concrete, but all the doors were modern, with electronic locks displaying either red or green lights. He led me to the second door on the right, one with a green light, and I found myself entering a perfectly normal lounge, like the kind of break room you'd find in any modern office. Green carpet covered the floor, like some wistful attempt at grass, and the walls were a tan that gave the illusion of warmth. A puffy couch and two chairs sat on the opposite side of the room, along with a table scattered with magazines. Best of all, the room had a counter with a sink—and a coffee maker.

"Make yourself at home," my guide told me. I was guessing

he was close to my age, eighteen, but his patchy attempts at growing a beard made him seem younger. "They'll come for you shortly."

My eyes had never left the coffee maker. "Can I make some coffee?"

"Sure," he said. "Whatever you like."

He left, and I practically ran to the counter. The coffee was pre-ground and looked as though it might very well have been here since the Cold War as well. As long as it was caffeinated, I didn't care. I'd taken a red-eye flight from California, and even with part of the day to recover, I still felt sleepy and bleary-eyed. I set the coffee maker going and then paced the room. The magazines were in haphazard piles, so I straightened them into neat stacks. I couldn't stand disorder.

I sat on the couch and waited for the coffee, wondering yet again what this meeting could be about. I'd spent a good part of my afternoon here in Virginia reporting to a couple of Alchemist officials about the status of my current assignment. I was living in Palm Springs, pretending to be a senior at a private boarding school in order to keep an eye on Jill Mastrano Dragomir, a vampire princess forced into hiding. Keeping her alive meant keeping her people out of civil war—something that would definitely tip humans off to the supernatural world that lurked beneath the surface of modern life. It was a vital mission for the Alchemists, so I wasn't entirely surprised they'd want an update. What surprised me was that they couldn't have just done it over the phone. I couldn't figure out what other reason would bring me to this facility.

The coffee maker finished. I'd only set it to make three

cups, which would probably be enough to get me through the evening. I'd just filled my Styrofoam cup when the door opened. A man entered, and I nearly dropped the coffee.

"Mr. Darnell," I said, setting the pot back on the burner. My hands trembled. "It—it's nice to see you again, sir."

"You too, Sydney," he said, forcing a stiff smile. "You've certainly grown up."

"Thank you, sir," I said, unsure if that was a compliment.

Tom Darnell was my father's age and had brown hair laced with silver. There were more lines in his face since the last time I'd seen him, and his blue eyes had an uneasy look that I didn't usually associate with him. Tom Darnell was a high-ranking official among the Alchemists and had earned his position through decisive action and a fierce work ethic. He'd always seemed larger than life when I was younger, fiercely confident and awe-inspiring. Now, he seemed to be afraid of me, which made no sense. Wasn't he angry? After all, I was the one responsible for his son being arrested and locked away by the Alchemists.

"I appreciate you coming all the way out here," he added, once a few moments of awkward silence had passed. "I know it's a long round-trip, especially on a weekend."

"It's no problem at all, sir," I said, hoping I sounded confident. "I'm happy to help with . . . whatever you need." I still wondered what exactly that could be.

He studied me for a few seconds and gave a curt nod. "You're very dedicated," he said. "Just like your father."

I made no response. I knew that comment *had* been intended as a compliment, but I didn't really take it that way.

Tom cleared his throat. "Well, then. Let's get this out of the way. I really don't want to inconvenience you any more than is necessary."

Again, I got that nervous, deferential vibe. Why would he be so conscientious of my feelings? After what I'd done to his son, Keith, I would've expected rage or accusations. Tom opened the door for me and gestured me through.

"Can I bring my coffee, sir?"

"Of course."

He took me back into the concrete corridor, toward more of the closed doors. I clutched my coffee like a security blanket, far more frightened than I'd been when first entering this place. Tom came to a stop a few doors down, in front of one with a red light, but hesitated before opening it.

"I want you to know . . . that what you did was incredibly brave," he said, not meeting my eyes. "I know you and Keith were—are—friends, and it couldn't have been easy to turn him in. It shows just how committed you are to our work— something that's not always easy when personal feelings are involved."

Keith and I weren't friends now or then, but I supposed I could understand Tom's mistake. Keith had lived with my family for a summer, and later, he and I had worked together in Palm Springs. Turning him in for his crimes hadn't been difficult for me at all. I'd actually enjoyed it. Seeing the stricken look on Tom's face, though, I knew I couldn't say anything like that.

I swallowed. "Well. Our work is important, sir."

He gave me a sad smile. "Yes. It certainly is."

The door had a security keypad. Tom punched in a series of about ten digits, and the lock clicked in acceptance. He pushed the door open, and I followed him inside. The stark room was dimly lit and had three other people in it, so I didn't initially notice what else the room contained. I knew immediately that the others were Alchemists. There was no other reason they'd be in this place otherwise. And, of course, they possessed the telltale signs that would have identified them to me even on a busy street. Business attire in nondescript colors. Golden lily tattoos shining on their left cheeks. It was part of the uniformity we all shared. We were a secret army, lurking in the shadows of our fellow humans.

The three of them were all holding clipboards and staring at one of the walls. That was when I noticed what this room's purpose was. A window in the wall looked through to another room, one much more brightly lit than this one.

And Keith Darnell was in that room.

He darted up to the glass separating us and began beating on it. My heart raced, and I took a few frightened steps back, certain he was coming after me. It took me a moment to realize he couldn't actually see me. I relaxed slightly. Very slightly. The window was a one-way mirror. He pressed his hands to the glass, glancing frantically back and forth at the faces he knew were there but couldn't see.

"Please, please," he cried. "Let me out. Please let me out of here."

Keith looked a little scragglier than the last time I'd seen him. His hair was unkempt and appeared as though it hadn't been cut in our month apart. He wore a plain gray jumpsuit, the kind you saw on prisoners or mental patients, that reminded me of the concrete in the hall. Most noticeable of all was the desperate, terrified look in his eyes—or rather, eye. Keith had lost one of his eyes in a vampire attack that I had secretly helped orchestrate. None of the Alchemists knew about it, just as none of them knew about how Keith had raped my older sister Carly. I doubted Tom Darnell would've praised me for my "dedication" if he'd known about my sideline revenge act. Seeing the state Keith was in now, I felt a little bad for him—and especially bad for Tom, whose face was filled with raw pain. I still didn't feel bad about what I'd done to Keith, however. Not the arrest or the eye. Put simply, Keith Darnell was a bad person.

"I'm sure you recognize Keith," said one of the Alchemists with a clipboard. Her gray hair was wound into a tight, neat bun.

"Yes, ma'am," I said.

I was saved from any other response when Keith beat at the glass with renewed fury. "Please! I'm serious! Whatever you want. I'll do anything. I'll say anything. I'll *believe* anything. Just please don't send me back there!"

Both Tom and I flinched, but the other Alchemists watched with clinical detachment and scrawled a few notes on their clipboards. The bun woman glanced back up at me as though there'd been no interruption. "Young Mr. Darnell has been spending some time in one of our Re-education Centers. An unfortunate action—but a necessary one. His trafficking in illicit goods was certainly bad, but his collaboration with vampires is unforgiveable. Although he *claims* to have no attachment to them . . . well, we really can't be certain. Even if he is telling the truth, there's also the possibility that this transgression might expand into something more—not just a collaboration with the Moroi, but also the Strigoi. Doing what we've done keeps him from that slippery slope."

"It's really for his own good," said the third clipboard-wielding Alchemist. "We're doing him a favor."

A sense of horror swept over me. The whole point of the Alchemists was to keep the existence of vampires secret from humans. We believed vampires were unnatural creatures who should have nothing to do with humans like us. What was a particular concern were the Strigoi—evil, killer vampires—who could lure humans into servitude with promises of immortality. Even the peaceful Moroi and their half human counterparts, the dhampirs, were regarded with suspicion. We worked with those latter two groups a lot, and even though we'd been taught to regard them with disdain, it was an inevitable fact that some Alchemists not only grew close to Moroi and dhampirs . . . but actually started to like them.

The crazy thing was—despite his crime of selling vampire blood—Keith was one of the last people I'd think of when it came to getting too friendly with vampires. He'd made his dislike of them perfectly obvious to me a number of times. Really, if anyone deserved to be accused of attachment to vampires . . .

. . . well, it would be me.

One of the other Alchemists, a man with mirrored sunglasses hanging artfully off his collar, took up the lecture. "You, Miss Sage, have been a remarkable example of someone able to work extensively with *them* and keep your objectivity. Your dedication has not gone unnoticed by those above us."

"Thank you, sir," I said uneasily, wondering how many times I'd hear "dedication" brought up tonight. This was a far cry from a few months ago, when I'd gotten in trouble for helping a dhampir fugitive escape. She'd later been proven innocent, and my involvement had been written off as "career ambition."

"And," continued Sunglasses, "considering your experience with Mr. Darnell, we thought you would be an excellent person to give us a statement."

I turned my attention back at Keith. He'd been pounding and shouting pretty much non-stop this whole time. The others had managed to ignore him, so I tried as well.

"A statement on what, sir?"

"We're considering whether or not to return him to Re-education," explained Gray Bun. "He's made excellent progress there, but some feel it's best to be safe and make sure any chance of vampire attachment is eradicated."

If Keith's current behavior was "excellent progress," I couldn't imagine what poor progress looked like.

Sunglasses readied his pen over his clipboard. "Based on what you witnessed in Palm Springs, Miss Sage, what is your opinion of Mr. Darnell's state of mind when it comes to vampires? Was the bonding you witnessed severe enough to warrant further precautionary measures?" Presumably, "further precautionary measures" meant more Re-education.

While Keith continued to bang away, all eyes in my room were on me. The clipboard Alchemists looked thoughtful and curious. Tom Darnell was visibly sweating, watching me with fear and anticipation. I supposed it was understandable. I held his son's fate in my hands.

Conflicting emotions warred within me as I regarded Keith. I didn't just dislike him—I hated him. And I didn't hate many people. I couldn't forget what he'd done to Carly. Likewise, the memories of what he'd done to others and me in Palm Springs were still fresh in my mind. He'd slandered me and made my life miserable in an effort to cover up his blood scam. He'd also horribly treated the vampires and dhampirs we were in charge of looking after. It made me question who the real monsters were.

I didn't know exactly what happened at Re-education Centers. Judging from Keith's reaction, it was probably pretty bad. There was a part of me that would have loved to tell the Alchemists to send him back there for years and never let him see the light of day. His crimes deserved severe punishment—and yet, I wasn't sure they deserved *this* particular punishment.

"I think . . . I think Keith Darnell is corrupt," I said at last. "He's selfish and immoral. He has no concern for others and hurts people to further his own ends. He's willing to lie, cheat, and steal to get what he wants." I hesitated before continuing. "But . . . I don't think he's been blinded to what vampires are. I don't think he's too close to them or in danger of falling in with them in the future. That being said, I also don't think he should be allowed to do Alchemist work for the foreseeable future. Whether that would mean locking him up or just putting him on probation is up to you. His past actions show he doesn't take our missions seriously, but that's because of selfishness. Not because of an unnatural attachment to *them*. He . . . well, to be blunt, is just a bad person."

Silence met me, save for the frantic scrawling of pens as the clipboard Alchemists made their notes. I dared a glance at Tom, afraid of what I'd see after completely trashing his son. To my astonishment, Tom looked . . . relieved. And grateful. In fact, he seemed on the verge of tears. Catching my eye, he mouthed, *Thank you.* Amazing. I had just proclaimed Keith to be a horrible human being in every way possible. But none of that mattered to his father, so long as I didn't accuse Keith of being in league with vampires. I could've called Keith a murderer, and Tom would have probably still been grateful if it meant Keith wasn't chummy with the enemy.

It bothered me and again made me wonder who the real monsters were in all of this. The group I'd left back in Palm Springs was a hundred times more moral than Keith.

"Thank you, Miss Sage," said Gray Bun, finishing up her notes. "You've been extremely helpful, and we'll take this into consideration as we make our decision. You may go now. If you step into the hall, you'll find Zeke waiting to take you out."

It was an abrupt dismissal, but that was typical of Alchemists. Efficient. To the point. I gave a polite nod of farewell and one last glance at Keith before opening the door. As soon as it shut behind me, I found the hallway mercifully silent. I could no longer hear Keith.

Zeke, as it turned out, was the Alchemist who had originally led me in. "All set?" he asked.

"So it seems," I said, still a bit stunned over what had just taken place. I knew now that my earlier debriefing on the Palm Springs situation had simply been a convenience for the Alchemists. I'd been in the area, so why not have an in-person meeting? It hadn't been essential. This—seeing Keith—had been the real purpose of my cross-country trip.

As we walked back down the hallway, something caught my attention that I hadn't noticed before. One of the doors had a fair amount of security on it—more so than the room I'd just been in. Along with the lights and keypad, there was also a card reader. At the top of the door was a deadbolt that locked from outside. Nothing fancy, but it was clearly meant to keep whatever was behind the door inside.

11

I stopped in spite of myself and studied the door for a few moments. Then, I kept walking, knowing better than to say anything. Good Alchemists didn't ask questions.

Zeke, seeing my gaze, came to a halt. He glanced at me, then the door, and then back at me. "Do you want . . . do you want to see what's in there?" His eyes darted quickly to the door we'd emerged from. He was low-ranking, I knew, and clearly feared getting in trouble with the others. At the same time, there was an eagerness that suggested he was excited about the secrets he kept, secrets he couldn't share with others. I was a safe outlet.

"I guess it depends on what's in there," I said.

"It's the reason for what we do," he said mysteriously. "Take a look, and you'll understand why our goals are so important."

Deciding to risk it, he flashed a card over the reader and then punched in another long code. A light on the door turned green, and he slid open the deadbolt. I'd half-expected another dim room, but the light was so bright inside, it almost hurt my eyes. I put a hand up to my forehead to shield myself.

"It's a type of light therapy," Zeke explained apologetically. "You know how people in cloudy regions have sun lamps? Same kind of rays. The hope is that it'll make people like *him* a little more human again—or at least discourage them from thinking they're Strigoi."

At first, I was too dazzled to figure out what he meant. Then, across the empty room, I saw a jail cell. Large metal bars covered the entrance, which was locked with another card reader and keypad. It seemed like overkill when I caught sight of the man inside. He was older than me, mid-twenties if I had to guess, and had a disheveled appearance that made Keith look neat and tidy. The man was gaunt and curled up in a corner, arms draped over his eyes against the light. He wore handcuffs and feet cuffs and clearly wasn't going anywhere. At our entrance, he dared a peek at us and then uncovered more of his face.

A chill ran through me. The man was human, but his expression was as cold and evil as any Strigoi I'd ever seen. His gray eyes were predatory. Emotionless, like the kinds of murderers who had no sense of empathy for other people.

"Have you brought me dinner?" he asked in a raspy voice that had to be faked. "A nice young girl, I see. Skinnier than I'd like, but I'm sure her blood is still succulent."

"Liam," said Zeke with a weary patience. "You know where your dinner is." He pointed to an untouched tray of food in the cell that looked like it had gone cold long ago. Chicken nuggets, green beans, and a sugar cookie. "He almost never eats anything," Zeke explained to me. "It's why he's so thin. Keeps insisting on blood."

"What . . . what *is* he?" I asked, unable to take my eyes off of Liam. It was a silly question, of course. Liam was clearly human, and yet . . . there was something about him that wasn't right.

"A corrupt soul who wants to be Strigoi," said Zeke. "Some guardians found him serving those monsters and delivered him to us. We've tried to rehabilitate him but with no luck. He keeps going on and on about how great the Strigoi are and how he'll get back to them one day and make us pay. In the meantime, he does his best to pretend he's one of them."

"Oh," said Liam, with a sly smile, "I *will* be one of them. They will reward my loyalty and suffering. They will awaken me, and I will become powerful beyond your miniscule mortal dreams. I will live forever and come for you—all of you. I will feast on your blood and savor every drop. You Alchemists pull your strings and think you control everything. You delude yourselves. You control nothing. You *are* nothing."

"See?" said Zeke, shaking his head. "Pathetic. And yet, this is what could happen if we didn't do the job we did. Other humans could become like him—selling their souls for the hollow promise of immortality." He made the Alchemist sign against evil, a small cross on his shoulder, and I found myself echoing it. "I don't like being in here, but sometimes . . . sometimes it's a good reminder of why we have to keep the Moroi and the others in the shadows. Of why we can't let ourselves be taken in by them."

I knew in the back of my mind that there was a huge difference in the way Moroi and Strigoi interacted with humans. Still, I couldn't formulate any arguments while in front of Liam. He had me too dumbstruck—and afraid. It was easy to believe every word the Alchemists said. This was what we were fighting against. This was the nightmare we couldn't allow to happen.

I didn't know what to say, but Zeke didn't seem to expect much.

"Come on. Let's go." To Liam, he added, "And you'd better eat that food because you aren't getting any more until morning. I don't care how cold and hard it is."

Liam's eyes narrowed. "What do I care about human food when soon I'll be drinking the nectar of the gods? Your blood will be warm on my lips, yours and your pretty girl's." He began to laugh then, a sound far more disturbing than any of Keith's screams.

That laughter continued as Zeke led me out of the room.

The door shut behind us, and I found myself standing in the hall, numbed. Zeke regarded me with concern.

"I'm sorry . . . I probably shouldn't have shown you that."

I shook my head slowly. "No . . . you were right. It's good for us to see. To understand what we're doing. I always knew . . . but I didn't expect anything like that."

I tried to shift my thoughts back to everyday things and wipe that horror from my mind. I looked down at my coffee. It was untouched and had grown lukewarm. I grimaced.

"Can I get more coffee before we go?" I needed something normal. Something human.

"Sure."

Zeke led me back to the lounge. The pot I'd made was still hot. I dumped out my old coffee and poured some new. As I did, the door burst open, and a distraught Tom Darnell came in. He seemed surprised to see anyone here and pushed past us, sitting on the couch and burying his face in his hands. Zeke and I exchanged uncertain looks.

"Mr. Darnell," I began. "Are you okay?"

He didn't answer me right away. He kept his face covered, his body shaking with silent sobs. I was about to leave when he looked up at me, though I got the feeling he wasn't actually *seeing* me. "They decided," he said. "They decided about Keith."

"Already?" I asked, startled. Zeke and I had only spent about five minutes with Liam.

Tom nodded morosely. "They're sending him back . . . back to Re-education."

I couldn't believe it. "But I . . . but I told them! I told them he's not in league with vampires. He believes what . . . the rest of us believe. It was his choices that were bad."

"I know. But they said we can't take the risk. Even if Keith seems like he doesn't care about them—even if *believes* he doesn't—the fact remains he still set up a deal with one. They're worried that willingness to go into that kind of partnership might subconsciously influence him. Best to take care of things now. They're . . . they're probably right. This is for the best."

That image of Keith pounding on the glass and begging not to go back flashed through my mind. "I'm sorry, Mr. Darnell."

Tom's distraught gaze focused on me a little bit more. "Don't apologize, Sydney. You've done so much . . . so much for Keith. Because of what you told them, they're going to reduce his time in Re-education. That means so much to me. Thank you."

My stomach twisted. Because of me, Keith had lost an eye. Because of me, Keith had gone to Re-education in the first place. Again, the sentiment came to me: he deserved to suffer in some way, but he didn't deserve *this*.

"They were right about you," Tom added. He was trying to smile but failing. "What a stellar example you are. So dedicated. Your father must be so proud. I don't know how you live with those creatures every day and still keep your head about you. Other Alchemists could learn a lot from you. You understand what responsibility and duty are."

Since I'd flown out of Palm Springs yesterday, I'd actually been thinking a lot about the group I'd left behind—when the Alchemists weren't distracting me with prisoners, of course. Jill, Adrian, Eddie, and even Angeline . . . frustrating at times, but in the end, they were people I'd grown to know and care about. Despite all the running around they made me do, I'd missed that motley group almost the instant I left California. Something inside me seemed empty when they weren't around.

Now, feeling that way confused me. Was I blurring the lines between friendship and duty? If Keith had gotten in trouble for one small association with a vampire, how much worse was I? And how close were any of us to becoming like Liam?

Zeke's words rang inside my head: *We can't let ourselves be taken in by them.*

And what Tom had just said: *You understand what responsibility and duty are.*

He was watching me expectantly, and I managed a smile as I pushed down all my fears. "Thank you, sir," I said. "I do what I can."

CHAPTER 2

I DIDN'T SLEEP THAT NIGHT. Part of it was simply the time change. My flight back to Palm Springs was scheduled for six in the morning—which was three in the morning in the time zone my body still thought it was in. Sleeping seemed pointless.

And, of course, there was the teeny-tiny fact that it was kind of hard to relax after everything I'd witnessed over at the Alchemist bunker. If I wasn't envisioning Liam's freaky eyes, then I was replaying the constant warnings I'd heard about those who got too close to vampires.

It didn't help the situation that I had an inbox full of messages from the gang in Palm Springs. Normally, I checked my e-mail automatically on my phone when I was out and about. Now, in my hotel room, staring at the various messages, I found myself filled with doubt. Were these truly professional? Were they too friendly? Did they blur the lines of Alchemist protocol? After seeing what had happened to Keith, it was more obvious than ever that it didn't take much to get in trouble with my organization.

One message was from Jill, with a subject line reading: *Angeline . . . sigh.* This wasn't a surprise to me, and I didn't bother reading it yet. Angeline Dawes, a dhampir recruited to be Jill's roommate and provide an extra layer of security, had had a little trouble fitting into Amberwood. She was always in trouble for something, and I knew whatever it was this time, there was nothing I could do about it right now.

Another message was from Angeline herself. I also didn't read it. The subject was: READ THIS! SO FUNNY! Angeline had only recently discovered e-mail. She had not, so it seemed, discovered how to turn off the caps-lock key. She also had no discrimination when it came to forwarding jokes, financial scams, or virus warnings. And speaking of that last one . . . we'd had to finally install child protection software on her laptop, in order to block her from certain websites and ads. That had come after she'd accidentally downloaded four viruses.

It was the last e-mail in my inbox that gave me pause. It was from Adrian Ivashkov, the only person in our group who wasn't posing as a student at Amberwood Preparatory School. Adrian was a twenty-one-year-old Moroi, so it would have been kind of a stretch passing him off in high school. Adrian was along because he and Jill had a psychic bond that had been inadvertently created when he'd used his magic to save her life. All Moroi wielded some type of elemental magic, and his was spirit—a mysterious element tied to the mind and healing. The bond allowed Jill to see Adrian's thoughts and emotions, which was troubling to both of them. His staying near her helped them work out some of the bond's kinks. Also, Adrian had nothing better to do.

His message's subject was: SEND HELP IMMEDIATELY. Unlike Angeline, Adrian knew the rules of capitalization and was simply going for dramatic effect. I also knew that if I had any doubts about which of my messages related to my job, this was hands-down the most nonprofessional one in the set. Adrian wasn't my responsibility. Yet, I clicked the message anyway.

Day 24. Situation is growing worse. My captors continue to find new and horrific ways to torture me. When not working, Agent Scarlet spends her days examining fabric swatches for bridesmaid dresses and going on about how in love she is. This usually causes Agent Boring Borscht to regale us with stories of Russian weddings that are even more boring than his usual ones. My attempts at escape have been thwarted thus far. Also, I am out of cigarettes. Any assistance or tobacco products you can send will be greatly appreciated.

—Prisoner 24601

I began smiling in spite of myself. Adrian sent me some kind of message like this nearly every day. This summer, we had learned that those who were forcibly turned Strigoi could be turned back with the use of spirit. It was still a tricky, complicated process . . . made more so by the fact that there were so few spirit users. Even more recent events had suggested that those restored from being Strigoi could never be turned again. That had electrified Alchemists and Moroi alike. If there was some magical way to prevent Strigoi conversion, freaks like Liam would no longer be a problem.

That was where Sonya Karp and Dimitri Belikov came in—or, as Adrian called them in his angst-filled letters, "Agent

Scarlet" and "Agent Boring Borscht." Sonya was a Moroi; Dimitri was a dhampir. Both had once been Strigoi and had been saved by spirit magic. The two of them had come to Palm Springs last month to work with Adrian in a sort of think tank to figure out what might protect against Strigoi turning. It was an extremely important task, one that could have huge ramifications if successful. Sonya and Dimitri were some of the hardest working people I knew—which didn't always mesh with Adrian's style.

A lot of their work involved slow, painstaking experiments— many involving Eddie Castile, a dhampir who was also under-cover at Amberwood. He was serving as the control subject since, unlike Dimitri, Eddie was a dhampir untouched by spirit or a Strigoi history. There wasn't much I could do to help Adrian with his frustration over his research group—and he knew it. He just liked playing up the drama and venting to me. Mindful of what was essential and nonessential in the Alchemist world, I was on the verge of deleting the message, but . . .

One thing made me hesitate. Adrian had signed his e-mail with a reference to Victor Hugo's *Les Misérables*. It was a book about the French Revolution that was so thick, it could easily double as a weapon. I had read it in both French and English. Considering Adrian had once gotten bored while reading a par-ticularly long menu, I had a hard time imagining he'd read the Hugo book in any language. So how did he know the reference? *It doesn't matter, Sydney*, a stern Alchemist voice said inside my head. *Delete it. It's irrelevant. Adrian's literary knowledge (or lack thereof) is no concern of yours.*

But I couldn't do it. I *had* to know. This was the kind of detail that would drive me crazy. I wrote back with a quick message: *How do you know about 24601? I refuse to believe you read the book. You saw the musical, right?*

I hit send and received a response back from him almost immediately: *SparkNotes.*

Typical. I laughed out loud and immediately felt guilty. I shouldn't have responded. This was my personal e-mail account, but if the Alchemists ever felt the need to investigate me, they'd have no qualms about accessing it. This kind of thing was damning, and I deleted the e-mail exchange—not that it mattered. No data was ever truly lost.

By the time I landed in Palm Springs at seven the next morning, it was painfully obvious that I had surpassed my body's limits to subsist on caffeine. I was too exhausted. No amount of coffee would help anymore. I nearly fell asleep at the airport's curb, waiting for my ride. When it arrived, I didn't notice until I heard my name called.

Dimitri Belikov jumped out of a blue rental car and strode toward me, grabbing hold of my suitcase before I could utter a word. A few nearby women stopped talking to stare at him admiringly. I got to my feet. "You don't have to do that," I said, even though he was already loading my suitcase into the trunk.

"Of course I do," he said, his words lightly touched with a Russian accent. He gave me a small smile. "You looked like you were asleep."

"I should be so lucky," I said, getting into the passenger side. Even if I'd been wide awake, I knew Dimitri would've taken my suitcase anyway. That's how he was, a lost remnant of chivalry in the modern world, ever-ready to help others.

That was only one of the many striking things about Dimitri. His looks alone were certainly enough to make many halt in their tracks. He had dark brown hair pulled back into a short ponytail, with matching brown eyes that seemed mysterious and alluring. He was tall, too—about 6'7"—rivaling some Moroi. Dhampirs were indistinguishable from humans to me, so even I could admit that he scored pretty high on the attractiveness scale.

There was also an energy around him that you couldn't help but be affected by. He was always on alert, always ready for the unexpected. I'd never seen his guard down. He was constantly ready to strike. He was dangerous, no question, and I was comforted that he was on our side. I always felt safe around him—and a little wary.

"Thanks for the ride," I added. "I could've called a taxi." Even as I spoke, I knew my words were as useless as when I'd told him he didn't need to help me with my bag.

"It's no problem," he assured me, driving toward suburban Palm Springs. He wiped sweat off his brow and somehow made that look attractive. Even this early in the morning, the heat was beginning to build. "Sonya insisted. Besides, no experiments today."

I frowned at that. Those experiments and the amazing potential they represented to prevent the creation of more Strigoi were vastly important. Dimitri and Sonya knew that and were dedicated to the cause—especially on weekends, when Adrian and Eddie didn't have classes—which made this news so puzzling. My own work ethic had a hard time understanding why there'd be no research happening on a Sunday.

"Adrian?" I guessed. Maybe he wasn't "in the mood" for research today.

"Partially," said Dimitri. "We're also missing our control subject. Eddie said he had some conflict and couldn't make it."

My frown deepened. "What conflict could Eddie have?"

Eddie was intensely dedicated too. Adrian sometimes called him mini-Dimitri. Although Eddie was going to high school and completing assignments just like me, I knew he'd drop any homework in an instant to help out with the greater good. I could think of only one thing that would take precedence over helping find a "cure" for being Strigoi. My heart suddenly raced.

"Is Jill okay?" She had to be. Someone would have told me, right? Eddie's main purpose in Palm Springs—and mine—was to keep her safe. If she was in danger, it would trump everything else.

"She's fine," said Dimitri. "I talked to her this morning. I'm not sure what's going on, but Eddie wouldn't be away without good reason."

"I suppose not," I murmured, still concerned.

"You worry as much as me," teased Dimitri. "I didn't think that was possible."

"It's my job to worry. I always have to make sure everyone's okay."

"Sometimes it's not a bad thing to make sure you're okay too. You might find it actually helps others."

I scoffed. "Rose always joked about your 'Zen Master Wisdom.' Am I getting a taste of it? If so, I can see why she was helpless against your charms."

This earned me one of Dimitri's rare, genuine laughs. "I think so. If you ask her, she'll claim it was the staking and decapitation. But I'm sure it was the Zen wisdom that won her in the end."

My answering smile immediately melted into a yawn. It was amazing that I could joke with a dhampir. I used to have panic attacks being in the same room with them or Moroi. Slowly, over the last six months, my anxiety had begun to ease up. I'd never shake the feeling of "otherness" I got from all of them, but I'd come a long way. Part of me knew it was a good thing that I still drew that line between them and humans, but it was also good to be flexible in order to make my job smoother. *Not too flexible,* that inner Alchemist voice warned.

"Here we are," said Dimitri, pulling up in front of my dorm at Amberwood Prep. If he'd noticed my shift in mood, he didn't say so. "You should get some rest."

"I'll try," I said. "But I need to find out what's going on with Eddie first."

Dimitri's face turned all-business. "If you can find him, you should bring him over tonight, and we can see about getting a little work done. Sonya would love it. She has some new ideas."

I nodded, reminding myself that that was the kind of standard we needed to adhere to. Work, work, work. We had to remember our higher goals. "I'll see what I can do."

I thanked him again and then headed inside, filled with resolve to carry out my mission. So, it was a bit disappointing when my lofty goals were shattered so quickly.

"Miss Melrose?"

I turned immediately at the sound of the last name I'd assumed here at Amberwood. Mrs. Weathers, our plump, elderly dorm matron, was hurrying over to me. Her face was lined with worry, which couldn't bode well.

"I'm so glad you're back," she said. "I trust you had a good family visit?"

"Yes, ma'am." If by "good," she meant "terrifying and unsettling."

Mrs. Weathers beckoned me over to her desk. "I need to talk to you about your cousin."

I held back a grimace as I recalled Jill's e-mail. Cousin Angeline. All of us attending Amberwood were doing so under fake family connections. Jill and Eddie were my siblings. Angeline was our cousin. It helped explain why we were always together and getting involved with each other's business.

I sat down with Mrs. Weathers and thought longingly of my bed. "What's happened?" I asked.

Mrs. Weathers sighed. "Your cousin is having trouble with our dress code."

That was a surprise. "But we have uniforms, ma'am."

"Of course," she said. "But not outside of classes."

That was true. I was in khaki dress pants and a green short-sleeved blouse, along with a small gold cross I always wore. I did a mental rundown of Angeline's wardrobe, trying to recall if I'd ever seen anything concerning about it. Probably the most appalling part was its quality. Angeline had come from the Keepers, a mixed community of humans, Moroi, and dhampirs who lived in the Appalachian Mountains. Along with a lack of electricity and plumbing, the Keepers chose to make a lot of their clothing or at least wear it into threads.

"Friday night, I saw her wearing the most appallingly short jean shorts," continued Mrs. Weathers with a shudder. "I immediately chastised her, and she told me they were the only way she could be comfortable in the heat outside. I gave her a warning and advised she find more appropriate attire. Saturday, she appeared in the same shorts *and* a tank top that was totally indecent. That was when I suspended her to the dorm for the rest of the weekend."

"I'm sorry, ma'am," I said. Really, I had no idea what else to say. I'd spent the weekend caught up in the epic battle to save humanity, and now . . . jean shorts?

Mrs. Weathers grew hesitant. "I know . . . well, I know this isn't really anything you should be involved in. It's a parental matter. But, seeing as how you're so responsible and look out for the rest of your family . . . "

I sighed. "Yes, ma'am. I'll take care of it. Thank you for not taking more severe action against her."

I went upstairs, my small suitcase growing heavier with each step. When I reached the second floor, I stopped, unsure what to do. One more floor would take me to my room. This floor would take me to "Cousin Angeline." Reluctantly, I turned into the second floor hall, knowing the sooner this was dealt with, the better.

"Sydney!" Jill Mastrano opened the dorm room's door, her light green eyes shining with joy. "You're back."

"So it seems," I said, following her inside. Angeline was there as well, lounging on her bed with a textbook. I was pretty sure that was the first time I'd ever seen her study, but the house arrest probably limited her recreational options.

"What did the Alchemists want?" asked Jill. She sat cross-legged on her own bed and began absentmindedly playing with the strands of her curly, light brown hair.

I shrugged. "Paperwork. Boring stuff. Sounds like things were a little more exciting here." That was delivered with a pointed look at Angeline.

The dhampir girl jumped off her bed, face furious and blue eyes flashing. "It wasn't my fault! That Weathers woman was completely out of line!" she exclaimed, a slight southern drawl in her words.

A quick scan of Angeline showed nothing too concerning.

Her jeans were threadbare but decent, as was her T-shirt. Even her mop of strawberry blonde hair was tame for a change, tied back in a ponytail.

"What on earth did you wear that got her so upset then?" I asked.

Scowling, Angeline went to her dresser and produced a pair of jean shorts with the most ragged hem I'd ever seen. I thought they'd unravel before my eyes. They were also so short that I wouldn't have been surprised if they showed underwear when she wore them.

"Where did you get those?"

Angeline almost looked proud. "I made them."

"With what, a hacksaw?"

"I had two pairs of jeans," she said pragmatically. "It was so hot out, I figured I might as well turn one into shorts."

"She used a knife from the cafeteria," said Jill helpfully.

"Couldn't find the scissors," explained Angeline.

My bed. Where was my bed?

"Mrs. Weathers mentioned something about an indecent shirt too," I said.

"Oh," said Jill. "That was mine."

I felt my eyebrows rise. "What? I know you don't own anything 'indecent.'" Before Angeline had come along a month ago, Jill and I had been roommates.

"It's not," agreed Jill. "Except, it's not really Angeline's size."

I glanced between the two girls and understood. Jill was tall and slim, like most Moroi, with a figure much coveted among human fashion designers, a figure I would've killed to have. Jill had even done some modeling. With that figure came a modest chest. Angeline's chest . . . was not so modest. If she wore a tank top in Jill's size, I imagined the shirt's structural integrity would indeed be stretched to indecent limits.

"Jill wears that tank top all the time and doesn't get in trouble," said Angeline defensively. "I figured there wouldn't be a problem if I borrowed it."

My head was starting to hurt. Still, I supposed this was better than the time Angeline had been caught making out with a guy in the boys' bathroom. "Well. This is easily fixed. We can go—well, I can go since you're stuck here—and get you some clothes *in your size* tonight."

"Oh," Angeline said, suddenly turning more upbeat, "you don't have to. Eddie's handling it."

If not for Jill nodding along, I would've thought it was a joke. "Eddie? Eddie's buying you clothes?"

Angeline sighed happily. "Isn't that nice of him?"

Nice? No, but I understood why Eddie would do it. Getting decent clothes for Angeline was the last thing he probably wanted to do, but he would do it. Like me, he understood duty. And now I could guess why Eddie had canceled the experiments—and been vague about his reasons for doing so.

I immediately took out my cell phone and called him. He answered right away, like always. I was certain he was never more than three feet from his phone at all times. "Hello, Sydney. Glad you're back." He paused. "You *are* back, right?"

"Yeah, I'm with Jill and Angeline. I understand you've been doing some shopping."

He groaned. "Don't get me started. I just walked into my room."

"You want to swing by with your purchases? I need the car back anyway."

There was a moment's hesitation. "Would you mind coming over here? As long as Jill's okay. She *is* okay, right? She doesn't need me? Because if she does—"

"She's fine." His dorm wasn't far, but I'd been hoping for a quick nap. Nonetheless, I found myself agreeing, just like I always did. "Okay. I'll meet you in the lobby in about fifteen minutes?"

"Sounds good. Thanks, Sydney."

As soon as I disconnected, Angeline asked excitedly, "Is Eddie coming over?"

"I'm going to him," I said.

Her face fell. "Oh. Well, I guess it doesn't matter since I have to stay here anyway. I can't wait until I'm free to train again. I'd like to get some more one-on-one time with him." I hadn't realized how focused Angeline was on her training. In fact, she seemed really excited about the prospect of it.

I left their room and was surprised to find Jill right behind me once the door shut. Her eyes were wide and anxious. "Sydney . . . I'm sorry."

I regarded her curiously, wondering now if she'd done something. "For what?"

She gestured toward the door. "For Angeline. I should have done better at keeping her out of trouble."

I almost smiled. "That's not your job."

"Yeah, I know . . . " She glanced down, letting some of her long hair fall forward. "But still. I know I should be more like you. Instead, I've just been . . . you know. Having fun."

"You're entitled to it," I said, trying to ignore the subtle commentary on me.

"I should still be more responsible," she argued.

"You are responsible," I assured her. "Especially compared to Angeline." My family had a cat back in Utah that I was pretty sure was more responsible than Angeline.

Jill's face brightened, and I left her so that I could return the suitcase to my room. Angeline's arrival and my work in busting Keith had earned me my own private room in the dorm, something I treasured. Inside it, everything was quiet and orderly. My perfect world. The one place that the chaos of my life couldn't touch. The neatly made bed was asking to be slept in. Begging, really. *Soon*, I promised it. *I hope.*

Amberwood Prep was divided into three campuses, East (where the girls were housed), West (where the boys were), and Central (containing all the academic buildings). A shuttle bus ran between them on a regular schedule, or brave souls could walk between them in the heat. I usually didn't mind the temperatures, but walking seemed like a lot of work today. So, I took the shuttle to West Campus and tried to stay awake.

The lobby of the boys' dorm was a lot like my own, people coming and going to either catch up on academic work or simply enjoy the Sunday off. I glanced around, but Eddie wasn't here yet.

"Hey, Melbourne."

I turned and found Trey Juarez approaching, a grin on his tanned face. He was a senior like me and had picked up the Melbourne nickname after one of our teachers proved incapable of remembering Melrose. Honestly, with all these names, it was a wonder I knew who I was anymore.

"Hey, Trey," I said. Trey was a bona fide high school football star—but also pretty brainy, no matter how much he tried to hide it. We got along well as a result, and my help in restoring his athletic status last month had gone a long way to raise my stock in his eyes. A backpack hung on one of his shoulders. "Are you finally going to finish that chem lab write-up?"

"Yup," he said. "Me and half the cheerleading squad. You want to join us?"

I rolled my eyes. "Somehow I doubt there'll be much work going on. Besides, I'm meeting Eddie."

Trey gave an easy shrug and brushed some unruly black hair out of his eyes. "Your loss. See you tomorrow." He took a couple of steps and then glanced back at me. "Hey, are you dating anyone?"

I immediately started to say no, and then a panicked thought occurred to me. I had a tendency to take things very literally. Friends of mine here, Kristin and Julia, had been trying to train me up in the subtleties of high school social life. One of their chief lessons was that what people said wasn't always what they meant—particularly in romantic matters.

"Are you . . . are you asking me out?" I asked, taken aback. This was the last thing I needed right now. How should I respond? Should I say yes? Should I say no? I'd had no idea helping him with chemistry homework would be so alluring. I should've made him do it on his own.

Trey looked as startled by the thought as I was. "What? No. Of course not."

"Thank God," I said. I liked Trey, but I had no interest in dating him—or figuring out what the appropriate way to say "no" would be.

He shot me a wry look. "You don't have to look *that* relieved."

"Sorry," I said, trying to mask my embarrassment. "Why'd you ask?"

"Because I know the perfect guy for you. I'm pretty sure he's your soul mate."

We were back in familiar territory now: logic vs. lack of logic. "I don't believe in soul mates," I said. "It's statistically unreasonable that there's only one ideal person for everyone in the world." And yet, for half a moment, I wished it was kind of possible. It'd be nice to have someone who understood some of the things that went on in my head.

Trey rolled his eyes. "Okay. Not a soul mate. How about just someone you could maybe go out with once in a while and have a nice time with?"

I shook my head. "I don't have time for anything like that." And I didn't. Keeping everything in order with the group, and pretending to be a student, was a full time job as it was.

"I'm telling you, you'd like him. He goes to a public school and just started at Spencer's." Spencer's was a coffee shop Trey worked at, an arrangement that yielded me discounts. "The other day, he was going off on unaerobic vs. aerobic respiration, and I was thinking, 'You know who this sounds like? Melbourne.'"

"It's *an*aerobic respiration," I corrected. "And it still doesn't mean I have the time. Sorry." I had to admit, I was immensely curious about how that topic would have come up between baristas, but figured it was best not to encourage Trey.

"Okay," he said. "Don't say I never tried to help you."

"Wouldn't dream of it," I assured him. "Hey, there's Eddie."

"My cue to go then. See you guys." Trey gave a mock salute

to Eddie and me. "Don't forget my offer if you want a hot date, Melbourne."

Trey left, and Eddie shot me an astonished look. "Did Trey just ask you out?"

"No. He's just got some co-worker he wants to set me up with."

"Maybe that's not a bad idea."

"It's a terrible idea. Let's go outside."

The desert heat didn't seem to care that it was October, and I led us to a bench right by the dorm's stucco walls. Partial shade from some nearby palm trees offered mild relief. People swore the temperature would taper soon, but I'd seen no sign of change. Eddie handed me my car keys and a shopping bag from a local superstore.

"I had to guess at size," he told me. "When in doubt, I went big. Figured it was safer that way."

"Probably." I sat down on a bench and rifled through his purchases. Jeans, khakis, a few solid colored T-shirts. They were very practical, very much something a no-nonsense guy like Eddie would pick out. I approved. "The size actually looks right. Good eye. We'll have to send you out shopping more often."

"If that's what I have to do," he said, face serious. I couldn't help but laugh in surprise.

"I was joking." I put the shirts back in the bag. "I know that couldn't have been fun." Eddie's face gave nothing away. "Oh, come *on*. It's okay. You don't have to play stoic with me. I know you didn't enjoy it."

"I'm here to do a job. Doesn't matter if I enjoy it or not."

I started to protest but then thought better of it. After all, wasn't that my philosophy too? Sacrificing my own wants for higher goals? Eddie was intensely dedicated to this mission. He never backed down. I expected nothing less from him than single-minded focus.

"So, does that mean you're up for some experiments tonight?" I asked.

"Of cours—" He stopped and reconsidered. "Are Jill and Angeline coming?"

"No. Angeline's still under house arrest."

"Thank God," he said with visible relief.

His reaction was probably the most surprising thing to happen today. I couldn't imagine why Eddie would look so relieved. Aside from his guardian loyalty to Jill, he was also crazy about her. He would've done anything for her, even if it wasn't his job, but refused to share his feelings with her. He thought he was unworthy of a princess. An uneasy thought occurred to me.

"Are you . . . are you avoiding Jill because of her and Micah?"

Micah was Eddie's roommate, a nice guy who caused Eddie all sorts of therapy-worthy trauma because he bore so much similarity to Eddie's dead best friend, Mason. Micah also had a weird pseudo-dating relationship with Jill. None of us were happy about it, since (aside from the Keepers) humans dating Moroi or dhampirs was strictly taboo. We'd finally decided it would be impossible to keep Jill from a social life, and she swore nothing serious or physical was going on between her and Micah. They just spent a lot of time together. And flirted incessantly. He didn't know the truth about her, but I wondered at what point he'd want more from their relationship. Eddie kept insisting it was better for Jill to have a casual relationship with a human than one with an "unworthy" dhampir like him, but I knew it had to be torturous.

"Of course not," said Eddie sharply. "It's not Jill I want to avoid. It's Angeline."

"Angeline? What's she done now?"

Eddie ran a hand through his hair in frustration. His was a sandy blond, not far from my own, which was a dark gold. The similarity made it easy to pass ourselves off as twins. "She won't leave me alone! She's always dropping these suggestive comments when I'm around . . . and she won't stop staring at me. Like, you wouldn't think that'd be creepy, but it is. She's always watching. And I can't avoid her because she's with Jill a lot of the time, and I have to keep Jill safe."

I thought back on recent interactions. "Are you sure you're reading this right? I've never noticed anything."

"That's because you don't notice that kind of thing," he said. "You cannot imagine how many excuses she finds to rub up against me."

After seeing her homemade jean shorts, I actually could imagine it. "Huh. Well, maybe I can talk to her."

Like that, Eddie snapped back to all-business. "No. It's my problem, my personal life. I'll deal with it."

"Are you sure? Because I can—"

"Sydney," he said gently. "You're the most responsible person I know, but this isn't what you're here to do. You don't have to take care of everything and everyone."

"I don't mind," I said automatically. "It *is* what I'm here for." But even as I said it, I wondered if that was true. A bit of the anxiety from the bunker returned, making me question if what I did was truly Alchemist responsibility or the desire to help those who—against protocol—had become my friends.

"See? Now you sound just like I did earlier." He stood up

and flashed me a grin. "You want to come with me to Adrian's? Be responsible together?"

His words were meant as a compliment, but they echoed too close to what the Alchemists had told me. And Mrs. Weathers. And Jill. Everyone thought I was so amazing, so responsible and controlled.

But if I was so amazing, then why was I always so unsure if I was doing the right thing?

CHAPTER 3

EVEN THOUGH EDDIE had told me not to worry about Angeline, the curious part of me couldn't help but prod him about it on the drive over to Adrian's apartment. "How are you going to handle it?" I asked. "Have a heart-to-heart?"

He shook his head. "Mostly I was going to simply avoid her unless absolutely necessary. Hopefully she'll lose interest."

"Well. I guess that's one method. But, I mean, you're a pretty direct person." If faced with a roomful of Strigoi, he would've walked in without hesitation. "Maybe you should try that kind of approach instead. Just confront her and tell her honestly that you're not interested."

"That's easy in theory," he said. "Not so much in person."

"Seems easy to me."

Eddie was skeptical. "That's because you've never had to do it."

Going to Adrian's was a lot easier than it once had been for me. His apartment used to belong to Keith and was also the site where a Moroi named Lee and two Strigoi had died. Those were hard memories to shake. The Alchemists had offered the apartment to me, since I'd also taken on full responsibility for · Palm Springs, but I'd yielded it to Adrian. I hadn't been sure I wanted to live there, and he'd been pretty desperate for his own place. When I'd seen how happy the apartment made him, I knew I'd made the right choice.

Adrian opened the door before we'd barely had a chance to knock. "The cavalry! Thank God."

I hid a smile as Eddie and I stepped inside. The first thing that always hit me about this place was the sunny yellow paint Adrian had put up on the walls. He was convinced it helped the mood and had warned us not to question his "artistic sensibili- ties." The fact that the yellow clashed pretty terribly with his secondhand plaid furniture was apparently irrelevant. Or maybe I just wasn't "artistic" enough to appreciate it. Nonetheless, I actually found the erratic style comforting. It bore little resem- blance to Keith's decorating, making it a *little* easier to blot out the events of that awful night. Sometimes, when I looked around the living room, my breath would catch as visions of the vicious Strigoi attack and Lee's death haunted me. Adrian's stamp on the apartment was like light chasing away the grue- some shadows of the past.

Sometimes when I was down, Adrian's personality had a similar effect.

"Nice blouse, Sage," he told me, deadpan. "It really brings out the khaki in your pants."

His sarcasm aside, he looked supremely delighted to see us. He had the tall, lean build that most Moroi guys did, along with their typically pale (though not Strigoi-pale) skin. I hated to admit it, but he was more good-looking than he had any right to be. He wore his dark brown hair stylishly messy and had eyes that sometimes seemed too green to be real. Adrian had on one of those button-up printed shirts that were trendy with guys lately, with a blue pattern on it I liked. He smelled like he'd been smoking recently, which I didn't like.

Dimitri and Sonya were sitting at the kitchen table going over a bunch of papers with hand-written notes on them. The papers were kind of haphazardly scattered around, which made me wonder how much work they could really be accomplishing. I would have had those pages neatly stacked and organized by topic.

"Glad you're back, Sydney," said Sonya. "I've needed a little female support here." The prettiness of her red hair and high cheek bones was tainted by the fact that she showed her fangs when she smiled. Most Moroi were taught early to avoid that, to prevent detection from humans. Sonya had no qualms about doing it in private. It still bugged me.

Dimitri smiled at me. It made his already handsome face even more so, and I knew that "Zen master wisdom" wasn't the reason Rose had fallen for him. "I'm guessing you didn't take a nap."

"Too much to do," I said.

Sonya gave Eddie a curious look. "We've been wondering where you were."

"Busy at Amberwood," said Eddie vaguely. He'd mentioned in the car that it might be best if Angeline's indiscretion and his forced shopping weren't mentioned. "You know, keeping an eye on Jill and Angeline. Besides, I was waiting until Sydney came back since she wanted to see what we were doing." I let the white lie slide.

"How *is* Angeline?" asked Dimitri. "Is she improving?"

Eddie and I exchanged glances. So much for avoiding her indiscretions. "Improving how exactly?" I asked. "In combat, in following the dress code, or in keeping her hands to herself?"

"Or in turning off caps-lock?" added Eddie.

"You noticed that too?" I asked.

"Hard not to," he said.

Dimitri looked surprised, which was not a common thing. He wasn't caught off guard very often, but then, no one could really prepare for what Angeline might do.

"I didn't realize I needed to be more specific," said Dimitri after a pause. "I meant combat."

Eddie shrugged. "There's a little improvement, but it's hard to get through to her. I mean, she's absolutely dead set on protecting Jill, but she's also convinced she already knows how. She's got years of that sloppy training drilled into her. It's hard to break that. Plus, she's . . . easily distracted."

I had to swallow a laugh.

Dimitri still looked troubled. "She has no time for distraction. Maybe I should talk to her."

"No," said Eddie firmly, in a rare show of contradicting Dimitri. "You've got plenty to do here. She's my responsibility to train. Don't worry."

Adrian pulled up a chair, turning it backwards so he could rest his chin on its back. "What about you, Sage? I know we don't have to worry about you violating the dress code. Did you have fun at your Alchemist spa this weekend?"

I set down my bag and walked over to the refrigerator. "If by spa, you mean underground bunker. And it was just business." I made a face as I looked inside. "You promised to get me diet pop."

"I did promise that," said Adrian, no remorse whatsoever. "But then I read some article that said those artificial sweeteners aren't good for you. So, I figured I'd watch out for your health." He paused. "You're welcome."

Dimitri said what we were all thinking. "If you want to start tackling healthy habits, I could suggest a few."

If Eddie or I had said that, it would have rolled right off Adrian—particularly since it was completely valid. But coming from Dimitri? That was different. There was a huge amount of tension between the two men, tension that had been building for a long time. Dimitri's girlfriend, a notorious dhampir named Rose Hathaway, had briefly dated Adrian. She hadn't meant to hurt him, but she'd been in love with Dimitri the whole time. So, there was no way that situation could have ended well. Adrian still carried a lot of scars from that and was particularly bitter toward Dimitri.

"Wouldn't want to inconvenience you," said Adrian, a bit too coolly. "Besides, when not hard at work with this research, I'm actually conducting a side experiment on how cigarettes and gin increase charisma. As you might guess, the results are looking very promising."

Dimitri arched an eyebrow. "Wait, go back. Did you say hard at work?"

Dimitri's tone was light and playful, and again, I was struck by the double standard here. If I'd made that comment, Adrian's response would've been something like, "Absolutely, Sage. I'll probably win the Nobel Prize for this." But for Adrian, Dimitri's words were a call to battle. I saw a glint of something hard in Adrian's eyes, a stirring of some old pain, and it bothered me. That wasn't his way. He always had a smile and a quip, even if they were often irreverent or inappropriate. I'd gotten used to that. I kind of liked it.

I glanced at Adrian with a smile that I hoped looked genuine, rather than a desperate attempt to provide distraction. "Research, huh? I thought you were a gambling man."

It took Adrian a few moments to drag his gaze from Dimitri and fix it on me. "I've been known to roll the dice now and then," he said warily. "Why?"

I shrugged. "No reason. Just wondering if you'd put your charisma research on hold and step up for a challenge. If you went twenty-four hours without cigarettes, I'd drink a can of pop. *Regular* pop. The whole can."

I saw the glimmer of Adrian's earlier smile returning. "You would not."

"I totally would."

"Half a can would put you into a coma."

Sonya frowned. "Are you diabetic?" she asked me.

"No," said Adrian, "but Sage is convinced one extraneous calorie will make her go from super skinny to just regular skinny. Tragedy."

"Hey," I said. "You think it'd be a tragedy to go an hour without a cigarette."

"Don't question my steel resolve, Sage. I went without one for *two* hours today."

"Show me twenty-four, and then I'll be impressed."

He gave me a look of mock surprise. "You mean you aren't

already? And here I thought you were dazzled from the moment you met me."

Sonya shook her head indulgently at the two of us, like we were adorable children. "You're missing out, Sydney," she remarked, tapping the open pop in front of her. "I need about three of these a day to keep me focused on all this work. No detrimental effects so far."

No detrimental effects so far? Of course not. Moroi never had any. Sonya, Jill . . . they could all eat whatever they wanted and still keep those amazing bodies. Meanwhile, I labored over every calorie and still couldn't reach that level of perfection. Fitting into these size four khakis had been a triumph this morning. Now, looking at Sonya's slender build, I felt enormous by comparison. I suddenly regretted my comment about drinking a can of pop, even if it had succeeded in distracting Adrian. I supposed I could rest easy knowing that him skipping cigarettes for a day was impossible. I'd never be called to pay up on my sugary wager.

"We should probably get to work. We're losing time." That was Dimitri, getting us back on track.

"Right," said Adrian. "This is five minutes of valuable research wasted. Up for more fun, Castile? I know how much you love sitting around." Because they were trying to find something special about Dimitri, Sonya and Adrian would often sit the two dhampirs side by side and study their auras in fine detail. Their hope was that Dimitri's Strigoi conversion had left some sign that would help explain the immunity to being turned again. It was a valid idea, though not something that someone as active as Eddie enjoyed.

He didn't complain, of course. Eddie wore a look as tough and determined as Dimitri. "Tell me what you need."

"We want to do another aura study," said Sonya. Looked like poor Eddie would be doing some more sitting around. "Last time we focused on any sign of spirit. This time, we want to show both of you some pictures and see if they trigger any color changes in your auras." I nodded in approval. A lot of psychological experiments attempted similar techniques, though they usually monitored physiological responses instead of mystical auras.

"I still say it's a waste," said Adrian. "They're both dhampirs, but that doesn't mean we can assume any different reactions they have are because Belikov was a Strigoi. Everyone's unique. Everyone's going to respond differently to pictures of kittens or spiders. My old man? He hates kittens."

"Who could hate kittens?" asked Eddie.

Adrian made a face. "He's allergic."

"Adrian," said Sonya. "We've already been over this. I respect your opinion but still think we can learn a lot." I was actually impressed that Adrian had an opinion. So far, I'd kind of felt like he was just going along with everything Sonya and Dimitri told him to do and that he didn't give these experiments much thought. And, although I wasn't familiar with the auras that surrounded all living creatures, I could understand his point that individual differences would throw off their research.

"All data is useful in this case," said Dimitri. "Especially since we haven't found anything so far. We know there's something different about former Strigoi. We can't rule out any chance to observe it."

Adrian's lips tightened, and he made no further protest. Maybe it was because he felt overruled, but I had a feeling it was because he just didn't want to engage with Dimitri.

With the attention off me, I settled into the living room with a book and tried to stay awake. They didn't need me. I'd simply come to keep Eddie company. Occasionally, I'd check the others' progress. Dimitri and Eddie watched as Sonya flipped through different images on her laptop. In turn, Adrian and Sonya watched the dhampirs closely and made notes on paper. I almost wished I could see the bands of color and light and wondered if there really were any noticeable differences. Studying Eddie and Dimitri, I sometimes would notice a change in facial expression when particularly cute or horrific images showed up on the screen, but for the most part their work remained a mystery to me.

Curious, I walked over to Sonya when they were about halfway through. "What do you see?" I asked in a low voice.

"Colors," she said. "Shining around all living things. Eddie and Dimitri have different colors, but they have the same reactions." She changed the picture on the screen to one of a factory spilling black smoke into an otherwise clear sky. "Neither of them like this. Their auras dim and turn troubled." She flipped to the next image, a smile on her lips. Three kittens appeared on the screen. "And now they warm up. Affection is very easy to spot in an aura. So far, they react in normal ways. There's no sign in Dimitri's aura that he's different from Eddie." I returned to the couch.

After a couple of hours, Sonya called a halt. "I think we've seen what we needed to. Thank you, Eddie."

"Happy to help," he said, rising from his chair and

stretching. He seemed relieved both that it was over and that it had involved something slightly more interesting than staring off into space. He was active and energetic, and didn't like captivity.

"Although . . . we've got a few other ideas," she added. "Do you think you guys can power through a little longer?" Naturally, she asked just as I was yawning.

Eddie regarded me with sympathy. "I'll stay, but you don't have to. Go sleep. I'll get a ride home."

"No, no," I said, stifling a second yawn. "I don't mind. What are your other ideas?"

"I was hoping to do something similar with Eddie and Dimitri," she explained. "Except this time, we'd use sounds instead of images. Then I'd like to see how they respond to direct contact with spirit."

"I think that's a good idea," I said, not really sure what that last one would entail. "Go for it. I'll wait."

Sonya glanced around and seemed to notice I wasn't the only one who looked tired. "Maybe we should get some food first." Eddie brightened up at that.

"I'll go," I offered. It was a sign of my progress that vampires talking about "food" no longer made me hyperventilate. I knew she didn't mean blood, not if the dhampirs and I were being involved. Besides, there was no feeder around. Feeders were humans who willingly gave blood to Moroi for the high it produced. Everyone here knew better than to even joke about that around me. "There's a good Thai carryout place a few blocks away."

"I'll help," said Adrian eagerly.

"*I'll* help," said Sonya. "The last time you ran an errand, you were gone two hours." Adrian scowled but didn't deny the charge. "Our aura observations have been identical anyway. You can get them started on the sounds without me."

Sonya and I took everyone's orders and set out. I didn't really feel like I needed help, but I supposed carrying food for five people—even for a few blocks—could get unwieldy. I soon learned she had other motives for coming along, though.

"It feels good to get outside and stretch my legs," she said. It was early evening, with significantly less sun and heat—a condition the Moroi loved. We walked along a side street leading toward downtown, lined with cute apartments and small businesses. All around us, huge palm trees loomed, providing an interesting contrast to the eclectic urban setting. "I've been cooped up there all day."

I smiled at her. "And here I thought Adrian was the only one who got cabin fever from the work you guys do."

"He just complains the most," she explained. "Which is kind of funny since he also probably gets out the most, between his classes and his cigarette breaks." I'd nearly forgotten about the two art classes Adrian was taking at a local college. He usually kept his latest projects on display, but there'd been none in the living room lately. I hadn't realized until that moment how much I missed them. I might give him a hard time, but sometimes those artistic glimpses into the way he thought were fascinating.

Sonya gave me a brief recap of her wedding plans as we walked the short distance to the Thai restaurant. Her relationship with dhampir Mikhail Tanner was kind of epic on a lot of levels, I supposed. First, dhampirs and Moroi didn't generally get involved in serious relationships. Usually, they were just casual affairs that resulted in the reproduction of more dhampirs. In addition to the scandal of even being involved, Mikhail had actually wanted to hunt down Sonya when she was a Strigoi to free her from that twisted state. Rose had attempted the same with Dimitri, believing death was better than being a Strigoi. Mikhail had failed, but their love had remained steadfast enough through the ordeal that when she'd defied the odds and been restored, they'd immediately gotten back together. I couldn't even begin to imagine love like that.

"We're still deciding on flowers," she continued. "Hydrangeas or lilies. I'm guessing I know what your vote is for."

"Actually, I'd say hydrangeas. I'm around too many lilies already."

She laughed at that and suddenly knelt near a flower bed filled with gladiolas. "More than you know. There are lilies sleeping in this bed."

"They're out of season," I pointed out.

"Nothing's ever out of season." Sonya glanced around covertly and then rested her fingers on the earth. Moments later, dark green shoots appeared, growing taller and taller until a red trumpet lily opened up on top. "Ah. Red. Alchemists ones are white—oh, are you okay?"

I had backed up so far on the sidewalk that I'd nearly walked into the street. "You . . . you shouldn't do that. Someone might see."

"No one saw," she said, getting to her feet. Her face softened. "I'm so sorry. I forget sometimes how you feel about this. It was wrong of me."

"It's okay," I said, not sure that it was. Vampire magic always made my skin crawl. Vampires, creatures who needed blood, were bad enough. But being able to manipulate the world with magic? Even worse. That lily, although beautiful, took on a sinister edge now. It shouldn't have existed this time of the year.

No more was said about magic, and we soon reached the main strip downtown, where the Thai restaurant was. We placed a giant carryout order and were told it would take about fifteen minutes. Sonya and I lingered outside, admiring downtown Palm Springs in twilight. Last-minute shoppers were out before the boutiques closed, and all the restaurants were hopping with those coming and going. Many of them had outdoor tables on the sidewalk, and friendly conversation buzzed around us. A large fountain, tiled in bright colors, fascinated children and inspired tourists to stop for photo ops. Sonya was easily distracted by the various plants and trees that the city used to beautify the streets. Even without spirit's ability to affect living things, she was still quite the gardener.

"Hey you! Elder Melrose!"

I turned and winced when I saw Lia DiStefano striding toward me. Lia was a fashion designer with a shop here in downtown Palm Springs. I hadn't realized we were standing directly across from her store. If I had, I would've waited inside the restaurant. Lia was short but had an overwhelming presence, enhanced by the flamboyant gypsy style she often chose for her personal attire.

"I've been calling you for weeks," she said, once she reached our side of the street. "Why don't you answer?"

"I've been really busy," I said straight-faced.

"Uh-huh." Lia put her hands on her hips and tried to stare me down, which was kind of amazing since I was taller. "When are you going to let your sister model for me again?"

"Miss DiStefano," I said patiently, "I've told you before. She can't do it anymore. Our parents don't like it. Our religion doesn't allow faces to be photographed."

Last month, Jill's runway-perfect build and gorgeous, ethereal features had attracted Lia's attention. Seeing as having your picture taken en masse was kind of a bad way to stay in hiding, we'd only agreed to let Jill walk in Lia's fashion show because all the models wore Venetian masks. Lia had been on me ever since to let Jill model again. It was hard because I knew Jill wanted to, but she understood as well as I did that her safety came first. Claiming we were part of some obscure religion had often explained away our weird behaviors to others, so I'd figured it would get Lia off my back. It hadn't.

"I never hear from these parents of yours," Lia said. "I've watched your family. I see how it is. *You're* the authority. You're the one I have to go through. I have the chance to do a major magazine spread for my scarves and hats, and Jill was born to do it. What's it going to take to get her? You want a cut of the pay?"

I sighed. "It's not about the money. We can't show her face. If you want to put her in a Venetian mask again, then be my guest."

Lia scowled. "I can't do that."

"Then we're at an impasse."

"There must be *something*. Everyone has a price."

"Sorry." There was no price in the world she could offer to get me to shirk my duty to Jill and the Alchemists.

A restaurant clerk stuck his head outside and called that our order was ready, mercifully freeing us from Lia. Sonya chuckled as we loaded up on our bags and headed back down

51

the street to make the walk to Adrian's. The sky was still purple with the last of the day's light, and street lamps made whimsical patterns on the sidewalk as they cast their light through the leaves of palm trees.

"Did you ever imagine your job here would involve dodging aggressive fashion designers?" Sonya asked.

"No," I admitted. "Honestly, I never foresaw half the stuff this job has—"

"Sonya?"

A young man appeared seemingly out of nowhere, blocking our path. He was no one I knew and looked to be a little older than me. He wore his black hair in a buzz cut and was staring curiously at Sonya.

She came to a halt and frowned. "Do I know you?"

He brightened. "Sure. Jeff Eubanks. Remember?"

"No," she said politely, after a few moments of study. "You must have me mistaken for someone else. I'm sorry."

"No, no," he said. "I know it's you. Sonya Karp, right? We met in Kentucky last year."

Sonya stiffened. She'd made Kentucky her home while she was a Strigoi. I knew those couldn't be pleasant memories.

"I'm sorry," she repeated, voice strained. "I don't know what you're talking about."

The guy was undaunted, still smiling as though they were best friends. "You've come a long ways from Kentucky. What brings you out here? I just transferred for work."

"There's some mistake," I told him sternly, nudging Sonya forward. I didn't know what that mistake could be exactly, but Sonya's attitude was all I needed. "We have to go."

The guy didn't follow us, but Sonya remained silent for most of the walk home.

"Must be hard," I said, feeling like I should say something. "Meeting people from your past."

She shook her head. "He's not. I'm certain of it. I've never met him."

I'd figured she just wanted to avoid all associations with being a Strigoi. "You're sure? He wasn't just some casual acquaintance?"

She shot me a wry look. "Strigoi don't have casual acquaintances with humans. They have them for dinner. That guy shouldn't have known who I was."

"He was human? Not dhampir?" I couldn't tell the difference, but Moroi could.

"Definitely."

Sonya had stopped again and was glancing back at the guy's retreating figure. I followed her gaze. "There must be some reason he recognized you. He seems pretty harmless."

That got me another smile. "Come now, Sydney. I figured you'd been around us long enough to know."

"Know what?"

"Nothing's ever as harmless as it seems."

CHAPTER 4

SONYA DIDN'T SAY ANYTHING about the mysterious encounter to the rest of the gang at Adrian's, so I respected her silence. Everyone else was too preoccupied with dinner and the experiments to notice much else. And once they conducted the second wave of experiments, even I grew too distracted to give much thought to the guy on the street.

Sonya had said she wanted to see how Eddie and Dimitri responded to direct spirit. This was accomplished by her and Adrian focusing their magic at the dhampirs one at a time.

"It's sort of like what we'd do if we were trying to heal them or make something grow," Sonya explained to me. "Don't worry—this isn't going to make them supersized or anything. It's more like we're coating them with spirit magic. If Dimitri's got some lasting mark from when he was healed, I'd imagine it would react with our magic."

She and Adrian coordinated their timing and did Eddie first. Initially, there was nothing to see—just the two spirit users

54

staring at Eddie. He looked uncomfortable under the scrutiny. Then, I saw a silvery shimmer run over his body. I stepped back, amazed—and unnerved—at seeing a physical manifestation of spirit. They repeated the process on Dimitri, with the same results. Apparently, on an unseen level, things were the same too. There was nothing notable about Dimitri's response. All of them took this in stride as part of the scientific process, but seeing that magic actually embrace the two men had creeped me out.

As Eddie and I drove back to Amberwood that night, I found myself sitting as far away from him as I could in the car, as though residual magic might leak over and touch me. He chatted with me in our usual, friendly way, and I had to work hard to hide my feelings. Doing so made me feel guilty. This was Eddie, after all. My friend. The magic, even if it could've hurt me, was long since gone.

A good night of sleep went a long ways to shake both my anxiety and guilt, leaving the magic a distant memory when I woke and prepared for classes the next day. Even though being at Amberwood was an assignment, I'd kind of come to love the elite school. I'd been homeschooled before this, and while my dad had certainly taught tough curriculum, he'd never gone beyond what he felt was necessary. Here, even if I surpassed what my classes were learning, there were plenty of teachers ready to encourage me to push farther. I hadn't been allowed to go to college, but this was a nice substitute.

Before I could get on to it, I had to chaperone a training session with Eddie and Angeline. Even though he might want to avoid her, he wouldn't—not with Jill's safety on the line. Angeline was part of Jill's defense. I settled down in the grass with a cup of coffee, still wondering if he wasn't just imagining Angeline's interest. I'd recently acquired a one-cup coffee maker for my dorm room, and while it couldn't compare to a coffee shop, it had gotten me through a number of rough mornings. A yawn smothered my greeting as Jill sat down beside me.

"Eddie never trains me anymore," she said wistfully, as we watched the spectacle. Eddie was trying to patiently explain to Angeline that headbutting, while suitable in a bar brawl, was not always the best tactic with Strigoi.

"I'm sure he will if he gets more time," I said, though I wasn't sure at all. Now that he could admit his feelings for Jill to himself, he was nervous about touching her too much. That, and a chivalrous part of him didn't want Jill risking herself anyway. It was ironic because Jill's fierceness in wanting to learn self-defense (rare in a Moroi) was what had attracted him to her. "Angeline was recruited as protection. He's got to make sure she can handle it."

"I know. I just feel like everyone's trying to coddle me." She frowned. "In PE, Micah won't let me do anything. After I had all that trouble starting out, he's now paranoid I'll hurt myself. I keep telling him I'm fine, that it was just the sun . . . but well, he keeps jumping in. It's sweet . . . but it drives me crazy sometimes."

"I've noticed it," I admitted. I was in the same PE class. "I don't think that's why Eddie won't train you, though. He knows you can do it. He's proud that you can . . . he just thinks that if he's doing his job, you shouldn't have to learn. Kind of weird logic."

"No, I get it." Her earlier dismay shifted to approval as she turned back to the training session. "He's so dedicated . . . and, well, good at what he does."

"The knee's an easy way to disable someone," Eddie told Angeline. "Especially if you're caught without a weapon and have to—"

"When are you going to teach me to stake or decapitate?" she interrupted, hands on her hips. "All the time, it's hit here, dodge this, blah, blah, blah. I need to practice killing Strigoi."

"No, you don't." Eddie was the picture of patience and back in the determined, ready mode I knew so well. "You're not here to kill Strigoi. Maybe we can practice that at a later time, but right now, your priority is keeping *mortal* assassins away from Jill. That takes precedence over anything else, even our lives." He glanced over at Jill for emphasis, and there was a flash of admiration in his eyes as he looked at her.

"Seems like decapitation would kill Moroi just the same," Angeline grumbled. "And besides, you *did* have a Strigoi problem last month."

Jill shifted uneasily beside me, and even Eddie paused. It was true—he *had* had to kill two Strigoi recently, back when Adrian's apartment had been Keith's. Lee Donahue had led the Strigoi to us. He was a Moroi who'd once been Strigoi. After he was returned to his natural state, Lee had wanted desperately to become a Strigoi again. He was the reason we'd learned that those restored by spirit seemed to have some Strigoi resistance. The two Strigoi he'd called to help him had tried to convert him but ended up killing him instead—a better fate than being undead, in my opinion.

Those Strigoi had then turned on the rest of us and

inadvertently revealed something unexpected and alarming (if not to them, then to me). My blood was inedible. They'd tried to drink from me and been unable to. With all the fallout from that night, no one among the Alchemists or Moroi had paid much attention to that small detail—and I was grateful. I was terrified that one of these days someone would think to put me under a microscope.

"That was a fluke," said Eddie at last. "Not one that's likely to happen again. Now watch the way my leg moves, and remember that a Moroi will probably be taller than you."

He did a demonstration, and I cast a quick look at Jill. Her face was unreadable. She never talked about Lee, whom she'd dated briefly. Micah had gone a long way to distract her on the romantic front, but having your last boyfriend want to become a bloodthirsty monster couldn't be an easy thing to get over. I had a feeling she was still in pain, even if she did a great job at hiding it.

"You're too rigid," Eddie told Angeline, after several attempts.

She completely relaxed her body, almost like a marionette. "So, what? Like this?"

He sighed. "No. You still need some tension."

Eddie moved behind her and attempted to guide her into position, showing her how to bend her knees and hold her arms. Angeline took the opportunity to lean back into him and brush her body suggestively against his. My eyes widened. Okay. Maybe he wasn't imagining things.

"Hey!" He leapt backwards, a look of horror on his face. "Pay attention! You need to learn this."

Her expression was pure angelic innocence. "I am. I'm just trying to use your body to learn what to do with mine."

So help me, she batted her eyelashes. Eddie moved back even farther.

I realized I should probably intervene, no matter what Eddie had said about handling his own problems. An even better savior came when the school's thirty-minute warning bell rang. I jumped up.

"Hey, we should go if we want to get to breakfast in time. Right now."

Angeline gave me a suspicious look. "Don't you usually skip breakfast?"

"Yeah, but I'm not the one putting in a hard morning's work. Besides, you still need to change and—wait, you're in your uniform?" I hadn't even noticed. Whenever Eddie and Jill trained, it was always in casual workout clothes—just like he wore now. Angeline had actually come out today in an Amberwood uniform, skirt and blouse, that were showing the wear and tear of a morning's battle.

"Yeah, so?" She tucked in her blouse where it had started to come undone. The side of it was smudged with dirt.

"You should change," I said.

"Nah. This is fine."

I wasn't so sure, but at least it was better than the jean shorts. Eddie did leave to put on his uniform and never came back for breakfast. I knew he liked his breakfasts, and since he was a guy, he could change clothes pretty quickly. My guess was he was sacrificing food to stay away from Angeline.

I heard my name called as we entered the cafeteria and caught sight of Kristin Sawyer and Julia Cavendish waving to me. Aside from Trey, they were the two closest friends I'd made at Amberwood. I still had miles to go in ever being socially savvy, but those two had helped me a lot. And with all the supernatural intrigue my job involved, there was something comforting about being around people who were normal . . . and, well, human. Even if I couldn't be fully honest with them.

"Sydney, we have a fashion question for you," Julia said. She tossed her blonde hair over one shoulder, her usual sign that what she was about to say was of utmost importance.

"A fashion question for me?" I was almost ready to glance back and see if maybe there was another Sydney standing behind me. "I don't think anyone's ever asked that."

"You have really nice clothes," Kristin insisted. She had dark skin and hair, as well as an athletic air that contrasted with Julia's more girly nature. "Too nice, actually. If my mom were ten years younger, cool, and had a lot more money, she'd dress just like you." I didn't know if that was a compliment or not, but Julia didn't give me a chance to ruminate.

"Tell her, Kris."

"Remember that counseling internship I wanted next semester? I scored an interview," Kristin explained. "I'm trying to decide if I should wear pants and a blazer or a dress."

Ah, that explained why they were coming to me. An interview. Anything else they could have pulled from a fashion magazine. And while I could admit that I probably *was* the authority on such practical matters . . . well, I was kind of disappointed that was what I'd been summoned for. "What color are they?"

"The blazer's red, and the dress is navy."

I studied Kristin, taking in her features. On her wrist was a scar, the remnant of an insidious tattoo I'd helped remove, back when Keith's shady tattoo ring had run rampant. "Do the dress. Wait . . . is it a dress you'd wear to church or to a nightclub?"

"Church," she said, not sounding happy about it.

"Dress for sure then," I said.

Kristin flashed a triumphant look at Julia. "See? I told you that's what she'd say."

Julia looked doubtful. "The blazer's more fun. It's bright red."

"Yeah, but 'fun' isn't usually what you want to portray at an interview," I pointed out. It was hard to keep a straight face with their banter. "At least not for this kind of job."

Julia still didn't seem convinced, but she also didn't try to talk Kristin out of my sound fashion advice. A few moments later, Julia perked up. "Hey, is it true Trey set you up with some guy?"

"I . . . what? No. Where'd you hear that?" Like I had to ask. She'd undoubtedly heard it from Trey himself.

"Trey said he'd talked to you about it," said Kristin. "How this guy's perfect for you."

"It's a great idea, Syd," said Julia, face as serious as if we were discussing a life or death matter. "It'd be good for you. I mean, since school started, I've gone out with . . . " She paused and silently counted out names on her fingers. " . . . four guys. You know how many you've gone out with?" She held up a fist. "That many."

"I don't need to go out with anyone," I argued. "I have enough complications already. I'm pretty sure that would add more."

"What complications?" laughed Kristin. "Your awesome grades, killer body, and perfect hair? I mean, okay, your family's a little out there, but come on, everyone has time for a date now and then—or lots, in Julia's case."

"Hey," said Julia, though she didn't deny the charge.

Kristin pushed forward, making me think she was more suited to a legal internship than a counseling one. "Skip homework for once. Give this guy a shot, and we can all go out together sometime. It'd be fun."

I gave them a forced smile and murmured something noncommittal. *Everyone has time for a date now and then.* Everyone but me, of course. I felt a surprising pang of longing, not for a date but just for social interaction. Kristin and Julia went out a lot with a larger group of friends and love interests and often invited me on their outings. They thought my reticence was because of homework or, perhaps, no suitable guy to go with me. I wished it were that simple, and suddenly, it was as though there was a huge chasm separating me from Kristin and Julia. I was their friend, and they had welcomed me to every part of their lives. Meanwhile, I was full of secrets and half truths. Part of me wished I could be open with them and able to confide all the woes of my Alchemist life. Heck, part of me just wished I really could go on one of these outings and let go of my duties for a night. It would never work, of course. We'd be out at a movie, and I'd probably get texted to come cover up a Strigoi slaying.

This mood wasn't uncommon for me, and it began lightening as I started my school day. I fell into the rhythm of my schedule, comfortable in its familiarity. Teachers always assigned the most work over weekends, and I was pleased to be able to turn in all that I'd done on my plane rides. Unfortunately, my last class of the day derailed all the progress of my mood. Actually, *class* wasn't the right word. It was an independent study I had with my history teacher, Ms. Terwilliger.

Ms. Terwilliger had recently revealed herself to be a magic user, a witch of sorts or whatever those people referred to themselves as. Alchemists had heard rumors of them, but it was nothing we had a lot of experience with or facts about. To our knowledge, only Moroi wielded magic. We utilized it in our lily tattoos—which had trace amounts of vampire blood—but the thought of humans producing it in the same way was crazy and twisted.

That was why it was such a surprise when Ms. Terwilliger not only revealed herself to me last month but also ended up kind of tricking me into wielding a spell. It had left me shocked and even feeling dirty. Magic was not for humans to use. We had no right to manipulate the world like that; it was a hundred times worse than what Sonya had done to the red lily on the street. Ms. Terwilliger insisted I had a natural affinity for magic and had offered to train me. Why she wanted this, exactly, I wasn't sure. She'd gone on and on about the potential I had, but I could hardly believe she'd want to train me without a reason of her own. I hadn't figured out what that might be, but it didn't matter. I'd refused her offer. So, she'd found a work-around.

"Miss Melbourne, how much longer do you think you'll be on the Kimball book?" she called from her desk. Trey had picked up "Melbourne" from her, but unlike him, she seemed to constantly forget that wasn't my actual name. She was in her forties, with mousy brown hair and a perpetually cunning glint in her eyes.

I looked up from my work, forcing politeness. "Two more days. Three at most."

"Make sure to translate all three of the sleep of spells," she said. "Each has its own nuances."

"There are four sleep spells in this book," I corrected.

"Are there?" she asked innocently. "I'm glad to see they're making an impression."

I hid a scowl. Having me copy and translate spell books for research was how she taught me. I couldn't help but learn the texts as I read them. I hated that I'd been ensnared, but it was too late in the school year to transfer out. Besides, I could hardly complain to the administration that I was being forced to learn magic.

So, I dutifully copied her spell books and spoke as little as possible during our time together. Meanwhile, I simmered with resentment. She was well aware of my discomfort but made no attempts to alleviate the tension, leaving us in a stalemate. Only one thing brightened those sessions.

"Look at that. It's been nearly two hours since my last cappuccino. It's a wonder I can function. Would you be kind enough to run to Spencer's? That should finish us out for the day." The last bell had rung fifteen minutes ago, but I'd been putting in some overtime.

I was already closing the spell book before she finished speaking. When I'd begun as her assistant, I'd resented the constant errands. Now, I looked forward to the escape. Not to mention my own caffeine fix.

When I reached the coffee shop, I found Trey was just starting his shift, which was great—not just because he was a friendly face, but because it meant discounts. He began making my order before I even placed it since he knew the drill by now. Another barista offered to help, and Trey gave him meticulous instructions on what to do.

"Skinny vanilla latte," said Trey, grabbing the caramel for

Ms. Terwilliger's cappuccino. "That's sugar-free syrup and skim. Don't mess it up. She can sniff out sugar and 2% milk a mile away." I suppressed a smile. Maybe I couldn't reveal Alchemist secrets to my friends, but it was nice to know they at least knew my coffee preferences backwards and forwards.

The other barista, who looked to be our age, gave Trey a droll look. "I'm well aware of what skinny means."

"Nice attention to detail," I teased Trey. "I didn't know you cared."

"Hey, I live to serve," he said. "Besides, I need your help tonight with that lab write-up from chem. You always find things I miss."

"It's due tomorrow," I chastised. "You had two weeks. I'm guessing you didn't get much done in your cheerleader study session."

"Yeah, yeah. Will you help me out? I'll even go to your campus."

"I'll be up late with a study group—a real one." The opposite sex was banned from our dorms after a certain hour. "I could meet you on Central Campus afterward if you want."

"How many campuses does your school have?" asked the other barista, setting down my latte.

"Three." I reached eagerly for the coffee. "Like Gaul."

"Like what?" asked Trey.

"Sorry," I said. "Latin joke."

"Omnia Gallia in *tres partes divisa est*," said the barista.

I jerked my head up. Not much could have distracted me from coffee, but hearing Julius Caesar quoted at Spencer's certainly did.

"You know Latin?" I asked.

"Sure," he said. "Who doesn't?"

Trey rolled his eyes. "Only the rest of the world," he muttered.

"Especially classical Latin," continued the barista. "I mean, it's pretty remedial compared to Medieval Latin."

"Obviously," I said. "Everyone knows that. All the rules became chaotic in the post-Empire decentralization."

He nodded agreement. "Although, if you compare it to the Romance languages, the rules start to make sense when you read them as part of the larger picture of the language's evolution."

"This," interrupted Trey, "is the most messed-up thing I've ever seen. And the most beautiful. Sydney, this is Brayden. Brayden, Sydney." Trey rarely used my first name, so that was weird, but not nearly as weird as the exaggerated wink he gave me.

I shook Brayden's hand. "Nice to meet you."

"You too," he said. "You're a Classics fan, huh?" He paused, giving me a long, considering look. "Did you see the Park Theatre Group's production of *Antony and Cleopatra* this summer?"

"No. Didn't even know they performed it." I suddenly felt kind of lame for not having known that, as though I should be up on all arts and culture events in the greater Palm Springs area. I added by way of explanation, "I only moved here a month ago."

"I think they have a couple performances left in the season." Brayden hesitated once more. "I'd see it again if you wanted to go. Though I'll warn you—it's one of those reinterpreted Shakespeare productions. Modern clothes."

"I don't mind. That kind of reinterpretation is what makes

Shakespeare timeless." The words rolled automatically off my lips. As they did, I suddenly had one of those epiphany moments where I realized there was more going on than I'd initially thought. I replayed Brayden's words. Between that and Trey's enormous grin, I soon had a startling realization. This was the guy Trey had been telling me about. My "soul mate." *And he was asking me out.*

"This is a great idea," said Trey. "You kids should totally go see that play. Make a whole day of it. Grab some dinner and hang out at the library or whatever it is you do for fun."

Brayden met my eyes. His were hazel, almost like Eddie's but with a little green. Not as much green as Adrian's, of course. No one's eyes were that amazingly green. Brayden's brown hair occasionally picked up glints of gold in the light and was cut in a no-nonsense way that showed off the angles of his cheekbones. I had to admit, he was pretty cute. "They perform Thursday through Sunday," he said. "I've got a debate tournament over the weekend . . . could you do it Thursday night?"

"I . . . " Could I? There was nothing planned, so far as I knew. About twice a week, I took Jill to the home of Clarence Donahue, an old Moroi who had a feeder. Thursday wasn't a scheduled feeding night, though, and technically I wasn't obligated to go to experiment nights.

"Of course she's free," Trey jumped in before I could even answer. "Right, Sydney?"

"Yes," I said, shooting him a look. "I'm free."

Brayden smiled. I smiled back. Nervous silence fell. He seemed as unsure as I was about how to proceed. I would have thought it was cute, if I wasn't so worried that I looked ridiculous.

Trey elbowed him sharply. "This is the part where you ask for her number."

Brayden nodded, though he didn't look like he appreciated the elbowing. "Right, right." He pulled a cell phone out of his pocket. "Is it Sydney with a *y* or *i*?" Trey rolled his eyes. "What? I'm guessing the former, but as naming conventions become increasingly untraditional, you never know. I just want to get it right in my phone."

"I would have done the same thing," I agreed. I then told him my phone number.

He looked up and smiled at me. "Great. I'm looking forward to it."

"Me too," I said, and actually meant it.

I left Spencer's in a daze. I had a date. How on earth did I have a date?

Trey hurried out to me a few moments later, catching me as I was unlocking my car. He still wore his barista apron. "Well?" he asked. "Was I right, or was I right?"

"About what?" I asked, though I had a feeling I knew what was coming.

"About Brayden being your soul mate."

"I told you—"

"I know, I know. You don't believe in soul mates. Still," he grinned, "if that guy isn't perfect for you, then I don't know who is."

"Well, we'll see." I balanced Ms. Terwilliger's cup on top of the car, so I could drink from my own. "Of course, he doesn't like modern Shakespearean interpretations, so that might be a deal breaker."

Trey stared at me in disbelief. "Seriously?"

"No," I said, giving him a look. "I'm kidding. Well, maybe." The latte Brayden had made me was pretty good, so I was willing to give him the benefit of a doubt on the Shakespeare thing. "Why do you care so much about my romantic life anyway?"

Trey shrugged and stuffed his hands into his pockets. Already, beads of sweat were forming on his tanned skin from the late afternoon sun. "I don't know. I guess I feel like I owe you for everything that went down with the tattoos. That and all your homework help."

"You don't really need my help with that. And the tattoos . . . " I frowned, as an image of Keith beating on the glass flashed through my mind. Keith's vampire blood ring had resulted in high-inducing tattoos that had wreaked havoc on Amberwood. Trey, of course, didn't know about my personal interest in the matter. He just knew I'd gotten rid of those who were using the tattoos to unfair advantage in sports. "I did it because it was the right thing to do."

That made him smile. "Of course. Still, it's saved me a lot of grief with my dad."

"I should hope so. You don't have any competition on the team now. What more could your dad want?"

"Oh, there's always something else he thinks I could be the best at. It's not just football." Trey had hinted at that before.

"I know what that's like," I said, thinking of my own father. A moment of silence fell between us.

"It doesn't help that my perfect cousin's coming into town soon," he said finally. "Makes everything I do look completely lame. You got a cousin like that?"

"Er, not really." Most of my cousins were on my mom's side, and my dad tended to shy away from her family.

"You probably *are* the perfect cousin," Trey grumbled. "Anyway, yeah, there're always these expectations in the family . . . always these tests. Football's given me some respectability for now." He winked at me. "That and my awesome chem grade."

That last comment wasn't lost on me. "Fine. I'll text you when I get back tonight. We'll make it happen."

"Thanks. And I'll give Brayden a talking-to so he doesn't try anything on Thursday."

My mind was still full of Latin and Shakespeare. "Try what?"

Trey shook his head. "Honestly, Melbourne, I don't know how you've survived this long in the world without me."

"Oh," I said, blushing. "*That.*" Great. Now I had something else to worry about.

Trey scoffed. "Between you and me, Brayden's probably the last guy in the world you have to worry about. I think he's as clueless as you are. If I didn't care about your virtue so much, I'd actually probably give him a lecture on *how* to try something."

"Well, thanks for keeping my best interests at heart," I said dryly. "I always wanted a brother to watch out for me."

He studied me curiously. "Don't you have, like, three brothers?"

Oh no.

"Er, I meant figuratively." I tried not to panic. I rarely slipped up on our background story. Eddie, Adrian, and Keith had all been passed off as my brothers at some point. "None of them are really that concerned about my dating life. What *I'm* concerned about, though, is getting into air conditioning." I opened my car door, and a wave of heat rolled out. "I'll talk to you tonight and help you with the lab."

Trey nodded, looking like he wanted to get back inside as well. "And I'll help *you* if you have any more questions about dating."

I hoped my scathing look told him my opinion on that, but once he was gone and I was blasting the car's air conditioning, my arrogance faded. Anxiety took its place. The question I'd asked myself earlier repeated in my head.

How on earth was I going to get through this date alive?

CHAPTER 5

WORD OF MY UPCOMING DATE spread fast.

I could only presume Trey had told Kristin and Julia, who had in turn told Jill and Eddie and God only knew who else. . . . So, I shouldn't have been surprised when I got a call from Adrian just after dinner. He started talking before I could even say hello.

"Really, Sage? A date?"

I sighed. "Yes, Adrian. A date."

"A real date. Not, like, doing homework together," he added. "I mean like where you go out to a movie or something. And a movie that's not part of a school assignment. Or about something boring."

"A *real* date." I figured I wouldn't give him the specifics on the Shakespeare play.

"What's the lucky guy's name?"

"Brayden."

There was a pause. "Brayden? That's his real name?"

"Why are you asking if everything's real? You think I'd make any of this up?"

"No, no," Adrian assured me. "That's what's so unbelievable about it. Is he cute?"

I glanced at the clock. It was time for me to meet my study group. "Gee, maybe I should just send you a picture to review?"

"Yes, please. And a full background check and life history."

"I have to go. Why do you care so much anyway?" I finally asked in exasperation.

His answer took a long time, which was uncharacteristic. Adrian was usually ready with a dozen witty quips. Maybe he couldn't decide which one to use. When he finally responded, it was in that usual sarcastic way of his—though the levity sounded a little forced. "Because it's one of those things I never expected to see in my lifetime," he told me. "Like a comet. Or world peace. I'm just used to you being single."

For some reason, that bothered me. "What, you don't think any guy would ever be interested in me?"

"Actually," said Adrian, sounding remarkably serious, "I can imagine lots of guys being interested in you."

I was certain he was teasing me and had no time for his jokes. I said goodbye and headed off to my study group, which, thankfully, was pretty dedicated and got a lot of work done. But when I met up with Trey at the library later, he was less than focused. He couldn't stop going on and on about how brilliant he was in getting Brayden and me together.

"This date hasn't even happened, and I'm already tired of it," I said. I spread Trey's lab paperwork out on the table before us. The numbers and formulas were comforting, far more concrete and orderly than the mysteries of social interaction. I tapped the lab assignment with my pen. "Pay attention. We don't have a lot of time."

He shrugged off my concerns. "Can't you just finish it?"

"No! I left enough time so that you could do it yourself. I'll help, but that's it."

Trey was intelligent enough to figure out most of it on his own. Using me was just another way for him to dodge looking smart. He let the date go and focused on the work. I thought I was free of Brayden interrogation until, just as were wrapping up, Jill and Micah came strolling by, hand in hand.

They were with a group of other people, which didn't surprise me. Micah was easygoing and popular, and Jill had inherited a large circle of friends by going out with him. Her eyes sparkled with happiness as someone in the group told a funny story that made them all laugh. I couldn't help a smile myself. This was a far cry from when Jill had first come to Amberwood and been treated as an outcast for unusual looks and odd behaviors. She was thriving with this new social status. Maybe it would help her embrace her royal background. My smile faded when Jill pulled Micah away from the group and hurried over to our table. Her eager expression worried me.

"Is it true?" she asked. "Do you have a date?"

"For the love of—you know it's true! And you told Adrian, didn't you?" I gave her a pointed look. Their psychic bond wasn't active 100 percent of the time, but something told me she knew about his earlier phone call to me. When the bond was "on," she could see into his mind, observing both his feelings and actions. It only worked one way, however. Adrian had no such insight. She turned sheepish.

"Yeah . . . I couldn't help it when Micah told me . . . "

"I heard it from Eddie," Micah added quickly, as though that might get him off the hook. He had red hair and blue eyes that were always cheerful and friendly. He was one of those people you couldn't help but like, which made it harder to undo the tangled web Jill had woven by dating him.

"Hey, I did *not* tell Eddie," said Trey defensively.

I turned my gaze on him. "But you told other people. And they told Eddie."

Trey gave a half shrug. "I might have mentioned it here and there."

"Unbelievable," I said.

"What's this guy like?" asked Jill. "Is he cute?"

I thought about it. "Pretty cute."

She perked up. "Well, that's promising. Where's he taking you? Somewhere good? Night on the town? Fancy dinner? Micah and I had an awesome time at Salton Sea. It's so pretty. You could go there, have a romantic picnic." Her cheeks turned pink and she stopped for breath, as if realizing she was talking too much. Rambling was one of Jill's most endearing traits.

"We're going to see Shakespeare in the park," I said.

That got me silence.

"*Antony and Cleopatra.* It's good." I suddenly felt the need to defend myself. "A classic. Brayden and I both appreciate Shakespeare."

"His name is *Brayden*?" asked Micah in disbelief. "What kind of a name is *that*?"

Jill frowned. "*Antony and Cleopatra* . . . is that romantic?"

"Kind of," I said. "For a while. Then everyone dies in the end."

Jill's horrified expression told me that I wasn't really improving matters.

"Well," she said. "I hope you have, um, fun." A few moments of awkwardness ensued, then her eyes lit up again. "Oh! Lia called me tonight. She said you two talked about me modeling for her again?"

"She what?" I exclaimed. "That's not quite how I'd put it. She asked if you could do some print ads. I said no."

"Oh." Jill's face fell a little. "I understand. From what she said . . . I just thought. Well. I thought maybe there was a way . . . "

I gave her a meaningful look. "I'm sorry, Jill. I wish there was a way. But you know why you can't."

She nodded sadly. "I understand. It's okay."

"You don't need a modeling campaign to be beautiful to me," said Micah gallantly.

That brought a smile back to her face that faded when she saw a nearby clock. Her transient moods reminded me of Adrian's, and I wondered if some of that was the effect of the bond. "Ugh. Curfew's coming. We'd better head out. You coming, Sydney?"

I glanced at Trey's lab. It was complete and, I knew, absolutely perfect. "I'll leave in just a couple minutes."

She and Micah left. Glancing over at Trey, I was surprised to find him staring at her retreating figure intently. I nudged him.

"Hey. Don't forget to put your name on this, or it was all for nothing."

It still took him several seconds to drag his gaze away. "That's your sister, isn't it?" His dismal tone made it sound more like a statement than a question, as though he were revealing some unfortunate fact.

"Um, yeah. You've seen her like a hundred times. She's gone to this school for a month."

He frowned. "I just never thought much about it . . . never got a good look at her before. I don't have any classes with her."

"She was front and center in that fashion show."

"She had a mask on." His dark eyes studied me. "You guys don't look alike at all."

"We get that a lot."

Trey still looked troubled, and I had no idea why. "You're smart to keep her out of modeling," he said at last. "She's too young."

"It's a religious thing," I said, knowing Trey wouldn't quiz me for many details on our "faith."

"Whatever it is, keep her out of the public eye." He scrawled his name on the lab and shut his textbook. "You don't want her plastered all over magazines or something. Lots of creepy people out there."

Now I was the one left staring. I agreed with him. Too much exposure meant the Moroi dissidents could find Jill. But why would Trey feel that way, too? His claims that she was too young were sound, I supposed, but there was something vaguely unsettling about the exchange. The way he'd watched her walk away was too weird. But then, what other reason aside from concern could he have?

The normality of the next couple of days was welcome— normality being relative around here, of course. Adrian kept sending me e-mails, asking me to rescue him (while also offering unsolicited dating advice). Ms. Terwilliger continued her passive aggressive attempts to teach me magic. Eddie continued in his fierce dedication to Jill. And Angeline continued her not-so-subtle advances on Eddie.

After watching her "accidentally" spill her water bottle all over her white T-shirt at practice with him one day, I knew something would have to be done, no matter what Eddie had said about his personal life. Like so many awkward and unpleasant tasks in our cohort, I had a feeling I was the one who would have to do it. I figured this would be some sort of stern, heart-to-heart talk about the proper way to solicit someone's attention, but on the night of my date with Brayden, it was soon made clear to me that I was apparently the last person who should be giving dating advice.

"You're wearing *that*?" demanded Kristin, pointing an accusing finger at the outfit I'd neatly set out on my bed. She and Julia had taken it upon themselves to inspect me before I went out. Jill and Angeline had tagged along without invitation, and I couldn't help but notice that everyone seemed a lot more excited about this than I was. Mostly I was a tangle of nerves and fear. This was what it must feel like to go into a test without having studied. It was a new experience for me.

"It's not a school uniform," I said. I'd had enough sense to know wearing that would be unacceptable. "And it's a color. Kind of."

Julia held up the top I'd selected, a crisp cotton blouse with short sleeves and a high, button-up collar. The whole thing was a soft shade of lemon yellow, which I thought would score me points with this group since everyone accused me of not wearing colors. I'd even combined it with a pair of jeans. She shook her head. "This is the kind of shirt that says, 'You're never getting in here.'"

"Well, why would he?" I demanded.

Kristin, sitting cross-legged in my desk chair, tilted her head thoughtfully as she studied the shirt. "I think it's more like a shirt that says, 'I'm going to have to end this date early so I can go prepare my Power Point presentation.'"

That sent them into fits of laughter. I was about to protest when I noticed Jill and Angeline going through my closet. "Hey! Maybe you should ask before doing that."

"All your dresses are too heavy," said Jill. She pulled out one made of soft, gray cashmere. "I mean, at least this is sleeveless, but it's still too much for this weather."

"Half my wardrobe is," I said. "It's made for four seasons. I didn't really have a lot of time to switch to all summer stuff before coming here."

"See?" exclaimed Angeline triumphantly. "Now you know my problem. I can cut a couple inches off of that, if you want."

"No!" To my relief, Jill put the dress away. A few moments later, she produced a new find.

"What about this?" She held up a hanger carrying a long white tank top made of light, crinkly material with a scoop neckline.

Kristin glanced at Angeline. "Think you could make the neckline lower?"

"The neckline's low enough already. And that's not a shirt you wear on its own," I protested. "It's meant to be tucked in under a blazer."

Julia rose from the chair. She tossed her hair; this was

serious business. "No, no . . . this might work." She took the shirt from Jill and laid it across the jeans I'd set out. She studied it for a few moments and then returned to my closet—which was apparently free game for everyone. After a quick search, she pulled out a skinny leather belt with a tan snakeskin pattern. "I thought I remembered you wearing this." She laid the belt over the white shirt and stepped back. After a bit more scrutiny, she gave it a nod of approval. The others crowded in to look.

"Good eye," said Kristin.

"Hey, I found the shirt," Jill reminded her.

"I can't wear the shirt alone," I said. I hoped my protests covered up my anxiety. Had I really been that off on the yellow shirt? I'd been certain it was date-appropriate. How was I going to survive tonight if I couldn't even dress right?

"If you want to put a blazer on over it in this weather, be my guest," said Julia. "But I don't think you have to worry about it showing too much. This wouldn't even be worth Mrs. Weathers's notice."

"Neither would the yellow blouse," I pointed out.

They decided my clothing was a done deal and moved on to hair and makeup advice. I drew the line there. I wore makeup every day—very nice, very expensive makeup applied to make the most of my features in a way that made it look as though I didn't even have makeup on. I wasn't going to change that natural look, no matter how adamantly Julia swore pink eye shadow would be "hot."

None of them put up much of a fight on my hair. It was currently in a layered cut that went just past my shoulders. There was exactly one way it could be styled, worn down with the layers carefully arranged with a hair dryer. Any other style looked messy, and of course, I already had it in the perfect configuration today. No point messing with a good thing. Besides, I think they were all too excited that I'd agreed to wear the white tank top—once I'd tried it on to verify that it wasn't transparent.

My only nod to jewelry was my little gold cross. I fastened it around my neck and said a silent prayer that I'd get through this. Although Alchemists used crosses a lot, we weren't exactly part of any traditional Christian faith or practice. We had our own religious services and believed in God, that He was a great force of goodness and light that infused every bit of the universe. With all that responsibility, He probably didn't care much about one girl going on a date, but maybe He could spare a second to make sure it wasn't *too* painful.

They all traipsed down the stairs with me when the time came for Brayden to pick me up. (Actually, it was a little earlier than the appointed time, but I hated being late.) The girls had all come up with reasons for needing to meet him, from Jill's "It's a family thing" to Kristin's "I can spot an asshole in five seconds." I wasn't confident in that last one, seeing as she'd once speculated that Keith might be a good catch.

All of them were also full of unsolicited advice.

"You can split the cost of dinner *or* the play," said Julia. "Not both. He needs to pick up the whole bill on one of them."

"Better if he pays for everything, though," said Kristin.

"Still order something, even if you don't want to eat it," added Jill. "If he's buying dinner, you don't want to let him off cheap. He's gotta work for you."

"Where are you guys getting all of this?" I asked. "What does it matter if I—oh, come *on*."

We'd reached the lobby and found Eddie and Micah sitting

on a bench together. They at least had the decency to look embarrassed.

"Not you guys too," I said.

"I was just here to see Jill," said Micah unconvincingly.

"And I was here to, um . . . " Eddie faltered, and I held up a hand to stop him.

"Don't bother. Honestly, I'm surprised Trey isn't here with a camera or something. I figured he'd want to immortalize every moment of this debacle of a—oh. Hey, over here." I put on a smile as Brayden stepped into the lobby. Apparently I wasn't the only one who liked to be early.

Brayden seemed a little surprised that I had an entourage. I couldn't blame him since I was kind of surprised I had one too.

"It's nice to meet all of you," said Brayden, friendly, even if a little bewildered.

Eddie, while uncomfortable with Angeline's advances, could be perfectly outgoing in less bizarre social situations. He played up the brotherly role and shook Brayden's hand. "I hear you guys are seeing a play tonight."

"Yes," said Brayden. "Although, I prefer the term drama. I've actually already seen this production, but I'd like to watch it again with an eye toward alternative forms of dramatic analysis. The standard Freytag method can get a little clichéd after a while."

This left everyone speechless. Or maybe they were just trying to figure out what he'd said. Eddie glanced at me then back to Brayden. "Well. Something tells me you guys are going to have a great time together."

Once we were able to extract ourselves from my well-wishers Brayden said, "You have very . . . devoted family and friends."

"Oh," I said. "That. They just, uh, happened to all be going out together at the same time we were. To study."

Brayden glanced at his watch. "Not too late for that, I suppose. If I can, I always do my homework right after school because—"

"If you put it off, you never know if something unexpected might happen?"

"Exactly," he said.

He smiled at me. I smiled back.

I followed him to visitor parking, over to a shiny, silver Ford Mustang. I nearly swooned. Immediately, I reached out and ran my hand along the car's smooth surface. "Nice," I said. "Brand new, next model year. These new ones will never quite have the character of the classics, but they certainly make up for it in fuel economy and safety."

Brayden looked pleasantly surprised. "You know your cars."

"It's a hobby," I admitted. "My mom is really into them." When I'd first met Rose Hathaway, I'd had the incredible experience of driving a 1972 Citroën. Now I owned a Subaru named Latte. I loved it, but it wasn't exactly glamorous. "They're works of art and engineering."

I noticed then that Brayden had come with me to the passenger side. For half a second, I thought he expected me to drive. Maybe because I liked cars so much? But then, he opened the door and I realized he was waiting for me to get in. I did, trying to remember the last time a guy had opened a car door for me. My conclusion: never.

Dinner wasn't fast food, but it wasn't anything fancy either. I wondered what Julia and Kristin's opinion would be on that. We ate at a very California type of café, that served all organic sandwiches and salads. Every menu item seemed to feature avocado.

"I would've taken you somewhere nicer," he told me. "But I didn't want to risk being late. The park's a few blocks away, so we should be able to get a good spot. I . . . I hope that's okay?" He suddenly looked nervous. It was such a contrast to the confidence he had shown when talking about Shakespeare. I had to admit, it was kind of reassuring. I found myself relaxing a little bit. "If it's not, I'll find a better place—"

"No, this is great," I told him, glancing around the café's brightly lit dining room. It was one of those places where we ordered at a counter and then brought a number to our table. "I'd rather be early, anyway." He'd paid for all of our food. I tried to make sense of the dating rules my friends had bombarded me with. "What do I owe you for my ticket?" I asked tentatively.

Brayden looked surprised. "Nothing. It's on me." He smiled tentatively back.

"Thank you," I said. So, he was paying. That would make Kristin happy, although it made me a little uneasy—through no fault of his. With the Alchemists, I was always the one picking up the bills and handling the paperwork. I wasn't used to someone else doing it. I guess I just had trouble shaking that feeling that I had to take care of everything because no one else could do it right.

Academics had always been a breeze for me. But at Amberwood, learning how to hang out with people my own age in a normal way had been a much more difficult task. I'd gotten better, but it was still a struggle trying to figure out the proper things to say to my peers. With Brayden, there were no such problems. We had an endless supply of topics, both of us eager to put forth all we knew on anything and everything. Most of the meal was spent discussing the intricacies of the organic certification process. It was pretty awesome.

Trouble came when, as we were finishing up, Brayden asked if I wanted to get dessert before we left. I froze, suddenly in a dilemma. Jill had said to make sure I ordered enough to not come across as a cheap date. Without even thinking about it, I'd ordered an inexpensive salad—simply because it sounded good. Was I now on the hook to order more so I'd seem like someone Brayden had to work for? Was this worth breaking all my own rules about sugar and dessert? And honestly, what did *Jill* know about dating etiquette anyway? Her last boyfriend had been homicidal, and her current one was oblivious to the fact that she was a vampire.

"Uh, no thank you," I said at last. "I'd rather make sure we get to the park on time."

He nodded as he rose from the table and gave me another smile. "I was thinking the same thing. Most people don't seem to think punctuality is that important."

"Important? It's essential," I said. "I'm always at least ten minutes early."

Brayden's grin widened. "I aim for fifteen. To tell you the truth . . . I really didn't want dessert anyway." He held the door open for me as we stepped outside. "I try to avoid getting too much sugar."

I nearly came to a standstill in astonishment. "I totally agree—but my friends always give me a hard time about it."

Brayden nodded. "There are all sorts of reasons. People just don't get it, though."

I walked to the park, stunned. No one had ever understood me so quickly and easily. It was like he had read my mind.

Palm Springs was a desert city, filled with long stretches of sandy vistas and stark, rocky mountain faces. But it was also a city that mankind had been shaping for a long time, and many places—Amberwood, for example—had been given lush, green makeovers in defiance of the natural climate. This park was no exception. It was a huge expanse of green lawn, ringed with leafy deciduous trees instead of the usual palms. A stage had been set up at one end, and people were already seeking out the best spots. We chose one in the shade that had a great view of the stage. Brayden took out a blanket to sit on from his backpack, along with a worn copy of *Antony and Cleopatra*. It was marked up with notes and sticky tabs.

"Did you bring your own?" he asked me.

"No," I said. I couldn't help but be impressed. "I didn't bring many books from home when I moved here."

He hesitated, as though unsure he should say what he was thinking. "Do you want to read along with mine?"

I'd honestly figured I would just watch the play, but the scholar in me could certainly see the perks of having the original text along. I was also curious about what kind of notes he'd made. It was only after I'd said yes that I realized why he was nervous. Reading along with him meant we had to sit very, very close together.

"I won't bite," he said, smiling when I didn't move right away.

That broke the tension, and we managed to move into positions that allowed us both to see the book with *almost* no touching. There was no avoiding our knees brushing one another, but we both had jeans on, and it didn't make me feel like my virtue was at stake. Also, I couldn't help but notice he smelled like coffee—my favorite vice. That wasn't a bad thing. Not bad at all.

Still, I was very conscious of being so close to someone. I didn't *think* I was getting any romantic vibes. My pulse didn't race; my heart didn't flutter. Mostly I was aware that this was the closest I'd sat to anyone, maybe in my life. I wasn't used to sharing my personal space so much.

I soon forgot about that as the play started. Brayden might not like Shakespeare performed in modern clothing, but I thought they did an admirable job. Following along with the text, we caught a couple of spots where the actors messed up a line. We shot each other secret, triumphant looks, gleeful that we were in on something others didn't know about. I kept up with Brayden's annotations too, nodding at some and shaking my head at others. I couldn't wait until we discussed this on the ride home.

We were all leaning forward intently during Cleopatra's dramatic death scene, intensely focused on her last lines. Off to my side, I heard the crinkling of paper. I ignored it and leaned forward further. The paper crinkled again, this time much louder. Looking over, I saw a group of guys sitting nearby who appeared to be about college-aged. Most of them were watching the performance, but one was holding an item wrapped in a brown paper bag. The bag was too big for the object and had been rolled down several times. He glanced around nervously, trying to be discreet and unroll the paper in small batches. It was obvious that was actually making more noise than if he'd just gone for it and unrolled it all at once.

This went on for another minute, and by then, a few others nearby were glancing over at him. He finally managed to open the bag and then, still in slow motion, carefully lowered his hand inside. I heard the *pop* of a cap and the guy's face lit up in triumph. Still keeping the object concealed, he lifted the bag to his mouth and drank out of what was very obviously a bottle of beer or some other alcohol. It had been pretty apparent right away from the bag shape.

I clapped a hand over my mouth, in an attempt to smother my laughter. He reminded me so much of Adrian. I could absolutely see Adrian smuggling in alcohol to an event like this and then going to all sorts of pains to be covert, thinking that if he just did everything slowly enough, no one would catch on to him. Adrian, too, would probably have the misfortune of opening the bottle right in the middle of the play's most tense scene. I could even picture a similarly delighted look on his face, one that said, *No one knows what I'm doing!* When, of course, we all knew. I didn't know why it made me laugh, but it did.

Brayden was too focused on the play to notice. "Ooh," he whispered to me. "This is a good part—where her handmaidens kill themselves."

The two of us had plenty to debate and analyze on the way back to Amberwood. I was almost disappointed when his car pulled up to my dorm. As we sat there, I realized we'd come to another critical dating milestone. What was the correct procedure here? Was he supposed to kiss me? Was I supposed to let him? Had that been the real price of my salad?

Brayden seemed nervous too, and I braced myself for the worst. When I looked down at my hands in my lap, I noticed they were shaking. *You can do this*, I told myself. *It's a rite of passage*. I started to close my eyes, but when Brayden spoke, I opened them quickly.

As it turned out, Brayden's buildup of courage wasn't for a kiss, so much as a question.

"Would you . . . would you like to go out again?" he asked, giving me a shy smile.

I was surprised at the mix of emotions this triggered. Relief was foremost, of course. I'd now have time to research books on kissing too. At the same time, I was kind of disappointed that the swagger and confidence he'd shown in dramatic analysis didn't carry through here. Some part of me thought his line should've been more like, "Well, after that night of perfection, I guess we have no choice but to go out again." Immediately, I felt stupid for such a sentiment. I had no business expecting him to be more at ease with this when I was sitting there with my hands shaking.

"Sure," I blurted out.

He breathed a sigh of relief. "Cool," he said. "I'll e-mail you."

"That'd be great." I smiled. More awkward silence fell, and suddenly, I wondered if the kiss might be coming after all.

"Do you . . . do you want me to walk you to the door?" he asked.

"What? Oh, no. Thank you. It's right there. I'll be fine. Thank you." I realized I was on the verge of sounding like Jill.

"Well, then," said Brayden. "I had a really nice night. Looking forward to next time."

"Me too."

He held out his hand. I shook it. Then I left the car and went inside.

I shook his hand? I replayed the moment in my head, feeling dumber and dumber. *What is wrong with me?*

As I walked through the lobby, kind of dazed, I took out my cell phone to see if I had any messages. I'd turned it off tonight, figuring if ever there was a time I'd earned peace, this was it. To my astonishment, no one had needed anything in my absence, though there was one text message from Jill, sent about fifteen minutes ago: *How was your date with Brandon? What's he like?*

I unlocked my dorm door and stepped inside. *His name is Brayden*, I texted back. I pondered the rest of her question and took a long time in trying to decide how to respond.

He's just like me.

CHAPTER 6

"YOU SHOOK HIS HAND?" Adrian asked incredulously.

I shot an accusing look at Eddie and Angeline. "Is nothing private around here?"

"No," said Angeline, as bluntly honest as ever. Eddie actually chuckled. It was a rare moment of camaraderie between them.

"Was it supposed to be a secret?" he asked. We were over at Clarence Donahue's house for Jill and Adrian's biweekly blood feedings. Jill was off right now with Clarence's human housekeeper, Dorothy, who doubled as his feeder. I could take a lot of Moroi things in stride now, but drinking blood—*human* blood—made me shudder every time. My best coping mechanism was trying to forget why we were here.

"No," I admitted. Julia and Kristin had grilled me for date details a couple of days ago, so I'd given them some. I supposed I had to accept that once I told them anything, it would inevitably get back to everyone in the world. No doubt my Amberwood family had then passed it on to Adrian.

"Really?" Adrian was still hung up on the end of my date. *"His hand?"*

I sighed and sank back into a sleek leather sofa. Clarence's house always reminded me of some stereotypical haunted manor from the outside—but inside it was modern and well furnished. "Look, it just happened—okay, you know what? Never mind. This is none of your business. Just let it go." But something in Adrian's expression told me he would not, in fact, be letting it go anytime soon.

"With all that red-hot passion, it's a wonder you guys can stay away from each other," said Adrian, deadpan. "Is there going to be a second date?"

Eddie and Angeline looked at me expectantly. I hesitated. This was information I hadn't given up to Julia and Kristin, largely because it had only just been arranged. "Yes," I said at last. "We're going on a, um, windmill tour later this week."

If I'd wanted to shut them all up, I'd definitely succeeded. They all looked stunned.

Adrian spoke first. "I'm going to assume that means he's flying you to Amsterdam on his private jet. If so, I'd like to come along. But not for the windmills."

"There's a huge windmill farm north of Palm Springs," I explained. "It's one of the only ones in the world that does public tours."

More blank looks.

"Wind energy is a powerful renewable resource that could have a huge impact on our country's future!" I said in exasperation. "This is a cool thing."

"'Cool,'" said Adrian. "'Wind.' I see what you did there, Sage. Pretty clever."

"It wasn't meant to be a—"

The sitting room's stained glass French doors opened, and Dimitri and Sonya entered with our host Clarence in tow. I hadn't seen him since I arrived and gave him a polite smile, glad for the distraction from my so-called love life.

"Hello, Mr. Donahue," I said. "It's nice to see you again."

"Eh?" The elderly Moroi man squinted in my direction, and after a few moments, recognition lit his features. He had white hair and always dressed as though he were at a formal dinner party from about fifty years ago. "There you are. Glad you could stop by, my dear. What brings you over?"

"Jill's feeding, sir." We did this two times every week, but Clarence's mind wasn't quite what it used to be. He'd been pretty scattered since we first met, but the death of his son, Lee, had seemed to push the old man even farther over the edge—particularly since he didn't seem to believe it. We'd told him gently—a number of times—that Lee had died, leaving out the Strigoi part. Each time we did, Clarence insisted Lee was just "away right now" and would be back. Scattered or not, Clarence was always kind and relatively harmless—for a vampire, of course.

"Ah, yes, naturally." He settled into his massive armchair and then glanced back toward Dimitri and Sonya. "So you'll be able to fix the window locks?" There had apparently been some other discussion going on before they joined us.

Dimitri seemed to be trying to find a nice way to respond. He was as amazing to look at as ever, dressed in jeans and a T-shirt, with a long leather duster over it all. How anyone could survive wearing a coat like that in Palm Springs was beyond me, but if anyone could, I supposed it was him. Usually he only wore it inside, but sometimes, I'd see it outside too. I'd mentioned this odd wardrobe choice to Adrian a couple of weeks ago: "Isn't Dimitri hot?" Adrian's response hadn't been entirely unexpected: "Well, yeah, according to most women, at least."

Dimitri's face was the picture of politeness as he addressed Clarence's concerns. "I don't believe there's anything wrong with the ones you have," Dimitri said. "Everything is sealed up pretty tightly."

"So it seems," said Clarence ominously. "But you don't know how resourceful *they* are. I'm not behind the times, you know. I know there are all sorts of technologies out there that you can put in. Like lasers that tell you if someone's breaking in."

Dimitri arched an eyebrow. "You mean a security system?"

"Yes, exactly," said Clarence. "That'll keep the hunters out."

This turn in conversation wasn't exactly a surprise to me. Clarence's paranoia had also increased recently—and that was saying something. He lived in constant fear of what he claimed were vampire hunters, humans who . . . well, hunted vampires. For the longest time, he'd claimed they were responsible for his niece's death and that reports of her being killed by a Strigoi were incorrect. It turned out he was half-right. Her death hadn't been the result of a Strigoi attack—it had been caused by Lee, in a desperate attempt to change back from a Moroi to a Strigoi. Clarence refused to accept that, however, and persisted in his beliefs about the hunters. My assurances that the Alchemists had no records of any groups like that existing since the Middle Ages hadn't gone very far. Consequently, Clarence was always making people do "security checks" of his house. Since Sonya and Dimitri were actually staying with him throughout the experimentation, that tedious task often fell to them.

"I'm not really qualified to install a security system," said Dimitri.

"Really? There's something you can't do?" Adrian's voice was so soft that I could barely hear him, and he was sitting right next to me. I doubted even the others, with their superior hearing, could've made out his words. *Why does he still let Dimitri get to him?* I wondered.

"You'd have to call professionals," Dimitri continued to Clarence. "I'm guessing you wouldn't want a bunch of strangers coming in and out of your house."

Clarence frowned. "That's true. It'd be very easy for the hunters to infiltrate them."

Dimitri was the picture of patience. "I'll do daily checks of all the doors and windows while I'm here—just to be sure."

"That would be wonderful," said Clarence, some of his tension easing. "Admittedly, I'm not really the hunters' usual type. Not dangerous enough. Not anymore." He chuckled to himself. "Still. You never know what could happen. Best to be safe."

Sonya gave him a gentle smile. "I'm sure everything will be fine. You have nothing to worry about."

Clarence met her eyes, and after a few seconds, a smile slowly spread over his face as well. His rigid posture slackened. "Yes, yes. You're right. Nothing to worry about."

I shivered. I'd been around Moroi enough to know what had happened. Sonya had just used compulsion—only a whisper of it—to calm Clarence. Compulsion, the ability to force your will on others, was a skill all Moroi possessed to varying degrees. Spirit users were the strongest, rivaling Strigoi. Using compulsion on others was taboo among the Moroi, and there were serious consequences for those who abused it.

I was guessing Moroi authorities would overlook her soothing a nervous old man, but the small act still unsettled me. Compulsion in particular had always struck me as one of the most insidious Moroi powers. And had Sonya *really* needed to use it? She was already so kind and soothing. Wouldn't that be enough for Clarence? Sometimes I wondered if they just used magic for the sake of doing so. Sometimes I wondered if it was being used around me . . . without me even knowing.

Clarence's talk of vampire hunters always triggered a mix of amusement and unease around everyone. With him pacified (even if I didn't like the means), we were all able to relax a little bit. Sonya leaned back against the loveseat, drinking some fruity drink that looked perfect on a hot day like this. From her dirty clothes and haphazard hairstyling, I was willing to bet she'd been outside—not that she still didn't look beautiful. Most Moroi avoided this kind of intense sun, but her love of plants was so great that she'd been risking it to work on some of the ailing flowers in Clarence's garden. Heavy sunscreen could work wonders.

"I'm not going to be around much longer," she told us. "A few more weeks at most. I need to go back and work on some wedding plans with Mikhail."

"When's the big day again?" Adrian asked.

She smiled. "It's in December." That surprised me until she added, "There's a huge, tropical greenhouse near the Court that we're going to use. It's gorgeous—not that it matters.

Mikhail and I could be married anywhere. All that counts is that we're together. Of course, if we're able to choose, then why not go all out?"

Even I smiled at that. Leave it to Sonya to find a spot of green in the middle of a Pennsylvania winter.

"Dimitri may stay on," she continued. "But it'd be great if we could make some kind of progress before I go. The aura tests so far have been . . . "

"Useless?" suggested Adrian.

"I was going to say inconclusive," she replied.

Adrian shook his head. "So all that time we spent was wasted?"

Sonya didn't answer and instead took another sip of her drink. I was willing to bet it was non-alcoholic—she didn't self-medicate the way Adrian did—and that Dorothy could make me one if I wanted. Yet, I was also willing to bet it was terrible for me. Maybe I'd see if there was any Diet Coke in the kitchen.

Sonya leaned forward, an eager glint in her eye. "Dimitri and I were talking and realized there's something obvious we've been missing. Actually, I should say avoiding, but not pursuing it would be a waste."

"What's that?" asked Adrian.

"Blood," said Dimitri.

I winced. I didn't like it when this topic came up. It reminded me of exactly what kind of people I was with.

"Obviously, there's something about restored Strigoi that protects them—us," he said. "We've looked for magical signs, but the answer might be more physical. And from the report I read, the Strigoi had trouble drinking L—*his* blood." Dimitri had been about to say Lee, but had amended his choice out of respect for Clarence. The old man's dazed, happy look made it hard to tell if he understood what we were discussing at all.

"They complained about it," I agreed. "But that didn't seem to stop them from drinking it." Strigoi could be forcibly created if a Strigoi drained a victim's blood and then fed Strigoi blood back to him or her. Lee had asked Strigoi to do this for him, but all draining him had achieved was death.

"We'd like to take a sample of Dimitri's blood and then compare it to yours, Eddie," said Sonya. "Blood can hold all sorts of magical properties, which might show us how to fight Strigoi."

I kept my face as blank as possible, praying no one would notice me. *Blood can hold all sorts of magical properties.* Hopefully, in all this talk, no one would recall the mystery of why my blood was inexplicably revolting to Strigoi. And really, why should they? I'd never been restored. I wasn't a dhampir. There was no reason at all they'd want me in these experiments. And yet, if that was true, why was I suddenly sweating?

"We can send it to a lab for the chemical part and try to read any magical properties off it too," Sonya continued. She sounded apologetic, but Eddie didn't look concerned.

"No problem," he said. "Whatever you need." He meant it too, I knew. Losing blood was a million times easier for him than being inactive. Besides, he probably lost more blood in daily practice than he'd even need to give up for this experiment.

"If you need another dhampir," said Angeline. "You can use me too. Me and Eddie could help you. We'd be a team. Sydney wouldn't have to keep coming along, especially now that she's got a boyfriend."

There were so many things wrong with that, I didn't know where to start. The confidence Eddie had shown over giving blood vanished at "we'd be a team."

"We'll consider it," said Sonya. There was a sparkle in her eye, and I remembered her saying she could see affection in auras. Could she detect Angeline's crush? "For now, I'd rather not take you away from your schoolwork. It's less important for Eddie since he's already graduated, but you should keep up with it." Angeline looked unhappy about that. She'd had a number of difficulties with her classes, not to mention some outright embarrassments—like when she'd been asked to create a map of Central America and had shown up with one of Nebraska and Kansas. She put on a cocky face, but I knew Amberwood overwhelmed her sometimes.

Jill joined us, looking bright and refreshed. Ideally, Moroi drank blood every day. They could survive on this twice-a-week schedule, but I'd noticed that Jill grew tired and run-down the farther she got from feedings.

"Your turn, Adrian," she said.

He was yawning and looked startled at being noticed. I don't think he'd really been interested in Sonya's blood experiments. As he stood up, he glanced over at me. "Will you walk with me a sec, Sage?" Before I could even lodge my protest, he said, "Don't worry, I'm not taking you to the feeding. I just want to ask you a quick question."

I nodded and followed him out of the room. As soon as we were away from the others, I said, "I do *not* want to hear any more 'witty' commentary on Brayden."

"My commentary's hilarious, not witty. But that's not what

I wanted to talk about." He came to a halt in the hallway, outside what I suspected was Dorothy's room. "So, it seems my old man's coming to San Diego on business next weekend."

I leaned against the wall and crossed my arms, already getting a bad feeling about this.

"He doesn't know why I'm here, of course, or that I'm with Jill. He doesn't even know what city I'm in. He just thinks I'm partying in California, up to no good as usual." I wasn't surprised that Mr. Ivashkov wouldn't know the true reason for Adrian being here. Jill's "resurrection" was top secret, as were her whereabouts. We couldn't risk any extra people—not even someone who might not mean her harm—finding out where she was.

What did surprise me was that Adrian was working so hard to act like he didn't care what his father thought—but he obviously did. Adrian's face was convincing, but there was a note of bitterness in his voice that gave him away. "Anyway," Adrian continued, "he said he'd meet me for lunch if I wanted. Normally, I'd blow it off . . . but I'd kind of like to know what's going on with my mom—they never tell me when I call or e-mail." Again, I picked up mixed emotions from him. Adrian's mother was serving time in a Moroi prison for crimes of intrigue. You wouldn't know it by his cocky attitude and sense of humor, but it must have been hard on him.

"Let me guess," I said. "You want to borrow my car." I was sympathetic to those with difficult fathers, even Adrian. But my compassion only went so far and didn't extend to Latte. I couldn't risk any dents. Besides, the idea of being stuck without any way to get around scared me, especially when vampires were involved.

"No way," he said. "I know better than that."

He did? "Then what do you want?" I asked, surprised.

"I was hoping you'd drive me."

I groaned. "Adrian, it takes two hours to get there."

"It's pretty much a straight shot down the highway," he pointed out. "And I figured you'd drive a four-hour round-trip before giving up your car to someone else."

I eyed him. "That's true."

He took a step closer, a disconcertingly earnest expression all over his face. "Please, Sage. I know it's a lot to ask, so I'm not even going to pretend you'd benefit. I mean, you can spend the day in San Diego doing whatever you want. It's not the same as going to see solar panels or whatever with Brady, but I'd owe you—literally and figuratively. I'll pay you gas money."

"It's *Brayden*, and where in the world would you get gas money?" Adrian lived on a very tight allowance his father gave him. It was part of why Adrian was taking college classes, in the hopes that he'd get financial aid next semester and have a bit more of an income. I admired that, though if we were all actually still in Palm Springs come January, it'd mean the Moroi had some serious political problems.

"I . . . I'd cut back on things to come up with the extra money," he said after a few moments of hesitation.

I didn't bother hiding my surprise. "Things" most likely meant alcohol and cigarettes, which was where his meager allowance usually went. "Really?" I asked. "You'd give up drinking to go see your dad?"

"Well, not permanently," he said. "That'd be ridiculous. But maybe I could switch to something slightly cheaper for a while. Like . . . slushes. Do you know how much I love those? Cherry, especially."

"Um, no," I said. Adrian was easily distractible by wacky topics and shiny objects. "They're pure sugar."

"Pure deliciousness, you mean. I haven't had a good one in ages."

"You're getting off topic," I pointed out.

"Oh. Right. Well, whether I have to go on a slush-based diet or whatever, you'll get your money. And that's the other reason . . . I'm kind of hoping the old man might agree to up my income. You probably don't believe it, but I *hate* always borrowing from you. It's easy for my dad to dodge phone calls, but face-to-face? He can't escape. Plus, he thinks it's more 'manly' and 'respectable' to ask for something directly. Classic Nathan Ivashkov honor."

Once again, the bitterness. Maybe a little anger. I studied Adrian for a long time as I thought about my next response. The hall was dim, giving him the advantage. He could probably see me perfectly while some details were more difficult for me. Those green, green eyes I so often admired in spite of myself simply looked dark now. The pain on his face, however, was all too apparent. He hadn't yet learned to hide his feelings from Jill and the bond, but I knew he kept that lazy, devil-may-care attitude on for the rest of the world—well, for everyone except me lately. This wasn't the first time I'd seen him vulnerable, and it seemed weird to me that I, of all people, was the one he kept baring his emotions to. Or was it weird? Maybe this was just my social ineptitude confusing me again. Regardless, it pulled at something within me.

"Is that really what this is about? The money?" I asked, tucking my other questions aside. "You don't like him. There has to be something more here."

"The money's a big part. But I meant what I said earlier . . . about my mom. I *need* to know how she is, and he won't tell me about her. Honestly, I think he just wants to pretend it never happened—either for that reputation of his or maybe . . . maybe because it hurts him. I don't know, but like I said, he can't dodge if I'm right there. Plus . . . " Adrian glanced away a moment before mustering the courage to meet my eyes again. "I don't know. It's stupid. But I thought . . . well, maybe he'd be impressed that I was sticking to college this time. Probably not, though."

My heart ached for him, and I suspected that last part—earning his dad's approval—was bigger than Adrian was letting on. I knew all about what it was like to have a father who continually judged, whom nothing was ever good enough for. I understood as well the warring emotions . . . how one day you could say you didn't care, yet be yearning for approval the next. And I certainly understood motherly attachment. One of the hardest parts of being in Palm Springs was the distance from my mom and sisters.

"Why me?" I blurted out. I hadn't meant to touch on those earlier questions, but I suddenly couldn't help myself. There was too much tension here, too much emotion. "You could've asked Sonya or Dimitri to drive you. They probably would've even let you borrow their rental car."

The ghost of a smile flashed across Adrian's face. "I don't know about that. And I think you know why I don't want to risk being trapped in a car with our Russian friend. As for the rest . . . I don't know, Sage. There's something about you . . . you don't judge like the others. I mean, you do. You're more judgmental than any of them in some ways. But there's an honesty to it. I feel . . . " The smile left his face as he faltered for words. "Comfortable around you, I guess."

There was no way I could stand against that, though I find it ironic he was allegedly most comfortable around me when Moroi gave me panic attacks half the time. *You don't have to help*, an inner voice warned me. *You don't owe him anything. You don't owe any Moroi anything that isn't absolutely necessary. Have you forgotten Keith? This isn't a part of your job.* The bunker came back to me, and I recalled how one vampire deal had landed Keith in Re-education. How much worse was I? Social interaction was an inevitable part of this assignment, but I was blurring all the lines around it again.

"Okay," I said. "I'll do it. E-mail me what time you need to leave."

That's when the funniest part came. He looked totally floored. "Really?"

I couldn't help but laugh. "You gave me that whole pitch and didn't really think I'd agree, did you?"

"No," he admitted, still clearly amazed. "I can't always tell with you. I cheat with people, you know. I mean, I'm good at reading faces, but I pick up a lot from auras and act like I just have amazing insight. I haven't learned to totally understand humans, though. You've got the same colors but a different feel."

Auras didn't weird me out as much as other vampire magic, but I still wasn't entirely comfortable with them. "What color is mine?"

"Yellow, of course."

"Of course?"

"Smart, analytic types usually have yellow. You've got a little purple here and there, though." Even in the dimness, I could see a mischievous spark in his eyes. "That's what makes you interesting."

"What's purple mean?"

Adrian put his hand on the door. "Gotta go, Sage. Don't want to keep Dorothy waiting."

"Come on. Tell me what purple is." I was so curious, I nearly grabbed his arm.

He turned the knob. "I will if you want to join us."

"Adrian—"

Laughing, he disappeared inside the room and shut the door. With a shake of my head, I started to return to the others and then decided to seek out my Diet Coke after all. I lingered with it in the kitchen for a while, leaning against the granite countertops and staring absentmindedly at the brilliant copper pots hanging from the ceiling. Why had I agreed to drive Adrian? What was it about him that managed to crack all the propriety and logic I built my life around? I understood why I often had a soft spot for Jill. She reminded me of my younger sister, Zoe. But Adrian? He wasn't like anyone I knew. In fact, I was fairly certain there was *no one* in the entire world quite like Adrian Ivashkov.

I delayed so long that when I returned to the living room, Adrian was on his way back too. I sat down on the couch, nursing the last of my Diet Coke. Sonya brightened upon seeing me.

"Sydney, we just had a wonderful idea."

Maybe I wasn't always the quickest in picking up social cues, but I did notice this wonderful idea was addressed to me, and not Adrian and me.

"We were just talking about the reports from the night of

the . . . incident." She gave Clarence a meaningful look, and I nodded in understanding. "Both the Moroi and the Alchemists said the Strigoi had trouble with your blood too, correct?"

I stiffened, not liking this at all. It was a conversation I'd lived in fear of. The Strigoi who'd killed Lee hadn't just had "trouble" with my blood. Lee's had tasted strange to them. Mine had been disgusting. The one who'd tried to drink from me hadn't been able to tolerate it at all. She'd even spit it out.

"Yes . . . " I said carefully.

"Obviously, you're not a restored Strigoi," said Sonya. "But we'd like to take a look at your blood too. Maybe there's something about it that could help us. A small sample should suffice."

All eyes were on me, even Clarence's. The room started to close in as a familiar panic filled me. I had thought a lot about why the Strigoi hadn't liked my blood—actually, I'd tried to avoid thinking about it. I didn't want to believe there was anything special about me. There couldn't be. I didn't want to attract anyone's attention. It was one thing to facilitate these experiments and another to actually be a subject. If they wanted me for one test, they might want me for something else. And then something else. I'd end up locked away, poked and prodded.

There was also the fact that I just didn't want to give up my blood. It didn't matter that I liked Sonya and Dimitri. It didn't matter that the blood would be drawn with a needle, not teeth. The basic concept was still there, a taboo stemming from the most rudimentary of Alchemist beliefs: giving blood to vampires was wrong. It was *my* blood. Mine. No one—especially vampires—had any business with it.

I swallowed, hoping I didn't look like I wanted to bolt. "It was only one Strigoi's opinion. And you know they don't like humans as well as . . . you guys." That was part of why the Moroi lived in such fear and had seen their numbers reduced over time. They were the crème de la crème of Strigoi cuisine. "That's probably all it was."

"Perhaps," said Sonya. "But there's no harm done in checking." Her face was alight with this new idea. I hated turning her down . . . but my principles on this matter were too strong. It was everything I'd been raised to believe.

"I think it's a waste of time," I said. "We know spirit has to be involved, and I have no connection to that."

"I do think it would be helpful," she said. "Please."

Helpful? From her point of view, yes. She wanted to rule out every possibility. But my blood had nothing to do with Strigoi conversions. It couldn't.

"I . . . I'd rather not." A tame response, considering the emotions churning inside me. My heart was starting to race, and the walls were still closing in on me. My anxiety increased as I was visited by an old feeling, the awful realization that I was outnumbered here at Clarence's. That it was me and a roomful of vampires and dhampirs. Unnatural creatures. Unnatural creatures who wanted my blood . . .

Dimitri studied me curiously. "It won't hurt, if that's what you're afraid of. We don't need any more than what a doctor would take."

I shook my head adamantly. "No."

"Both Sonya and I have training in this sort of thing," he added, trying to reassure me. "You don't have to worry about—"

"She said no, okay?"

All the eyes that had been on me suddenly jerked toward Adrian. He leaned forward, fixing his gaze on Sonya and Dimitri, and I saw something in those pretty eyes I'd never seen before: anger. They were like emerald fire.

"How many times does she have to refuse?" Adrian demanded. "If she doesn't want to, then that's all there is to it. This has nothing to do with her. This is *our* science project. She's here to protect Jill and has plenty to do there. So stop harassing her already!"

"'Harassing' is kind of a strong word," Dimitri said, calm in the face of Adrian's outburst.

"Not when you keep pushing someone who wants to be left alone," countered Adrian. He shot me a concerned look before fixing his anger back on Sonya and Dimitri. "Stop ganging up on her."

Sonya glanced uncertainly between us. She looked legitimately hurt. As astute as she was, I don't think she'd realized how much this bothered me. "Adrian . . . Sydney . . . we aren't trying to upset anyone. We just really want to get to the bottom of this. I thought all of you did too. Sydney's always been so supportive."

"It doesn't matter," growled Adrian. "Take Eddie's blood. Take Belikov's blood. Take your own for all I care. But if she doesn't want to give hers, then that's all there is to it. She said no. This conversation is done." Some distant part of me noticed that this was the first time I'd ever seen Adrian stand up to Dimitri. Usually, Adrian simply tried to ignore the other man—and hoped to be ignored in return.

"But—" began Sonya.

"Let it go," said Dimitri. His expression was always difficult to read, but there was a gentleness in his voice. "Adrian's right."

Unsurprisingly, the room was a little tense after that.

There were a few halting attempts at small talk that I hardly noticed. My heart was still in overtime, my breath still coming fast. I worked hard to calm down, reassuring myself that the conversation was done, that Sonya and Dimitri weren't going to interrogate me or forcibly drain my blood. I dared a peek at Adrian. He no longer looked angry, but there was still a fierceness there. It was almost . . . protective. A strange, warm feeling swirled in my chest, and for a brief moment, when I looked at him, I saw . . . safety. That wasn't usually the first sentiment I had around him. I shot him what I hoped was a grateful look. He gave me a small nod in return.

He knows, I realized. *He knows how I feel about vampires.* Of course, everyone knew. Alchemists made no secret about how we believed most vampires and dhampirs were dark creatures who had no business interacting with humans. Because I was with them so often, however, I didn't think my cohort here in Palm Springs really understood how deeply that belief ran. They understood it in theory but didn't really feel it. They had no reason to since they hardly ever saw any evidence of it in me.

But Adrian understood. I didn't know how, but he did. I thought back on the handful of times I'd freaked out around them since being in Palm Springs. Once had been at a mini-golf course when Jill had used her water magic. Another time had been with the Strigoi and Lee, when Adrian had offered to heal me with his magic. Those were small lapses of control for me, ones none of the others had even noticed. Adrian had.

How was it that Adrian Ivashkov, who never seemed to take anything seriously, was the only one among these "responsible" people who had paid attention to such small details? How was he the only one to really understand the magnitude of what I was feeling?

When the time came to leave, I drove Adrian home along with the rest of us Amberwood students. More silence persisted in the car. Once Adrian had been dropped off, Eddie relaxed and shook his head.

"Man. I don't think I've ever seen Adrian so mad. Actually, I've never seen Adrian mad at all."

"He wasn't that mad," I said evasively, eyes on the road.

"He seemed pretty mad to me," said Angeline. "I thought he was going to jump up and attack Dimitri."

Eddie scoffed. "I don't think it was going to quite reach that point."

"I dunno," she mused. "I think he was ready to take on anyone who messed with you, Sydney."

I continued staring ahead, refusing to look at any of them. The whole encounter had left me feeling confused. Why had Adrian protected me? "I offered to do him a favor next weekend," I said. "I think he feels like he owes me."

Jill, sitting beside me in the passenger seat, had been quiet thus far. With the bond, she might know the answer. "No," she said, a puzzled note in her voice. "He would have done it for you regardless."

CHAPTER 7

I SPENT MOST OF THE NEXT DAY wrestling with my refusal to help Sonya, ruminating over the decision as I went from class to class. There was a part of me that felt bad about not giving blood for the experiments. After all, I knew what they were doing was useful. If there was a way to protect Moroi from becoming Strigoi, then that could theoretically be applied to humans too. That could revolutionize the way the Alchemists operated. People like that creepy guy Liam being held at the bunker would no longer be a threat. He could be "sterilized" and released, with no fear of him falling prey to the corruption of Strigoi. I knew also that Sonya and the others were running into walls with their research. They couldn't find any reason for what had made Lee impervious to turning Strigoi.

At the same time, despite the worthiness of the cause, I still felt staunchly opposed to giving up my own blood. I really was afraid that doing so would subject me to more and more experiments. And I just couldn't face that. There was nothing special about me. I hadn't undergone a massive transformation via spirit. Lee and I hadn't had anything in common. I was the same as any other human, any other Alchemist. I just apparently had bad tasting blood, which was fine by me.

"Tell me about the charm spell," Ms. Terwilliger said one afternoon. It was a few days after Clarence's, and I was still mulling over those events even while ostensibly doing work in her independent study.

I looked up from the book in front of me. "Which variant? The charisma one or the meta one?"

She was sitting at her desk and smiled at me. "For someone so against all of this, you certainly learn well. The meta one."

That had been a recent spell I'd had to learn. It was fresh in my mind, but I made sure to sigh heavily and let her know in a passive aggressive way how inconvenient this was for me. "It allows the caster to have short-term control of someone. The caster has to create a physical amulet that he or she wears . . . " I frowned as I considered that part of the spell. "And then recite a short incantation on the person being controlled."

Ms. Terwilliger pushed her glasses up her nose. "Why the hesitation?"

She noticed every slip. I didn't want to engage in this, but she was my teacher, and this was part of my assignment so long as I was stuck in this miserable session. "It doesn't make sense. Well, none of it makes sense, of course. But logically, I'd think you need something tangible to use on the vict—subject. Maybe they'd have to wear an amulet. Or drink something. It's hard for me to believe the caster is the only one who needs enhancement. I feel like they would need to connect with the subject."

"You touched on the key word," she said. "'Enhancement.' The amulet enhances the spell caster's will, as does the incantation. If that's been done correctly—and the caster is advanced and strong enough—that'll push the power of command on to the subject. Perhaps it doesn't seem tangible, but the mind is a powerful tool."

"Power of command," I muttered. Without thinking about it, I made the Alchemist sign against evil. "That doesn't seem right."

"Is it any different from the kind of compulsion your vampire friends do?"

I froze. Ms. Terwilliger had long since admitted to knowing about the world of Moroi and Strigoi, but it was still a topic I avoided with her. My tattoo's magic wouldn't stop me from discussing the vampire world with those who knew about it, but I didn't want to accidentally reveal any details about my specific mission with Jill. Nonetheless, her words were startling. This spell was very much like compulsion, very much like what I'd seen Sonya do to soothe Clarence. Vampires could simply wield it unaided. This spell required a physical component, but Ms. Terwilliger had told me that was normal for humans. She said magic was inborn for Moroi but that we had to wrest it from the world. To me, that just seemed like more reason why humans had no business dabbling in such affairs.

"What they do isn't right either," I said, in a rare acknowledgment of the Moroi with her. I didn't like that the abilities I found so twisted and wrong were allegedly within human reach too. "No one should have that kind of power over another."

Her lips quirked. "You're very haughty about something you have no experience with."

"You don't always need experience. I've never killed anyone, but I know murder is wrong."

"Don't discount these spells. They could be a useful defense," she said with a shrug. "Perhaps it depends on who's using it—much like a gun or other weapon."

I grimaced. "I don't really like guns either."

"Then you may find magical means to be a better option." She made a small, graceful motion with her hands, and a clay pot on the windowsill suddenly exploded. Sharp fragments fell to the floor. I jumped out of my desk and backed up a few feet. Was that something she'd been able to do this whole time? It had seemed effortless. What kind of damage could she do if she really tried? She smiled. "See? Very efficient."

Efficient and simple, as easy as a vampire wielding elemental magic with a thought. After all the painstaking spells I'd seen in these books, I was stunned to see such "easy" magic. It kicked what Ms. Terwilliger had been advocating up to a whole new—and dangerous—level. My whole body tensed as I waited for some other horrific act, but judging from the serene look on her face, that was the only show of power she had in mind—for now. Feeling a little foolish at my reaction, I sat back down.

I took a deep breath and chose my words carefully, keeping my anger—and fear—pushed down. It wouldn't do to have an outburst in front of a teacher. "Ma'am, why do you keep doing this?"

Ms. Terwilliger tilted her head like a bird. "Doing what, dear?"

"This." I jabbed the book in front of me. "Why do you keep making me work on this against my will? I hate this, and you know it. I don't want anything to do with it! Why do you want me to learn it at all? What do you get out of it? Is there some witch club where you get a finder's fee if you bring in a new recruit?"

That quirky smile of hers returned. "We prefer the term coven, not witch club. Though that does have a nice ring. But, to answer your question, I don't get anything out of it—at least, not in the way you're thinking. My coven can always use strong members, and you have the potential for greatness. It's bigger than that, however. Your perennial argument is that it's wrong for humans to have this kind of power, right?"

"Right," I said through gritted teeth. I'd made that argument a million times.

"Well, that's absolutely true—for some humans. You worry this power will be abused? You're right. It happens all the time, which is why we need good, moral people who can counter those who would use the magic for selfish and nefarious reasons."

The bell rang, freeing me. I stood up and gathered my things together. "Sorry, Ms. Terwilliger. I'm flattered that you think I'm such an upstanding person, but I'm already caught up in one epic battle of good versus evil. I don't need another."

I left our session feeling both troubled and angry and hoped the next two months of this semester would speed by. If this Alchemist mission continued into next year, then creative writing or some other elective would become a very viable choice for my schedule. It was a shame too because I'd really loved Ms. Terwilliger when I first met her. She was brilliant and knew her subject area—history, not magic—and had encouraged me in that. If she'd shown the same enthusiasm for teaching me history as she did magic, we wouldn't have ended up in this mess.

My dinners were usually spent with Julia and Kristin or "the family." Tonight was a family night. I found Eddie and Angeline already at a table when I entered East's cafeteria, and as usual, he seemed grateful for my presence.

"Well, why not?" Angeline was saying as I sat down with my tray. It was Chinese food night, and she held chopsticks, which seemed like a bad idea. I'd tried to teach her how to use them once, with no luck. She'd gotten angry and stabbed an eggroll so hard that the sticks had broken.

"I just . . . well, it's not my thing," Eddie said, clearly groping for an answer to whatever her question was about. "I'm not going at all. With anyone."

"Jill will be there with Micah," pointed out Angeline slyly. "Won't you need to come keep an eye on her since it's not at the school?"

Eddie's answer was a pained look.

"What are you talking about?" I finally asked.

"The Halloween Dance," said Angeline.

That was news to me. "There's a Halloween Dance?"

Eddie dragged himself from his misery to give me a surprised look. "How do you not know? There are signs everywhere."

I stirred around my steamed vegetables. "They must not be anywhere I've been."

Eddie gestured with his fork to something behind me. Turning, I looked back toward the food line I'd just been in. There, hanging above it on the wall, was an enormous banner that read HALLOWEEN DANCE. It listed the date and time and was decorated with badly drawn pumpkins.

"Huh," I said.

"How can you memorize entire books but miss something like that?" asked Angeline.

"Because Sydney's brain only records 'useful' information," Eddie said with a smile. I didn't deny it.

"Don't you think Eddie should go?" pushed Angeline. "He needs to watch out for Jill. And if he goes, we might as well go together."

Eddie shot me a desperate look, and I tried to find him a way out of this. "Well, yeah, of course he'll go . . . especially if it's off-site." The banner mentioned some venue I'd never heard of. We'd seen no sign of the Moroi who were after Jill, but an unknown place presented new dangers. Inspiration hit. "But that's the thing. He'll be on-duty. He'll spend the whole time checking the place out, watching for mysterious people. It'd be a waste for him to, uh, go with you. You probably wouldn't have much fun. Better to go with someone else."

"But *I* should be protecting Jill too," she argued. "Isn't that why I'm here? I need to learn what to do."

"Well, yeah," he said, obviously trapped by her logic. "You'll have to go with me in order to look after her."

Angeline brightened. "Really? Then we can go together!"

Eddie's look of pain returned. "No. We're going together. Not *together*."

Angeline didn't seem to be fazed by the nuances. "I've never been to a dance," she admitted. "Well, I mean, back home, we have them all the time. But I don't think they'll be like the ones here."

That I agreed with. I'd seen the types of social events the Keepers had. They involved raucous music and dancing around bonfires, along with some kind of toxic homemade alcohol that probably even Adrian wouldn't touch. The Keepers also didn't think a social event was a success if at least one fight didn't break out. It was actually kind of amazing that Angeline hadn't gotten into one yet here at Amberwood. I should have counted myself lucky that her only transgressions were dress code violations and talking back to teachers.

"Probably not," I said neutrally. "I don't know. I've never been to a dance either."

"You're going to this one, aren't you?" asked Eddie. "With Brody?"

"Brayden. And I don't know. We haven't even had our second date. I don't want things to move too fast."

"Right," Eddie said. "Because there's no bigger sign of commitment than a Halloween dance."

I was about to get him back by suggesting maybe he and Angeline should go *together* after all when Jill and Micah joined us. Both were laughing and had a hard time settling down to explain what was so funny.

"Janna Hall finished a men's suit in sewing club tonight," said Jill between giggles. Once again, I felt a rush of joy at seeing her so happy. "Miss Yamani said it's the only guy's outfit she's seen in there in five years. Of course, Janna needed a model, and there's only one guy in there . . . "

Micah attempted a tormented look but was quickly smiling again. "Yeah, yeah. I did the manly thing and stepped up. That suit was awful."

"Aw," said Jill. "It wasn't that awful—okay, it really was. Janna didn't try to go by any size guidelines, so the pants were huge. Like, tents. And since she didn't make any belt loops, he had to hold it all up with a sash."

"Which barely held when they made me do a runway walk," said Micah, shaking his head.

Jill gave him a playful nudge. "Everyone probably would've loved if it hadn't held."

"Remind me to never ever sign up for an all-girls club again," said Micah. "Next semester, I'm taking something like shop or karate."

"You won't do it again? Not even for me?" Jill managed a look that was amazingly both pouty and alluring. That, I realized, was more effective than any charm spell or compulsion.

Micah groaned. "I'm helpless."

I didn't consider myself particularly sentimental—and still disapproved of their timid romance—but even I smiled at their antics. At least, I did until I caught sight of Eddie's face. He wasn't giving away much, to be fair. Maybe hanging around Dimitri had provided some tips on the guardian poker face. But Eddie wasn't Dimitri yet, and I could see the faintest signs of pain and longing.

Why did he do this to himself? He'd refused to tell Jill how he felt. He took the noble stance that he was her protector and nothing more. Some part of me could understand that. What I couldn't understand was why he kept torturing himself by endorsing her going out with his roommate, of all people. Even with his hang-up over Micah and Mason, Eddie was forcing himself to constantly watch the girl he wanted with someone else. I had no relatable experience, but it had to be agonizing.

Eddie caught my eye and gave a small shake of his head. *Let it go*, he seemed to be saying. *Don't worry about me. I'll be fine.*

Angeline soon piped in with more talk about the dance, interrogating Jill and Micah about whether they'd be going. She also brought up her plans to go "with" Eddie. That pulled him out of his melancholy mood, and although I knew she annoyed him, I wondered if that was better than continually being tormented by Jill and Micah's relationship.

Of course, the conversation came to a halt—as did Eddie's problem—when Micah frowned and pointed out what the rest of us had missed. "Why would you go to the dance together? Aren't you guys cousins?"

Eddie, Jill, and I froze. Another cover story mess-up. I couldn't believe this had now slipped past me twice. I should have mentioned this as soon as Angeline brought up the dance. In the school's eyes, we were all related.

"So?" asked Angeline, missing the point.

Eddie cleared his throat. "Um, third cousins. But still. We're not really going together. It's more of a joke."

That effectively killed the topic, and he couldn't help smiling triumphantly.

Brayden picked me up immediately after school the next day so that we could make the windmill tour on time. Ms. Terwilliger had even let me go a few minutes early, after promising I'd get her a cappuccino on our way back to Amberwood. I was excited to see Brayden and the tour, yet as I got into his car, I felt a brief pang of doubt. Did I have any business doing these sorts of fun, personal activities? Especially now that the cover story had slipped a couple of times. Maybe I was spending too much time on me and not enough on the mission.

Brayden had lots to tell me about the debate competition he'd attended over the weekend. We analyzed some of the more difficult topics he'd come across and laughed at the easy ones that had stumped the opposing team. I'd feared dating for years but was again pleasantly surprised at how easy it was to talk to him. It was a lot like the Shakespearean outing: an endless source of topics that we both knew lots about. It was the rest of the experience that still left me unsettled—the "date" stuff. The dating books I'd read since our last outing mostly advised on when to have sex, which was completely useless since I had yet to figure out holding hands.

The giant windmills were pretty impressive. They didn't have the sleek beauty of cars that I loved, but I felt the same awe at the engineering they represented. Some of the windmills were over a hundred feet tall, with blades half the size of a football field. Moments like these made me marvel at human ingenuity. Who needed magic when we could create these kinds of wonders?

Our tour guide was a cheery girl in her mid-twenties who clearly loved her job and all that wind energy represented. She knew all sorts of trivia about it—but not quite enough to satisfy Brayden.

"How do you address the energy inefficiency that comes from the turbines needing wind speeds that fall into such a narrow range?"

Then: "What's your response to studies showing that simply improving the filters in the conversion of fossil fuels would result in less carbon dioxide emissions than this sort of energy production?"

And later: "Can wind power really be treated as a viable option when—after considering the cost of construction and other maintenance—consumers end up paying more than they would for traditional forms of electricity?"

I couldn't be certain, but I think our guide wrapped up the tour early. She encouraged some of the other tourists to come back anytime but said nothing as Brayden and I walked past her.

"That woman was sadly uninformed," he told me, once we were back on the highway.

"She knew plenty about the windmills and their facility," I pointed out. "I'm guessing the latest controversies just don't get brought up much on these tours. Or," I paused, smiling, "how to deal with, um, forceful tourists."

"I was forceful?" he asked, seeming legitimately surprised. He had gotten so caught up in his ideas that he didn't even realize it. It was endearing.

I tried not to laugh. "You came on strong, that's all. I don't think they were prepared for someone like you."

"They should be. Wind power's got promise, true, but for now, there are all sorts of expenses and efficiency problems that need to be addressed. It's useless otherwise."

I sat there for several moments, trying to decide how best I should respond. None of the advice I'd gotten from the books or my friends really prepared me for how to handle discussions about alternative energy sources. One of the books—one I'd chosen not to finish—had a decidedly male-centric view that said women should always make men feel important on dates. I suspected that Kristin and Julia's advice right now would have been to laugh and toss my hair—and not let the discussion progress.

But I just couldn't do that.

"You're wrong," I said.

Brayden—who was a big advocate of safe driving—actually took his eyes off the road for a few seconds to stare at me. "What did you say?"

Aside from learning that he had a vast store of extensive and random knowledge like I did, I'd also picked up on something else central to Brayden's personality. He didn't like to be wrong. This was no surprise. I didn't either, and we had a lot in common that way. And, from the way he'd discussed school and even his debate competition, I'd also deduced people never told him he was wrong—even if by chance he was.

Maybe it wasn't too late to do the hair-tossing thing. Instead, I just rushed on.

"You're wrong. Maybe wind isn't as efficient as it could be, but the fact that it's even being developed is a vast improvement over the outdated, archaic energy sources our society's been dependent on. Expecting it to be as cost-efficient as something that's been around much, much longer is naïve."

"But—"

"We can't deny that the cost is worth the benefits. Climate change is increasingly becoming a problem, and wind's reduced carbon dioxide emissions could have a significant impact. Furthermore—and most importantly—wind is renewable. It doesn't matter if other sources are cheap if they're going to run out on us."

"But—"

"We need to be progressive and look towards what's going to save us later. To focus strictly on what's cost-efficient now—while ignoring the consequences—is short-sighted and will ultimately lead to the downfall of the human race. Those who think otherwise are only perpetuating the problem, unless they can come up with other solutions. Most don't. They just complain. That's why you're wrong."

I paused to catch my breath and then dared a glance at Brayden. He was watching the road, but his eyes were impossibly wide. I don't think he could have been more shocked if I'd slapped him. Immediately, I berated myself for what I'd said. *Sydney, why didn't you just bat your eyelashes?*

"Brayden?" I asked tentatively when almost a minute passed with no response. More stunned silence met me.

Suddenly, without warning, he pulled the car sharply off the highway and onto the shoulder. Dust and gravel kicked up around us. In that moment, I was absolutely certain he was going to demand I get out and walk back to Palm Springs. And we were still miles from the city.

Instead, he caught hold of my hands and leaned toward me. "You," he said breathlessly. "Are amazing. Absolutely, positively, exquisitely amazing." And then he kissed me.

I was so surprised, I couldn't even move. My heart raced, but it was more from anxiety than anything else. Was I doing it right? I tried to relax into the kiss, letting my lips part slightly, but my body stayed rigid. Brayden didn't pull back in revulsion, so that was a good sign. I'd never kissed anyone before and had been worrying a lot about what it'd be like. The mechanics of it turned out not to be so difficult. When he did finally pull away, he was smiling. A good sign, I guessed. I smiled back tentatively because I knew it was expected. Honestly, a secret part of me was a little disappointed. That was it? That's what the big deal was? It hadn't been terrible, but it hadn't sent me soaring to new heights either. It had been exactly what it seemed like, lips on lips.

With a great sigh of happiness, he turned and began driving again. I could only watch him with wonder and confusion, unable to form any response. What had just happened? That was my first kiss?

"Spencer's, right?" Brayden asked when we exited to downtown shortly thereafter.

I was still so baffled by the kiss that it took me a moment to remember I'd promised Ms. Terwilliger a cappuccino. "Right."

Just before we turned the corner toward the street Spencer's was on, Brayden suddenly made an unexpected stop at a florist shop. "Be right back," he said.

I nodded wordlessly, and five minutes later, he returned and handed me a large bouquet of delicate, pale pink roses. "Thank you?" I said, making it more of a question. Now, in addition to the kiss and "amazing" declaration, I'd somehow earned flowers too.

"They're not adequate," he admitted. "In traditional floral symbolism, orange or red would have been more appropriate. But it was either these or some lavender ones, and you just don't seem like a purple person."

"Thank you," I said, more firmly this time. As I breathed in the roses' sweet scent on the way to Spencer's, I realized that no one had ever given me flowers before.

We reached the coffee shop soon thereafter. I got out of the car, and in a flash, Brayden was right by my side so that he could shut the door for me. We went inside, and I was almost relieved to see Trey working. His teasing would be a nice return to normality, seeing as my life had just detoured into Crazyland.

Trey didn't even notice us at first. He was speaking intently to someone on the other side of the counter, a guy a little older than us. The guy's tanned skin, black hair, and similar facial features tipped me off pretty quickly that he and Trey were related. Brayden and I waited discreetly behind the guy, and Trey finally looked up, an astonishingly grim expression on his face that was pretty out of character. He looked surprised when he saw us, but then seemed to relax a little.

"Melbourne, Cartwright. Here for a little post-windmill caffeine?"

"You know I never drink caffeine after four," said Brayden. "But Sydney needs something for her teacher."

"Ah," said Trey. "The usual for you and Ms. T?"

"Yeah, but make mine iced this time."

Trey gave me a knowing look. "Need to cool down a little, huh?"

I rolled my eyes.

The guy ahead of us was still standing around, and Trey nodded toward him while grabbing two cups. "This is my cousin Chris. Chris, this is Sydney and Brayden."

This must have been Trey's "perfect" cousin. At a glance, I saw little that marked him as better than Trey, except maybe his height. Chris was pretty tall. Not Dimitri-tall, but still tall. Otherwise, they both had similar good looks and an athletic build. Chris even had some of the same bruises and scrapes Trey often sported, making me wonder if there was a family connection to sports as well. Regardless, Chris hardly seemed like anyone Trey should be intimidated by, but then, I was biased by our friendship.

"Where are you here from?" I asked.

"San Francisco," said Chris.

"How long are you in town?" asked Brayden.

Chris gave Brayden a wary look. "Why do you want to know?"

Brayden looked surprised, and I didn't blame him. Before either of us could figure out the next move in the small-talk handbook, Trey hurried back over. "Relax, C. They're just being nice. It's not like they work for some spy agency."

Well, Brayden didn't.

"Sorry," said Chris, not actually sounding that sorry. That was a difference between the cousins, I realized. Trey would've laughed off his mistake. He never actually would have made the mistake. There were definitely different levels of friendliness in this family. "A couple weeks."

Neither Brayden nor I dared say anything after that, and mercifully, Chris chose that opportunity to leave, with a promise to call Trey later. When he was gone, Trey shook his head apologetically and set the completed coffees on the counter. I reached for my wallet, but Brayden waved me away and paid.

Trey handed Brayden back his change. "Next week's schedule's already up."

"It is?" Brayden glanced over at me. "Mind if I go in the back room for a second? Figuratively, of course."

"Go ahead," I said. As soon as he was gone, I turned frantically to Trey. "I need your help."

Trey's eyebrows rose. "Words I never thought I'd hear from you."

That made two of us, but I was at a loss, and Trey was my only source of help right now. "Brayden got me flowers," I declared. I wasn't going to mention the kiss.

"And?"

"And, why'd he do it?"

"Because he likes you, Melbourne. That's what guys do. They buy dinner and gifts, hoping that in return you'll—um, like them back."

"But I argued with him," I hissed, glancing anxiously at the door Brayden had gone through. "Like, just before he got me the flowers, I gave him this big lecture about how he was wrong about alternative sources of energy."

"Wait, wait," said Trey. "You told . . . you told Brayden Cartwright he was wrong?"

I nodded. "So why'd he react like he did?"

Trey laughed, a big, full laugh that I was certain would draw Brayden back. "People don't tell him he's wrong."

"Yeah, I figured."

"And girls especially don't tell him he's wrong. You're probably the only girl who's ever done it. You're probably the only girl smart enough to do it."

I was getting impatient. "I get that. So why the flowers? Why the compliments?"

Trey shook his head and looked like he was about to start laughing again. "Melbourne, if you don't know, then I'm not going to tell you."

I was too worried about Brayden returning to comment further on Trey's useless "advice." Instead, I said, "Is Chris the perfect cousin you were talking about?"

Trey's smirk faded. "That's the one. Anything I can do, he can do better."

I immediately regretted asking. Trey, like Adrian, was one of those people I didn't like seeing troubled. "Well. He didn't seem so perfect to me. Probably I'm biased from being around you all the time. You set the standard for perfection."

That brought Trey's smile back. "Sorry about his attitude. He's always been like that. Not the most charming branch of the Juarez family tree. That's me, of course."

"Of course," I agreed.

He was still smiling when Brayden returned, but when I cast a glance backward as I was leaving the coffee shop, Trey's expression had darkened again. His thoughts were turned inward, and I wished I knew how to help.

On the drive back to Amberwood, Brayden said shyly, "Well. Now I know my schedule for the next two weeks."

"That's . . . good," I said.

He hesitated. "So . . . I know when I can go out again. If, that is, I mean. If you want to go out again."

That would've surprised me, if I wasn't already stumped by everything else that had happened today. Brayden wanted to go out with me again? Why? *Girls especially don't tell him he's wrong. You're probably the only girl who's ever done it. You're probably the only girl smart enough to do it.* More importantly, did *I* want to go out with him again? I glanced over at him and then down at the roses. I thought about his eyes when he'd gazed at me in the stopped car. I realized then the odds of me ever finding a guy who thought Shakespeare and wind farms were fun were pretty infinitesimal.

"Okay," I said.

His narrowed his eyes in thought. "Isn't there some kind of dance your school's having? Do you want to go to that? People go to those, right?"

"That's what I keep hearing. How'd you know about it?"

"The sign," he said. Then, as if on cue, he pulled into the driveway in front of my dorm. Hanging over the main door was a sign decorated with cobwebs and bats. GET YOUR SCARE ON AT THE HALLOWEEN DANCE.

"Oh," I said. "That sign." Eddie was right. I really did have selective data storage. "I guess we can go. If you want to."

"Sure. I mean, if you want to."

Silence. We both laughed.

"Well, then," I said. "I guess we're going."

Brayden leaned toward me, and I panicked until I saw that he was trying to get a better look at the sign. "A week and a half away."

"Enough time to get costumes, I suppose."

"I suppose. Although . . . "

And that's when the next crazy thing happened. *He held my hand*.

I admit, I hadn't been expecting much, especially after my mixed reaction to the roadside kiss. Still, as he laid his hand over mine, I was surprised to feel that it was again just like . . . well, like touching someone's hand. I'd at least thought there might be goose bumps or a little heart fluttering. My biggest emotional reaction was worry over what to do with my hand. Lace fingers? Squeeze his hand back?

"I'd like to go out sooner," he said. That hesitancy returned. "If you want to."

I looked down at our hands and tried to figure out how I felt. He had nice hands. Smooth, warm. I could get used to holding those hands. And of course, he smelled like coffee. Was that enough to build love on? Again, that uncertainty nagged me. What right did I have to any of this? I wasn't in Palm Springs for my own entertainment. There was no "me" in Alchemy. Well, phonetically there was, but that wasn't the point. I knew my superiors wouldn't approve of any of this.

And yet, when would I get this chance again? When would I ever get flowers? When would someone look at me with this kind of fervor? I decided to take the plunge.

"Sure," I said. "Let's go out again."

CHAPTER 8

GOING OUT AGAIN didn't really happen until the weekend. Brayden and I were both over-achieving enough to manage weeknight outings and still finish homework—but neither of us liked to do it if we could avoid it. Besides, my weeknights usually had some other conflict with the gang, be it a feeding or the experiments. Eddie had given his blood this week, and I'd made a point to not be around when it happened, lest Sonya try to pitch to me again.

Brayden had wanted to go out Saturday, but that was the day I'd promised to drive Adrian to San Diego. Brayden compromised on breakfast, catching me before I hit the road, and we went out to a restaurant adjacent to one of Palm Springs' many lush golf resorts. Although I had long since offered to pull my share, Brayden continued picking up the bills and doing all the driving. As he pulled up in front of my dorm to drop me off afterward, I saw a surprising and not entirely welcome sight awaiting me: Adrian sitting outside on a bench, looking bored.

"Oh geez," I said.

"What?" asked Brayden.

"That's my brother." I knew there was no avoiding this. The inevitable had happened. Adrian would probably cling to Brayden's bumper until he got an introduction. "Come on, you can meet him."

Brayden left the car idling and stepped out, casting an anxious glance at the NO PARKING sign. Adrian jumped up from his seat, a look of supreme satisfaction on his face.

"Wasn't I supposed to pick you up?" I asked.

"Sonya had some errands to run and offered to drop me here while she was out," he explained. "Figured we'd save you some trouble." Adrian had known what I was doing this morning, so I wasn't entirely sure his motives had been all that selfless.

"This is Brayden," I told him. "Brayden, Adrian."

Adrian shook his hand. "I've heard so much about you." I didn't doubt that but wondered who exactly he'd heard it from.

Brayden gave a friendly smile back. "I've actually never heard of you. I didn't even know Sydney had another brother."

"You never mentioned me?" Adrian shot me a look of mock hurt.

"It never came up," I said.

"You're still in high school, right?" asked Adrian. He nodded toward the Mustang. "You must have a side job to make those car payments, though. Unless you're one of those slackers who just tries to get money off of their parents."

Brayden looked indignant. "Of course not. I work almost every day at a coffee shop."

"A coffee shop," repeated Adrian, managing to convey a

million shades of disapproval in his tone. "I see." He glanced over at me. "I suppose it could be worse."

"Adrian—"

"Well, it's not like I'm going to work there forever," protested Brayden. "I've already been accepted to USC, Stanford, and Dartmouth."

Adrian nodded thoughtfully. "I guess that's respectable. Although, I've always thought of Dartmouth as the kind of school people go to when they can't get into Yale or Harv—"

"We really need to go," I interrupted, grabbing hold of Adrian's arm. I attempted to tug him toward the student parking lot and failed. "We don't want to get caught in traffic."

Brayden glanced at his cell phone. "Traffic patterns should be relatively light going west this time of the day, but being a weekend, you never know how tourists might alter things, especially with the various attractions in San Diego. If you look at traffic models applying the Chaos Theory—"

"Exactly," I said. "Better safe than sorry. I'll text you when I get back, okay? We'll figure out the rest of this week."

For once, I didn't have to stress about handshaking or kissing or anything like that. I was too fixated on dragging Adrian away before he could open his mouth and say something inflammatory. Brayden, while passionate about academic topics and me disagreeing with him, tended to otherwise be pretty mild-mannered. He hadn't exactly been upset just now, but that was certainly the most agitated I'd ever seen him. Leave it to Adrian to work up even the most easygoing people.

"Really?" I asked, once we were safely inside Latte. "You couldn't have just said 'nice to meet you,' and let it go?"

Adrian pushed back the passenger seat, managing the most lounging position possible while still wearing a seatbelt. "Just looking out for you, sis. Don't want you ending up with some deadbeat. Believe me, I'm an expert on that kind of thing."

"Well, I appreciate your insider knowledge, but I'll manage this on my own, thanks just the same."

"Come on, a barista? Why not some business intern?"

"I like that he's a barista. He always smells like coffee."

Adrian rolled down a window, letting the breeze ruffle his hair. "I'm surprised you let him drive you around, especially considering the way you freak out if anyone touches the controls in your car."

"Like the window?" I asked pointedly. "When the air conditioning's on?" Adrian took the hint and raised the window back up. "He wants to drive. So I let him. Besides, I like that car."

"That *is* a nice car," Adrian admitted. "Though I never took you for the type to go for status symbols."

"I don't. I like it because it's an interesting car with a long history."

"Translation: status symbol."

"Adrian." I sighed. "This is going to be a long ride."

In actuality, we made pretty good time. Despite Brayden's speculations, traffic moved easily, enough that I felt I deserved a coffee break halfway through. Adrian got a mocha—"Can you spot me this one time, Sage?"—and maintained his usual breezy conversation style throughout most of the trip. I couldn't help but notice, when we were about thirty minutes out, he grew more withdrawn and thoughtful. His banter dropped off, and he spent a lot of time gazing out the window.

I could only assume the reality of his seeing his dad was

setting in. It was certainly something I could relate to. I'd be just as anxious if I was about to see mine. I didn't really think Adrian would appreciate a shared psychotherapy session, though, so I groped for a safer topic to draw him out of his blue mood.

"Have you guys learned anything from Eddie and Dimitri's blood?" I asked.

Adrian glanced at me in surprise. "Didn't expect you to bring that up."

"Hey, I'm curious about the science of it. I just didn't want to participate."

He accepted this. "Not much to tell so soon. They sent the samples off to a lab—one of your labs, I think—to see if there's anything physically different between the two. Sonya and I did pick up a . . . oh, I don't know how to describe it. Like, a 'hum' of spirit in Belikov's blood. Not that him having magic blood should surprise anyone. Most people seem to think everything he does is magic."

"Oh, come on," I said. "That's unfair."

"Is it? You've seen the way Castile worships him. He wants to be just like Belikov when he grows up. And even though Sonya's usually the spokesperson for our research, she won't breathe without checking with him beforehand. 'What do you think, Dimitri?' 'Is this a good idea, Dimitri?' 'Please give us your blessing so that we can fall down and worship you, Dimitri.'"

I shook my head in exasperation. "Again—unfair. They're research partners. Of course she's going to consult him."

"She consults him more than me."

Probably because Adrian always looked bored during their research, but I figured it wouldn't help to bring that up. "They've both been Strigoi. They've kind of got a unique insight to this."

He didn't respond for several moments. "Okay. I'll give you points for that. But you can't argue that there was any competition between me and him when it came to Rose. You saw them together. I never had a chance. I can't compare."

"Well, why do you have to?" Part of me also wanted to ask what Rose had to do with this, but Jill had told me numerous times that for Adrian, *everything* came back to Rose.

"Because I wanted her," Adrian said.

"Do you still want her?"

No answer. Rose was a dangerous topic; one I wished we hadn't weirdly stumbled into.

"Look," I said. "You and Dimitri are two different people. You shouldn't compare yourself to him. You shouldn't try to be like him. I mean, I'm not going to sit here and rip him apart or anything. I like Dimitri. He's smart and dedicated, insanely brave and ferocious. Good in a fight. And he's just a nice guy."

Adrian scoffed. "You left out dreamy and ruggedly handsome."

"Hey, you're pretty easy on the eyes too," I teased, quoting something he'd told me a while ago. He didn't smile. "And don't underestimate yourself. You're smart too, and you can talk yourself out of—and into—anything. You don't even need magical charisma."

"So far I'm not seeing a lot of difference between me and a carnival con-man."

"Oh, stop," I said. He could make me laugh even with the most serious of topics. "You know what I mean. And you're also one of the most fiercely loyal people I know—and caring, no matter how much you pretend otherwise. I see the way you look after Jill. Not many people would've traveled across the country to help her. And almost no one would have done what you did to save her life."

Again, Adrian took a while to respond. "But what are loyal and caring really worth?"

"To me? Everything."

There was no hesitation in my answer. I'd seen too much backstabbing and calculation in my life. My own father judged people not by who they were but by what they could do for him. Adrian did care passionately about others underneath all of his bravado and flippancy. I'd seen him risk his life to prove it. Considering I'd had someone's eye cut out to avenge my sister . . . well. Devotion was definitely something I could appreciate.

Adrian didn't say anything else for the rest of the drive, but at least I didn't get the impression he was brooding anymore. Mostly he seemed thoughtful, and that wasn't so concerning. What did make me a little uneasy was that I often caught sight of him studying me in my periphery. I replayed what I'd said over and over in my mind, trying to figure out if there'd been anything to warrant such attention.

Adrian's father was staying at a sprawling San Diego hotel with a vibe similar to the resort Brayden and I had eaten breakfast at. Businessmen in suits mingled with pleasure seekers in tropical prints and flip-flops. I'd almost worn jeans to breakfast and was glad now for my choice of a gray skirt and short-sleeved blouse with a muted blue and gray print. It had a tiny ruffled trim, and the skirt had a very, very faint herringbone pattern. Normally, I wouldn't have worn such contrasting textures together, but I'd liked the boldness of the look. I'd pointed it out to Jill before I left the dorm for breakfast. It'd taken her a while to even find the contrasting textures, and when she did, she'd rolled her eyes. "Yeah, Sydney. You're a real rebel."

Meanwhile, Adrian was in one of his typical summer outfits, jeans and a button-up shirt—though of course the shirt was untucked, with the sleeves rolled up and a few top buttons undone. He wore that look all the time, and despite its casual façade, he often made it appear dressy and fashionable. Not today, however. These were the most worn-out jeans I'd ever seen him wear—the knees were on the verge of having holes. The dark green shirt, while nice quality and a perfect match for his eyes, was wrinkled to inexplicable levels. Sleeping in it or tossing it on the floor wouldn't achieve that state. I was pretty sure someone would have to actually crumple it into a ball and sit on it for it to look that bad. If I'd noticed it back at Amberwood (and hadn't been so distracted getting him away from Brayden), I would've insisted on ironing the shirt before we left.

He still looked good, of course. He *always* looked good, no matter the condition of his clothing and hair. It was one of the more annoying things about him. This rumpled look made him come across as some pensive European model. Studying him as we took the elevator to the second floor lobby, I decided it couldn't be a coincidence that the most disheveled outfit I'd ever seen Adrian in had fallen on the day he had a father-son visit. The question was: why? He'd complained that his dad always found fault with him. Dressing this way seemed like Adrian was just providing one more reason.

The elevator opened, and I gasped as we stepped out. The back wall of the lobby was almost entirely covered with windows that offered a dramatic view of the Pacific. Adrian chuckled at my reaction and took out his cell phone. "Take a closer look while I call the old man."

He didn't have to tell me twice. I walked over to one of the glass walls, admiring the vast, blue-gray expanse. I imagined that on cloudy days, it would be hard to tell where sky ended and ocean began. The weather was gorgeous out today, full of sun and a perfectly clear azure-blue sky. On the lobby's right side, a set of doors opened up onto a Mediterranean style balcony where diners were enjoying lunch out in the sun. Looking down to ground level, I caught sight of a sparkling pool as blue as the sky, surrounded in palm trees and sunbathers. I didn't have the same longing for water that a magic user like Jill possessed, but I *had* been living in the desert for almost two months. This was amazing.

I was so transfixed with the beauty outside that I didn't notice Adrian's return. In fact, I didn't even notice he was standing right beside me until a mother calling for her daughter—also named Sydney—made me glance aside. There, I saw Adrian only inches away, watching me with amusement.

I flinched and stepped back a little. "How about some warning next time?"

He smiled. "I didn't want to interrupt. You looked happy for a change."

"For a change? I'm happy lots of times."

I knew Adrian well enough to recognize the sign of an incoming snarky comment. At the last second, he changed course, his expression turning serious. "Does that guy—that Brendan guy—"

"Brayden."

"Does that Brayden guy make you happy?"

I looked at Adrian in surprise. These kinds of questions were almost always a setup from him, but his neutral face made it hard to guess his motives this time.

"I guess," I said at last. "Yeah. I mean, he doesn't make me unhappy."

That brought Adrian's smile back. "Red-hot answer if ever there was one. What do you like about him? Aside from the car? And that he smells like coffee?"

"I like that he's smart," I said. "I like that I don't have to dumb myself down around him."

Now Adrian frowned. "You do that a lot for people?"

I was surprised at the bitterness in my own laugh. "'A lot?' Try all the time. Probably the most important thing I've learned at Amberwood is that people don't like to know how much you know. With Brayden, there's no censoring for either of us. I mean, just look at this morning. One minute we were talking Halloween costumes, the next we were discussing the ancient Athenian origins of democracy."

"I'm not going to claim to be a genius, but how the hell did you make that leap?"

"Oh," I said. "Our Halloween costumes. We're dressing Greek. From the Athenian era."

"Of course," he said. And this time, I could tell the snark was about to return. "No sexy cat costumes for you. Only the most dignified, feminist attire will do."

I shook my head. "Feminist? Oh, no. Not Athenian women. They're about as far from feminist as you can—well, forget it. It's not really important."

Adrian did a double take. "That's it, isn't it?" He leaned

toward me, and I nearly moved back . . . but something held me where I was, something about the intensity in his eyes.

"What?" I asked.

He pointed at me. "You stopped yourself just now. You just dumbed it down for me."

I hesitated only a moment. "Yeah, I kind of did."

"Why?"

"Because you really don't want to hear about ancient Athens, any more than you wanted to hear Brayden talk about Chaos Theory."

"That's different," said Adrian. He hadn't moved away and was still standing so, so close to me. It seemed like that should've bothered me, but it didn't. "He's boring. You make learning fun. Like a children's book or after school special. Tell me about your . . . um, Athenian women."

I tried not to smile. I admired his intentions here but knew he really wasn't up for a history lesson. Again, I wondered what game was going on. Why was he pretending to be interested? I tried to compose an answer that would take less than sixty seconds.

"Most Athenian women weren't educated. They mostly stayed inside and were just expected to have kids and take care of the house. The most progressive women were the hetaerae. They were like entertainers and high-class prostitutes. They were educated and a little flashier. Powerful men kept their wives at home to raise children and then hung out with hetaerae for fun." I paused, unsure if he'd followed any of that. "Like I said, it's not really important."

"I don't know," said Adrian thoughtfully. "I find prostitutes vastly important."

"Well. How refreshing to see that things haven't changed," a new voice cut in.

We both flinched and looked up at the scowling man who had just joined us.

Adrian's father had arrived.

"Well. How refreshin
new voice cut in.
We both flinched an
d just joined us.
s father he a

CHAPTER 9

THOSE OF US WHO KNEW what to look for could instantly spot Moroi by their pale complexions and tall, slim builds. To most human eyes, those features stood out but weren't a vampire tip-off. Humans just noted the features as striking and unusual, much as Lia regarded Jill as the perfect ethereal runway form. I didn't want to play upon stereotypes, but after a quick assessment of Mr. Ivashkov's Moroi-paleness, long face, dour look, and silver hair, I kind of wondered that he didn't get mistaken for a vampire more often. No, *vampire* wasn't really the correct term, I decided. More like undertaker.

"Dad," said Adrian stiffly. "Always a pleasure."

"For some of us." His father studied me, and I saw his eyes fall on my cheek. He extended a hand. I took it, proud that shaking hands with Moroi was a non-event for me now. "Nathan Ivashkov."

"Sydney Sage," I replied. "It's very nice to meet you, sir."

"I met Sage while I was bumming around out here,"

explained Adrian. "She was nice enough to give me a ride from L.A. today since I don't have a car."

Nathan looked at me in astonishment. "That's a long drive." Not nearly as long as the drive from Palm Springs, but we'd figured it would be safest—and more believable—to let him think Adrian was in Los Angeles.

"I don't mind, sir," I said. I glanced over at Adrian. "I'll go get some work done. You want to text me when you're ready to go?"

"Work?" he asked in disgust. "Come on, Sage. Go buy a bikini and enjoy the pool while you're hanging around."

Nathan looked between us incredulously. "You made her drive you out here, and now you're just going to make her wait around for your convenience?"

"Really," I said. "I don't—"

"She's an Alchemist," continued Nathan. "Not a chauffeur. There's a big difference." Actually, there were days at Amberwood I doubted that. "Come, Miss Sage. If you've wasted your day driving my son here, the least I can do is buy you lunch."

I shot a panicked look at Adrian. It wasn't panicked because I was afraid of being with Moroi. I'd long since gotten used to these sorts of situations. What I was unsure of was if Adrian really wanted me around for his family reunion. That hadn't been part of the plan. Also, I wasn't sure that I really wanted to be around for said reunion either.

"Dad—" Adrian attempted.

"I insist," said Nathan crisply. "Pay attention and learn common courtesy." He turned and began walking away, assuming we'd follow. We did.

"Should I find a reason to leave?" I whispered to Adrian.

"Not when he uses his 'I insist' voice," came the muttered response.

For a moment, catching sight of the gorgeous terrace restaurant and its sunny ocean view, I thought I could handle the Ivashkovs. Sitting out there in that warmth and beauty would be well worth the drama. Then, Nathan walked right past the balcony doors and led us to the elevator. We followed obediently. He took us down to the hotel's ground floor, to a pub called The Corkscrew. The place was dim and windowless, with low-hanging wood beams and black leather booths. Oak barrels lined the walls, and what light there was came filtered through red glass lamps. Aside from a lone bartender, the pub was empty, which didn't entirely surprise me this time of day.

What did surprise me was that Nathan had taken us here instead of the ritzy outdoor restaurant. The guy was dressed in an expensive suit that looked like it had come straight from a Manhattan boardroom. Why he'd ignore a trendy, elite restaurant for lunch and instead choose a stuffy, dark—

Dark.

I nearly groaned. Of course the terrace wasn't an option, not with Moroi. The sunny afternoon that made such enchanting conditions for me would have resulted in a pretty miserable lunch for the Ivashkovs—not that either of them looked like they planned on enjoying this one anyway.

"Mr. Ivashkov," said the bartender. "Nice to see you back."

"Can I get food delivered down here again?" asked Nathan.

"Of course."

Again. This subterranean lair had probably been Nathan's mainstay for all meals since arriving in San Diego. I allowed the terrace one last, wistful thought and then followed Nathan and Adrian inside. Nathan selected a corner table intended for eight people. Maybe he liked his space. Or maybe he liked pretending he was presiding over a corporate meeting. The bartender gave us menus and took drink orders. I got coffee. Adrian ordered a martini, earning disapproving looks from his father and me.

"It's barely noon," said Nathan.

"I know," said Adrian. "I'm surprised I held out that long too."

Nathan ignored the comment and turned to me. "You're very young. You must have just started with the Alchemists."

"They start us all young," I agreed. "I've been working on my own for a little over a year."

"I admire that. Shows a great deal of responsibility and initiative." He nodded thanks as the bartender set down a bottle of sparkling water. "It's no secret how the Alchemists feel about us, but at the same time, your group does a lot of good for us. Your efficiency is particularly remarkable. Too bad my own people don't pay more attention to that example."

"How are things with the Moroi?" I asked. "With the queen?"

Nathan almost smiled. "Are you saying you don't know?"

I did—at least, I knew what the Alchemists knew. "It's always different hearing an insider's perspective, sir."

He chuckled. It was a harsh sound, like laughing wasn't something Nathan Ivashkov had much practice with. "The situation's better than it was. Not great, though. That girl's smart, I'll give her that." I assumed "that girl" was Vasilisa Dragomir, teenage queen of the Moroi and Rose's best friend. "I'm sure she'd rather be passing dhampir laws and hereditary laws—but she knows those are only going to anger her opponents. So, she's finding ways to compromise on other issues and has won a few of her enemies over to her already."

The hereditary laws. Those were of interest to me. There were twelve royal lines among the Moroi, and Vasilisa and Jill were the only two left in theirs. Current Moroi law said a monarch had to have at least one other family member, which was how Jill had become such a political game piece. Even hardcore assassins would have a difficult time taking out a well-guarded queen. Removing her half sister would provide the same results, however, and invalidate Vasilisa's rule. That was why Jill had ended up in hiding.

Nathan's thoughts followed the same lines. "She's also smart to hide that bastard sister of hers." I knew he meant "bastard" in the sense of an illegitimate child, not an insult, but I still winced. "Rumor has it your people know something about that. Don't suppose you'd give me an insider's perspective on it?"

I shook my head and tried to keep my tone friendly. "Sorry, sir. Insight only goes so far."

After a few moments of silence, Nathan cleared his throat. "Well, Adrian. What is it you wanted?"

Adrian took a sip of his martini. "Oh, did you just notice I was here? I thought you'd come to see Sydney."

I sank into my chair a little. This was exactly the kind of situation I'd wanted to avoid.

"Why must every question yield some difficult answer with you?" asked Nathan wearily.

"Maybe it's the kinds of questions you ask, Dad."

This pub wasn't going to be big enough to hold the rapidly increasing tension. Every instinct told me to become invisible, but I found myself speaking anyway.

"Adrian's in college," I said. "Taking art classes. He's very talented." Adrian shot me a questioning—but amused—look at that. Some of his pieces were quite good. Others—especially when he'd been drinking—looked like he'd accidentally spilled paint on canvas. I'd helpfully told him so on a number of occasions.

Nathan looked unimpressed. "Yes. He's done that before. It didn't last."

"Different time, different place," I said. "Things can change. People can change."

"But often, they don't," declared Nathan. The bartender returned to take our lunch orders, though none of us had even looked at the menus yet. "I'll just order for us all, shall I?" Nathan opened the menu and scanned it quickly. "Bring us a platter of the garlic butter mushrooms, the goat cheese fondue, the bacon-wrapped scallops, and the fried oyster Caesar salad. Enough for three on the salad, obviously."

The bartender made a couple of quick notes and was gone before I could even say a word.

"Heavy-handed much, Dad?" asked Adrian. "You didn't even ask if we minded you ordering."

Nathan looked unconcerned. "I've eaten here before. I know what's good. Trust me, you'll like it."

"Sage won't eat any of that."

This really would be easier, I decided, if they'd both just pretend I didn't exist.

"Why ever not?" asked Nathan, looking at me curiously. "Are you allergic to seafood?"

"She only eats healthy stuff," said Adrian. "Everything you just got is dripping in fat."

"A little butter won't hurt her. You'll both see that I'm right. It's all good. Besides," Nathan added, pausing to sip at his water. "I *did* order a salad for the table. Lettuce is healthy."

I didn't even attempt to point out that no amount of Romaine was going to make up for *fried* oysters or Caesar dressing. I wouldn't have had a chance to speak up anyway because Adrian was on a roll and—I noticed with some surprise—halfway through his martini.

"You see?" he said in disgust. "That's exactly how you operate. You assume you know best for everyone. You just go ahead and make these decisions, not bothering to consult with anyone, because you're so certain you're right."

"In my vast experience," said Nathan coldly, "I *am* usually right. When you too possess that kind of experience—when you can actually claim to be an authority on, well, *anything*—then you can also be trusted with important decisions."

"This is lunch," Adrian argued back. "Not a life or death decision. All I'm saying is that you could have at least made some effort to include others. Obviously, your 'vast experience' doesn't apply to normal courtesies."

Nathan glanced over at me. "Have I been anything but courteous to you, Miss Sage?"

My chair, much to my dismay, didn't swallow me up or offer to hide me.

Adrian finished his martini in a gulp and held up the glass to catch the bartender's eye. "Leave her out of it," Adrian told his father. "Don't try to manipulate her into proving your point."

"I hardly need to manipulate anyone into proving my point," said Nathan. "I think it's made."

"Lunch will be fine," I blurted out, fully aware that this

altercation between father and son really had nothing to do with my eating habits. "I need to try more things anyway."

"Don't give in to him, Sydney," warned Adrian. "That's how he gets away with walking all over people—especially women. He's done it to my mom for years." The bartender silently appeared and replaced the empty martini glass with a full one.

"Please," said Nathan, with a heavy sigh. "Let's leave your mother out of this."

"Should be easy enough," said Adrian. I could see lines of tension in his face. His mother was a sensitive topic. "Seeing as you *always* do. I've been trying to get an answer out of you for weeks on how she's doing! Hell, I've just been trying to figure out where she's even at. Is that so hard for you to give up? She can't be in maximum security. They must let her get letters."

"It's better that you don't have contact with her while she's incarcerated," said Nathan. Even I was amazed at how coldly he spoke about his wife.

Adrian sneered and took a sip of his new martini. "There we are again: you knowing what's best for everyone. You know, I'd really, really like to think you're keeping this avoidance attitude with her because it hurts too much. I know that if the woman *I* loved was locked away, I'd be doing everything in my power to reach her. For you? Maybe it's too hard. Maybe the only way you can cope without her is to block her out—and by keeping me away too. I could almost understand that."

"Adrian—" began Nathan.

"But that's not it, is it? You don't want me to have contact—and you probably aren't having contact—because you're embarrassed." Adrian was really getting worked up now. "You want to distance us and pretend what she did doesn't exist. You want to pretend that *she* doesn't exist. She's ruined the family reputation."

Nathan fixed his son with a steely look. "Considering your own reputation, I'd think you would see the wisdom in not associating with someone who has done what she's done."

"What, screw up?" Adrian demanded. "We *all* screw up. Everyone makes mistakes. That's what she did. It was bad judgment, that's all. You don't cut off the people you love for mistakes like that."

"She did it because of you," said Nathan. His tone left no question about what he thought of that decision. "Because you couldn't leave well enough alone with that dhampir girl. You had to flaunt your relationship with her, nearly getting yourself in as much trouble as her in your aunt's murder. That's why your mother did what she did—to protect you. Because of your irresponsibility, she's in prison now. All of this is your fault."

Adrian went pale—more so than usual—and looked too shocked to even attempt any response. He picked up his martini again, and I was almost certain I could see his hands shaking. It was right around then that two waiters from the upstairs restaurant showed up with our food. We stared in silence as they arranged our place settings and artfully laid out the platters of food. Looking at all that food made me nauseous, and it had nothing to do with the oil or salt content.

"Mr. Ivashkov," I began, despite every reasonable voice in my head screaming at me to shut up. "It's unfair to blame Adrian for her choices, especially when he didn't even realize what she was doing. I know he would do anything for her. If he'd been able to stop this—or take her place—he would have."

"You're sure of that, huh?" Nathan was piling his plate with food and seemed quite excited about it. Neither Adrian nor I had an appetite. "Well, Miss Sage, I'm sorry to shatter your illusions, but it seems you—like so many other young women—have been fooled by my son's fast-talking ways. I can assure you, he has never done anything that didn't serve his own interests first. He has no initiative, no ambition, no follow-through. From a very early age, he was constantly breaking rules, never listening to what others had to say if it didn't suit what he wanted. I'm not really surprised his college attempts have failed—and I assure you, this one will too—because he barely made it out of high school. It wasn't even about the drinking, the girls, and the stunts he pulled . . . he just didn't care. He ignored his work. It was only through our influence and checkbook that he managed to graduate. Since then, it's been a constant downward spiral."

Adrian looked like he'd been slapped. I wanted to reach out and comfort him, but even I was still in shock from Nathan's words. Adrian clearly was too. It was one thing to go on and on about how you thought your father was disappointed in you. It was an entirely different thing to hear your father explain it in excruciating detail. I knew because I had been in both situations.

"Honestly, I don't even mind the drinking so much, so long as it knocks him out and keeps him quiet," continued Nathan, through a mouth full of goat cheese. "You think his mother suffers now? I assure you, she's far better off. She was up countless nights, crying over whatever trouble he'd gotten himself into. Keeping him away from her now isn't about me or him. It's for her. At least now, she doesn't have to hear about his latest antics or worry about him. Ignorance is bliss. She's in a better place not having contact with him, and I intend to keep it that way." He offered the scallops to me, as though he hadn't just delivered a huge chastisement without taking a breath. "You really should try this. Protein's good for you, you know."

I shook my head, unable to find words.

Adrian took a deep breath. "Really, Dad? I come all the way here to see you, to ask you to give me some way to contact her . . . and this is all I get? That she's better off not talking to me?" Looking at him, I had a feeling he was working very hard to stay calm and reasonable. Breaking into snarky Adrian retorts wouldn't win him any ground, and he knew it.

Nathan looked startled. "Is that the only reason you came here?" It was clear from his tone that he thought it was a foolish reason.

Adrian bit his lip, probably again to hold back his true feelings. I was impressed at his control. "I also thought . . . well, that maybe you'd want to hear how I was doing. I thought you might be glad to know I was doing something useful." I gasped.

For a moment, his father simply stared. Then, his confusion melted into one of those awkward laughs. "Ah. You're joking. I was puzzled for a moment."

"I'm done with this," said Adrian.

In a flash, he downed his martini and was out of his seat, heading toward the door. Nathan continued eating undisturbed, but I was on my feet as well. It was only when I was halfway across the pub, trying to catch up with Adrian, that Nathan bothered to say anything else.

"Miss Sage?" Every part of me wanted to run after Adrian,

but I paused to glance back at his father. Nathan had taken out his wallet and was flipping through a stack of bills. "Here. Allow me to pay you for your gas and your time."

He held the cash out, and I almost laughed. Adrian had forced himself to come here for all sorts of reasons, money being one of them. He'd never gotten a chance to ask for it, yet here his father was, offering it up. I didn't move.

"I don't want anything from you," I said. "Unless it's an apology to Adrian."

Nathan gave me another blank look. He seemed sincerely confused. "What do I have to apologize for?"

I left.

Adrian had either taken the stairs or immediately caught an elevator because there was no sign of him outside the pub. I went back up to the lobby and peered around anxiously. A bellman passed by, and I flagged him down.

"Excuse me. Where's the nearest place you can smoke?"

He nodded back toward the front door. "Far side of the circle drive."

I thanked him and practically ran outside. Sure enough, over in the designated smoking area, Adrian was leaning against an ornate fence in the shade of an orange tree, lighting up. I hurried over to him.

"Adrian," I exclaimed. "Are you okay?"

He took a long drag on his cigarette. "Is that really a question you want to ask, Sage?"

"He was out of line," I said adamantly. "He had no business saying any of that about you."

Adrian inhaled on the cigarette again and then dropped it to the sidewalk. He stamped the cigarette out with the toe of his shoe. "Let's just go back to Palm Springs."

I glanced back at the hotel. "We should get you some water or something. You took down that vodka pretty fast."

He nearly smiled. Nearly. "Takes a lot more than that to make me sick. I won't throw up in your car. I promise. I just don't want to stick around and risk seeing him again."

I complied, and before long, we were back on the road again. We'd spent less time in San Diego than it had taken to drive there. Adrian stayed silent, and this time, I didn't try to coax him out or distract him with meaningless conversation. No words of mine would help. I doubted anyone's words would help. I didn't blame Adrian for his mood. I'd feel the same way if my father had laid into me like that in public. Still, I wished there was something I could do to ease Adrian's pain. Some small comfort to give him a moment of peace.

My chance came when I saw a small gas station outside of Escondido with a sign reading BEST SLUSHES IN SOUTHERN CALIFORNIA HERE AT JUMBO JIM'S! I remembered his joke about switching to a slush-based diet. I turned my car off the highway, even though I knew it was silly. What was a slush compared to the disaster we'd just left behind? Still, I had to do something—anything—to make Adrian feel better. He didn't even seem to notice we'd stopped there until I was getting out of the car.

"What's up?" he asked, managing to drag himself out of his dark thoughts. The look on his face tore me apart. "You've got half a tank."

"Be right back," I said.

I returned five minutes later, a cup in each hand, and

managed to knock on his window. He got out of the car, truly puzzled now. "What's going on?"

"Slushes," I said. "Cherry for you. You have to drink it out here, though. I'm not risking the car."

Adrian blinked a couple of times, as though maybe I was a mirage brought on by too much sunlight. "What is this? A pity party for me? Because I'm so pathetic?"

"It's not always about you," I scolded. "I saw the sign and wanted a slush. Figured you'd want one too. If you don't, I'll throw it away and just drink mine."

I only got one step away before he stopped me and took the bright red slush. We leaned against the car together and drank without talking for a while. "Man," he finally said, when we were about halfway through. There was a look of wonder in his eyes. "I'd forgotten how good these are. What kind did you get?"

"Blue raspberry."

He nodded and slurped loudly on his. That dark mood still hung around him, and I knew a childhood beverage wasn't going to undo what his father had done anytime soon. The best I could hope for was a few moments of peace for him.

We finished shortly thereafter and tossed the cups in the trash. When we got back in Latte, Adrian sighed wearily and rubbed his eyes. "God, those are awesome. I think I needed that. The vodka may have hit me harder than I thought. Glad you decided to branch out into something that isn't coffee for a change."

"Hey, if they'd had coffee flavor, you know I would've gotten it."

"That's disgusting," he said. "There isn't enough sugar in the world to make that even remotely—" He stopped and gave me a startled look. In fact, he looked so shocked that I stopped backing up and kicked the car back into park.

"What's wrong?" I asked.

"The slush. That thing's like 99 percent sugar. You just drank one, Sage." He seemed to interpret my silence as though perhaps I hadn't understood. "You just drank liquid sugar."

"Maybe you drank liquid sugar," I said. "Mine was sugar free." I hoped I sounded convincing.

"Oh." I couldn't tell if he was relieved or disappointed. "You freaked me out there for a minute."

"You should've known better."

"Yeah. I suppose so." He fell back into his blue mood, the slushes only a temporary distraction. "You know what the worst part of all that was?"

I knew we were back to his father, not slushes. "What?"

"You'd think it'd be that I didn't get the money or that he just ripped my life apart or that he has no faith in me sticking to college. But that's okay. I'm used to that from him. What really bothers me is that I really did ruin my mom's life."

"I can't imagine you did," I said, shocked at his words. "Like you pointed out, we still love people who make mistakes. I'm sure she loves you too. Anyway, that's something you need to discuss with her—not him."

He nodded. "The other thing that bothered me . . . well, he said all that in front of you."

That was a shock too. I brushed it off, feeling a little flustered that he would think so much of my opinion. Why should he care? "Don't worry about me. I've been with much more abrasive people than him."

"No, no . . . I mean . . . " Adrian looked at me and then

quickly averted his eyes. "After what he said about me, I can't stand the thought that you might think less of me."

I was so surprised that I couldn't muster a response right away. When I did, I just blurted out the first thing that came to mind. "Of course I don't." He still wouldn't look at me, apparently not believing my words. "Adrian." I laid my hand over his and felt a warm spark of connection. He jerked his head toward me in astonishment. "Nothing he said could change what I think of you. I've had my mind made up about you for a long time . . . and it's all good."

Adrian looked away from me and down to where my hand covered his. I blushed and pulled away. "Sorry." I'd probably freaked him out.

He glanced back up at me. "Best thing that's happened to me all day. Let's hit the road."

We got back on the highway, and I found myself distracted by two things. First was my hand. It still tingled and felt warm from where I'd touched his, which was kind of funny. People always thought vampires were cold, but they weren't. Certainly not Adrian. The sensation was fading the longer I drove, but I kind of wished it'd stay.

The other thing that kept distracting me was all that sugar I'd just consumed. I kept running my tongue over my teeth. My whole mouth was coated in sickening sweetness. I wanted to brush my teeth and then drink a bottle of mouthwash. *Liquid sugar.* Yes, that was exactly what it had been. I hadn't wanted to drink one, but I'd known if I'd just brought a slush for Adrian, he really would've read that as pity and refused. I had to act as though I'd wanted one too, with him as an afterthought. He seemed to have believed my lie about the drink's sugar content, though a quick trip into the gas station would have quickly alerted him to the fact that Jumbo Jim's most certainly didn't carry sugar-free slushes. I'd asked them. They'd laughed.

Skipping lunch wasn't going to compensate for those calories, I thought glumly. And I wasn't going to get that sugary taste out of my mouth anytime soon. With as quickly as Adrian had sunk back into his depression, I suddenly felt stupid for even attempting this ruse. A slush couldn't change what his father had said, and I'd be a pound up on the scale tomorrow. This probably hadn't been worth it.

Then, I thought back to that brief moment by the car, and Adrian's fleeting look of contentment, followed later by: *God, those are awesome. I think I needed that.*

A brief moment of peace in the midst of his dark despair. That was what I had wanted, and that was what I had gotten. Was it worth it? I rubbed my fingertips together, still feeling that warmth.

Yes, I decided. Yes, it was worth it.

CHAPTER 10

THE SAN DIEGO TRIP continued to bother me, even though I knew I should let it go. As I often reminded myself, Adrian wasn't my concern, not like Jill and the others. Yet, I couldn't stop thinking about the terrible confrontation with him and Nathan—or Adrian's face afterwards. I felt even worse when a worried Eddie came to talk to me about Jill during breakfast on the following Monday.

"Something's wrong with her," he told me.

Immediately, I looked up toward the cafeteria line, where Jill was waiting with her tray. There was a vacant look on her face, like she was barely aware of her surroundings. Even with no magical talent for auras, I could practically see the misery radiating off of her.

"Micah's noticed it too," Eddie added. "But we don't know anything that could be upsetting her this much. Is it because of Lia? Or is she being harassed again?"

In that moment, I wasn't sure who I felt worse for: Adrian,

Jill—or Eddie. There was practically as much pain in Eddie as there was in Jill. *Oh, Eddie,* I thought. *Why do you keep doing this to yourself?* He was clearly worried about her but wouldn't dare approach her or offer comfort.

"There's nothing wrong with Jill. It's Adrian, and she's feeling it through the bond. He's going through a rough time." I offered no more details on Adrian's situation. It wasn't my story to tell.

Eddie's face darkened a little. "It's not fair that she has to endure his moods."

"I don't know," I said. "Seems like it might be a fair trade for her being alive." Adrian using spirit to bring Jill back from the dead was still a troubling matter for me. Every bit of Alchemist training I had said that kind of magic was wrong, far worse than any of the other magic I'd witnessed. One could even argue that what he'd managed was only a few steps away from the undead immortality of Strigoi. At the same time, whenever I saw Jill bright and alive, I was convinced that Adrian had done a good thing. I'd meant it when I said as much to him in San Diego.

"I suppose," said Eddie. "I wish there was a way she could block him out. Or at least a way to make him a little less moody."

I shook my head. "From what I've heard, Adrian was like that long before Jill was shadow-kissed."

Still, that conversation stuck with me, and I spent the day asking myself: what could I do to make Adrian happier? A new father obviously wasn't possible. I would have tried that on myself years ago if I could. Slushes were also out, partially because they only offered ten minutes of comfort and because I was still recovering from the last one. An idea finally came to me later on, but it wasn't one I could easily implement. In fact,

I knew my superiors would say it was nothing I should even attempt—which is why I decided to do it in a way that wouldn't leave an e-mail or paper trail. I couldn't do it today, however, so I made a mental note to deal with it later. Besides, who could say? Maybe Adrian would shake off the effects of his fatherly encounter on his own.

These hopes were actually reinforced when I saw Jill the next day at a school assembly. Assemblies like this were still a new concept to me, and we'd had exactly two since school started. One had been a welcoming gathering during our first week. The other had been a pep rally to cheer on the football team before Homecoming. Today's was called "Healthy Lifestyles." I couldn't figure out what it was about or why it was important enough to interrupt my chemistry class.

We were seated by grade in the school's gym, putting Jill and me in separate sections of the bleachers. Craning my neck to get a glimpse of her, I saw her sitting down near the front with Angeline and several friends she'd made through Micah. They'd welcomed her easily once they got to know her, which wasn't a surprise with how nice she was. Even Laurel, a girl who'd once tormented Jill, now gave her a friendly look. Angeline said something that made Jill laugh, and, overall, there was definitely an improvement in Jill's attitude. A very big improvement, judging from how much she was giggling. My spirits rose. Maybe Adrian really had bounced back.

"Can someone tell me what this is about?" I asked. I had Eddie and Micah on one side of me, Trey on the other.

"It's this group that comes to school and gives presentations about things like drugs and safe sex," explained Micah. He was pretty active in student government, so I wasn't surprised he knew about today's agenda.

"Those are kind of big topics," I said. "Isn't this just supposed to be an hour? Doesn't seem like they can really provide thorough coverage of these issues."

"I think it's just supposed to be a quick overview," said Trey. "Not like they're trying to do a seminar or anything."

"Well," I declared. "They should."

"Did we miss anything?" Julia and Kristin pushed their way through others and squeezed themselves in between Trey and me. Trey didn't seem to mind.

"We're trying to explain the point of this to Sydney," Trey told them.

"I thought the point was to get out of class," said Julia.

Kristin rolled her eyes. "This'll show you what you were missing by being homeschooled, Sydney."

Nothing could have prepared me for the spectacle that followed—mostly because never in my craziest dreams had I imagined weighty social issues would be addressed in musical numbers. The group performing for us called themselves Koolin' Around, and the inappropriate use of that *K* was nearly enough to make me walk out then and there. Before each song, they'd give a quick and totally vague info-blurb about the topic or—even worse—a skit. These little lectures always began with, "Hey, kids!"

The first song was called "STDs Are Not for Me." That was when I took out my math homework.

"Come on," Eddie told me, laughing. "It's not that bad. And people should know about this stuff."

"Exactly," I said, not looking up from my homework. "In trying to be 'hip' and 'relatable,' they're trivializing issues that need to be taken more seriously."

The only time I tuned in again was when Koolin' Around had moved on to the evils of alcohol. One of the lyrics in their particularly atrocious song was, "Don't listen to what your friends say / Bourbon will totally ruin your day."

"Ugh. That's it," I muttered. I sought out Jill again. She was watching with kind of a stunned disbelief, but just like earlier, there was none of that despair or melancholy. Some gut instinct told me why she'd had the mood change. Adrian hadn't snapped out of his gloom. Most likely he was drinking his way through it. Sometimes Jill would pick up some of the sillier side effects of intoxication—like the giggling I'd observed earlier—but eventually, alcohol actually numbed the spirit bond. The bright side of his indulgence was that it spared her some of his depression. The down side was that she could actually suffer the physical effects of a hangover later.

Koolin' Around mercifully reached their last song, a big production number celebrating the joys of feeling good and living a healthy, happy lifestyle. They pulled up members of the student body to dance with them, earning a variety of reactions. Some students just stood there frozen and embarrassed, wearing expressions that said they were counting the seconds until this ended. Other students—particularly those who normally sought attention in class—made the biggest, most outlandish spectacle they could of themselves.

"Sydney."

The warning note in Eddie's voice stopped me as I was about to return to my homework. That kind of concern could only be reserved for Jill, and I immediately looked at her again. Only, she wasn't the issue. Angeline was. One of the Koolin' Around members was trying to coax her out and even grabbed her hand. Angeline shook her head emphatically, but the guy seemed oblivious. Angeline might be okay around wild dances in the backwoods of West Virginia, but this was not a situation she was comfortable with.

To be fair, what happened next wasn't entirely her fault. He really should have left her alone when she said no, but I guess he was too caught up in his feel-good mood. He actually managed to drag her to her feet, and that's when Angeline made her disapproval perfectly clear.

She punched him.

It was pretty impressive since the guy had almost a foot on her in height. I supposed that came from Eddie's training in how to take out taller Moroi. The guy staggered backward and fell, hitting the floor hard. There was a gasp from most of the students sitting nearby, though only one of the band members—a guitarist—noticed. The rest kept on singing and dancing. The guitarist hurried forward to her fallen colleague and must have threatened Angeline's personal space because Angeline punched her too.

"Eddie, do something!" I said.

He turned to me in astonishment. "Like what? I'd never make it there in time."

It was true. We were two thirds of the way up in the bleachers, surrounded by others. I could only watch helplessly as the rest of the spectacle unfolded. The band soon caught on that something was terribly wrong, and their music faltered, finally coming to silence. Meanwhile, a group of teachers had rushed the floor, trying to pry Angeline away from Koolin' Around's bass player. There was a frantic look in her eyes, like a trapped animal that had gone beyond reason and only wanted escape. The teachers finally managed to restrain her, but not before she'd thrown a speaker at the lead singer (she missed) and punched the school's shop teacher.

Trey leaned forward, mouth gaping. *"That's* your cousin? Wow."

I didn't even bother responding. All I could think about was how in the world I was going to do damage control this time. Fighting was a serious offense in and of itself. I couldn't even imagine what attacking a motivational musical group would elicit.

"She took out, like, three people twice her size!" Kristin exclaimed. "And I mean *took out.* Knocked them to the floor."

"Yeah, I know," I said dismally. "I'm right here. I saw it all."

"How was she even able to do that?" asked Julia.

"I taught her some moves," remarked Eddie in disbelief.

Unsurprisingly, no one even bothered sending this to Mrs. Weathers. Angeline was referred directly to the principal *and* vice principal. After her display, maybe they felt there was safety in numbers. It may have been Mrs. Weathers's recommendation or simply the fact that our fictitious parents (and "cousin" Angeline's) were notoriously hard to get a hold of, but I was asked to accompany her when she met with the administration.

My pre-briefing with Angeline was short and to the point. "You will act apologetic and contrite," I told her as we sat outside the principal's office.

"What's contrite mean?"

"Apologetic."

"Then why didn't you just say—"

"And," I continued. "If pushed for reasons, you will say you were overwhelmed and panicked. You'll say you don't know what came over you."

"But I didn't—"

"And you will not mention how stupid they were or say anything negative whatsoever."

"But they are—"

"In fact, don't speak at all unless you're asked something directly. If you let me handle this, it'll be over fast."

Angeline apparently took that to heart because she crossed her arms and glared at me, refusing to say anything else.

When we were ushered into the office, the principal and vice principal—Mrs. Welch and Mr. Redding, respectively—were both sitting on the same side of one desk. They were side by side, presenting a united front that again made me think they feared for their lives.

"Miss McCormick," began Mrs. Welch. "I hope you know that what you did was completely out of line." McCormick was Angeline's fake last name around here.

"Violence and fighting of any kind are not tolerated at Amberwood," said Mr. Redding. "We have high standards—standards meant to ensure the safety of everyone at this school—and expect our students to adhere to them. None of your other violations of school rules come close to what you did today."

"Even if we didn't have those other transgressions on file, there can be no question here," said Mrs. Welch. "There is no place for you at Amberwood."

My stomach sank. Expulsion. Although the Keepers weren't entirely uneducated, her academic background had hardly been up to that of average high school students in the modern world. She was in a lot of remedial classes, and getting her into Amberwood at all had been quite a feat. Expulsion wasn't as bad as someone investigating how a petite girl like her could do so much damage, but it still wasn't an outcome I wanted. I could already imagine one of my superiors asking, *why didn't you realize how volatile the school was making her?* To which I would have to respond: *because I've been too busy going on dates and helping vampires who aren't my concern.*

"Do you have anything to say for yourself before we notify your parents?" asked Mrs. Welch. They looked at Angeline expectantly.

I braced myself for an irrational tirade. Instead, Angeline managed to produce some tears which, I had to admit, certainly looked contrite. "I . . . I panicked," she said. "I don't know what came over me. So much happened at once, and that guy was so scary, and I just freaked out. I felt threatened. I wanted everyone to get away from me . . . "

I was nearly convinced, probably because it was seeded with truth. Angeline had had a number of flustered moments at Amberwood, no matter her bravado. There were more people at the school than had been in her mountain community, and she'd been so overwhelmed in her first week that we'd had to take turns escorting her to class. I really should've been paying more attention to her.

Mr. Redding looked a tiny bit sympathetic—but not enough to change his mind. "I'm sure that must have been hard, but it was hardly reason for you to act in that way. Injuring three people and damaging expensive audio visual equipment were in no way appropriate responses." *Understatement.*

I was tired of the formalities and needed to fix things before they escalated further. I leaned forward in my chair. "You know what else isn't appropriate? A thirty-year-old guy—because that's how old he was, no matter how young and cool they were trying to be—*grabbing* a fifteen-year-old girl. It was bad enough that he did so when she clearly didn't want to go with him. The point is he never should have touched her in the first place. She's a minor. If a teacher did that, he'd be fired. I've read the book teachers are given from your HR department." It had been an attempt to see if Ms. Terwilliger was abusing me. "Medical emergencies and breaking up a fight are the only times teachers can lay hands on students. Now, you might argue that that guy wasn't a teacher or employed by the school, but his group was invited here by the school—which is obligated to keep its students safe. You're a private school, but I'm certain the California Department of Education would have a few things to say about what happened here today—as will Angeline's father, who's a lawyer." He was actually the leader of a bunch of mountain vampires and had multiple wives, but that was beside the point. I looked back and forth between Mrs. Welch and Mr. Redding's faces. "Now then. Shall we renegotiate your position?"

Angeline was in awe after we left the office and went back to our dorm. "Suspension," she exclaimed, a bit too much joy in her voice for my liking. "I really just get to skip class? That sounds more like a reward."

"You still have to keep up with your homework," I warned. "And you can't leave the dorm. Don't even *think* about sneaking out because that will get you expelled, and I won't be able to save you again."

"Still," she said, practically skipping, "this was all pretty easy."

I came to a halt in front of her, forcing her to face me. "It was not easy. You got off on a technicality. You've continually resisted efforts to follow the rules around here, and today—well, that was off the charts. You aren't back home. The only time you should even think about fighting here is if Jill is attacked. That's why you're here. Not to do whatever you want. You said you were up to the challenge of protecting her. If you get expelled—and it's a miracle you weren't—she's at risk. So get in line or start packing for home. And for God's sake, leave Eddie alone."

Her face had been kindling with anger as I spoke, but that last bit caught her off guard. "What do you mean?"

"I mean, you constantly throwing yourself at him."

She sniffed. "That's how you show a guy you like him."

"Maybe among the uncivilized! Here you need to back off and start acting like a responsible human being—er, dhampir. Whatever. You're making him miserable! Besides, you're supposed to be cousins. You're screwing up our cover."

Angeline's jaw dropped. "I . . . I'm making him miserable?"

I almost felt bad for her. The look of shock on her face was so great that it was obvious she really hadn't known what she was doing to Eddie was wrong. I was too worked up to feel much sympathy right then, though. Jill had acted out when we'd first arrived, and that had been just as frustrating. I'd come to enjoy our peace, and now Angeline was threatening all of that. Unlike Jill, she didn't seem to realize it, and I didn't know if that made things better or worse.

I left an upset and frustrated Angeline off at her dorm room and also verified with Jill that Adrian had indeed been drinking. That and my agitation were more than enough to make me want to leave campus, if only for the escape. Brayden had asked earlier if I wanted to go out, but I wasn't up to that. I sent a quick text: *Can't go out tonight. Family stuff.* Then I headed off to Clarence's.

I'd called ahead to make sure Dimitri and Sonya were there since I had no interest in having a one-on-one visit with the ancient Moroi. He wasn't around when I arrived. I found Dimitri and Sonya huddled over some cards with blots of dried blood, speculating on how to proceed.

"It'd be interesting to get Strigoi blood and see if anything happened when I applied spirit," she was saying. "Do you think you could manage that?"

"Gladly," said Dimitri.

They noticed me. As soon as she looked up, Sonya asked, "What's wrong?"

I didn't even bother asking how she knew. My face probably said more than my aura did. "Angeline got into a brawl with a motivational group at school."

Dimitri and Sonya exchanged looks. "Maybe we should go get some dinner," he said. He grabbed a set of keys from the table. "Let's go downtown."

I never would've imagined that I'd look forward to going out with a Moroi and a dhampir. It was yet another sign of how far I'd advanced—or regressed, by Alchemist standards. Compared to most of the other people in my life, Dimitri and Sonya were grounded and stable. It was refreshing.

I gave them a rundown of Angeline's behavior, as well as my thinly veiled legal threat. That part seemed to amuse Sonya.

"Smart," she said, twirling spaghetti on a fork. "Maybe you should be in law school instead of the Alchemists."

Dimitri found it less funny. "Angeline came here to do a job. She wanted out of the Keepers and swore she'd devote every waking minute to protecting Jill."

"There has been a bit of a culture shock," I admitted, unsure as to why I was defending Angeline. "And those guys today . . . I mean, if they'd tried to get me to join their sing-along, I probably would've punched them too."

"Unacceptable," said Dimitri. He used to be a combat instructor, and I could understand why. "She's here on a mission. What she did was reckless and irresponsible."

Sonya gave him a sly smile. "And here I thought you had a soft spot for reckless young girls."

"Rose never would have done anything like that," he countered. He paused to reconsider, and I could've sworn there was the hint of a smile there. "Well, at least not in such a public setting."

Once the Angeline topic was put to rest, I brought up the reason I'd come here. "So . . . no experiments today?"

Even Sonya's good nature faltered. "Ah. No, not exactly. We've gone over some notes on our own, but Adrian hasn't been . . . he hasn't been quite up to the research this week. Or up to going to class."

Dimitri nodded. "I was over there earlier. He could barely answer the door. No idea what he'd been drinking, but whatever it was, he'd had a lot." Considering their rocky relationship, I would've expected disdain in discussing Adrian's vices. Instead, Dimitri sounded disappointed, as though he'd expected better.

"That's what I wanted to talk to you about," I said. I'd eaten little of my dinner and was nervously tearing a roll into pieces. "Adrian's current mood isn't entirely his fault. I mean, it is, but I can kind of understand it. You know we saw his dad this weekend, right? Well . . . it didn't go well."

There was a knowing glint in Dimitri's dark eyes. "I'm not surprised. Nathan Ivashkov isn't the easiest man to get along with."

"He sort of tore down everything Adrian's been trying to do. I tried to make a case for Adrian, but Mr. Ivashkov wouldn't listen. That's why I was wondering if you guys could help."

Sonya couldn't hide her surprise. "I'd gladly help Adrian, but something tells me Nathan's not going to really put much stock in what we have to say."

"That's not what I was thinking." I gave up on the bread and dropped all the pieces to my plate. "You guys are both close to the queen. Maybe you could get her to tell Adrian's dad how . . . I don't know. What an asset he's been. How much he's been helping. Obviously, she couldn't explain exactly what he's doing, but anything might help. Mr. Ivashkov won't listen to Adrian or anyone else, but he'd have to take a commendation from the queen seriously. If she'd do it."

Dimitri looked thoughtful. "Oh, she'd do it. She's always had a soft spot for him. Everyone seems to."

"No," I said stubbornly. "Not everyone. There's a split. Half condemn him and write him off as useless like his dad. The other half just shrug and indulge him and say, 'Well, that's Adrian.'"

Sonya studied me carefully, a trace of that amusement returning. "And you?"

"I don't think he should be babied or disregarded. If you expect him to do great things, he will."

Sonya said nothing right away, and I shifted uncomfortably under her scrutiny. I didn't like when she looked at me like this. It was about more than auras. It was like she could see into my heart and soul.

"I'll speak to Lissa," she said at last. "And I'm sure Dimitri will too. In the meantime, let's hope that if we follow your advice and expect Adrian to sober up soon, he will."

We had just paid the check when Dimitri's cell phone rang. "Hello?" he answered. And like that, his face transformed. That fierceness I so associated with him softened, and he practically glowed. "No, no. It's always a good time for you to call, Roza." Whatever the response on the other end was, it made him smile.

"Rose," said Sonya to me. She stood up. "Let's give them a little privacy. You want to take a walk?"

"Sure," I said, rising as well. Outside, dusk was falling. "There's a costume store a few blocks away I actually want to check—if they're still open."

Sonya glanced at Dimitri. "Meet us there?" she whispered. He gave a quick nod. Once we were outside in the warm evening air, she laughed. "Ah, those two. In a fight, they're lethal. Around each other, they melt."

"Is that how you and Mikhail are?" I asked, thinking there wasn't much melting with Brayden and me, no matter how much I enjoyed spending time with him.

She laughed again and glanced up at the sky, painted in shades of orange and blue. "Not exactly. Every relationship is different. Everyone loves differently." There was a long pause as she chose her next words. "That was a nice thing you chose to do for Adrian."

"There was no choice to be made," I countered. We crossed onto a busier street, full of brightly lit stores with water misters outside that were meant to cool off hot shoppers. I winced at what that mist was doing to my hair. "I had to help. He didn't deserve that kind of treatment. I can't imagine how Adrian's put up with that his whole life. And would you believe that what worried Adrian the most was that I would think less of him?"

"Actually," said Sonya softly, "I can very much believe that."

The costume store was still open, thanks to extended Halloween hours, but only for ten more minutes. Sonya wandered around the aisles with no real goal, but I headed immediately for the historical section. They had exactly one Greek-style dress left, a plain white gown with a gold plastic belt. I knelt down to take a better look. Opening the package, I felt the fabric. It was cheap, probably flammable. The dress was also an XL, and I wondered if Jill had learned enough in sewing club to take it in for me. With less than a week until the dance, my options were limited.

"Really?" a voice beside me said. "Haven't you insulted me enough without resorting to this trash?"

Standing above me was Lia DiStefano. Her curly hair was bound up with a bright red scarf, and a voluminous peasant blouse made her petite body look like it had wings. She peered down at me disapprovingly with kohl-lined eyes.

"Are you following me?" I asked, getting to my feet. "Every time I'm downtown, here you are."

"If I were following you, I never would have let you set foot in here in the first place." She pointed at the costume. "What is *that*?"

"My outfit for Halloween," I said. "I'm going Greek."

"It's not even the right size."

"I'll get it taken in."

She tsked. "I'm so appalled, I don't even know where to start. You want a Greek dress? I'll make you one. A good one. Not this monstrosity. My God. People know you know me. If you were seen in that, it'd ruin my career."

"Yeah, because what I wear to a high school dance will really make or break you."

"When's your dance?" she asked.

"Saturday."

"Easy," she declared. She gave me a once-over and nodded in satisfaction. "Easy measurements too. Is your sister dressing just as badly?"

"Not sure," I admitted. "She talked about making a fairy dress in sewing club. A blue one, I think."

Lia blanched. "Even worse. I'll make her a dress too. I've already got her measurements."

I sighed. "Lia, I know what you're trying to do, and it won't work. Jill absolutely cannot model for you again. It doesn't matter how much bribery you try."

Lia attempted an innocent look that was in no way convincing. "Who said anything about bribery? I'm doing this out of charity. It'd be a disgrace to let you two go out in anything less than the best."

"Lia—"

"Do not buy that," she warned, pointing at the costume. "It's a waste. You might as well set your money on fire—although, it probably wouldn't light as fast as that dress. I'll let you know when your costumes are ready." With that, she turned on her high wooden heels and walked away, leaving me staring.

"Did you get a costume?" Sonya asked me later, once the closing store forced us to leave.

"Weirdly, yes," I said. "But not from there."

Dimitri apparently wasn't done with his call, since he hadn't joined us yet. We strolled leisurely back toward the restaurant, wanting to give him more time with Rose. Other stores were closing, and the tourists were beginning to thin out. I explained the meeting with Lia. Sonya found it more amusing than I did.

"Well, don't knock it," she said. "If a designer wants to make you something, you're not obligated to give her anything else. Maybe she could help me out with bridesmaid dresses."

We crossed a less busy street and cut through a narrow alley with a brick building on one side and a tree-filled church lawn on the other. I'd admired the church on our way over, but now, in only a short time, evening had filled it with shadows and given it a foreboding look and feel. I was glad I wasn't walking through here alone. It felt strange to be reassured by a vampire's presence.

"Lia *does* make amazing things," I admitted. "But I don't know if we should encourage her."

"Fair enough," said Sonya. "Maybe one of these days, you'll help me look for dresses. You've got a really good sense of—"

She suddenly spun around toward the darkened church-yard. There was a look of fear on her face, but I saw nothing alarming—at first. Seconds later, four figures in black jumped out from behind the trees. One of them threw me against the brick wall while the other three pinned Sonya to the ground. I pushed back against my captor, but a muscled arm held me tightly. In the faint light, I saw a glimmer of something I never expected to see on the streets of Palm Springs: a sword.

The dark figure poised it over Sonya's neck. "Time to go back to Hell," he said.

CHAPTER 11

I'M NOT A PHYSICAL PERSON. I'm decent in volleyball, and Eddie once taught me to throw a punch. But I make no claims to having the kind of training that guardians get. I certainly don't have their reflexes. So, in this situation, unable to break free of restraint, I pretty much did the only thing I could.

I screamed.

"Help! Somebody help!"

My hope was that it would delay Sonya's captors from decapitating her or whatever it was they planned to do. I also hoped it would, well, bring help. We'd departed from the main downtown roads but were still close enough that someone should hear me—especially since there had still been a decent number of people out earlier.

One of the attackers holding Sonya flinched, so I supposed I was partially successful. My own captor clamped a hand over my mouth and pushed me harder against the brick wall. Then, a strange thing happened. He—because he had the right build to be male, even though I couldn't make out his face—froze. He was still holding me, but his body had gone rigid. It was almost like he was shocked or surprised. I wasn't sure why. Surely someone screaming for help when assaulted wasn't that weird. I didn't think I could overpower him but still hoped I might take advantage of his stunned state. I pushed forward again, trying to get out of his grip. I only managed to move a few inches before he locked me back into place.

"We need to go!" exclaimed one of Sonya's captors. Another guy. From what I could tell, they all were. "Someone will come."

"This'll only take a second," growled the one holding the sword. "We need to rid the world of this evil."

I watched in terror, my heart seizing in my chest. I was afraid for myself, but I was especially afraid for Sonya. I'd never seen a decapitation. I didn't want to start now.

Half a second later, I found myself suddenly free. Someone new had joined our fray, someone who ripped my captor away and tossed him easily to the pavement. It looked painful, and the guy landed with a grunt. Even in this poor lighting, the height and coat gave my savior away. It was Dimitri.

I'd seen him fight before, but it never got old. He was captivating. He never stopped moving. Every action was graceful and lethal. He was a dancer of death. Ignoring the guy he'd just thrown, Dimitri surged toward the others. He immediately went for the guy with the sword. A swift kick from Dimitri sent the assailant flying backward. He dropped the sword and barely managed to catch hold of one of the churchyard trees.

Meanwhile, one of the men holding Sonya simply turned tail and ran back toward downtown. Dimitri didn't pursue. His attention now was on the last guy, who was foolishly attempting to fight back. This freed Sonya, however, and she wasted no time getting to her feet and scurrying over to my side. I was rarely touchy-feely with anyone—certainly not Moroi—but I clung to her without even thinking twice. She did the same, and I could feel her trembling. Once, as a Strigoi, she'd been a force to be reckoned with. As a Moroi, one who'd just had a sword at her throat, things were understandably different.

The guy facing down Dimitri actually managed a couple of good dodges. His mistake came when he attempted to hit Dimitri. It opened his guard, and like that, Dimitri punched him hard in the face. The tall guy who'd hit the tree earlier attempted an attack, but he was an idiot if he thought Dimitri was distracted. Dimitri dispatched him easily, and he landed near the guy Dimitri had just punched. The tall one struggled to his feet and looked like he wanted to attack again. His friend grabbed hold of him and tugged him away. After a moment's struggle between them, the two finally ran off. Dimitri didn't pursue. His attention was all on Sonya and me.

"Are you okay?" he asked, swiftly striding over to us.

I managed a weak nod, even though I was shaking uncontrollably.

"Let's get out of here," said Dimitri. He put a hand on each of our shoulders and began to steer us away.

"Wait," I said, moving toward the churchyard. "We should take the sword."

I scanned in front of me, but it was even darker than before. Dimitri found the sword right away with his superior eyesight. He tucked it under his duster, and the three of us quickly got out of there. We walked to Adrian's apartment, since it was much closer than Clarence's property outside of town. Even so, the brief trip seemed to take forever. I kept feeling like we could be attacked again at any moment, but Dimitri continued giving us assurances, while still pushing us at a good pace.

Adrian was surprised to see us at his door. He also looked pretty drunk, but I didn't care. All I wanted was the security of his four walls.

"What . . . what's going on?" he asked, as Dimitri urged Sonya and me inside. Adrian's eyes looked at each of us, resting longest on me. "Are you okay? What happened?"

Dimitri gave Sonya and me a once-over, double-checking for injuries despite our protests. He reached out and gently held my chin, turning my non-tattooed cheek toward him. "A little scraped," he said. "Not serious, but you should clean it." I touched the spot he'd indicated and was astonished to see blood on my fingers. I didn't even remember getting hurt but supposed it had come from the brick wall.

Sonya had no physical marks but admitted to having a pretty bad headache from where she'd hit the ground.

"What happened?" Adrian asked again.

Dimitri held up the sword he'd retrieved from the scene. "Something a little more serious than a mugging, I think."

"I'd say so," said Sonya, sitting on the couch. Her attitude was amazingly calm for what we'd just endured. She touched the back of her head and winced. "Particularly since they called me a creature of evil before you showed up."

Dimitri arched an eyebrow. "They did?"

I hadn't moved once I'd reached the living room. I simply stood there with my arms wrapped around myself, feeling numbed. Movement seemed too difficult. Thinking seemed too difficult. As Dimitri examined the sword, however, something caught my eye and made my sluggish brain slowly begin to function again.

Seeing my interest, he held the sword out to me. I took it, careful of the blade, and examined the hilt. It was covered with engravings.

"Do those mean something to you?" he asked.

My mind was still cloudy with fear and adrenaline, but I ignored it and tried to dredge up some facts. "These are old alchemy symbols," I said. "From the Middle Ages, back when our group was just a bunch of medieval scientists trying to turn lead into gold."

That was all the history books knew about my society. That, and we'd eventually given up on gold. The organization had later found more sophisticated compounds, including vampire blood. Interacting with vampires had eventually evolved into our current cause, as ancient Alchemists realized the terrible and dark temptations vampires represented. Our cause became a holy one. The chemistry and formulas my society had once worked on for personal gain became the tools needed to hide the existence of vampires, tools we now supplemented with technology.

I tapped the largest symbol, a circle with a dot in the center. "This is actually the symbol for gold. This other one is silver. These four triangle things are the basic elements—earth, air, water, and fire. And these . . . Mars and Jupiter, which tie into iron and tin. Maybe the sword's composition?" I frowned and studied the rest of the metal. "No gold or silver actually in it, though. Their symbols can also refer to the sun and moon. Maybe these aren't physical at all. I don't know."

I handed the sword back to Dimitri. Sonya took it from him,

studying what I'd pointed out. "So, are you saying this is an Alchemist weapon?"

I shook my head. "Alchemists would never use something like this. Guns are easier. And the symbols are archaic. We use the periodic table now. Easier to write 'Au' for gold instead of drawing that sun symbol."

"Is there any reason these would be on a weapon? Some greater symbolism or meaning?" Dimitri asked.

"Well, again, if you go back, the sun and gold were the most important to the ancient Alchemists. They revolved around this whole idea of light and clarity." I touched my cheek. "Those things are still important in some ways—it's why we use this gold ink. Aside from the benefits, the gold marks us as . . . pure. Sanctified. Part of a holy cause. But on a sword . . . I don't know. If whoever did this was going off the same symbolism, then maybe the sword is sanctified." I thought back to the attackers' words, about returning to Hell. I grimaced. "Or maybe its owners feel it's serving some kind of holy duty."

"Who were these guys anyway?" asked Adrian. "Do you think Jill's at risk?"

"They knew about vampires. But they were human," said Dimitri.

"Even I could tell that," I agreed. "The one was pretty tall, but he was no Moroi." Admitting our assailants had been human was difficult—and baffling—for me. I'd always believed the Strigoi were evil. That was easy. Even Moroi couldn't always be trusted, which was why the thought of Moroi assassins coming after Jill didn't seem that far-fetched. But humans . . . the people I was supposed to be protecting? That was tough. I'd been attacked by my own kind, the so-called good guys, not the fanged fiends I'd been taught to fear. It was a jolt to my worldview.

Dimitri's face grew even grimmer. "I've never heard of anything like this—mainly because most humans don't know about Moroi. Aside from the Alchemists."

I gave him a sharp look. "This had nothing to do with us. I told you, swords aren't our style. Neither are attacks."

Sonya set the sword down on the coffee table. "No one's making accusations about anyone. I assume it's an issue you'll both want to bring up to your groups." Dimitri and I nodded. "Although, I think we're overlooking a key point here. They were treating me like a Strigoi. A sword's not the easiest way to kill someone. There'd have to be a reason."

"It's the only way a human could kill a Strigoi, too," I murmured. "Humans can't charm a silver stake. I suppose they could set you on fire, but that's not practical in an alley."

Silence fell as we all mulled this over. At last, Sonya sighed. "I don't think we're going to get anywhere tonight, not without talking to others. Do you want me to heal that?"

It took me a moment to realize she was talking to me. I touched my cheek. "No, it'll heal fast on its own." That was one of the side effects of the vampire blood in our lily tattoos. "I'll go clean it before I go."

I walked to the bathroom as confidently as I could. When I reached it and saw my reflection in the mirror, I lost it. The scrape wasn't bad, not at all. Mostly, what upset me was what it represented. Sonya had had the blade to her throat, but my life had been in danger too. I had been attacked, and I'd been helpless. I wet a washcloth and tried to bring it to my face, but my hands were shaking too badly.

"Sage?"

Adrian appeared in the doorway, and I quickly tried to blink away the tears that had started to fill my eyes. "Yeah?"

"You okay?"

"Can't you tell from my aura?"

He didn't answer but instead took the washcloth from me before I dropped it. "Turn," he commanded. I did, and he dabbed the scrape with it. With him standing so close to me, I could see that his eyes were bloodshot. I could also smell the alcohol on him. Nonetheless, his hand was steadier than mine. Again, he asked, "You okay?"

"I'm not the one who had a sword to my throat."

"That's not the question I asked. Are you hurt anywhere else?"

"No," I said, looking down. "Just maybe . . . maybe my pride."

"Your pride?" He paused to rinse the washcloth. "What does that have to do with anything?"

I looked up but still didn't meet his eyes. "I can do a lot of things, Adrian. And—at the risk of sounding egotistical—I mean, well, I can do a lot of pretty awesome things that most people can't."

There was amusement in his voice. "Don't I know it. You can change a tire in ten minutes while speaking Greek."

"Five minutes," I said. "But when my life's on the line—when others' lives are on the line—what good am I? I can't fight. I was completely helpless out there. Just like when the Strigoi attacked us and Lee. I can only stand and watch and wait for people like Rose and Dimitri to save me. I . . . I'm like a storybook damsel in distress."

He finished cleaning my cheek and set the washcloth down. He cupped my face in his hands. "The only thing true about what you just said was the storybook damsel part—and that's only because you're pretty enough to be one. Not the distress thing. Everything else you just said was ridiculous. You're not helpless."

I finally looked up. In our conversations, Adrian wasn't usually the one accusing me of being ridiculous. "Oh? So I am like Rose and Dimitri?"

"No. No more than I am. And, if memory serves, *someone* told me recently it was useless trying to be like other people. That you should only try to be yourself."

I scowled at having my words thrown back at me. "This isn't the same situation at all. I'm talking about taking care of myself, not impressing someone."

"Well, there's your other problem, Sage. 'Taking care of yourself.' These encounters you've had—Strigoi, crazy guys with swords. Those aren't exactly normal. I don't think you can really get down on yourself for not being able to fight back against those kinds of attacks. Most people couldn't."

"*I* should be able to," I muttered.

His eyes were sympathetic. "Then learn. That same person who likes giving me advice once told me not to be a victim. So don't be. You've learned how to do a million other things. Learn this. Take a self-defense class. Get a gun. You can't be a guardian, but that's not the only way to protect yourself."

A cluster of emotions boiled within me. Anger. Embarrassment. Reassurance. "You've got a lot to say for a drunk guy."

"Oh, Sage. I've got a lot to say, drunk or sober." He released me and stepped away. I felt oddly vulnerable without him near. "What most people don't get is that I'm more coherent like this. Less chance for spirit to make me crazy." He tapped the side of his head and rolled his eyes.

"Speaking of which . . . I'm not going to give you any lectures about that," I said, glad to shift the topic from me. "Lunch with your dad sucked. I get it. If you want to drown that out, it's fine. But please, just keep Jill in mind. You know what this does to her—not now, maybe, but later."

The ghost of a smile flickered across his lips. "You're always the voice of reason. Just try listening to yourself once in a while."

The words were familiar. Dimitri had said something similar, that I couldn't take care of others without taking care of myself first. If two people as wildly different as Adrian and Dimitri had the same opinion, then *maybe* there was something to it. It gave me a lot to think about when I returned to Amberwood later.

One of the good things about Adrian's intoxication was that Jill hadn't been able to witness our talk. So the next day over lunch when I gave Jill, Eddie, and Angeline a recap of what had happened, I was able to edit the story and leave out my own breakdown. Jill and Angeline's reactions were about what I expected. Jill was concerned and kept asking over and over if Sonya and I were okay. Angeline regaled us with tales of all the things she would've done to the attackers and how, unlike Dimitri, she would have chased them through the streets. Eddie was quiet and didn't say much until the other two had left, Angeline back to her room and Jill to get ready for class.

"I thought something was wrong with you today," he said.

"Especially at breakfast, when Angeline called a tomato a vegetable and you didn't correct her."

I managed a half smile at his joke. "Yeah. Well, it's the kind of thing that sticks with you. I mean, maybe not for you guys. Random sword attacks in dark alleys are normal for you, right?"

He shook his head, face serious. "You can't ever take any attack in stride. People who do get careless. You have nothing to feel bad about."

I'd been stirring some sketchy looking mashed potatoes and finally gave up. "I don't like being unprepared. For anything. Don't get me wrong—I've been there when you and Rose fought Strigoi. I was helpless then too . . . but that's different. They're larger than life . . . beyond a human's scope. I don't really expect myself to be able to fight then. But what happened last night—even with the sword—was only one step away from a mugging. Mundane. And they were human, like me. I shouldn't have been so ineffectual."

"Do you want me to teach you some tricks?" he asked kindly.

That brought my smile back. "What you do is a little larger than life too. Maybe I'd be better doing something a little more suited to my level. Adrian said I should get a gun or take a self-defense class."

"That's good advice."

"I know. Scary, huh? The Alchemists do gun-training, but I'm not a fan. I do pretty well at classes and theory, though."

He chuckled. "Very true. Well, if you change your mind, let me know. After working with Angeline, I'm ready for anything. Although . . . to be fair, she's backed off a little."

I thought back to my last real conversation with her. Her

fight and suspension had only been yesterday but felt like years ago. "Oh. I sort of had a talk with her."

"What kind of talk?" he asked, surprised. "I told you not to worry about my personal life. It's my problem."

"I know, I know. But it just kind of happened. I told her that her behavior was out of line and that she needed to stop. She was pretty mad at me, though, so I wasn't sure if it had gotten through."

"Huh. I guess it did." The next words obviously were a big concession. "Maybe she's not as bad as I thought."

"Maybe," I agreed. "And look at it this way. At least her suspension means you don't have to worry about her at the dance."

From the way his face lit up, it was clear he hadn't realized that yet. A few moments later, he toughened up again. "If there are attacks going on like this, I'm going to have to be extra cautious with Jill—especially at the dance." I hadn't thought there was any way Eddie could be more cautious, but probably he'd prove me wrong. "I kind of wish Angeline was going."

Most of my classes were distracting enough to keep me from thinking too much about last night, but Ms. Terwilliger's independent study was different. It was too quiet, too low-key. It gave me a lot of time in my own head, bringing back all the fear and self-doubt I'd been trying to ignore. For once, I copied and notated the spells without really memorizing them. Usually, I couldn't help myself. Today, my mind wasn't there.

We were almost halfway through the period when I finally tuned in enough to really process what I was working on. It was a spell from Late Antiquity that allegedly made the victim think scorpions were crawling on him or her. Like so many of

Ms. Terwilliger's spell books, the formula was convoluted and time consuming.

"Ms. Terwilliger?" I hated to ask anything of her, but recent events weighed too heavily on me.

She looked up in surprise from her paperwork. After the cold war we'd entered into, she'd grown used to me never speaking unless spoken to. "Yes?"

I tapped the book. "What good are these so-called offensive spells? How would you ever use them in a fight when they require concoctions that take days to prepare? If you're attacked, there's no time for anything like that. There's hardly any time to think."

"Which one are you looking at?" she asked.

"The scorpion one."

She nodded. "Ah, yes. Well, that's more of a premeditated one. If you've got someone you don't like, you work on this and cast it. Quite effective for ex-boyfriends, I might add." Her face grew distracted, and then she focused back on me. "There are certainly ones that would be more useful in the kind of situation you're describing. Your fire charm, if you recall, had a lot of prep work but could be used quite quickly. There are others that can be cast on extremely short notice with few components—but as I've said in the past, those types require considerable skill. The more advanced you are, the less you need ingredients. You need a lot more experience before you're at a level to learn anything like that."

"I never said I wanted to learn anything like that," I snapped. "I'm just . . . making an inquiry."

"Oh? My mistake. It almost sounded like you were, dare I say, interested."

"No!" I was grateful that the healing magic in my tattoo had cleared up most of the bruising on my face from last night. I didn't want her to suspect that I might have serious motivation for protection. "See, this is why I never say anything in here. You read too much into it and just use it to further your agenda to torment me."

"Torment? You read books and drink coffee in here—exactly what you'd be doing if you weren't here."

"Except that I'm miserable," I told her. "I hate every minute of this. I'm almost ready to stop coming and risk the academic fallout. This is all sick and twisted and—"

The last bell of the day cut me off before I said something I'd regret. Almost immediately, Trey appeared in the doorway. Ms. Terwilliger began packing up and looked over at him with a smile, as though everything in here was perfectly normal.

"Why, Mr. Juarez. How nice of you to show up now, seeing as you couldn't make it to my class this morning."

Looking back, I realized she was right. Trey hadn't been in her history class or our chemistry class. "Sorry," he said. "I had some family stuff to take care of."

"Family stuff" was an excuse I used all the time, though I doubted Trey's had involved taking vampires on a blood feeding run.

"Can you, uh, tell me what I missed?" he asked.

Ms. Terwilliger slung her bag over her shoulder. "I have an appointment. Ask Miss Melbourne—she'll probably explain it more thoroughly than I can. The door will lock behind you when you two leave."

Trey sat down in a nearby desk and pulled it up to face mine while I produced our history and chemistry assignments, since

I assumed he'd need the latter as well. I nodded toward the duffle bag he had on the floor beside him.

"Off to practice?"

He leaned over to copy the assignments, his dark hair falling around the sides of his face. "Wouldn't miss it," he said, not looking up as he wrote.

"Right. You only miss classes."

"Don't judge," he said. "I would've been there if I could."

I let it go. I'd certainly had my fair share of weird personal complications come up before. While he wrote, I turned on my cell phone and found I had a text message from Brayden. It was one word, a record for him: *Dinner?*

I hesitated. I was still worked up over last night, and although Brayden was fun, he wasn't the comfort I needed right now. I texted back: *Not sure. I've got some work to do tonight.* I wanted to look up some self-defense options. That was the reassurance I needed. Facts. Options. Brayden's quick response followed: *Late dinner? Stone Grill at 8?* I considered it and then texted back that I'd be there.

I had just set down my phone when another text message buzzed. Unexpectedly, it was from Adrian. *How r u feeling after last night? Been worried about u.* Adrian was articulate in e-mail but often resorted to abbreviations in texts—something I could never bring myself to do. Even reading it was like listening to nails on a chalkboard for me, yet something touched me about his concern, that he was worried about my well-being. It was soothing.

I wrote back: *Better. I'm going to find a self-defense class.* His response time was nearly as fast as Brayden's: *Let me know what u find. Maybe I'll take one 2.* I blinked in surprise. I certainly hadn't seen that coming. There was only one thing I could send back: *Why?*

"Geez," said Trey, closing up his notebook. "Miss Popularity."

"Family stuff," I said.

He scoffed and shoved the notebook into his backpack. "Thanks for these. And speaking of family stuff . . . your cousin. Is it true she was expelled?"

"Suspended for two weeks."

"Really?" He stood up. "That's it? I thought it'd be a lot worse."

"Yeah. It nearly was. I persuaded them to go easy on her."

Trey laughed outright at that. "I can only imagine. Well, I guess I can wait two weeks then."

I frowned. "For what?"

"To ask her out."

I was speechless for a few seconds. "Angeline?" I asked, just in case he thought I had another cousin. "You want to ask out . . . Angeline?"

"Sure," he said. "She's cute. And taking out three guys and a speaker? Well . . . I'm not going to lie. That was pretty hot."

"I can think of a lot of words to describe what she did. 'Hot' isn't one of them."

He shrugged and moved toward the door. "Hey, you've got your turn-ons, I've got mine. Windmills for you, brawling for me."

"Unbelievable," I said. Yet, I wondered if it really was. I supposed we did all have our own "turn-ons." Trey's lifestyle was certainly different from mine. He was devoted to his sport and always had bruises on him from practice, even now. They were more severe than usual. I couldn't understand his passions any more than he could understand my love of knowledge. My phone buzzed again.

"Better get back to your fan club," said Trey. He left, and a strange thought occurred to me. Were all of Trey's recent bruises really from sports? He kept making a lot of references to his family, and I suddenly wondered if something far more insidious than I'd suspected was keeping him away. It was a troubling idea, one I didn't have a lot of experience with. Another buzz from the phone pulled me out of my worries.

I checked the phone and found another text from Adrian—a long one that spanned two messages. It was a response to my question about him taking a self-defense class.

It'll give me a reason to avoid S&D. Besides, u aren't the only one who might need protection. Those guys were human and knew S was a vampire. Maybe vampire hunters r real. Ever think Clarence might be telling the truth?

I stared at the phone in disbelief, processing Adrian's words and the implications of last night's attack.

Ever think Clarence might be telling the truth?

No. Until that moment, I hadn't.

CHAPTER 12

WHEN I SHOWED UP for my dinner date, Brayden was sitting at a booth with a laptop. "I got here early," he explained. "Figured I should get in some work. Did you get yours done?"

"I did, actually. I was researching self-defense classes. You won't believe what I found."

I sat down on his side of the booth so that I could use his laptop. Like usual, he smelled like coffee. I'd never get tired of that, I decided. I directed him to a website I'd found just before coming here. The site looked like one I could have made about ten years ago and had a lot of over-the-top animated images on it. *Wolfe School of Defense – Malachi Wolfe, instructor.*

"Really?" Brayden asked. "Malachi Wolfe?"

"He can't help his name," I said. "And look—he's actually got a number of awards and commendations." Some of the awards were even recent. Most were from at least a few years ago. "Here's the best part."

I clicked on a link entitled "Upcoming Classes." Malachi Wolfe had a pretty busy schedule, but there was one promising part. He was holding a four-week class, starting tomorrow, that met once a week.

"This isn't exactly the kind of instructor I'd had in mind," I admitted, "but it starts right away."

"Not a very long course," added Brayden. "But it'd give you a good intro. Why the interest?"

An image of the alley flashed back into my mind, the figures in the dark and the helpless feeling as I was shoved against the wall. My breath started to catch, and I had to remind myself that I was no longer in the alley. I was in a well-lit restaurant, with a boy who liked me. I was safe.

"Just, uh, something I feel it's important for a woman to learn," I said. "Although . . . it's open to men and women both."

"Trying to sign me up?" At first I thought he was being serious, but when I looked up, he was smiling.

I grinned. "If you want. I was thinking of—my brother. He wants to do this too."

"Probably best if I don't. Although, I was going to take martial arts as a college elective." Brayden shut off his laptop, and I moved back over to the other side of the booth. "Anyway, you've got a pretty tight-knit family. Not sure if I should force myself into that."

"Probably a smart idea," I agreed, thinking that he didn't know the half of it.

Dinner was good, as was our subsequent conversation about thermodynamics. Despite the compelling topic, however, I found my mind was wandering a lot. I had to keep tuning back into what Brayden was saying. The attack and Adrian's offhand comment about vampire hunters had given me a lot to think about.

Still, we stayed at the restaurant for a long time. So much so that when we left, I saw it was completely dark. I wasn't parked that far away—and not even in a remote spot—but suddenly, the anticipation of a walk alone in the dark made me freeze up. Brayden was saying something about seeing me at the dance and then noticed my reaction.

"What's wrong?" he asked.

"I . . . " I stared off down the street. Two blocks. That's how close my car was. There were people out. And yet, I was choking up. "Would you walk me to my car?"

"Sure," he said. He didn't even think twice about it, but I was mortified the entire way. As I'd told Eddie and Adrian, I didn't usually need help from others. Needing it for something like this was especially humiliating. *Rose wouldn't need an escort,* I thought. *Even Angeline wouldn't. She'd probably beat up a few pedestrians on the way, just to stay in practice.*

"Here we are," said Brayden, once we reached Latte. I wondered if he thought less of me for needing an escort.

"Thanks. I'll see you Saturday?"

He nodded. "You sure you want to meet there? I can pick you up."

"I know. And I wouldn't mind going in your car. No offense, Latte." I gave the car's side a comforting pat. "But I'll have to drive my brother and sister. Easier this way."

"Okay," he said. The smile he gave me was almost shy, contrasting with his earlier confidence in academic topics. "Can't wait to see your costume. I got mine from a theatrical company.

Not an ideal reproduction of Athenian garb, of course, but the best I could find."

I'd nearly forgotten that I'd left my costume in the hands of Lia. Brayden wasn't the only one interested in seeing what I'd be wearing.

"Looking forward to it," I said.

After a few moments, I wondered why he wasn't leaving. He still wore that shyness and uncertainty, as though he were trying to work up the nerve to say something. Only, as it turned out, speaking wasn't what he wanted to do. With a great show of courage, he stepped forward and kissed me. It was nice, though once again a little underwhelming.

From the look on Brayden's face, however, he might have been sent to new heights. Why didn't I have the same reaction? Maybe I'd done something wrong after all. Or maybe I was deficient?

"See you Saturday," he said.

I made a mental note to add kissing to my list of research topics.

I got back to Amberwood and texted Adrian as I was walking into my dorm. *There's a defense class that starts tomorrow night. $75.* Despite his interest last night, I was a little skeptical of whether he'd snapped out of his depression enough to be up for something like this. I wasn't even sure if he was going to his art classes anymore. A minute later, I got his answer: *I'll be there.* This was followed by another text: *Can u spot me the cash?*

Jill was walking into the dorm, just as I was, both of us barely getting in before curfew. She didn't even notice me and instead looked troubled and pensive. "Hey," I called. "Jill?"

She stopped halfway through the lobby and blinked in

surprise upon seeing me. "Oh, hey. Were you out with your boyfriend?"

I winced. "Not sure I'd call him that yet."

"How many times have you gone out?"

"Four."

"He's taking you to the dance?"

"I'm meeting him there."

She shrugged. "Sounds like a boyfriend to me."

"Sounds like you're quoting something from Kristin and Julia's dating guidebook."

That brought a fleeting smile, but it didn't last. "I think it's just common sense."

I studied her, still trying to get a feel for her mood. "Are you okay? You looked like something was bothering you. Is it . . . is it Adrian? Is he still upset?" For a moment, I was actually more worried about Adrian than her.

"No," she said. "I mean, well, yes. But he's a little better. He's excited about learning self-defense with you." The bond would never cease to amaze me. I'd only communicated with Adrian a minute ago.

"'Excited?'" I asked. That seemed like an astonishingly strong reaction.

"It's a distraction. And a distraction's the best thing for him in these moods," she explained. "He is still upset, though. He's still depressed over his dad."

"I shouldn't have taken him to San Diego," I murmured, more to myself than her. "If I'd refused, he wouldn't have been able to get there."

Jill looked skeptical. "I don't know. I think he would've found a way, with or without you. What happened between them was going to happen eventually." She sounded remarkably wise.

"I just feel terrible seeing Adrian like this," I said.

"These moods come and go for him. Always have." Jill got a faraway look in her eyes. "He's laid off the drinking a little bit—for my sake. But then that just opens him up for . . . well, it's hard to explain. You know how spirit drives people insane? When he's down like this and sober, it makes him more vulnerable."

"Are you saying Adrian's going crazy?" That was not a complication I was ready for.

"No, not exactly." She pursed her lips as she thought. "He just gets a little scattered . . . weird. You'll know it when you see it. He kind of makes sense but kind of not. Gets dreamy and rambles. But not in the way I do. It's got like a—I don't know— mystical feel. But it's not actually magical. It's just him kind of . . . losing it temporarily. It never lasts and, like I said, you'll know it when you see it."

"I think I might have . . . " An unexpected memory flashed back to me, of just before Sonya and Dimitri had arrived. I'd been at Adrian's, and he'd looked at me strangely, like he was just noticing me for the first time. Thinking about it still sent chills through me.

My God, Sage. Your eyes. How have I never noticed them? The color . . . like molten gold. I could paint those . . .

"Girls?" Mrs. Weathers was at her desk, shutting things down for the night. "You need to get to your rooms."

We nodded obediently and moved toward the stairs. When we reached Jill's floor, I stopped her before she could leave.

"Hey—if Adrian's not the problem, then what was bothering you when you came in? Is everything okay?"

"Huh? Oh, that." She flushed in a cute kind of way. "Yeah. I guess. I don't know. Micah . . . um, well, he kissed me tonight. For the first time. And I guess I was just kind of surprised at how I felt about it."

I was surprised they hadn't kissed before and supposed I should be grateful. Her words resonated with me. "What do you mean? Did it feel a lot less exciting than you expected? Like you were just touching someone's lips? Like you were kissing a relative?"

She gave me a puzzled look. "No. That's crazy. Why would you think that?"

"Um, just guessing." I suddenly felt silly. Why had it felt that way for *me*?

"It was great, actually." A faraway look came over her. "Well, almost. I couldn't quite get into it as much as I wanted because I was worried about my fangs. It's easy to hide them talking and smiling. But not while kissing. And all I kept thinking was, 'What am I going to say if he notices?' And then I started thinking about what you and everyone else said. About how this thing with Micah isn't a good idea and how I can't keep things hands-off forever. I like him. I like him a lot. But not enough to risk exposing the Moroi . . . or endanger Lissa."

"That's a noble attitude."

"I guess. I don't want to end things yet, though. Micah's so nice . . . and I love all the friends I've made by being with him. I guess I'll just see what happens . . . but it's hard. It's a wake-up call." She looked so sad as she went into her room.

Continuing on to mine, I felt bad for Jill . . . but at the

same time, I was relieved. I'd stressed over her casual dating of Micah, worried we'd be facing some dramatic, romantic situation where she refused to give him up because their love was too great and transcended their races. Instead, I should have had more faith in her. She wasn't as immature as I sometimes thought. Jill was going to realize the truth and resolve this on her own.

Her words about Adrian also stuck with me, particularly when I picked him up the next evening for our first self-defense class. He got into my car with a cheery attitude, seeming neither depressed nor crazy. He was, I noticed, dressed very nicely, in clothes that would have been an excellent choice for the visit to his father. He noticed my attire as well.

"Wow. I don't think I've ever seen you in anything so . . . casual." I had on olive green yoga pants and an Amberwood T-shirt.

"The class description said to dress in comfortable workout clothes—like I texted you earlier." I gave his raw silk shirt a meaningful look.

"This is very comfortable," he assured me. "Besides, I don't own any workout clothes."

As I shifted the car into drive, I caught sight of Adrian's left hand. At first, I thought he was bleeding. Then, I realized it was red paint.

"You're painting again," I said in delight. "I thought you'd stopped."

"Yeah, well. You can't take painting classes and not paint, Sage."

"I thought you'd stopped those too."

He gave me a sidelong glance. "Nearly did. But then

I remembered I'd convinced some girl that if she gave me a chance and got me into those classes, I'd follow through on them. That'll teach me."

I smiled and pulled into traffic.

I'd left a little early so that Adrian and I had time to take care of our registration. When I'd called the Wolfe School of Defense earlier today, an agitated man had told me to just show up with the money since we were down to the last minute. The address was outside of downtown, in a residence set on sprawling grounds that had made no attempts to go green and thwart the climate. The desert still held claim here, giving the house a dismal, forlorn look. If not for WOLFE printed on the mailbox, I would've thought we had the wrong place. We pulled up into the gravel drive—no other cars were there—and stared.

"This is the kind of place you see in movies," said Adrian. "Where careless people run into serial killers."

"At least it's still light out," I said. Ever since the alley, darkness had taken on a whole new menace for me. "Can't be that bad."

Adrian opened the car door. "Let's find out."

We rang the doorbell and were immediately met with the sounds of barking and scampering feet. I stepped back uneasily. "I hate poorly trained dogs," I muttered to Adrian. "They need to behave and be kept in line."

"Just like the people in your life, huh?" asked Adrian.

The door opened, and we were met by a fifty-something man with a grizzled blond beard. He was wearing Bermuda shorts and a Lynyrd Skynyrd T-shirt. Also, he had an eye patch.

"This is incredible," I heard Adrian murmur. "Beyond my wildest dreams."

I was taken aback. The eye patch made me think of Keith's glass eye, which in turn made me think of my role in him acquiring it. It wasn't a memory I liked being reminded of, and I wondered at the odds of running into another one-eyed man. This guy nudged the herd of dogs aside—which appeared to be some sort of Chihuahua mix—and barely managed to step outside without them following before he shut the door.

"Yeah?" he asked.

"We're, uh, here for the class. The self-defense class." I felt the need to clarify, in case he also taught about dog breeding or riding the high seas. "I'm Sydney, this is Adrian. I called this morning?"

"Ah, right, right." He scratched his beard. "You got the money? Cash only."

I produced one hundred and fifty dollars and handed it over. Out of habit, I nearly asked for a receipt, but then thought better of it. He stuffed the cash into the pocket of his shorts.

"Okay," he said. "You're in. Go ahead and wait in the garage until the others show up. The side door's unlocked." He gestured to a large, industrial looking building—twice the size of the house—over on the far side of the lot. Without waiting around to see if we'd comply, he slipped back inside to the barking dogs.

The garage's interior, I was relieved to see, was the first thing here that looked like it had some semblance of legitimacy. There were clean mats on the floor and mirrors on some of the walls. A TV and VHS player sat on a cart, along with some defense-related tapes covered in dust. Slightly more disconcerting was some of the decor, like a pair of nunchucks hanging on the wall.

"Don't touch those!" I warned, seeing Adrian head toward them. "That's not the kind of guy whose stuff you want to mess with."

Adrian stayed hands-off. "Do you think we'll get to learn to use these?"

"Weapons weren't in the class description. It's about basic self-defense and hand-to-hand."

"Why bother then?" Adrian strolled over to a glass case displaying several types of brass knuckles. "That's the kind of stuff Castile does all day. He could have showed us."

"I wanted someone a little more approachable," I explained.

"What, like Captain McTropicalShorts back there? Where on earth did you find him anyway?"

"Just did an Internet search." Feeling a need to defend my research, I added, "He comes highly recommended."

"By who? Long John Silver?" Despite myself, I laughed.

Over the next half hour, the rest of our class trickled in. One was a woman who looked to be about seventy. Another was a mother who'd just had her fourth child and decided she needed to "learn to protect them." The last two women in the class were in their mid-twenties and wore T-shirts with angry girl-power catchphrases. Adrian and I were the youngest in the group. He was the only man, not counting our instructor, who asked that we simply refer to him as Wolfe.

I was beginning to get a bad feeling about all of this, particularly as class started. The six of us sat on the floor while Wolfe leaned against one of the mirrors and looked down upon us. "If you're here," he began. "You probably want to learn to use those right away." He pointed at the nunchucks.

I caught sight of Adrian's face in the mirror. His expression said, *Yes, that is exactly what I want to learn.*

"Well, too bad," said Wolfe. "You aren't ever going to use them. Not in this class, anyway. Oh, they've got their uses, believe me. Saved my ass more than once when I was out bow-hunting in Alaska a few years ago. But if you pay attention to what I'm going to tell you, you won't ever need to pick those up, seeing as we don't have a rabid moose problem here in Palm Springs."

The new mom raised her hand. "You used nunchucks on a moose?"

Wolfe got a haunted look in his eyes. "I used all sorts of things on that bastard. But that's neither here nor now. Because here's the thing. With a little common sense, you won't need weapons. Or fists. You."

To my shock, Wolfe pointed at me and fixed me with a steely, one-eyed stare.

"What did I tell you to do when you arrived?"

I gulped. "Give you cash, sir."

"And after that?"

"You told us to come wait out here."

He nodded in satisfaction, so apparently my answering of the obvious had gone well. "We're two miles from any other houses and about a mile from the highway. You don't know me, and let's face it, this place looks like something from a serial killer film." Out of the corner of my eye, Adrian flashed me a triumphant look. "I sent you out into a remote building with hardly any windows. You went inside. Did you look around as you were walking over here? Did you scan the surroundings in here before coming all the way inside? Did you check the exits?"

"I—"

"No, of course you didn't," he interrupted. "No one ever does. And *that* is the first rule of self-defense. Don't assume anything. You don't have to live your life in fear, but know what's around you. Be smart. Don't go blindly into dark alleys or parking lots."

And like that, I was hooked.

Wolfe was astonishingly well prepared. He had lots of stories and examples of attacks, ones that kept reminding me: *humans are some of the most vicious creatures out there, not vampires.* He showed us pictures and diagrams of various unsafe places, pointing out vulnerabilities and providing pretty practical advice that should've been obvious to most people—but wasn't. The more he spoke, the more foolish I felt about what had happened with Sonya. If those guys had wanted to attack Sonya badly enough, they would've found a way somehow. But there were a million things I could have done to be more cautious and possibly avoid the confrontation that went down that night. That idea turned out to be a huge part of Wolfe's philosophy: avoidance of danger in the first place.

Even when he finally moved on to discuss some very basic moves, his emphasis was on using them to get away—not to stick around and beat your attacker into the ground. He let us practice some of these moves in the last half hour of the class, having us pair up to work with classmates and a dummy since we didn't really want to hurt each other.

"Thank God," said Adrian, when we broke out to practice.

He and I were partners. "I thought I'd come to a fight class to learn how not to fight."

"But he's right," I said. "If you can avoid the fight, so much the better."

"But what if you can't?" asked Adrian. "Like with your sword-wielding friends? What do you do once you're in trouble?"

I tapped our blank-faced stuffed practice dummy. "That's what this is for."

Wolfe's main move today was on how to break out of some-one's hold if we were grabbed from behind. He had a couple of techniques which weren't much more complex than head-butting or stomping on feet. Adrian and I took turns being the attacker while the victim practiced the maneuvers—in slow motion and with almost no contact on our partners. That was what the dummies were for. I was about five inches shorter than Adrian and seemed pretty implausible as an attacker, which made us both laugh each time I made a move. Wolfe chastised us for not being serious enough but gave us high marks for learning the techniques.

This made me feel a little arrogant, enough so that when Adrian turned his back to get a water bottle, I sneaked up from behind and flung my arms around him, pinning his arms in turn. Wolfe had shown us how to break that type of hold, and I honestly thought Adrian had seen me coming enough to slip away before I even touched him. Apparently not. He froze, and for one moment, we stood locked in time. I could feel the silk of his shirt against my skin and the warmth of his body. The lin-gering scent of the overpriced cologne he wore floated around me. No smoke for a change. I'd always told him the cologne couldn't be worth what he spent, but suddenly, I reconsidered. It was amazing.

I was so awash in sensory overload that I was caught completely unaware when he *did* push me away.

"What are you doing?" he exclaimed. I'd thought he'd be impressed at my sneak attack, but there was neither approval nor humor on his face. My own smile faded.

"Testing if you could handle a surprise attack." My tone was hesitant. I didn't know what I'd done wrong. He looked uncomfortable. Almost upset. "What's the matter?"

"Nothing," he said gruffly. For a moment his eyes locked onto me with an intensity that left me breathless. Then, he glanced away, as though he couldn't handle looking at me. I felt more confused than ever. "Never thought I'd see the day when you'd throw your arms around a vam—someone like me."

I barely even noticed his public slipup. His words drew me up short. He was right. I'd touched him without even thinking about it—and not just a formal Moroi handshake, like usual. Sure, it was in the context of our class, but I knew that I never could have done this a few months ago. Touching him now had seemed perfectly natural. Was that why he was upset? Was he worried about the Alchemists and me?

Wolfe strolled by. "Nice work, girl." He gave Adrian a teeth-rattling slap on the back. "You were totally unprepared for her."

This seemed to distress Adrian even more, and I could've sworn I heard him mutter, "That's for damned sure."

Some of Adrian's swagger returned during the car ride home, but he was still quiet and thoughtful. I again tried to figure out his shift in mood. "Do you need to stop by Clarence's for blood?" Maybe the class had exhausted him.

"Nah," he said. "Don't want you to be late. But maybe . . . maybe you can come by this weekend, and we can do a group trip over there?"

"I've got the dance on Saturday," I said apologetically. "And I think Sonya was going to take Jill to Clarence's tomorrow after school. Probably she can pick you up too."

"I suppose," he said. He sounded disappointed, but one day wasn't that long to wait for blood. Maybe he was afraid Sonya would recruit him for experiments again—which wouldn't be a bad thing, I thought. Suddenly, he straightened up from his slouch. "Speaking of Sonya . . . I was thinking of something earlier. Something Wolfe said."

"Why, Adrian. Were you paying attention after all?"

"Don't start, Sage," he warned. "Wolfe's crazy, and you know it. But when he was giving all his words of wisdom, he mentioned that stuff about not giving out personal info to strangers and how victims are often staked out in advance. Remember?"

"Yeah, I was there," I said. "Like, an hour ago."

"Right, so. Those guys who attacked you and Sonya seemed to know she was a vampire—the wrong kind, but still. The fact that they showed up with a sword implies they did some research. I mean, it's possible they just noticed her on the street one day and were like, 'Ooh, vampire.' But maybe they've been watching her for a while."

Noticed her on the street . . . I gasped as a million pieces fell into place in my mind at once. "Adrian, you're a genius."

He flinched in surprise. "Wait. What?"

"The week before the attack. Sonya and I got dinner, and we were stopped by some random guy who claimed he knew her from Kentucky. She was pretty freaked out because she was a

Strigoi the whole time she was there, and obviously, she didn't hang out with humans a lot back then."

Adrian took a few moments to turn this over in his mind. "So . . . you're saying they've been checking into her for a while."

"Actually, you're saying that."

"Right. Because I'm a genius." More silence as we both considered the implications of Sonya's situation. When Adrian spoke again, his tone wasn't nearly so light. "Sage . . . last night. You never acknowledged my comment about vampire hunters."

"The Alchemists have no records of modern vampire hunters," I said automatically. "My dad once said that occasionally, some random human discovers the truth. I'd figured her attack was something like that—not some huge organized group or conspiracy."

"Is it remotely possible that somehow, somewhere, the Alchemists might have missed something? And what do you mean by 'modern' exactly?"

Alchemist history had been drilled into me nearly as much as the philosophies that governed our actions. "A long time ago—like, back in the Middle Ages—when the Alchemists were forming, a lot of factions had different ideas on how to deal with vampires. Nobody thought humans should associate with them. Those who eventually formed my group decided the best way was to work with Moroi just enough to keep them separate from humans. But there were others who didn't take that approach. They thought the best way to keep humans free was to eradicate vampires—through any means." I was relying on facts again, my old armor. If I reasoned away this argument, then I wouldn't have to acknowledge what it would mean if there were people actively hunting Moroi.

"Sounds like vampire hunters to me," Adrian pointed out.

"Yes, but they weren't successful. There were just too many vampires, Moroi and Strigoi, for a group like this to take out. The last records we have of them are from, oh, I'd say the Renaissance. Those hunters eventually faded away." Even I heard the uncertainty in my voice.

"You said that sword had alchemy symbols on it."

"Old ones."

"Old enough to be from the time that splinter group was breaking away?"

I sighed. "Yes. That old."

I wanted to close my eyes and sink into my seat. Cracks were appearing in my armor. I still wasn't entirely sure I could accept the idea of vampire hunters, but I could no longer rule out their possibility.

I could see Adrian studying me out of the corner of my eye. "Why the sigh?"

"Because this is all stuff I should have put together sooner."

He seemed very pleased at the acknowledgment. "Well, you don't believe in vampire hunters. Makes it hard to really consider them an actual threat when you operate in a world of facts and data, huh? But then . . . how would they have stayed under your radar for so long?"

Now that Adrian had given me the seeds, my mind was already working out the idea. "Because they're only killing Strigoi—if these hunters exist. If some group were taking out Moroi, your people would notice. The Strigoi aren't organized the same way, and even if they noticed, it's not like they're going to report killings to us. Plus, Strigoi are killed all the time by Moroi and dhampirs. A few dead ones would just be written off to you guys—if anyone even found them. Toss a Strigoi out in the sun, and you'd never even know they'd been there." Relief poured through me at my conclusion. If a group like this *did* exist, they couldn't be killing Moroi. Strigoi-hunting was still dangerous, however. Only Alchemists could be trusted to deal with those fiends' deaths and keep them secret from average humans.

"Could you ask other Alchemists about hunters?" Adrian asked.

"No, not yet. I might be able to dig through some records, but I could never bring this up officially. They'd stick to my dad's theory—that it was just some random, weird group of humans. Then they'd laugh me away."

"You know who wouldn't laugh you away?"

"Clarence," we both said in unison.

"Not a conversation I look forward to," I said wearily. "But he might really know something after all. And all his paranoia might pay off. All that home security? If this group really has it in their heads to come after Sonya, then she might be in even more danger than we realized."

"We need to tell Belikov. He excels at that protection thing. He won't sleep if we convince him she's in trouble—which seems likely after the sword attack." I noticed that this was the first time Adrian had ever spoken about Dimitri without bitterness. In fact, Adrian's words and praise sounded legitimate. He did believe in Dimitri's skill. I said nothing about my observation, though. If Adrian was going to get over his hatred of Dimitri, it needed to come gradually and without any outside "help."

I dropped Adrian off with plans to talk later. When I got back to Amberwood, I was immediately flagged down by Mrs. Weathers. *What now?* I was ready to hear that Angeline had set something on fire. Instead, Mrs. Weathers's face looked calm—pleasant, even—and I dared to hope for the best.

"Some things came for you, dear," she said. From a small office behind her desk, she produced two hangers with zipped garment bags on them. "A short, energetic woman dropped these off."

"Lia." I took the hangers, wondering what contents I'd find inside. "Thank you."

I started to turn away, but Mrs. Weathers spoke again. "One more thing. Ms. Terwilliger left something for you too."

I tried to keep my face neutral. I was already drowning in Ms. Terwilliger's latest assignments. What now? Mrs. Weathers handed me a large envelope that felt like it had a book in it. Scrawled on the outer side was: *Not classwork. Maybe you won't hate this.* I thanked Mrs. Weathers again and took my haul up to my room. After depositing the costumes on my bed unopened, I promptly tore into the envelope. Something about her note made me feel uneasy.

I wasn't entirely surprised to see it was another spell book. What did surprise me was that unlike the others I pored over for her, this one was new. Modern. There was no publisher listed on it, so it was probably someone's home project, but it had clearly been printed and bound within the last few years. That was startling. I'd pointedly never asked Ms. Terwilliger about her magic-using pals and their lifestyle but had always assumed they were reading the dusty old volumes she had me translate and copy. That they might be working from their own, new, and updated books hadn't even crossed my mind—though it should have.

I had no time to beat myself up, though, not once I got a look at the book's title. *The Invisible Dagger: Practical Spells for Offense and Defense.* Flipping through the pages, I saw that the spells were exactly as the title suggested but written in a more modern way than I was used to. Their origins were cited, times and places. Those varied wildly, but what didn't was the spells' efficiency. All were either the kind of spells that could be cast in very little time or ones that could be made in advance for immediate destructive effects—like the fire charm.

These were exactly the kinds of spells I'd been asking Ms. Terwilliger about.

Angry, I stuffed the book back in the envelope. How dare she try to lure me in with this? Did she think this would make up for everything she'd put me through? Mrs. Weathers would still be downstairs, and I had half a mind to drop the book off and tell her it had been sent to me in error. Or I could simply leave it on Ms. Terwilliger's desk first thing in the morning. I wished now I hadn't even opened it. "Returning to sender" unopened would have made a powerful statement, that she wasn't going to trick me into her magic ring by finding a topic of interest to me.

Mrs. Weathers knew about my connection to Ms. Terwilliger, though, and would simply tell me to return it tomorrow if I tried giving it back tonight. So, I'd have to hang on to this until the morning. I consoled myself by getting out some tape. I couldn't undo opening the envelope, but there'd be something psychologically soothing about resealing it.

Yet, as I started to unwind the tape, my mind spun back to my evening with Adrian and Wolfe. Wolfe had calmed me a bit in his constant reminders that most attacks were random and came from carelessness on the victim's part. Knowing that and what to look for had made me feel empowered. He'd offhandedly mentioned attacks of a more premeditated or personal nature, but those clearly weren't his focus. Nonetheless, they brought me back to my discussion with Adrian. What if there was truth to Clarence's stories? What if vampire hunters were real? We'd all known Sonya's attack wasn't random, but if she really was dealing with some faction that had existed since the Middle Ages . . . well, then. My and Adrian's fears would be correct. They would probably come for her again. No amount of avoiding isolated parking spots or walking confidently would stop them.

I looked down at the envelope and decided not to seal it quite yet.

CHAPTER 13

THE DAY OF THE DANCE, I seriously considered going back to the costume store and buying the flammable white costume.

Lia's dress was . . . a bit more than I had expected.

She had done a fair job copying the chiton style worn in ancient Greece, I'd give her that. The dress was sleeveless, pinned at my shoulders to drape into a neckline lower than I was comfortable with. The dress was floor length, and she'd somehow nailed my height perfectly without measuring me. That was where the historical resemblance ended. The material was some sort of silky, flowing fabric that draped around me and showed my figure better than you'd expect a dress like that to manage. Whatever the material was, it was nothing the Greeks could have produced, and it was . . . red.

I couldn't remember the last time I'd worn red. Maybe when I was a child. Sure, the Amberwood uniform variations sometimes had burgundy in them, but it was a subdued shade. This was a brilliant, flaming scarlet. I never wore colors that intense. I didn't like the attention they attracted. Amplifying it was the amount of gold she'd worked into the dress. Gold thread danced along the edge of the red fabric, glittering in the light. The belt was golden too—and not the cheap plastic of the costume's. The pins holding the dress were gold (or at least some high quality metal that appeared gold), as were the accessories she'd provided: a necklace and earrings made of little coins. She'd even given me a gold comb with little red crystals on it.

I tried it on in my dorm room and stared at the glittering, red display I made.

"No," I said aloud.

Someone knocked at my door, and I grimaced. It would take forever to change out of the elaborate dress, so I had no choice but to answer in costume. Fortunately, it was Jill. Her mouth opened to speak and then just hung there in silence when she saw me.

"I know," I said. "It's ridiculous."

She recovered herself a few seconds later. "No . . . no! It's amazing. Oh my God."

I hurried her into the room before our classmates could see me. She was also dressed for the dance, in a fairy confection of pale blue gauzy material that looked perfect on her willowy Moroi frame. "It's red," I told her. In case it wasn't obvious, I added: "I never wear red."

"I know," she said, wide-eyed. "But you should. It looks amazing on you. You should burn all your gray and brown clothes."

I shook my head. "I can't wear this. If we leave now, there's still time to go by the costume store and get something else."

Jill shook off her awed state and took on an adamant, fierce look that seemed kind of extreme for the situation. "No. Absolutely not. You are wearing that. It's going to blow your boyfriend away. And you should put on a little more makeup— I know, I know. You don't like anything crazy, but just darken the eyeliner and put on some lipstick. Just a little. You've got to match the dress's intensity."

"You see? Already this color is causing problems."

She wouldn't back down. "It'll take like a minute. And that's all we've got. If we don't leave soon, we're going to be late. Your boyfriend's always early, right?"

I didn't answer right away. She had me there. Brayden *was* always early, and as much as the costume pained me, I couldn't stand the thought of making him wait—especially since he wouldn't be able to get into the dance without an Amberwood student.

"Fine," I said, with a sigh. "Let's go."

Jill grinned triumphantly. "But first—the makeup."

I conceded to the makeup and then, at the last minute, added my cross necklace. It didn't go with the theme and was instantly swallowed by the more flamboyant gold jewelry, but it made me feel better. It was a piece of normality.

When we finally left, we found Eddie waiting for us in the lobby. He was dressed in normal clothes, his only nod to Halloween being a plain white half-mask that reminded me of the Phantom of the Opera. I was half-tempted to ask if he had a second one so that I could do a quick wardrobe change and just go masked.

He jumped up from his chair, his face going dreamy when he saw Jill in her blue, ethereal glory. Honestly, how could no one else see how crazy he was about her? It was so painfully obvious. He drank her in with his eyes, looking as though he might swoon then and there. Then, he flicked his gaze over to me and did a double-take. His expression wasn't lovestruck so much as dumbfounded.

"I know, I know." I could already see tonight's pattern forming. "It's red. I never wear red."

"You should," he said, echoing Jill. He glanced between her and me then shook his head. "Too bad we're 'related.' I'd ask you guys to dance. Seeing as my cousin already wants to go out with me, though, I suppose we shouldn't start any more rumors."

"Poor Angeline," said Jill, as we walked out to my car. "She really wanted to go."

"Seeing as there'll be speakers there, it's probably best she doesn't," I said.

Eddie paused when we reached Latte. "Can I drive? I feel like I should be a chauffeur tonight. You guys look like royalty." He grinned at Jill. "Well, you're *always* royalty." He opened one of the back doors and actually swept her a bow. "After you, milady. I'm here to serve."

Practical, stoic Eddie was rarely given to such dramatic shows, and I could tell it caught Jill off guard. "Th-thank you," she said, getting into the backseat. He helped her tuck her skirt inside, and she regarded him wonderingly, like she'd never noticed him before. After that, I could hardly deny his request and gave him the keys.

The Halloween dance was being held at a very pretty hall adjacent to some botanical gardens. Eddie and I had checked it out this week so that he could determine its safety. Micah was meeting Jill there, though for different reasons than Brayden meeting me. Supervised buses were shuttling most students from the school to the dance. Upperclassmen like Eddie and me were allowed to take our own transportation, along with family like Jill. No one would technically know if Micah dropped her off later, but for now, she could only leave campus in the family carpool.

"I hope I'm ready for this," I muttered, as we pulled into the parking lot. The dress had distracted me so much that I hadn't had time to ruminate over my other concern: going to a dance. All my old social anxieties returned. What did I do? What was normal here? I hadn't had the nerve to ask any of my friends.

"You'll be fine," said Eddie. "Your boyfriend and Micah will both be speechless."

I unfastened my seatbelt. "That's the third time I've heard 'your boyfriend.' What's going on with that? Why won't anyone say Brayden's name?"

Neither of them answered right away. Finally, Jill said sheepishly, "Because none of us can remember it."

"Oh, come on! I'd expect that from Adrian but not you guys. It's not that weird of a name."

"No," admitted Eddie. "But there's just something so . . . I don't know. Unmemorable about him. I'm glad he makes you happy, but I just start to tune out whenever he talks."

"I can't believe this," I said.

Brayden was waiting out front for us, no doubt having been there for at least ten minutes. My stomach fluttered as he looked me over from head to toe. He didn't comment, though his eyes widened a bit. Was that good or bad? I flashed my student ID to get him in the door, and Jill almost immediately joined Micah.

Eddie's brief romantic flare was gone as he shifted into business mode. A brief look of pain crossed his face, disappearing as quickly as it had appeared. I touched his arm.

"You going to be okay?" I asked softly.

He smiled back. "I'll be fine. Just have fun." He walked away, soon melting into the crowd of students. That left me alone with Brayden. Silence fell between us, which wasn't uncommon. It sometimes took us a few minutes to warm up and get the conversation going.

"So," he said, as we walked further inside. "You have a DJ. I wondered if it'd be that or a live band."

"Our school just had a bad experience with a live band," I said, thinking of Angeline.

Brayden didn't press for details and instead gazed around at the decor. Fake cobwebs and twinkling lights were strewn near the ceiling. Paper skeletons and witches hung on the walls. Over on a far table, students were scooping punch out of a giant plastic cauldron.

"Amazing, isn't it?" said Brayden. "How a pagan Celtic holiday has become such a commercial event."

I nodded. "And a very secular one. Well, aside from attempts to merge it into All Saints Day."

He smiled at me. I smiled back. We were safely in familiar academic territory.

"You want to check out the punch?" I asked. Some fast, bass-heavy song was on, drawing lots of people to the dance floor. Fast dancing wasn't really my style. I didn't know Brayden's take and was afraid he might want to join in.

"Sure," he said, looking relieved to have a purpose. Something told me he'd been to as many dances as I had: none.

The punch provided us with a reason to discuss sugar vs. artificial sweeteners, but my heart wasn't into it. I was too concerned about something else. Brayden hadn't said one word about my dress, and it was filling me with anxiety. Was he as shocked by it as I had been? Was he politely holding back his true thoughts? I could hardly expect compliments if I wasn't giving them, so I decided to take the plunge.

"Your costume's great," I said. "That's from the theatrical company, right?"

"Yes." He glanced down and smoothed out the folds of his tunic. "Not entirely accurate, of course, but it'll do." The tunic was knee-length, pinned on one shoulder, and made of very light, off-white wool. He had a woolen cape over it dyed in a dark brown that was accurate to the time period. Even with the cape, a fair amount of his arms and chest were exposed, showing a runner's body with a lightly muscled build. I'd always thought he was cute, but it wasn't until this moment I realized he might actually be *hot*. I expected that to trigger a stronger feeling in me, but it didn't.

He was waiting for me to say something. "Mine's not entirely, um, accurate either."

Brayden studied the red dress in a very clinical way. "No," he agreed. "Not at all. Well, the cut's not *that* far off, I suppose." He thought for several moments more. "But I still think it's very pretty on you."

I relaxed a little. Coming from him, "very pretty" was high praise. While he often had a lot to say about every other topic, he was thrifty with words when it came to emotions. I shouldn't have expected anything more than a simple statement of facts, so this was a big deal.

"Whoa, Melbourne. Where have you been hiding?" Trey strolled over to us and began liberally filling a cup with the fluorescent green punch. "You look badass. And hot." He shot Brayden an apologetic look. "Don't take that the wrong way. Just telling it like it is."

"Understood," said Brayden. I couldn't help a smile. Trey had been behaving weirdly around me for the last day or so, and it was nice to see him back to usual form.

Trey gave me another admiring look and then turned back to Brayden. "Hey, check it out. We both went for togas. Romans rule!" He held up a hand to high-five Brayden but didn't receive it.

"This is a Greek chiton," Brayden explained patiently. He studied Trey's homemade toga, which looked suspiciously like it had been made from a bed sheet. "That's, um, not."

"Greek, Roman." Trey shrugged. "What's the difference?"

Brayden opened his mouth, and I knew he was about to explain *exactly* what the difference was. I quickly rushed in. "Yours looks good on you," I told Trey. "Looks like all those hours of weight training paid off—*and* I finally get to see the tattoo."

Like Brayden's, Trey's tunic was draped over one shoulder, giving a glimpse of his lower back. Trey, like half the school, had a tattoo. But unlike the rest, his hadn't been part of the high-inducing, sinister vampire blood ones that had swept the student body. Trey's was a sun with highly stylized rays. It had been done in normal, dark blue tattoo ink. Eddie had told me about it, but I'd never gotten a look at it before, seeing as Trey didn't really go shirtless around me.

Some of Trey's enthusiasm dimmed, and he turned slightly,

keeping his back away from us. "Well, it's pretty softcore compared to yours. Nice to see it out again, by the way."

I absentmindedly touched my cheek. I usually covered the golden lily with makeup at school, but I figured here at the dance, I could claim it as part of the costume if any teachers grilled me about the dress code.

Another fast song came on, and Trey brightened again. "Time to show off my moves. You guys coming? Or are you going to supervise the punch all night?"

"I don't really do fast dancing," said Brayden. I nearly sagged in relief.

"Me either," I said.

Trey gave us a rueful smile before heading out. "Color me surprised."

Brayden and I spent a good deal of that evening by the punch, actually, continuing our discussion of Halloween's origins and the larger subjugation of pagan holidays. Friends of mine came by occasionally, and Kristin and Julia in particular couldn't stop gushing about my dress. Every so often, I'd also catch a glimpse of Eddie patrolling the crowds, silently and covertly. Maybe he should've been a ghost. He was almost always within sight of Jill and Micah but focusing on guardian mode seemed to have saved him from pining over her too much.

Both Brayden and I stopped talking when a slow song finally came on. We tensed and then exchanged glances, knowing what was coming. "Okay," he said. "We can only avoid this for so long."

I nearly burst out laughing, and he answered with a small smile. He too was fully aware of our social ineptitude. Somehow, that was comforting. "Now or never," I agreed.

We walked over to the dance floor, joining other couples locked in embraces. Calling what most of them were doing "dancing" was kind of a stretch. Most were just kind of stiffly rocking and rotating around. A few were simply using the opportunity to plaster themselves all over each other and make out. They were quickly pulled apart by chaperones.

I took hold of one of Brayden's hands, and he rested his other on my hip. Aside from the kiss, this was probably the most intimate contact we'd had so far. There were still a few inches between us, but I couldn't help but be overwhelmed at the change to my normal personal space boundaries. I reminded myself that I liked and trusted Brayden and that there was nothing weird about this. As usual, I didn't feel surrounded in hearts or rainbows, but I didn't feel threatened either. Attempting to shift my thoughts from our closeness, I listened to the song and immediately got a feel for its count. About a minute into the song, Brayden realized what I was doing.

"You . . . you can dance," he said in amazement.

I looked up at him in surprise. "Of course." I was hardly sweeping across the floor in some grand ballroom waltz, but all of my movements were timed to the song's beats. I couldn't really imagine how else you would dance. Brayden, meanwhile, was only one step removed from the rigid movements of most of the other couples. "It's not hard," I added. "It's just kind of mathematical."

Once I put it into those terms, Brayden got on board. He was a quick study and counted off the beats with me. Before long, we looked as though we'd been taking dance lessons forever. Even more surprising, I glanced up at him once, expecting to see him concentrating and counting. Instead, he was regar...ng me with a soft expression . . . an affectionate one, even. Flushing, I looked away.

Amazingly, the smell of coffee still clung to him, even though he hadn't worked today. Maybe no amount of showering could get rid of that scent. Yet, as much as I loved *eau de coffee*, I found myself thinking of the way Adrian's cologne had smelled at Wolfe's.

When the next fast song came on, Brayden and I took a break, and he excused himself to go talk to the DJ. When he returned, he refused to explain his mysterious errand, but he seemed supremely pleased with himself. Another slow song soon followed, and we headed back to the dance floor.

And for once, conversation between us stilled. It was enough to just dance for a while. *This is what it's like to lead a simple life*, I thought. *This is what people my age do. No grand machinations or fights between good and—*

"Sydney?"

Jill was standing beside us—a worried expression on her face. My inner alarms immediately went off, wondering what had caused such a sudden change from her happy, carefree attitude earlier. "What's wrong?" I asked. My first fear was for Adrian, that she'd sensed something through the bond. I shook the thought. I needed to be worrying about Moroi assassins, not his well-being.

Jill said nothing but simply nodded toward the punch table, almost exactly where Brayden and I had been earlier. Trey was back, talking animatedly to a girl in a Venetian mask. The mask was beautiful—an icy blue, decorated with silver leaves and flowers. The mask was also familiar. Jill had worn it in Lia's runway show and had been allowed to keep it. Equally familiar was this masked girl's outfit, a threadbare shirt and ragged jean shorts—

"No," I said, recognizing the long, strawberry blonde hair. "Angeline. How did she get here? Never mind." There were any number of people she could have sneaked here with. The chaperones probably wouldn't have noticed her on a shuttle bus. "We have to get her out of here. If she's caught, she'll be expelled for sure."

"The mask *does* hide her features," Jill pointed out. "Maybe no one will notice."

"Mrs. Weathers will," I said, sighing. "That woman's got a sixth sense for—oh. Too late."

Mrs. Weathers was chaperoning on the other side of the room, but her eagle eyes missed nothing. Peering over the crowded dance floor, I saw her begin making her way toward the punch. I didn't think she'd made a positive ID on Angeline yet, but her suspicions were definitely raised.

"What's wrong?" asked Brayden, glancing between Jill and me. No doubt we wore mirrored expressions of dismay.

"Our cousin's about to get in some serious trouble," I said.

"We have to do something." Jill's eyes were wide and anxious. "We have to get her out of here."

"How?" I exclaimed.

Mrs. Weathers had reached the refreshments table, just as Trey and Angeline began walking toward the dance floor. I saw her start to go after them, but Mrs. Weathers didn't get very far—because the punch bowl suddenly exploded.

Well, not the bowl itself. The punch inside exploded,

spraying out in a spectacular shower of bright green liquid. There were shrieks as several nearby people got splashed, but it was Mrs. Weathers who took the brunt of it.

I heard a sharp intake of breath from Brayden. "How in the world did that happen? That must have—Sydney?"

I'd cried out and jerked a few feet away, knowing exactly what had caused that bowl to explode. Brayden assumed my reaction was fear of injury. "It's okay," he said. "We're too far away for any glass to be over here."

Immediately, I looked at Jill. She gave me a small, helpless shrug that said, *Well, what else was I supposed to do?* My usual reaction to Moroi magic was disgust and fear. Tonight, shock and dismay were there too. We didn't need attention drawn to us. True, no one knew or would even guess that Jill had used vampire water magic to create the punch distraction, but it didn't matter. I didn't want any word of weird, unexplainable phenomena leaking out of Amberwood. We needed to stay under the radar.

"Are you okay?" Eddie had suddenly appeared by our side—or rather, Jill's side. "What happened?" He wasn't even looking at the punch. His focus was all on Jill, and just like earlier, she actually seemed to notice it. Brayden was the one who answered, his eyes alight with intellectual curiosity as he watched teachers scurry and try to clean up the mess.

"Some sort of chemical reaction, if I had to guess. Could be as simple as using baking soda. Or maybe some kind of mechanical device?"

I gave Eddie a pointed look. "It was a prank," I said. "Anyone could've done it."

Eddie looked at me, then looked back at Jill. He gave a slow nod. "I see. We should get you out of here," he told her. "You never know what—"

"No, no," I said. "Get *Angeline* out of here."

"Angeline?" Eddie's face registered disbelief. "But how . . . ?"

I directed him toward where she stood with Trey on the dance floor. They, like many others, were staring at the aftermath of the punch explosion with wonder. "I don't know how she got here," I said. "It's irrelevant. She needs to leave. Mrs. Weathers nearly caught her."

A knowing glint flashed in Eddie's eyes. "But the punch distracted her?"

"Yes."

His attention fell back on Jill, and he smiled. "Convenient timing."

She smiled back. "I guess we got lucky this time." Their gazes locked, and it was almost a shame to interrupt. "Go," I told Eddie. "Get Angeline."

He cast one last look at Jill and then jumped into action. I couldn't hear the conversation as he spoke with Angeline and Trey, but the look on his face would accept no arguments. I could see Trey yielding to family authority, and after a few more arguments, Angeline gave in as well. Eddie quickly escorted her out, and to my relief, neither Mrs. Weathers nor anyone else seemed to notice.

"Jill," I said. "It might be best if you and Micah leave early. You don't have to go right this second . . . but soon."

Jill nodded, face sad. "I understand."

Even if no one would connect her to this, it was best if she wasn't around. Already, I could see people gathering at the table and, like Brayden, trying to figure out what could have caused such a phenomenon. She vanished into the crowd. Brayden finally looked away from the spectacle. He started to say something to me and then suddenly jerked his head toward the DJ.

"Oh no," he said, face crestfallen.

"What?" I asked, half-expecting the DJ's table to collapse or a speaker to catch on fire.

"This song. I requested it for you . . . but it's almost over."

I tilted my head to listen. I didn't know the song, but it was slow and romantic and made me feel . . . well, kind of guilty. Here it was, a sentimental gesture from Brayden, ruined by my "family's" wacky hijinks. I caught hold of his hand.

"Well, it's not over yet. Come on."

We were able to dance to the last minute of it, but it was clear that Brayden was disappointed. I wanted to make it up to him somehow and, in spite of everything that had happened, still have the normal high school dance experience I'd wanted.

"The night's young," I teased. "I'll go request one for you, and then you can try to guess when it comes on." Considering I didn't listen to the radio, it probably wouldn't be that hard to guess. I made the request and then joined Brayden for another slow song. I was still a little anxious about what had happened earlier but told myself all was well now. Jill had left. Eddie had taken care of Angeline. All I had to do was relax and—

A vibration startled me as I danced. I was wearing a tiny, red dress purse over my shoulder. It was lost in the folds of my gown, but the buzz of my cell phone was unmistakable. Apologizing to Brayden, I stopped dancing to check the message. It was from Adrian: *We need 2 talk.*

Great, I thought as my heart sank. *Could this night be any more of a disaster?*

I texted back: *I'm busy.*

His response: *I'll be fast. I'm close by.*

A feeling of dread crept over me: *How close?*

The response was about as bad as I could expect: *The parking lot.*

CHAPTER 14

"OH, LORD," I SAID.

"What's wrong?" asked Brayden. "Is everything okay?"

"Hard to say." I put the phone back in my purse. "I hate to do this, but I have to go take care of something outside. I'll be back as quickly as I can."

"Do you want me to go with you?"

I hesitated. "No, it's okay." I had no idea what to expect out there. It was best if Brayden wasn't subjected to it. "I'll hurry."

"Sydney, wait." Brayden caught hold of my arm. "This . . . this is the song you requested, isn't it?" The one we'd been dancing to had just ended, and a new one was on—or, well, an old one. It was about thirty years old.

I sighed. "Yes. It is. I'll be fast, I promise."

The temperature outside was pleasant, warm but not oppressively so. We were allegedly due for a rare bit of rain. As I walked toward the parking lot, some of Wolfe's lessons came back to me. Check your surroundings. Watch for people lurking near cars. Stay in the light. Make sure to—

"Adrian!"

All reasonable thoughts vanished from my head. *Adrian was lying on my car.*

I ran over to Latte as fast as the dress would allow me. "What are you doing?" I demanded. "Get off of there!" I automatically checked for dents and scratches.

Adding insult to injury, Adrian was actually smoking as he lay on the hood and stared up at the sky. Clouds were moving in, but a half-moon could occasionally be seen. "Relax, Sage. I won't leave a scratch. Really, this is surprisingly comfortable for a family car. I would've expected—"

He turned his head toward me and froze. I had never seen him so still—or so quiet. His shock was so thorough and intense that he actually dropped his cigarette.

"Ahh," I cried, springing forward, lest the burning cigarette damage the car. It landed harmlessly on the asphalt, and I quickly stamped it out. "For the last time, will you get off of there?"

Adrian slowly sat up, eyes wide. He slid off the hood and didn't seem to leave any marks. Obviously, I'd have to check it later. "Sage," he said. "What are you wearing?"

I sighed and stared down at the dress. "I know. It's red. Don't start. I'm tired of hearing about it."

"Funny," he said. "I don't think I could ever get tired of looking at it."

Those words drew me up short, and a rush of heat went through me. What did he mean? Was I so outlandish-looking that he couldn't stop staring at the crazy spectacle? Surely . . . surely he wasn't implying that I was pretty . . .

I promptly got back on track, reminding myself that I needed to think about the guy inside, not out here. "Adrian, I'm on a date. Why are you here? On my car?"

"Sorry to interrupt, Sage. I wouldn't have been on your car if they'd let me into the dance," he said. A little of his earlier awe had faded, and he relaxed into a more typical Adrian pose, leaning back against Latte. At least he was standing and less likely to do damage.

"Yeah. They generally frown on letting twenty-something guys into high school events. What did you want?"

"To talk to you."

I waited for him to elaborate, but the only response I received was a brief flash of lightning above. It was Saturday, and I'd been around campus all day, during which he could've easily called. He'd known the dance was tonight. Then, inhaling the smell of alcohol that hung in the air around him, I knew nothing he did should really surprise me tonight.

"Why couldn't it have been tomorrow?" I asked. "Did you really have to come here tonight and—" I frowned and looked around. "How did you even get here?"

"I took the bus," he said, almost proudly. "A lot easier getting here than to Carlton." Carlton College was where he took art classes, and without his own transportation, he'd come to rely heavily on mass transit—something he'd never done before in his life.

I'd been hoping Sonya or Dimitri had dropped him off— meaning they'd pick him up again. But of course that wouldn't happen. Neither one of them would have brought a drunken Adrian here. "So I guess I have to take you home then," I said.

"Hey, I got myself here. I'll get myself home." He started to take out a cigarette, and I gave him a stern headshake.

"Don't," I said sharply. With a shrug, he put the pack away. "And I have to take you home. It's going to storm soon. I'm not going to make you walk in the rain." Another flash of lightning emphasized my words, and a faint breeze stirred the fabric of my dress.

"Hey," he said, "I don't want to be an incon—"

"Sydney?" Brayden came striding across the parking lot. "Everything okay?"

No, not really. "I'm going to have to leave for a little bit," I said. "I have to give my brother a ride home. Will you be okay waiting? It shouldn't be that long." I felt bad even suggesting it. Brayden didn't really know anyone at my school. "Maybe you could find Trey?"

"Sure," said Brayden uncertainly. "Or I can come with you."

"No," I said quickly, not wanting him and drunken Adrian in the car. "Just go back and have fun."

"Nice toga," Adrian told Brayden.

"It's a chiton," said Brayden. "It's Greek."

"Right. I forgot that was tonight's theme." Adrian gave Brayden an appraising look, glanced over at me, and then turned back to Brayden. "So. What do you think of our girl's ensemble tonight? Pretty amazing, huh? Like Cinderella. Or maybe a Greek Cinderella."

"There's really not much about it that's truly Greek," said Brayden. I winced. I knew he didn't mean to be insensitive, but his words stung a little. "The dress is historically inaccurate. I mean it's a very nice dress, but the jewelry's anachronistic, and the fabric's nothing that ancient Greek women would have had. Certainly not that color either."

"What about those other Greek women?" asked Adrian. "The flashy smart ones." His forehead wrinkled, as though it were taking every ounce of his brain to come up with the word he wanted. And, to my astonishment, he did. "The hetaerae." I honestly hadn't believed he'd retained anything from our conversation in San Diego. I tried not to smile.

"The hetaerae?" Brayden was even more astonished than I was. He gave me a scrutinizing look. "Yes . . . yes. I suppose—if such materials were hypothetically possible in that era—that this is something you'd expect to see find on a hetaera instead of the average Greek matron."

"And they were prostitutes, right?" asked Adrian. "These hetaerae?"

"Some were," agreed Brayden. "Not all. I think the usual term is courtesan."

Adrian was completely deadpan. "So. You're saying my sister's dressed like a prostitute."

Brayden eyed my dress. "Well, yes, if we're still speaking in hypothetical—"

"You know what?" I interrupted. "We need to go. It's going to rain any minute now. I'll take Adrian home and meet you back here, okay?" I refused to let Adrian continue to play whatever game he had going to torment Brayden—and, by extension, me. "I'll text you when I'm on my way back."

"Sure," said Brayden, not looking very sure at all.

He left, and I started to get into the car until I noticed Adrian trying—and failing—to open the passenger side door. With a sigh, I walked over and opened it for him. "You're drunker than I thought," I said. "And I thought you were pretty drunk."

He managed to get his body into the seat, and I returned to my own side just as raindrops splashed on my windshield. "Too drunk for Jailbait to feel," he said. "The bond's numb. She can have an Adrian-free night."

"That was very thoughtful of you," I said. "Though I'm guessing that's not the real reason you were hitting the bottle. Or why you came here. As far as I can tell, all you've accomplished is to mess with Brayden."

"He called you a prostitute."

"He did not! You baited him into that."

Adrian ran a hand through his hair and leaned against the window, watching the rapidly unfolding storm outside. "Doesn't matter. I've decided I don't like him."

"Because he's too smart?" I said. I remembered Jill and Eddie's earlier comments. "And unmemorable?"

"Nah. I just think you can do better."

"How?"

Adrian had no answer, and I had to ignore him for a bit as my attention shifted to the road. Storms, while infrequent, could come up fast and furious in Palm Springs. Flash floods weren't uncommon, and the rain was now pouring down in sheets, making visibility difficult. Fortunately, Adrian didn't live that far away. That was a double blessing because, when we were a couple blocks from his apartment, he said: "I don't feel so well."

"No," I moaned. "Please, please do not get sick in my car. We're almost there." A minute or so later, I pulled up at the curb outside his building. "Out. Now."

and I followed with an umbrella for myself.
over at me as we walked to the building, he asked,
we live in a desert, and you keep an umbrella in your car?"

"Of course I do. Why wouldn't I?"

He dropped his keys, and I picked them up, figuring I'd have an easier time unlocking the door. I flipped on the nearest light switch—and nothing happened. We stood there for a moment, together in the darkness, neither of us moving.

"I have candles in the kitchen," said Adrian, finally taking a few staggering steps in that direction. "I'll light some."

"No," I ordered, having visions of the entire building going down in flames. "Lie on the couch. Or throw up in the bathroom. I'll take care of the candles."

He opted for the couch, apparently not as sick as he'd feared. Meanwhile, I found the candles—atrocious air freshening ones that smelled like fake pine. Still, they cast light, and I brought a lit one over to him, along with a glass of water.

"Here. Drink this."

He took the glass and managed to sit up long enough to get a few sips. Then, he handed the glass back and collapsed against the couch, draping one arm over his eyes. I pulled up a nearby chair and sat down. The pine candles cast fragile, flickering light between us. "Thanks, Sage."

"Are you going to be okay if I leave?" I asked. "I'm sure the power will be on by morning."

He didn't answer my question. Instead, he said, "You know, I don't just drink to get drunk. I mean, that's part of it, yeah. A big part of it. But sometimes, alcohol's all that keeps me clearheaded."

"That doesn't make sense. Here," I prompted, handing the

water back to him. As I did, I cast a quick look at my cell phone's clock, anxious about Brayden. "Drink some more."

Adrian complied and then continued speaking, arm back over his eyes. "Do you know what it's like to feel like something's eating away at your mind?"

I'd been about to tell him I needed to leave, but his words left me cold. I remembered Jill saying something similar when she was telling me about him and spirit. "No," I said honestly. "I don't know what it's like . . . but to me, well, it's pretty much one of the most terrifying things I can imagine. My mind, it . . . it's who I am. I think I'd rather suffer any other injury in the world than have my mind tampered with."

I couldn't leave Adrian right now. I just couldn't. I texted to Brayden: *Going to be a little longer than I thought.*

"It is terrifying," said Adrian. "And weird, for lack of a better word. And part of you knows . . . well, part of you knows something's not right. That your thinking's not right. But what do you about that? All we can go on is what we think, how we see the world. If you can't trust your own mind, what can you trust? What other people tell you?"

"I don't know," I said, for lack of a better answer. His words struck me as I thought how much of my life had been guided by the edicts of others.

"Rose once told me about this poem she'd read. There was this line, 'If your eyes weren't open, you wouldn't know the difference between dreaming and waking.' You know what I'm afraid of? That someday, even with my eyes open, I still won't know."

"Oh, Adrian, no." I felt my heart breaking and sat down on the floor near the couch. "That won't happen."

He sighed. "At least with the alcohol . . . it quiets the spirit and then I know if things seem weird, it's probably because I'm drunk. It's not a great reason, but it's a reason, you know? At least you actually have a reason instead of not trusting yourself."

Brayden texted back: *How much longer?* Irritated, I answered back: *Fifteen minutes.*

I looked back up at Adrian. His face was still covered, though the candlelight did a fair job of illuminating the clean lines of his profile. "Is that . . . is that why you drank tonight? Is spirit bothering you? I mean . . . you seemed to be doing so well the other day . . . "

He exhaled deeply. "No. Spirit's okay . . . in as much as it ever is. I actually got drunk tonight because . . . well, it was the only way I could bring myself to talk to you."

"We talk all the time."

"I need to know something, Sage." He uncovered his face to look at me, and I suddenly realized how close I was sitting. For a moment, I almost didn't pay attention to his words. The flickering dance of shadow and light gave his already good looks a haunting beauty. "Did you get Lissa to talk to my dad?"

"What? Oh. That. Hang on one second." Picking up my cell phone, I texted Brayden again: *Better make that thirty minutes.*

"I know someone got her to do it," Adrian continued. "I mean, Lissa likes me, but she's got a lot going on. She wouldn't have just thought one day, 'Oh, hey. I should call Nathan Ivashkov and tell him how awesome his son is.' You got her to do it."

"I've actually never talked to her," I said. I didn't regret my actions at all but felt weird at being called out on them. "But

I, uh, may have asked Sonya and Dimitri to talk to her on your behalf."

"And then she talked to my old man."

"Something like that."

"I knew it," he said. I couldn't gauge his tone, if it was upset or relieved. "I knew someone had to have prompted her, and somehow I knew it was you. No one else would have done it for me. Not sure what Lissa told him, but man, she must have really won him over. He was crazy impressed. He's sending me money for a car. And upping my allowance back to reasonable levels."

"That's a good thing," I said. "Isn't it?"

My phone flashed with another text from Brayden. *The dance will nearly be over by then.*

"But why?" Adrian asked. He sat down on the floor beside me. There was an almost distraught look to him. He leaned closer to me and then seemed shocked as he realized what he was doing. He leaned back a little—but only a little. "Why would you do that? Why would you do that for me?"

Before I could answer, another text came in. *Will you even be back in time?* I couldn't help be annoyed that he wasn't more understanding. Without thinking, I typed back: *Maybe you should just leave now. I'll call you tomorrow. Sorry.* I flipped the phone over so I wouldn't see any other messages. I looked back at Adrian, who was watching me intently.

"I did it because he wasn't fair to you. Because you deserve credit for what you've done. Because he needs to realize you aren't the person he's always thought you were. He needs to see you for who you really are, not for all the ideas and preconceptions he's built up around you." The power in Adrian's gaze was so strong that I kept talking. I was nervous about meeting that stare in silence. Also, part of me was afraid that if I pondered my own words too hard, I'd discover they were just as much about my own father and me as Adrian and his. "It should have been enough for you to tell him who you are—to show him who you are—but he wouldn't listen. I don't like the idea of using others to do things we can do ourselves, but this seemed like the only option."

"Well," Adrian said at last. "I guess it worked. Thank you."

"Did he tell you how to get in touch with your mother?"

"No. His pride in me apparently didn't go that far."

"I can probably find out where she is," I said. "Or . . . or Dimitri could, I'm sure. Like you said before, they must let letters in."

He almost smiled. "There you go again. Why? Why do you keep helping me?"

There were a million answers on my lips, everything from *It's the right thing to do* to *I don't know*. Instead, I said, "Because I want to."

This time, I got a true smile from him, but there was something dark and introspective about it. He shifted closer to me again. "Because you feel bad for this crazy guy?"

"You aren't going to go crazy," I said firmly. "You're stronger than you think. The next time you feel that way, find something to focus on, to remind you of who you are."

"Like what? Got some magic object in mind?"

"Doesn't have to be magic," I said. I racked my brain. "Here." I unfastened the golden cross necklace. "This has always been good for me. Maybe it'll help you." I set it in his hand, but he caught hold of mine before I could pull back.

"What is it?" he asked. He looked more closely. "Wait . . . I've seen this. You wear this all the time."

"I bought it a long time ago, in Germany."

He was still holding my hand as he studied the cross. "No frills. No flourishes. No secret etched symbols."

"That's why I like it," I told him. "It doesn't need embellishment. A lot of the old Alchemist beliefs focused on purity and simplicity. That's what this is. Maybe it'll help you have clarity of mind."

He had been staring at the cross, but now he lifted his gaze to meet mine.

Some emotion I couldn't quite read played over his features. It was almost like he'd just discovered something, something troubling to him. He took a deep breath and, his hand still holding mine, pulled me toward him. His green eyes were dark in the candlelight but somehow just as enthralling. His fingers tightened on mine, and I felt warmth spread throughout me.

"Sage—"

The power suddenly came back on, flooding the room with light. Apparently, with no concern for electrical bills, he'd left all the lights on when he went out earlier. The spell was broken, and both of us winced at the sudden brightness. Adrian sprang back from me, leaving the cross in my hand.

"Don't you have a dance or a curfew or something?" he asked abruptly, not looking at me. "I don't want to keep you. Hell, I shouldn't have bothered you at all. Sorry. I assume that was Aiden texting you?"

"Brayden," I said, standing up. "And it's okay. He left, and I'm just going to go back to Amberwood now."

"Sorry," he repeated, moving toward the door with me. "Sorry I ruined your night."

"This?" I nearly laughed, thinking of all the crazy things I contended with in my life. "No. It'd take a lot more to ruin my night than this." I started to take a few steps and then paused. "Adrian?"

He finally looked directly at me, once again nearly knocking me over with his gaze. "Yeah?"

"Next time . . . next time you want to talk to me about something—anything—you don't have to drink to work up the courage. Just tell me."

"Easier said than done."

"Not really." I tried for the door again, and this time, he stopped me, resting a hand on my shoulder.

"Sage?"

I turned. "Yeah?"

"Do you know why I don't like him? Brayden?" I was so astonished he'd gotten the name right that I couldn't voice any answers, though several came to mind. "Because of what he said."

"What part?" Seeing as Brayden had said many things, in great detail, it wasn't entirely clear which Adrian was referring to.

"'Historically inaccurate.'" Adrian gestured at me with his other hand, the one not on my shoulder. "Who the hell looks at you and says 'historically inaccurate'?"

"Well," I said. "Technically it is."

"He shouldn't have said that."

I shifted, knowing I should move away . . . but I didn't. "Look, it's just his way."

"He shouldn't have said that," repeated Adrian, eerily serious. He leaned his face toward mine. "I don't care if he's not the emotional type or the complimentary type or what. No one can look at you in this dress, in all that fire and gold, and start talking about anachronisms. If I were him, I would have said, 'You are the most beautiful creature I have ever seen walking this earth.'"

My breath caught, both at the words and the way he said them. I felt strange inside. I didn't know what to think, except that I needed to get out of there, away from Adrian, away from what I didn't understand. I broke from him and was surprised to find myself shaking.

"You're still drunk," I said, putting my hand on the door knob.

He tilted his head to the side, still watching me in that same, disconcerting way. "Some things are true, drunk or sober. You should know that. You deal in facts all the time."

"Yeah, but this isn't—" I couldn't argue with him looking at me like that. "I have to go. Wait . . . you didn't take the cross." I held it out to him.

He shook his head. "Keep it. I think I've got something else to help center my life."

CHAPTER 15

I FELT SO BAD for Brayden the next day that I actually called him, as opposed to our usual texting and e-mailing.

"I'm so sorry," I said. "Running out like that . . . it's not my usual style. Not at all. I wouldn't have left if it wasn't a family emergency." Maybe that was stretching it. Maybe not.

"It's okay," he said. Without seeing his face, I couldn't tell if it really was okay. "I suppose things were winding down anyway."

I wondered what "things" he meant. Did he mean the dance itself? Or was he talking about us?

"Let me take you out to make up for it," I said. "You always do everything. I'll handle it for a change. Dinner will be on me, and I'll even pick you up."

"In the Subaru?"

I ignored the judgment in his tone. "Are you in or not?"

He was in. We made the necessary arrangements, and I hung up feeling better about everything. Brayden wasn't mad.

Adrian's visit hadn't ruined my fledgling relationship. Things were back to normal—at least for me.

I'd kept to myself the day after the dance, wanting to catch up on work and not stress about social matters. Monday morning started the school week again, back to business as usual. Eddie walked into East's cafeteria when I did, and we waited together in the food line. He wanted to know about Adrian's visit to the dance, and I gave a glossed-over version of the night, simply saying that Adrian had gotten drunk and needed a ride home. I made no mention of my role in getting the queen to act on his behalf or of me being "the most beautiful creature walking this earth." I certainly didn't mention the way I'd felt when Adrian had touched me.

Eddie and I walked over to a table and found the unusual sight of Angeline trying to cheer up Jill. Normally, I would've chastised Angeline for what she'd done at the dance, but there'd been no damage done . . . this time. Plus, I was too distracted by Jill. It was impossible for me to see her down without immediately assuming something was wrong with Adrian. Eddie spoke before I could, noticing what I hadn't.

"No Micah?" he asked. "He was out the door before me. I figured he would've beat me over here."

"You had to ask, didn't you?" Angeline grimaced. "They had a fight."

I swear, Eddie looked more upset about this than Jill. "What? He didn't say anything. What happened? You guys seemed to be having such a great time on Saturday."

Jill nodded morosely but didn't look up from her uneaten food. I could just barely catch sight of tears in her eyes. "We did.

So good that he actually talked to me yesterday and asked . . . well, he asked if I wanted to have Thanksgiving with his family. They're from Pasadena. He thought he could either get permission from the school or talk to you guys."

"That doesn't sound so bad," said Eddie cautiously.

"Thanksgiving with his family is serious! It's one thing for us to hang out together here, but if we start expanding that . . . becoming a couple outside of school . . . " She sighed. "It's going to go too fast. How long would I be able to hide what I am? And even if that wasn't an issue, it's not safe anyway. The whole point of me being here is that it's a safe, controlled environment. I can't just take off to meet strangers."

It was another step of progress to her accepting the difficulties of a "casual" relationship with Micah. I offered a neutral comment. "Sounds like you've thought a lot about this."

Jill looked up sharply, almost as if she hadn't even realized I was there. "Yeah. I guess I have." She scrutinized me for a few seconds, and weirdly, her distraught expression softened. She smiled. "You look really pretty today, Sydney. The way the light hits you . . . it's kind of amazing."

"Um, thanks," I said, uncertain as to what had prompted that comment. I was pretty sure there was nothing remarkable about me today. My hair and makeup were the same as ever, and I'd chosen a white shirt and plaid skirt uniform combo today. I had to make up for this weekend's color splurge.

"And the burgundy trim in your skirt really brings out the amber in your eyes," Jill continued. "It's not as good as the bright red, but still looks great. Of course, every color looks great on you, even the dull ones."

Eddie was still focused on Micah. "How'd the fight come about?"

Jill dragged her gaze from me, much to my relief. "Oh. Well. I told him I didn't know if I could do Thanksgiving. Probably if I'd just given him one reason, it would've all been fine. But I started freaking out, thinking about all the problems, and just went off on a ramble, saying we might go back to South Dakota or maybe family would come here or maybe you wouldn't let me . . . or, well, a bunch of other things. I guess it was pretty obvious I was kind of making it all up, and then he outright asked me if I didn't want to be with him anymore. Then I said I did but that it was complicated. He asked what I meant, but of course I couldn't explain it all, and from there . . . " She threw up her hands. "It all just kind of exploded from there."

I'd never thought much about Thanksgiving or meeting one's family as a rite of passage in dating. Brayden's family lived in southern California too . . . would I be expected to meet them someday?

"Micah's not the type to hold a grudge," said Eddie. "He's also pretty reasonable. Just tell him the truth."

"What, that I'm one of the last in a line of vampire royalty and my sister's throne is dependent on me staying in hiding and surviving?" Jill asked incredulously.

Amusement flickered in Eddie's eyes, though I could tell he was trying to stay serious for her sake. "That's one way, I suppose. But no . . . I meant, just give him the simplified version. You don't want to get too serious. You like him but just want to watch how fast things are going. It's not unreasonable, you know. You're fifteen and have been 'dating' for barely a month."

She pondered his words. "You don't think he'd be mad?"

"Not if he really cares about you," said Eddie vehemently. "If he really cares, he'll understand and respect your wishes—and be happy at just any chance of spending time with you."

I wondered if Eddie was referring to Micah or himself, but that was a thought best kept quiet. Jill's face lit up.

"Thanks," she told Eddie. "I hadn't thought of it that way. You're so right. If he can't accept my feelings, then there's no point to anything." She glanced over at a wall clock and jumped to her feet. "I think I'm going to go try to find him now before class." Like that, she was gone.

Good work, Eddie, I thought. *You may have just helped get the girl of your dreams back together with her boyfriend*. When Eddie caught my eye, the look on his face told me he was thinking the exact same thing.

Angeline watched Jill dart out of the cafeteria, her blue eyes narrowed in thought. "Even if they make up, I don't think it'll last. With their situation . . . it can't work."

"I thought you were all about vampire and human relationships," I said.

"Oh, sure. Back home, no problem. Even out in your world, no problem. But Jill's a special case. She's got to stay out of sight and stay safe if she's going to help her family. Dating him won't do that, and she knows it—no matter how much she wishes it weren't true. She'll do the right thing in the end. This is duty. It's bigger than personal wants. Jill gets that."

Angeline then declared she needed to get back to her room to catch up on homework. Eddie and I were left staring.

He shook his head in amazement. "I don't think I've ever seen Angeline so . . . "

" . . . subdued?" I suggested.

"I was thinking . . . coherent."

I laughed. "Come on, she's coherent plenty of times."

"You know what I mean," he argued. "What she just said? It was totally true. It was . . . wise. She understands Jill and this situation."

"I think she understands more than we give her credit for," I said, recalling how much better-behaved she'd been since the assembly—breaking into dances aside. "It's just taken her time to adjust, which makes sense, considering what a change this is. If you'd seen where she's from, you'd understand."

"I may have misjudged her," Eddie admitted. He seemed astonished by his own words.

Part of me had expected to get chastised by Trey today for having skipped out on Brayden at the dance. Instead, I found Trey missing again from our morning classes. I almost worried but then reminded myself that his cousin was still in town, possibly muddling Trey in "family stuff." Trey was competent. Whatever was going on, he could handle it. *Then why all the bruises?* I wondered.

When I reached Ms. Terwilliger's independent study, she was waiting expectantly for me, which I took as a bad sign. Usually, she was already hard at work at her own desk and just gave me a nod of acknowledgment when I took out my books. Today, she was standing in front of her desk, arms crossed, watching the door.

"Miss Melbourne. I trust you had an enjoyable weekend? You were certainly the belle of the ball at the Halloween dance."

"You saw me?" I asked. For a moment, I expected her to say she'd been watching the whole dance through a crystal ball or something.

"Well, certainly. I was there as a chaperone. My post was near the DJ, so I'm not surprised you didn't see me. That, and I hardly stood out the way you did. I must say, that was an exquisite neo-Greco reproduction you were wearing."

"Thanks." I was getting compliments left and right today, but hers were much less creepy than Jill's.

"Now then," said Ms. Terwilliger, all business again. "I thought it might be useful for us to discuss some of the spells you've been researching for my project. Notating them is one thing. Understanding them is another."

My stomach sank. I'd grown comfortable in my avoidance of her and the repetitive, almost mindless nature of annotating and translating spells. So long as we didn't have to actually delve into them, I felt reassured that I wasn't doing anything real with magic. I dreaded whatever she had in mind, but there was little I could make in the way of protest, so long as this was all couched in the terms of my study and didn't involve harm to myself or others.

"Would you be kind enough to close the door?" she asked. I did, and my feeling of unease increased. "Now. I wanted to examine that book I gave you further—the one on protective spells."

"I don't have it with me, ma'am," I said, relieved. "But if you want, I'll go get it from my dorm room and bring it back." If I timed the shuttle bus right—by which I meant, wrong—I could probably use up a huge part of our hour in the round-trip.

"That's all right. I obtained that copy for your personal use." She lifted a book from her desk. "I have my own. Let's take a look, shall we?"

I couldn't hide my dismay. We sat in adjacent student desks, and she began by simply going over the table of contents with me. The book was divided into three sections: Defense, Planned Attacks, and Instant Attacks. Each of those subsections was divided into levels of difficulty.

"Defense includes a lot of protective charms and evasion spells," she told me. "Why do you think those come first in the book?"

"Because the best way to win a fight is to avoid one," I said immediately. "Makes the rest superfluous."

She looked startled that I had come up with that. "Yes . . . precisely."

"That's what Wolfe said," I explained. "He's the instructor in a self-defense class I'm taking."

"Well, he's quite right. Most of the spells in this section do exactly that. This one . . . " She flipped a few pages into the book. "This one's very basic but extremely useful. It's a conceal-ment spell. Many physical components—which you'd expect from a beginner spell—but well worth it. You create an amulet and keep a separate ingredient—crumbled gypsum—on hand. When you're ready to activate it, add the gypsum, and the amu-let comes to life. It makes it nearly impossible for someone to see you. You can leave a room or area in safety, undetected, before the magic wears off."

The wording wasn't lost on me, and in spite of my inner resistance, I couldn't help but ask: "'Nearly impossible?'"

"It won't work if they actually know you're there," she explained. "You can't just cast it and become invisible—though there are more advanced spells for that. But if someone isn't actively expecting to see you . . . well, they won't."

She showed me others, many of which were basic and

amulet based, requiring a similar means of activation. One that she dubbed intermediate had kind of a reverse activation process. The caster wore an amulet that protected her when she cast the rest of the spell—one that made all people within a certain radius go temporarily blind. Only the caster retained sight. Listening, I still squirmed at the thought of using magic to directly affect someone else. Concealing yourself was one thing. But blinding someone? Making them dizzy? Forcing them to sleep? It crossed that line, using wrong and unnatural means to do things humans had no business doing.

And yet . . . deep inside, some part of me could see the usefulness. The attack had made me reconsider all sorts of things. As much as it pained me to admit it, I could even see how giving blood to Sonya might not be so bad. *Might*. I wasn't ready to do it yet by any means.

I listened patiently as she went through the pages, all the while wondering what her game was here. Finally, when we had five minutes left of class, she told me, "For next Monday, I'd like you to re-create one of these, just as you did with the fire amulet and write a paper on it."

"Ms. Terwilliger—" I began.

"Yes, yes," she said, closing the book and standing up. "I'm well aware of your arguments and objections, how humans aren't meant to wield such power and all of that nonsense. I respect your right to feel that way. No one's making you use any of this. I just want you to continue getting a feel for the construction."

"I can't," I said adamantly. "I won't."

"It's no different than dissecting a frog in biology," she argued. "Hands-on work to understand the material."

"I guess . . . " I relented, glumly. "Which one do you want me to do, ma'am?"

"Whichever you like."

Something about that bothered me even more. "I'd rather you choose."

"Don't be silly," she said. "You have freedom in your larger term paper and freedom in this. I don't care what you do, so long as the assignment's complete. Go with what interests you."

And that was the problem. In having me choose, she was making me get invested in the magic. It was easy for me to claim no part in it and point out that everything I did for her was under duress. Even if this assignment was technically dictated by her, that one small choice she'd given me forced me to become proactive.

So, I put the decision off—which was almost unheard of for me when it came to homework. Some part of me thought that maybe if I ignored the assignment, it would go away or she'd change her mind. Besides, I had a week. No point in stressing about it yet.

Although I knew we had no obligation to Lia for giving us the costumes, I still felt the appropriate thing to do was return them to her—just so there was no doubt of my intentions. Once Ms. Terwilliger released me, I packed up my and Jill's costumes into their garment bags and headed into downtown. Jill was sad to let hers go but conceded that it was the right thing to do.

Lia, however, felt otherwise.

"What am I going to do with these?" she asked when I showed up at her shop. Large rhinestone hoop earrings made her dazzling to look at. "They were custom made for you."

"I'm sure you can alter them. And I'm sure they're not far

off from your sample sizes anyway." I held the hangers out, and she obstinately crossed her arms. "Look, they were great. We really appreciate what you did. But we can't keep them."

"You *will* keep them," she stated.

"If you don't take them, I'll just leave them on your counter," I warned.

"And I'll have them shipped back to your dorm."

I groaned. "Why is this so important to you? Why can't you take no for an answer? There are plenty of pretty girls in Palm Springs. You don't need Jill."

"That's exactly it," said Lia. "Plenty of pretty girls that all blend into each other. Jill is special. She's a natural and doesn't even know it. She could be great someday."

"Someday," I repeated. "But not right now."

Lia attempted another approach. "The campaign is for scarves and hats. I can't do masks again, but I can put her in sunglasses—especially if we shoot outside. Tell me if you'd agree to this plan—"

"Lia, please. Don't bother."

"Just listen," she urged. "We'll go do a photo shoot. Afterward, you can go through all the pictures and throw out any that don't meet your weird religious criteria."

"No exceptions," I insisted. "And I'm leaving the dresses." I set them on a counter and headed out, ignoring Lia's protests about all the amazing things she could do for Jill. *Maybe someday*, I thought. *Someday when all of Jill's problems are gone.* Something told me that day was far away, however.

Although my loyalty to Spencer's was steadfast, a small French café caught my attention as I walked back to my car. Or rather, the scent of their coffee caught my attention. I had no obligations at school and stopped into the café for a cup. I had a book for English class on me and decided to do some reading at one of the café's small tables. Half of that time was spent texting back and forth with Brayden. He'd wanted to know what I was reading, and we were swapping our favorite Tennessee Williams quotes.

I'd barely been there for ten minutes when shadows fell over me, blocking the late afternoon sun. Two guys stood there, neither of whom I knew. They were a little older than me, one blond haired and blue eyed while the other was dark haired and deeply tanned. Their expressions weren't hostile, but they weren't friendly either. Both were well built, like those who trained regularly. And then, after a double-take, I realized I did recognize one of them. The dark-haired guy was the one who'd approached Sonya and me a while ago, claiming to know her from Kentucky.

Immediately, all the panic I'd been trying to suppress this last week came back to me, that sense of being trapped and helpless. It was only the realization that I was in a public place, surrounded by people, which allowed me to regard these two with astonishing calm.

"Yes?" I asked.

"We need to talk to you, Alchemist," said the blond guy.

I didn't twitch a muscle in my face. "I think you've got me mixed up with someone else."

"No one else around here has a lily tattoo," said the other guy. He'd said his name was Jeff, but I wondered if he'd told the truth. "It'd be great if you could take a walk with us." My tattoo was covered up today, but something told me these guys had been following me for a while and didn't need to see the lily to know it was there.

"Absolutely not," I said. I didn't even need Wolfe's reminders to know that was a terrible idea. I was staying here in the safety of the crowd. "If you want to talk, you'd best take a seat. Otherwise, go away."

I looked back down at my book, like I didn't have a care in the world. Meanwhile, my heart was pounding, and it took every ounce of control I had to keep my hands from shaking. A few moments later, I heard the sounds of metal scraping on concrete, and the two guys sat down opposite me. I looked back up at their impassive faces.

"You've got to go inside if you want coffee," I remarked. "They don't have service out here."

"We're not here to talk about the coffee," said Jeff. "We're here to talk about vampires."

"Why? Are you filming a movie or something?" I asked.

"We know you hang out with them," said Blond Hair. "Including that Strigoi, Sonya Karp."

Part of my tattoo's magic was to prevent Alchemists from revealing information about the vampire world to outsiders. We literally couldn't do it. The magic would kick in and prevent it if we tried. Since these guys seemed to already know about vampires, the tattoo wasn't going to censor my words. Instead, I chose to censor myself of my own free will. Something told me ignorance was the best tactic here.

"Vampires aren't real," I said. "Look, if this is some kind of a joke—"

"We know what you do," continued Blond Hair. "You don't

like them any more than we do. So why are you helping them? How could your group have gotten so muddled and lost sight of our original vision? Centuries ago, we were one united group, determined to see all vampires wiped from the face of the earth in the name of the light. Your brethren betrayed that goal."

I had another protest ready, and then I noticed a glint of gold in Jeff's ear. He was wearing a tiny earring, a small golden sphere with a dark dot in the middle. I couldn't help myself.

"Your earring," I said. "It's the sun symbol—the symbol for gold." And, I realized, it was exactly the same symbol that had been on the hilt of the sword we'd retrieved from the alley.

He touched his earring and nodded. "We haven't forgotten the mission—or our original purpose. We serve the light. Not the darkness that hides vampires."

I still refused to acknowledge anything they said about vampires. "You're the ones who attacked my friend and me in the alley last week." Neither one denied it.

"Your 'friend' is a creature of darkness," said Blond Hair. "I don't know how she's managed this current enchantment—making herself look like one of the *other* vampires—but you can't be fooled. She's evil. She'll kill you and countless others."

"You guys are crazy," I said. "None of this makes any sense."

"Just tell us where her main lair is," said Jeff. "We know it's not that apartment on the other side of downtown. We've been watching it and she hasn't returned since our last attempt to destroy her. If you won't actively help us, that information will be all we need to rid the world of her evil."

We've been watching it. Adrian's apartment. Chills ran through me. How long had they been spying on his place? And to what extent? Had they simply sat outside in a car, stakeout style? Did they have high tech surveillance equipment? Wolfe had warned against being stalked in parking lots, not in homes. The small comfort I had here was that they obviously didn't know about Clarence's. Their surveillance couldn't have been that thorough if no one had followed her yet. But had they followed me? Did they know where I went to school?

And with their own words, they were confirming the terrible reality I'd hardly dared speculate about. It was a reality that meant there were forces moving unseen beneath the Alchemists' seemingly all-knowing vision, forces working against our goals.

Vampire hunters were real.

With that realization came a hundred more terrifying questions. What did this mean for the Moroi? Was Jill in danger?

Was Adrian?

"The only thing I'm going to do is call the police," I said. "I don't know who you guys are or why you're obsessed with my friend, but neither of us have done anything to you. You're even crazier than I first thought if you think I'm going to tell you where she is so that you can stalk her."

Then, by the sheerest luck, I saw a patrolling police officer walking down the street. The two guys at my table followed my gaze and undoubtedly could guess my thoughts. It would be very easy to call her over. We'd filed no report about the alley attack, but accusing these guys of a recent assault would certainly detain them. In sync, they both rose.

"You're making a terrible mistake," Jeff said. "We could have had this problem eradicated ages ago if our groups worked together. First the Strigoi, then the Moroi. Your misguided descent into their corruption has nearly ruined everything. Fortunately, we still walk the true path." The fact that he'd just named the two groups was particularly alarming. These guys were scary, certainly, but less so if they were just talking about vampires in shadowy, vague terms. Using "Moroi" and "Strigoi" indicated extensive knowledge.

Blond Hair tossed down a small, homemade pamphlet. "Read this, and maybe you'll see the light. We'll be in touch."

"I wouldn't if I were you," I said. "Mess with me again, and I'll do a lot more than just have a pleasant chat." My words came out more fiercely than I'd expected. Maybe Dimitri and Wolfe were rubbing off on me.

Jeff laughed as the two of them began walking away. "Too bad you got so bogged down in books," he said. "You've got the spirit of a hunter."

CHAPTER 16

I WASTED NO TIME in getting the group together. This was *big*. I still didn't know the level of danger we were facing, but I refused to take any chances. I chose Clarence's house as a meeting spot, seeing as the hunters didn't know about it yet. It still made me nervous. I would've been nervous even if we'd been meeting in an Alchemist bunker.

And apparently, "hunters" wasn't even the right term. According to their low-quality pamphlet, they called themselves "The Warriors of Light." I wasn't sure they deserved that fancy title, especially since in their mission statement, they spelled "abyss" as "abiss." The pamphlet was really very sparse, simply stating that there was an evil walking among humanity and that the Warriors were the force there to destroy it. They urged their fellow humans to be ready and stay pure. None of the vampires were mentioned by name, for which I was glad. The pamphlet also didn't mention much about any of the shared history they claimed to have with the Alchemists.

Before we went to Clarence's, Eddie scoured Latte for any sort of tracking device. The very idea creeped me out, the same way being watched at Adrian's did. There was a feeling of violation to it all. It was only my lack of faith in their technology that made me feel somewhat better.

"It seems unlikely they'd be that advanced," I told Eddie, as he wiggled under the car. "I mean, that pamphlet looked like it had been made on a 1980s copy machine. I don't know if that's because they've had the pamphlets sitting around that long or if that's the actual machine they still use . . . but regardless, they don't scream high tech to me."

"Maybe," he agreed, voice slightly muffled. "But we can't take any chances. We don't know what they're capable of. And for all we know, they're trying to hook up with the Alchemists to score technology."

Chills ran through me. It was an outrageous thought: that the Alchemists and this violent fringe group could be related. It had been crazy when Adrian and I had speculated about it and was hard to accept even in the face of mounting evidence. At least now I had enough information to take to my superiors without being ridiculed. Even though I'd never heard of hunters like this, it seemed plausible that somewhere, at some point, they'd tried to connect with my organization. Hopefully someone in the Alchemists could help.

Eddie scooted out from under Latte. "You're clean. Let's head out."

Jill and Angeline were waiting nearby, both tense and anxious. Jill gave Eddie an admiring smile. "I didn't know you knew how to do any of this. I never would have even thought about it."

He wiped sweat off his forehead. "You thought guardian training was all about hitting and kicking?"

She flushed. "Pretty much, yeah."

"Can you tell me about some of this stuff sometime?" asked Angeline. "Seems like I should know it."

"Sure," said Eddie, sounding like he meant it. She beamed.

He'd been much easier around her ever since her attitude had become more serious and restrained. I think some of that good behavior had played a role in me getting permission for her to join us tonight. She was still technically on suspension, but I'd managed to get a special exemption on the grounds of our family's so-called religion. I'd used a similar excuse when Jill had been suspended last month, in order to take her to feedings. Even still, we were on very strict orders with Angeline tonight. She couldn't be out for more than two hours, and the price was adding an extra day of suspension to her sentence.

We took an abnormal route to Clarence's, and Eddie watched behind us carefully, looking for any signs of pursuit. He tried to explain some of the things I needed to watch for when I was on my own. I was so nervous, I hardly heard. After a tense ride, we made it safely to Clarence's. There, we found Adrian already waiting for us. Dimitri had apparently been downtown earlier and picked Adrian up—no doubt taking all the same precautions Eddie had for travel.

I'd given Eddie and Dimitri some of the info on the hunters, but everyone else required a more thorough explanation. We gathered in our usual spot, the formal living room, and Dimitri paced around the room, bracing for an attack at any moment. Clarence looked on from his chair with that typical distracted gaze. When I held up the pamphlet, however, he came to life.

"That's them!" he cried. I thought he might actually spring up from the chair and rip the pamphlet from my hands. "Those are their symbols!" Most of the same alchemical symbols that had been on the sword were strewn across the pamphlet's front. "That circle. I remember that circle."

"The gold symbol," I confirmed. "Or, I guess in their case, the sun symbol since they're so obsessed with light and dark."

Clarence looked around frantically. "They're back! We have to get out of here. I came to this city to escape them, but they've found me. We have no time. Where's Dorothy? Where's Lee? I must pack!"

"Mr. Donahue," I said, in as a gentle a tone as I could manage, "they don't know you're here. You're safe." I didn't know if I believed that and hoped I was convincing.

"She's right," said Dimitri. "And even if they did, you know I wouldn't let them hurt you." There was such confidence and strength in the way Dimitri spoke that I had a feeling that we'd believe him even if a group of Strigoi were invading, and he said, "It's fine, you're safe."

"If what you're saying is true," said Sonya, "*I'm* the one that's in danger." She seemed much calmer than I would be in that situation.

"They're not going to hurt you either," said Dimitri sharply. "Especially if you don't leave this house."

"The research—" she began.

"—is nothing compared to your safety," he finished. There

was a look in his eyes that said he would tolerate no arguments. "You need to get back to Court. You were planning on it anyway. Just make the trip early."

Sonya didn't look happy about that. "So I leave the rest of you in danger?"

"Maybe we aren't," said Eddie, though the tension in his body said otherwise. "From what Sydney said—and their mini-manifesto—their focus seems to be Strigoi, not Moroi." He glanced over at Jill. "Not that we can let our guard down. If they've mistaken Sonya for a Strigoi, who knows what other craziness they might do? Don't worry. I won't let them near you." Jill looked ready to swoon.

"That's a good idea," I said. "They still think the Moroi are a threat but not as much as the Strigoi."

"Kind of like the Alchemists," said Adrian. He was sitting in a corner armchair and had been quiet this whole time. I hadn't seen him since the night of the dance or had any communication with him, which was odd. Even when he wasn't sending me pathetic e-mails about the experiments, he almost always had some witty quip to pass along.

"True," I admitted, with a smile. "But we're not trying to kill any of you. Not even Strigoi."

"And there's the problem," said Dimitri. "These warriors are convinced Sonya used to be a Strigoi and is using some trick to disguise herself."

"Maybe they have some tracking or inventory system," Sonya mused. "They keep tabs on various Strigoi in the country and then try to hunt them down."

"And yet they didn't know about you," I pointed out to Dimitri. His face stayed neutral, but I knew it was hard for him to be reminded of his Strigoi days. "And from what I know . . . you were much more of a, um, notable figure than Sonya." He'd essentially been a Strigoi mobster. "So, if you're off their radar, they probably don't have an international presence—or at least not a Russian one."

Angeline leaned forward, hands clasped, and regarded Clarence with a smile sweet enough to justify her name. "How do you know about them? How did you first run into them?"

At first, he looked too terrified to answer, but I think her kindly attitude soothed him. "Well, they killed my niece, of course."

We all knew Lee had killed Clarence's niece, but the old man didn't believe this any more than he believed Lee was dead. "Did you see them when they did it?" asked Angeline. "Did you ever see them at all?"

"Not when Tamara died, no," he admitted. His eyes got a faraway look, as though he were staring straight into the past. "But I knew what signs to look for. I'd run into them before that, you see. Back when I was living in Santa Cruz. They like California, you know. And the Southwest. Goes back to their sun fixation."

"What happened in Santa Cruz?" asked Dimitri.

"A group of their young ones began stalking me. Trying to kill me."

The rest of us exchanged glances. "So they do go after Moroi," said Eddie. He actually moved closer to Jill.

Clarence shook his head. "Not usually. From what Marcus told me, they prefer Strigoi. These were young, undisciplined members of their order going off on their own, without the knowledge of their superiors. I assume it was the same type who killed Tamara."

"Who's Marcus?" I asked.

"Marcus Finch. He saved me from them a few years ago. Fended them off during an attack and later got in touch with their order to keep those ruffians away from me." Clarence shivered at the memory. "Not that I stayed around after that. I took Lee and left. That was when we moved to Los Angeles for a while."

"This Marcus," I said. "Was he a guardian?"

"A human. He was about your age then. He knew all about the hunters."

"I suppose he would if he got in touch with them," Dimitri speculated. "But he must be friendly to Moroi if he helped you?"

"Oh, yes," said Clarence. "Very much so."

Dimitri looked over at me. "Do you think—"

"Yes," I said, guessing his question. "I'll see if we can find this Marcus guy. It'd be nice to get a source of info that's not one of these crazy warriors. I'm also going to report on all of this, actually."

"Me too," said Dimitri.

Although Clarence wasn't the expert on the hunters that this mysterious Marcus was, the old Moroi still had a surprising amount of info to share—info none of us had wanted to hear before. He verified what we'd already deduced, about the hunters' "devotion to the light." The group's focus was Strigoi (for now), and all of their hunts were carefully planned and organized. They had a ritualized set of behaviors, particularly in regard to their younger members—which was why the rogue group harassing Clarence had been stopped. From what Clarence had gathered, the group was quite tough on their new recruits, emphasizing discipline and excellence.

With the clock ticking down on Angeline's reprieve, we needed to wrap things up shortly thereafter. I was also in charge of taking Adrian home, since we figured it'd be best to eliminate any chance of Dimitri being followed back to Clarence's. Besides, I could tell Dimitri was anxious to begin putting certain things in motion. He wanted to finalize Sonya's departure and also confer with the guardians—in case Jill needed to be removed. Her face reflected what I felt about that possible outcome. We'd both become attached to Amberwood.

While he was giving some last-minute instructions to Eddie, I pulled Sonya aside for a quiet word. "I . . . I've been thinking about something," I told her.

She studied me carefully, probably reading my aura and other body language. "What is it?" she asked.

"If you want . . . if you really want it, you can have some of my blood."

It was a huge, huge admission. Was it something I wanted to do? No. Absolutely not. I still had the same instinctive fears about giving my blood to Moroi, even for scientific purposes. And yet, yesterday's events—and even the alley attack—had begun making me re-analyze my worldview. Vampires weren't the only monsters out there. They were hardly monsters at all, especially next to these vampire hunters. How could I judge the enemy on race? I was being reminded more and more that humans were just as capable as vampires of evil—and that vampires were capable of good. It was actions that mattered, and Sonya and Dimitri's were noble ones. They were fighting to destroy the ultimate evil of all, and as squeamish as I felt about giving my blood, I knew the right thing was to help them.

Sonya knew what a sacrifice this was for me. Her face

stayed calm—no whoops of joy—and she nodded solemnly. "I have my collection kit here. I can take a sample before you leave, if you're sure."

So soon? Well, why not. It was best to get it over with—especially if Sonya would be leaving town soon anyway. We did it in the kitchen, which seemed slightly more sanitary than the living room. Sonya was no doctor, but whatever training she'd had, it was right in line with what I'd observed when getting physicals. Antiseptic, gloves, a new syringe. All the right procedures were followed, and after a quick poke of the needle, she had my blood sample.

"Thank you, Sydney," she said, handing me a plastic bandage. "I know how difficult this must have been for you. Believe me, this could really help us."

"I want to help," I told her. "I really do."

She smiled. "I know. And we need all the help we can get. After being one of them . . . " Her smile faded. "Well, I believe more than ever that their evil needs to be stopped. You might be the key."

For one second, her words inspired me—that I might somehow play a greater role in the fight against evil and possibly even stop it. Immediately, that thought was replaced by my old panic. No. *No.* I wasn't special. I didn't want to be. I would make a good faith effort to help, but surely nothing would come of it.

I returned to fetch the others. Adrian and Jill were having some earnest conversation in the corner. Eddie and Angeline were also talking, and I overheard her say, "I'll stay with Jill more at school, just to be safe. We can't have her be part of some accident or mistaken identity."

Eddie nodded and looked impressed that she'd suggested it. "Agreed." *Amazing*, I thought.

I left soon with my carpool and swung by downtown to drop Adrian off. As I pulled up in front of his building, I saw something that made my jaw drop. Awe and disbelief rolled through me. In what was probably the most ungraceful parking job I'd ever done in my life, I brought Latte to an abrupt stop and was out of the car the second I pulled my keys from the ignition. The others followed moments later.

"What," I breathed. "Is *that*?"

"Oh," said Adrian casually. "That's my new car."

I took a few steps forward and then stopped, afraid to approach it in the same way someone hesitated before royalty. "It's a 1967 Ford Mustang convertible," I said, knowing my eyes were probably bugging out of my face. I began walking around it. "The year they did a major overhaul and increased the size to keep up with other high-powered competition. See? It's the first model with the concave tail lights but the last to have the Ford block lettering up front until 1974."

"What in the world is that color?" asked Eddie, not sounding impressed at all.

"Springtime Yellow," Adrian and I said in unison.

"I would've guessed Lemon Chiffon," said Eddie. "Maybe you can get it repainted."

"No!" I exclaimed. I tossed my purse over onto the grass and carefully touched the car's side. Brayden's beautiful new Mustang suddenly seemed so ordinary. "It's been touched up, obviously, but this is a classic color. Which engine code is this? C, right?"

"Um . . . not sure," said Adrian. "I know it's got a V-8 engine."

"Of course it does," I said. It was hard not to roll my eyes. "A 289. I want to know what the horsepower is."

"It's probably in the paperwork," Adrian said lamely.

It was at that moment that I really processed Adrian's earlier words. I looked up at him, knowing my face must be filled with disbelief. "This is really your car?"

"Yup," he said. "I told you. The old man spotted me the money for one."

"And you got this one?" I peered in through the window. "Nice. Black interior, manual transmission."

"Yeah," said Adrian, a note of unease in his voice. "That's the problem."

I glanced back. "What is? The black is great. And the leather's condition is fantastic. So is the rest of the car."

"No, not the interior. The transmission. I can't drive a stick."

I froze. "You can't drive a stick?"

"Neither can I," said Jill.

"You don't have a license," I reminded her. Although, my mother had taught me to drive before I had a license—both automatic *and* manual transmission. I knew I shouldn't be surprised the stick was a lost art, as savage as such a lack seemed to me. That paled, of course, in comparison to the other obvious problem. "Why on earth would you buy a car like this if you can't drive a stick? There are dozens of cars—new cars—that have automatic transmission. It'd be a million times easier."

Adrian shrugged. "I like the color. It matches my living room."

Eddie snorted.

"But you can't drive it," I pointed out.

"I figure it can't be that hard." Adrian sounded remarkably unconcerned about what I found blasphemous. "I'll just practice taking it around the block a few times and figure it out."

I couldn't believe what I was hearing. "*What*? Are you out of your mind? You'll ruin it if you don't know what you're doing!"

"What else am I supposed to do?" he asked. "Are *you* going to teach me?"

I turned back to the beautiful Mustang. "Yes," I said adamantly. "If that's what it takes to save it from you."

"I can show you too," said Eddie.

Adrian ignored him and focused on me. "When we can start?"

I ran through my school schedule, knowing I'd have to make talking to the Alchemists about the Warriors of Light my top priority. Then, the obvious hit me. "Oh. When we see Wolfe this week. We'll take this out there."

"Is that really to help me?" asked Adrian. "Or do you just want to drive the car?"

"Both," I said, not embarrassed to admit it.

Angeline's clock at school was ticking, so the rest of us had to leave. I'd driven three blocks away when I realized I'd left my purse on the grass. With a groan, I looped around and returned to his building. My purse was there, but the Mustang was gone.

"Where's the car?" I asked, panicked. "No one could have stolen it that fast."

"Oh," said Jill from the backseat, sounding slightly nervous. "I saw through the bond. He, um, moved it."

It was handy having the bond as a source of information, but her words made me panic more than if the car actually had been stolen. "He *what*?"

"Not far," she said quickly. "Just behind the building. This street's got weird overnight parking rules."

I grimaced. "Well, I'm glad it won't get towed, but he should've had *me* move it! Even if it's not far, he could ruin the transmission."

"I'm sure it's fine," said Jill. There was a strange note to her voice.

I didn't respond. Jill was no car expert. None of them were. "It's like letting a toddler loose in a room full of china," I muttered. "What was he thinking? About any of this?"

No one had an answer for that. I got us back to Amberwood in time for Angeline's curfew and retreated to the sanity and calm of my room. As soon as I was satisfied my friends were safe and secure for the night, I e-mailed Donna Stanton—a high-up Alchemist whom I'd inexplicably developed a good relationship with—about the hunters and what we'd learned. I even took pictures of the pamphlet and e-mailed those as well. Once that was done, I sat back and tried to think if there was anything else at all I could provide her with that might help.

It was only when I'd exhausted all options (and refreshed my inbox a few times to see if she'd responded already) that I finally moved on to homework. As usual, I was pretty much caught up on every assignment—save one.

Ms. Terwilliger's.

That stupid book was on my desk, staring back at me, daring me to open it. I still had a number of days before her spell was due, time during which I could continue to procrastinate. I was beginning to accept, however, that this assignment wasn't going to go away. Considering how long some of the prep on these took, maybe it'd be best to bite the bullet and get it out of the way.

Resolved, I brought the book over to my bed and opened it to the table of contents, scanning some of the spells she'd gone over with me. My stomach twisted at most of them, every instinct telling me how wrong it was to even be attempting these. *Magic is for vampires, not humans.*

I still believed that to be true, but the analytical part of my mind couldn't help but apply some of the defensive spells to various situations. Much like my decision to give blood, recent events had made me look at the world differently. Was magic wrong? Yes. But that blindness spell would have certainly been useful in the alley. Another spell, one that temporarily immobilized people, could've been used if I'd wanted to flee from the hunters at the café. Sure, it only lasted thirty seconds, but that was more than enough time for me to have escaped.

On and on, I went down the list. They were all so wrong and yet . . . so useful. If I hadn't seen the fire charm I'd made ignite a Strigoi, I wouldn't have believed any of these were possible. But by all accounts, they were.

So much power . . . the ability to protect myself . . .

Immediately, I rebuked myself for such a thought. I had no need for power. That kind of thinking was what led freaks like Liam to want to be Strigoi. Although . . . was it really the same? I didn't want immortality. I didn't want to hurt others. I just wanted to protect myself and those I cared about. Wolfe had a lot to teach me, but his preventative techniques wouldn't help if determined vampire hunters cornered Sonya and me again. As time went on, it was becoming clear that the hunters were *very* determined.

I returned to the table of contents, finding several that would be useful and well within my capabilities to make. According to

Ms. Terwilliger, someone like me had excellent potential for magic because of inborn talent (which I didn't entirely believe) and the rigorous Alchemist training in measurement and attention to detail. It wasn't difficult to figure out how long it would take me to produce any of these likely candidates.

The question was which spell did I make? Which did I have time to make?

The answer was eerily simple.

I had time to make all of them.

CHAPTER 17

ADRIAN'S CAR DROVE LIKE A DREAM.

When I got behind the wheel, I nearly forgot to check for any pursuit. In fact, I nearly forgot that I was supposed to be taking us to Wolfe's and showing Adrian how to use a stick shift. Instead, I was caught up in the way the engine hummed around us and in the scent of the leather. Leaving his neighborhood, I had to restrain myself from flooring it in the crowded streets of downtown Palm Springs. This was a car screaming to be let loose on the open road. I had admired Brayden's Mustang, but I worshipped this one.

"I feel like I've just crashed someone's date," Adrian remarked, once we were getting on the highway. No one had tailed us out of downtown, making me feel much safer. "Like I'm intruding on you two. If you want to drop me off some-where, I'll understand."

"Huh?"

I'd been paying careful attention to the way the car built up to higher speeds, both through sound and feel. The Mustang was in stunning shape. People often have the idea that classic cars are expensive. They are—if they're in good condition. Most aren't. When something's sat around for years without care, it inevitably falls apart, which is why so many older cars are fixer-uppers. Not Adrian's. This had been maintained and restored throughout the years and had probably never left the state of California—meaning it hadn't faced harsh winters. That all added up to a high price tag, making it that much more ludicrous that Adrian had bought something he couldn't drive.

I groaned. "I'm sorry . . . I don't know what I was thinking." Well, I kind of knew. I'd been wondering what my odds of a ticket would be if I broke the speed limit to see how fast we could go. "I should've been walking you through this as soon as I started the car. I promise I will when we leave Wolfe's, all the steps. For now, I guess we can recap the basics. This is the clutch . . . "

Adrian didn't seem annoyed by my neglect. If anything, he looked amused and simply listened to my explanations with a small, quiet smile on his face.

Wolfe looked just as disreputable as he had last time, complete with the eye patch and what I suspected were the same Bermuda shorts as before. I hoped he'd done laundry since then. Despite his appearance, he was ready to go when our class assembled and seemed competent in his subject matter. Although he reminded us again about the importance of avoiding conflicts and being aware of one's surroundings, he quickly moved past those points and focused on actually practicing more physical ways of protecting oneself.

Considering how much Adrian had complained last time

about the "boring" safety talk, I figured he'd be excited that we were pretty much jumping right into some action. Instead, that amused look from the car vanished, and he grew increasingly tense as Wolfe explained what he wanted us to do in our part-nered practice sessions.

When the time actually came to practice, Adrian looked blatantly unhappy.

"What's the matter?" I asked. I suddenly remembered last time, when Adrian had freaked out over my "attack." Maybe he hadn't really expected he'd have to work here. "Come on, these are simple. You won't get dirty."

Even when teaching more combative actions, Wolfe was still an advocate of keeping things fast and simple. We weren't try-ing to learn to beat someone up. These maneuvers were effec-tive means of distracting an assailant so that we could escape. Most were done with the dummies, since we could hardly try to stick fingers in each other's eyes. Adrian went through those motions diligently, if silently. It was working directly with me that he seemed to have a problem with.

Wolfe noticed it too as he made his rounds. "Come on, boy! She can't try to escape if you don't try to hold her. She's not going to hurt you, and you won't hurt her."

The maneuver in question was actually one that would've been helpful the night I'd been grabbed in the alley. So, I was eager to practice it and frustrated that Adrian kept only half-heartedly helping. He was supposed to put an arm around my torso and attempt to cover my mouth. Unfortunately, his efforts were so weak and his hold so loose that I didn't need any special techniques to escape. I could have simply walked right out of his arms.

With Wolfe there, Adrian made a slightly better showing as an assailant but immediately resorted to his former ways once we were alone. "Let's switch," I said at last, nearly wanting to pull my hair out. "You try to escape me. Make up for last time."

I couldn't believe that Adrian's sluggish attitude had turned out to be the problem here. I'd expected the hang-up would be me not wanting to touch a vampire, but it didn't bother me at all. I wasn't thinking of him as a vampire. He was Adrian, and my partner in this class. I needed him to learn the move. It was all very pragmatic. If I didn't know better, I'd almost say that Adrian was afraid to touch *me*, which made no sense. Moroi didn't have those hang-ups. Was something wrong with me? Why wouldn't Adrian touch me?

"What's going on?" I demanded, once we were in the car and headed back to the city. "I get that you're not an athlete, but what happened in there?"

Adrian refused to meet my eyes and instead stared pointedly out the window. "I don't think this is really my thing. I was all about playing action hero before, but now . . . I don't know. This is a bad idea. It's more work than I thought." There was a flippant, dismissive tone in his voice that I hadn't heard in a while.

"What happened to you finishing things you started?" I asked. "You told me you had changed."

"That was for art," said Adrian quickly. "I'm still in those classes, aren't I? I didn't jump ship on those. I just don't want to do this one anymore. Don't worry. Now that I've got more money, I'll pay you back the class fee. You won't be out anything."

"That doesn't matter," I argued. "It's still a waste! Especially since what Wolfe's showing us isn't really that difficult. We're not ripping ourselves apart like Eddie and Angeline would. Why is this so hard for you to stick with and learn?" My earlier self-doubt returned. "Do you just not want to work with me? Is there . . . is there something wrong with me?"

"No! Of course not. Absolutely not," said Adrian. In my periphery, I saw him finally look at me. "Maybe there are only so many things I can learn at once. I mean, I'm supposed to also be learning to drive a stick shift. Not that I see that happening."

I wanted to slap myself on the forehead. In my frustration over class, I'd completely forgotten again about showing Adrian how to drive. I felt like an idiot, even though I was still mad at him for giving up on Wolfe. I checked the time. I had things to do tonight at Amberwood but felt obligated to make up for my shoddy teaching.

"We'll practice once we're back in your neighborhood," I promised. "We'll start slow, and I'll show you everything you need to do. I might even let you try driving around the block tonight if you seem like you're paying attention to the lesson."

The transformation in Adrian was remarkable. He went from sullen and uncomfortable to cheerful and energetic. I couldn't figure it out. Sure, I found cars and driving fascinating, but technically speaking, there was a lot more detail to learn about manual transmission than there was in Wolfe's evasive techniques. Why were those difficult for him, but the clutch was easy?

I stuck around for about an hour when we got back. To his credit, Adrian paid attention to every word I said, although his results were inconsistent whenever I quizzed him or actually let him try something. Sometimes he'd respond like a pro. Other times, he'd seem totally lost on things I could have sworn he'd picked up. By the end of the hour, I felt safe enough with him driving the car at low speeds on empty streets. He was a long way from the highway or stop-and-go traffic of a busy city.

"Looks like we've got more lessons in our future," I told him when we finished. I'd parked the car behind his building, and we were walking back toward the main entrance and Latte. "Do *not* take that car beyond a half-mile radius. I checked the odometer. I'll know."

"Noted," he said, still wearing that smirky smile. "When's the next lesson? You want to come back tomorrow night?"

"Can't," I said. "I'm going out with Brayden." I was surprised at how much I was looking forward to it. Not only did I want to make things up to him after the dance, but I also just wanted a dose of normality—well, at least the kind of normality Brayden and I had together. Plus, things with Adrian were feeling really weird . . .

"Oh." Adrian's smile fell. "Well. I understand. I mean, love and romance and all that."

"We're going to the textile museum," I said. "It's cool, though I'm not sure how much love and romance there'll really be there."

Adrian nearly came to a halt. "There's a textile museum here? What do people do there?"

"Well, they look at . . . um, textiles. There's actually a great exhibit on—"

I stopped as we reached the front of the building. There, behind Latte, was a familiar car, the rental that Sonya and Dimitri were using. I looked questioningly at Adrian.

"Were you expecting them tonight?"

"No," he said, resuming his walk to the door. "They've got

a key, though, so I suppose they can make themselves at home anytime. They do it a lot, actually. He eats my food, and she uses my hair stuff."

I followed him. "Hopefully it's just Dimitri."

After our recent revelations about the hunters, Sonya was pretty much under house arrest. Or so I thought. When we walked into the apartment, she was sitting on the couch. No Dimitri in sight. She glanced up at us from her laptop.

"Thank goodness you're here," she said, directing her words to me. "Jill said you two were out and I was hoping to catch you."

Something told me no good would come out of her wanting to "catch" me, but I had greater concerns. "What are you doing here?" I asked, half-expecting hunters to come through the door. "You're supposed to be at Clarence's until you leave town."

"Day after tomorrow," she confirmed. She stood; eyes alight with whatever had driven her here. "But I needed to talk to you now—face-to-face."

"I would've come to you," I protested. "It's not safe for you to be out."

"I'm fine," she said. "I made sure I wasn't followed. This was too important." She was breathless and excited.

More important than being caught by wannabe vampire hunters? Debatable.

Adrian crossed his arms and looked surprisingly disapproving. "Well, it's too late now. What's going on?"

"We got the results back from Sydney's blood," explained Sonya.

My heart stopped. *No*, I thought. *No, no, no.*

"Just like with Dimitri's blood, nothing physiological showed up," she said. "Nothing unusual with proteins, antibodies, or anything like that."

Relief poured through me. I'd been right. Nothing special about me, no inexplicable properties. And yet . . . at the same time, I felt a tiny pang of regret. I wasn't the one who would fix everything.

"We sent it to a Moroi lab this time, not an Alchemist one," Sonya continued. "One of the researchers—an earth user—felt a hum of earth magic. Just like how Adrian and I felt spirit in Dimitri's blood. The technician had other types of magic users examine your sample, and all four basic elements were detected."

That panic returned. She had me on an emotional roller coaster, one that left me nauseous. "Magic . . . in my blood?" A moment later, I understood. "Of course there is," I said slowly. I touched my cheek. "The tattoo has vampire blood and magic in it. That's what it is. There are different degrees of charms in it from different users. That would show up in my blood."

I shivered. Even with a logical explanation, it was a scary thing accepting that there was magic in my blood. Ms. Terwilliger's spells were still anathema to me, but at least there was some comfort in knowing they drew magic from *outside* of me. But knowing I had something internal? That was terrifying. And yet, I couldn't be surprised at this finding, not with the tattoo. Sonya nodded along. "Yes, of course. But there must be something about that combination that's repulsive to Strigoi. It may be the key to all of our work!"

To my surprise, Adrian took a few steps toward me, and there was a tension in his stance that was fiercely protective.

"So you know Alchemist blood has magic in it," he said. "That's no surprise. Case closed. What do you want from her now?"

"Another sample to start," said Sonya eagerly. "There's none left in the original vial I took, once all the testing was done. I know this sounds strange, but it'd also be useful if a Moroi could . . . well, taste your blood and see if it has the same repulsive quality as it did to Strigoi. Fresh blood would be ideal, but even I'm not deluded enough to ask you to submit to a feeding. We should simply be able to use your sample and—"

"No," I said. I stumbled backward, horrified. "Absolutely not. Whether it's from a neck or a vial, there's no way I'm giving my blood for anyone to *taste*. Do you know how wrong that is? I know you do it all the time with feeders, but I'm not one of them. I should never have given you the first sample. You don't need me for any of this. Spirit's the key. Lee's proof that former Strigoi are the ones you need to examine."

Sonya wasn't cowed by my outburst. She pushed forward, though her tone was gentler. "I understand your fear, but think of the applications! If something in your blood makes you resistant to Strigoi, then you could save countless lives."

"Alchemists aren't resistant," I said. "That tattoo isn't protecting us, if that's what you're getting at. Do you think that in all our history, there haven't been Alchemists who were turned Strigoi?"

"Well, of course," she said. Her words were hesitant, encouraging me.

"So, the magic you sensed in me is irrelevant. It's just the tattoo. All Alchemists have it. Maybe ours tastes bad, but Alchemist blood has nothing to do with Strigoi turning. It still happens to us." I was rambling but didn't care.

Sonya grew perplexed, her mind running through the implications of this news. "But do all Alchemists have bad-tasting blood? If so, how would a Strigoi be able to drain them?"

"Maybe it varies by person," I said. "Or maybe some Strigoi are tougher than others. I don't know. Regardless, *we* aren't the ones to focus on."

"Unless there's just something special about *you*," mused Sonya.

No. I didn't want that. I didn't want to be scrutinized, locked behind glass like Keith. I *couldn't* be. I prayed she wouldn't see how scared I was.

"There's plenty that's special about her," said Adrian dryly. "But her blood's not up for dispute. Why are you pushing this again after last time?"

Sonya glared at Adrian. "I'm not doing this for selfish reasons, you know that! I want to save our people. I want to save *all* our people. I don't want to see any new Strigoi added to the world. No one should live like that." A haunted look shone in her eyes, as a memory seized her. "That kind of bloodlust and complete lack of empathy for any other living creature . . . no one can imagine what it's like. You're hollow. A walking nightmare, and yet . . . you just don't care . . . "

"Funny attitude," said Adrian, "seeing as you purposely chose to become one."

Sonya paled, and I felt torn. I appreciated Adrian's defense but also pitied Sonya. She'd explained to me in the past about how spirit's instability—the same instability Adrian feared—had driven her to turning Strigoi. Looking back at her decision, she regretted it more than anything else in her life. She would've submitted herself for punishment, but no court knew how to handle her situation.

"Doing that was a mistake," she said coldly. "One I've learned from—which is why I'm so anxious to save others from that fate."

"Well, then find a way to do it without dragging Sydney into it! You know how she feels about *us* . . . " Adrian faltered as he glanced at me, and I was surprised to almost detect bitterness in his voice. "You know how the Alchemists feel. Keep involving her, and you'll get her in trouble with them. And if you're so convinced they've got the answers, ask them for volunteers and do experiments that way."

"I'd help with that," I offered. "Getting authorized subjects for you. I'd talk to my superiors. They'd like to see an end to Strigoi as much as you."

When Sonya didn't answer right away, Adrian guessed why. "She knows they'd say no, Sage. That's why she's appealing to you directly *and* why they didn't send your blood to an Alchemist lab."

"Why can't you both see how important this is?" asked Sonya, a desperate longing to do good in her eyes. It made me feel guilty and conflicted.

"I do," said Adrian. "You think I don't want to see every single one of those bastard Strigoi wiped from the face of the earth? I do! But not at the cost of forcing people to do things they don't want to."

Sonya gave him a long, level look. "I think you're letting your personal feelings interfere with this. Your emotions are going to ruin our research."

He smiled. "Well, then. Be glad you'll be free of me in two days."

Sonya glanced between the two of us, looked like she was about to protest, and then thought better of it. Without another word she left, her face defeated. Again, I felt torn. In theory, I knew she was right . . . but my gut just couldn't agree.

"I didn't mean to upset her," I said at last.

Adrian's face showed no sympathy. "She shouldn't have upset *you*. She knows how you feel."

I still felt a little bad, yet I couldn't shake the feeling that if I gave this, I'd be asked to give more and more. I recalled the day Eddie and Dimitri had been coated in spirit magic. No way could I risk getting involved to that level. I was already pushing my limits too far. "I know . . . but it's hard," I said. "I like Sonya. I gave her the first vial, so I can see why she thought the second would be easy."

"Doesn't matter," he said. "No is no."

"I really will mention it to the Alchemists," I said. "Maybe they'll want to help." I didn't think I'd get in *too* much trouble for the first vial. The Alchemists endorsed the initial experiments after all, and I'd probably get points for standing up to vampire peer pressure for the other sample.

He shrugged. "If they do, great. If not, it's not your responsibility."

"Well, thanks for gallantly coming to my defense again," I teased. "Maybe you'd be more into Wolfe's training if you got to protect someone else instead of yourself?"

The earlier smile returned. "I just don't like seeing people bullied, that's all."

"But you should come back to Wolfe with me," I urged. "You need a chance to try to get at me."

Like that, he was serious again. He looked away. "I don't know, Sage. We'll see. For now, we'll just focus on the driving—when you can get away from your boyfriend, of course."

I left shortly after that, still confused about his weird behavior. Was that some of spirit's crazy effects on the mind? One minute, he was brave and defensive. The next, he was down and obstinate. Maybe there was a pattern or some type of reasoning behind it all, but it was beyond my analytical abilities.

Back at Amberwood, I immediately headed for the library to get a book for my English class. Ms. Terwilliger had lightened up on my usual work so that I could "devote more time" to crafting her spells. Since her independent study—which was supposed to be my easy elective—took up more time than my other classes, it was refreshing to focus on something else for a change. As I was leaving the British Lit section, I caught sight of Jill and Eddie studying together at a table. That wasn't weird, exactly. What was weird was that Micah wasn't with them.

"Hey, guys," I said, slipping into a seat. "Hard at work?"

"Do you know how weird it is to be repeating my senior year?" asked Eddie. "I can't even blow it off either. I have to get decent grades to stay here."

I grinned. "Hey, all knowledge is worth having."

He tapped the papers in front of him. "Yeah? You got any knowledge on the first woman to win the Pulitzer Prize in fiction?"

"Edith Wharton," I said automatically. He scrawled

something onto his paper, and I turned to Jill. "How are things with you? Where's Micah?"

Jill had her chin propped in her hand and was gazing at me with the weirdest look. It was almost . . . dreamy. It took her a few moments to snap out of her daze and respond. The dreamy look became embarrassed and then dismayed. She glanced down at her book.

"Sorry. I was just thinking how good you look in taupe. What did you ask?"

"Micah?" I prompted.

"Oh. Right. He's got . . . stuff to do."

I was pretty sure that was the shortest explanation she'd ever given me. I tried to remember what I'd last heard on their status. "You guys patched things up, right?"

"Yeah. I guess. He understood about Thanksgiving." She brightened. "Hey, Eddie and I were talking about that. Do you think we could all have a big family-style Thanksgiving at Clarence's? Do you think he'd mind? We could all help, and it'd be lots of fun. I mean, aside from the cover, we really are like a family. Eddie says he can make the turkey."

"I think Clarence would love that," I said, happy to see her cheery again. Then, I replayed her words. I turned to Eddie incredulously. "You know how to make a turkey? How would you have learned that?" From what I knew, most dhampirs stayed nearly year-round at their schools from an early age. Not a lot of culinary time.

"Hey," he said, straight-faced. "All knowledge is worth having."

Jill laughed. "He wouldn't tell me either."

"You know, Angeline claims she can cook," said Eddie. "We

were talking about it at breakfast. She says she knows about cooking turkey too, so if we tag-team, we can pull it off. Of course, she'll probably want to hunt and kill her own."

"Probably," I said. It was amazing that he was talking about working with her on anything. It was even amazing that he could speak about her fondly, without a grimace. I was beginning to think more and more that her display at the assembly had been a good thing. We didn't need animosity in this group. "Well, I got what I came for, so I'm heading back. I'll see you in the morning."

"See you," said Eddie.

Jill said nothing, and when I glanced over, I saw that she was watching me again with that weird, enraptured look. She sighed happily. "Adrian had a great time with you at your class tonight, you know."

I nearly rolled my eyes. "The bond leaves no secrets. He didn't always seem to be having a good time."

"No, he really did," she assured me. A dopey smile crossed her features. "He loves that you love the car more than he does and thinks it's awesome you're getting so good in your defense class. Not that that's a surprise. You're always so good at everything, and you don't even realize it. You don't even realize half the things you do—like how you watch out for others and never even think about yourself."

Even Eddie looked a little astonished by that. He and I exchanged puzzled looks. "Well," I said awkwardly, really unsure how to handle this Sydney lovefest. I decided escape was my best option. "Thanks. I'll see you later and—hey. Where'd you get that?"

"Huh?" she asked, blinking out of her enraptured haze.

Jill was wearing a silk scarf painted in rich jewel tones, almost reminding me of a peacock's tail. It also reminded me of something else, but I couldn't quite put my finger on it. "The scarf. I've seen it before."

"Oh." She ran her fingers over the smooth material. "Lia gave it to me."

"What? When did you see her?"

"She stopped by the dorm yesterday to give the dresses back again. I didn't tell you because I knew you'd want to return them."

"I do," I said adamantly.

Jill sighed. "Come on, let's just keep them. They're so pretty. And you know she'll just bring them back anyway."

"We'll deal with that later. Tell me about the scarf."

"It's no big deal. She was trying to pitch me on this scarf collection—"

"Yeah, yeah, she told me too. How she could make it so no one recognized you." I shook my head, feeling a surprising amount of anger. Was nothing under my control anymore? "I can't believe she went behind my back! Please tell me you didn't sneak off with her to do a photo shoot."

"No, no," said Jill quickly. "Of course not. But you don't think . . . I mean, you don't think there's any way she could pull it off? Hide me?"

I tried to keep my tone gentle. After all, I was mad at Lia, not Jill. "Maybe. Maybe not. You know we can't take the chance."

Jill nodded, face sad. "Yeah."

I left feeling annoyed and was so distracted that I nearly ran into Trey. When he didn't respond to my greeting, I realized he was even more distracted than I was. There was a haunted look in his eyes, and he seemed exhausted.

"You okay?" I asked.

He managed a weak smile. "Yeah, yeah. Just feeling the pressure of everything. Nothing I can't handle. What about you? Don't they usually have to throw you out of this place? Or did you finally get tired of being here for eight hours?"

"I just needed one book," I said. "And I was actually only here ten minutes. I was out most of the night."

The smile fell, replaced by a frown. "Out with Brayden?"

"That's tomorrow. I had, um, family stuff tonight."

The frown deepened. "You go out a lot, Melbourne. You have a lot of friends outside school."

"Not that many," I said. "I'm not living a party lifestyle, if that's what you're getting at."

"Yeah, well. Be careful. I've heard about some scary stuff going on out there."

I remembered him being concerned for Jill too. I usually kept up on all the local news and had heard nothing alarming recently. "What, is there a crime ring in Palm Springs I should know about?"

"Just be careful," he said.

We started to part ways, and then I called to him, "Trey? I know it's your own business, but whatever's going on . . . if you want to talk, I'm here." It was a huge concession for me, seeing as I wasn't always the most socially adept person.

Trey gave me a wistful smile. "Noted."

I was kind of reeling as I went back to my dorm. Adrian, Jill, Trey. I suppose if you counted Eddie and Angeline getting along, everyone in my life was behaving weirdly. *All part of the job,* I thought.

As soon as I was back in my room, I called Donna Stanton with the Alchemists. I never could be sure what time zone she was in, so I wasn't too concerned about the late hour. She answered right away and didn't sound tired, which I took as a good sign. She hadn't responded to my e-mail about the Warriors, and I was anxious for news. They posed too big a threat to us to be ignored.

"Miss Sage," she said. "I was planning on calling you soon. I trust everything's okay with the Dragomir girl?"

"Jill? Yeah, she's fine. I wanted to check in on some other things. You got the info I sent you about the Warriors of Light?"

Stanton sighed. "That's what I was going to call you about. Have you had any more run-ins?"

"No. And they don't seem to have been following us any-more either. Maybe they gave up."

"Unlikely." Her next words took a long time to get out. "Not from what we've observed in the past."

I froze, momentarily speechless. "In the past? Do you mean . . . you've run into them before? I was hoping they were just some . . . I don't know. A crazy, localized group."

"Unfortunately, no. We've encountered them before. Sporadically, mind you. But they pop up everywhere."

I was still in disbelief. "But I was always taught that any hunters had disappeared centuries ago. Why has no one ever talked about this?"

"Honestly?" asked Stanton. "Most Alchemists don't know. We want to run an efficient organization, one that deals with the vampire problem in an organized, peaceful way. There are some people in our group who might want to take more extreme action. It's best then if the existence of our radical offshoot is kept secret. I wouldn't have even told you, but with all the contact you're having, you need to be prepared."

"Offshoot . . . then they are related to Alchemists!" I was sickened.

"Not for a very long time." She sounded equally disgusted. "There's almost no resemblance anymore. They're reckless and savage. The only reason we let them be is because they usually just go after Strigoi. This situation with Sonya Karp is more difficult. She hasn't had any more threats?"

"No. I just saw her tonight . . . which brings up the other reason I called . . . "

I gave Stanton a rundown of the various blood experiments, including my own donation. I painted it in very scientific terms, how it had seemed useful as extra data. I then made sure to sound properly appalled by the second request—which wasn't that difficult.

"Absolutely not," said Stanton. No hesitation. Often, Alchemist decisions went through chains of command, even with someone as high up as her. It was a sign of how much this went against Alchemist beliefs that she didn't even have to consult anyone. "Human control-blood is one thing. The rest she's suggesting is out of the question. I will not allow humans to be used in these experiments, especially when the evidence clearly shows the former Strigoi need to be the focus—not us. Besides, for all we know, this is some ploy on the Moroi part to get more of our blood for personal reasons."

I didn't believe that last part at all and tried to find a tactful way of saying so. "Sonya seems to sincerely believe this would help protect against Strigoi. She just doesn't seem to grasp how we feel about it."

"Of course she wouldn't," said Stanton dismissively. "None of them do."

She and I returned our focus to the vampire hunters. The Alchemists were doing some investigating on any sightings in the area. She didn't want me to do any active investigation myself, but I was to report in immediately if any other information came my way. She was assuming the Warriors of Light were operating nearby, and once she found out where, the Alchemists would "deal with them." I wasn't entirely sure what that meant, but her tone made me shiver. As she'd pointed out earlier, we weren't a particularly aggressive group . . . though we were excellent at getting rid of problems.

"Oh," I said, just as we were wrapping up. "Did you ever find out anything about Marcus Finch?" I'd tried locating Clarence's mysterious human, who'd helped against the hunters, but had found nothing. I'd hoped Stanton might have more connections.

"No. But we'll keep looking." A slight pause. "Miss Sage . . . I can't emphasize enough how pleased we are with the work you're doing. You've run into a few more complications than any of us expected, yet you handle them all efficiently and properly. Even your conduct with the Moroi is outstanding. A weaker person might have yielded to Karp's request. You refused and contacted me. I'm so proud I took the chance on you."

I felt a tightening in my chest. *So proud.* I couldn't remember the last time someone had said they were proud of me. Well, my mother did a lot, but no one tied to my work among the Alchemists did. For most of my life, I'd hoped my father would say he was proud. I'd finally given up on expecting that. Stanton was hardly a parental figure, but her words triggered happiness in me I hadn't known was waiting to come out.

"Thank you, ma'am," I said, when I could finally speak.

"Keep it up," she said. "When I can, I'll get you out of that place and into a position that doesn't involve so much contact with *them*."

And like that, my world came crashing down. I suddenly felt guilty. She really had given me a chance, and now I was deceiving her. I was hardly like Liam, ready to sell my soul to the Strigoi, but I also wasn't staying objective with my charges. Driving lessons. Thanksgiving. What would Stanton say if she knew about that? I was a sham, reaping glory I didn't deserve. If I was truly a dedicated Alchemist, I'd change my life here. I'd stop all extraneous activities with Jill and the others. I wouldn't even attend Amberwood—I'd accept the offer of outside accommodations. I'd only come here and see the gang when I absolutely was required to.

If I could do those things, *then* I'd truly be a good Alchemist.

And, I realized, I'd also be terribly, awfully lonely.

"Thank you, ma'am," I said.

It was the only response I could give.

CHAPTER 18

JILL DIDN'T GIVE ME any starry-eyed looks at breakfast the next morning, which was kind of a relief. Micah had surfaced again, and while they weren't as flirty as they'd been in the past, the two were chatting animatedly away about a science project she had. Eddie and Angeline were equally engrossed in conversation, making plans for when she was free of her suspension. Her blues eyes were alight with happiness as they talked, and I realized that she had legitimate feelings for him. She hadn't just been throwing herself at him for the sake of conquest. I wondered if he knew.

It would've been easy to feel like a fifth wheel here, but instead, I was pleased and content to see my little cohort getting along so well. Stanton's conversation had still left me conflicted, but there was nothing wrong with appreciating the peace around here. I would've been happier still if Trey's behavior had also normalized, but when I reached my history class later, he was absent yet again. I had no doubt he'd claim he had family stuff, but my earlier suspicions were returning, about whether his family might be responsible for his injuries. Should I report my worries to someone? Who? I didn't want to jump to conclusions either, which left me in a bind.

Eddie and I always sat near each other in that class, and I leaned toward him before the bell rang, pitching my voice low to address another concern. "Hey, have you noticed that Jill's been kind of acting weirdly around me?"

"She's got a lot going on," he said, ever quick to defend her.

"Yeah, I know, but you had to have noticed her last night. In the library? I mean—keeping in mind I'm terrible at figuring this stuff out—it was like she had a crush on me or something."

He laughed at that. "She was kind of laying it on thick, but I don't think you have to worry about some romantic complication. She just looks up to you a lot, that's all. Part of her still wants to be a brave fighter who rushes out fearlessly . . . " He paused as he savored that idea, a mix of pride and rapture on his face before he tuned back into me. "But at the same time, you're starting to show her there all sorts of ways to be powerful."

"Thanks," I said. "I think. But speaking of her being a brave fighter . . . " I studied him curiously. "Why don't you train her anymore? Don't you want her to hone her skills?"

"Oh, yeah. That. Well . . . there are a few reasons for it. One is I need to focus on Angeline. Another is that I just don't want Jill worried about that. *I'll* do the protecting." Those were exactly the reasons I'd guessed. The next one was not. "And I guess . . . the other thing is that I don't feel right being in contact with her like that. I mean, I know it means nothing to her . . . but it means something to me."

Again, my social skills took a moment to kick in. "You mean, you don't like that you have to touch her?"

Eddie actually blushed. "It doesn't bother me, that's the problem. Better for us to spend time together in a hands-off way."

I hadn't expected that, but I could understand it. Leaving Eddie to his own inner demons, I soon got caught up in the day and wondering what had happened to Trey. I'd hoped he'd come into class late, but he didn't. In fact, he didn't surface for the rest of the day, not even when I was finishing up my independent study. I'd thought he might come by again for homework.

"You look troubled," said Ms. Terwilliger, watching me pack up when the bell rang. "Worried about getting your project in on time?"

"No." I'd actually finished two of the charms, but I certainly wasn't going to tell her that. "I'm worried about Trey. He keeps missing school. Do you know why he's out? I mean, if you can tell me?"

"The office notifies us if a student will be out for the day, but they don't tell us the reason. If it makes you feel better, Mr. Juarez's absence was called in this morning. He hasn't disappeared." I almost mentioned my fears about his home but held off. I still needed more evidence.

Between worrying about Trey, Ms. Terwilliger's work, the Warriors, Brayden, and all my other myriad complications, I knew I couldn't waste any of my free time. Nonetheless, I went to Adrian's after school on a mission I couldn't refuse. On our way to Wolfe's class earlier this week, Adrian had mentioned offhandedly that he hadn't had the Mustang looked at by a mechanic before purchasing it. Although my own novice assessment hadn't found anything wrong with the car, I pushed for Adrian to get the car examined—which, of course, meant *I* had to look up a specialist and make the appointment. It was just before my textile museum date, but I was certain I had time to make it all work.

"The guy I bought it from seemed pretty trustworthy," Adrian told me, after we'd dropped the car off with the mechanic. He'd told us he'd look at it right away and that we could hang around and wait. His shop was on the outskirts of a suburban area, so Adrian suggested we go for a walk through the neighborhoods. "And it ran just fine when I did the test drive, so I figured everything was okay."

"That doesn't mean there aren't problems you can't see. It's best to be safe," I said, knowing I sounded preachy. "Bad enough you got a car you can't drive." Glancing over, I saw a small, half smile on his face.

"With your help, I'll be a pro in no time. Of course, if you don't want to help anymore, I'll just wing it and figure it out on my own."

I groaned. "You already know what I'd say about—wow."

The neighborhood we were in was pretty affluent. In fact, I'd say the houses bordered on being bona fide mansions. We stopped in front of one that looked like a cross between a hacienda and a southern plantation, large and sprawling with a pillared porch and pink stucco siding. The front yard was a mix of climates, green grass with palm trees lining the path to the house. The trees were like tropical sentries.

"Gorgeous," I said. "I love architecture. In another life, I'd have studied that—not chemicals and vampires." As we continued on, we saw more of the same, each house trying to outdo the others. All of them had high fences and hedges blocking their backyards. "I wonder what's back there. Pools, probably."

Adrian stopped in front of another. It was as yellow as his car and showed another mix of styles, like a southwest version of a medieval castle, complete with turrets. "Nice juxtaposition," he remarked.

I turned, knowing my eyes were wide as I stared at him. "Did you just use *juxtaposition* in a sentence?"

"Yes, Sage," he said patiently. "We use it all the time with art, when we're mixing different components. That, and I know how to use a dictionary." He turned from me and scanned the house, his eyes resting on a gardener who was out trimming some hedges. A sly smile crossed Adrian's lips. "You want to see the back? Come on."

"What are you—" Before I could say another word, Adrian strode up the granite pathway and cut across the lawn to where the guy was working. I didn't want anything to do with this, but the responsible part of me couldn't let Adrian get into trouble. I hurried after him.

"Are the owners home?" Adrian asked.

The gardener had stopped his clipping and stared at Adrian. "No."

"When will they be back?"

"After six."

I was astonished that the guy was answering these questions. If I'd been asked them, I would've assumed someone was staging a break-in. Then, I saw the glazed look in the gardener's eyes and realized what was going on.

"Adrian—"

Adrian's eyes never left the other man's face. "Take us to the backyard."

"Of course."

The gardener dropped his hedge clippers and headed for a gate on the side of the house. I tried to get Adrian's attention to stop this, but he was outpacing me. Our guide stopped at the gate, entered a security code, and led us to the back. My protests died on my lips as I gazed around.

This back property was almost three times the size of the front. There were more palm trees ringing the yard, along with a terraced garden full of plants, both native and non-native. A huge oval shaped pool dominated the space, its turquoise hue startling against the gray of the granite that surrounded it. On one side of the pool, several steps led up to a smaller, square pool. It could only hold a few people, and a waterfall poured out from it, down to the larger pool. Tiki torches and tables around the pools completed the lush setup.

"Thanks," Adrian told the gardener. "Go back to your work. It's okay if we're here. We'll see ourselves out."

"Of course," the man replied. He walked back the way we'd come in.

I snapped back to reality. "Adrian! You used compulsion on that guy. That . . . I mean, it's . . . "

"Awesome?" Adrian walked over to the steps leading up to the upper pool. "Yeah, I know."

"It's wrong! All of this. Breaking and entering, and compulsion . . . " I shivered, despite the sweltering heat. "It's immoral. Controlling someone else's mind. You know it! Your people and mine both agree."

"Eh, no harm done." He climbed to the top of the pool and stood on its edge, surveying his kingdom. The sun brought out chestnut glints in his brown hair. "Believe me, that guy was easy to control. Weak-willed. I barely had to use compulsion."

"Adrian—"

"Come on, Sage. Not like we're going to hurt anything. Check out this view."

I was almost afraid to go up there. It was so rare for any of the Moroi here to use their magic that it was easy for me to pretend it didn't exist. Seeing Adrian use it—the most insidious kind—made my skin crawl. As I'd told Ms. Terwilliger in our charm discussion, no one should be able to control another like that.

"Come on," Adrian repeated. "You're not worried I'm going to compel you up here, are you?"

"Of course not," I said. And I meant it. I didn't know why, but some part of me knew Adrian would never, ever harm me. Reluctantly, I went to join him, hoping that would encourage him to leave. When I reached the top, my jaw dropped. The intimate pool hadn't seemed that high, but it gave us a stunning view of the mountains off in the distance, rugged and majestic against the blue of the sky. The larger pool glittered below us, and the waterfall made it look like we'd entered some mystical oasis.

"Cool, huh?" he asked. Adrian sat down on the small pool's edge, rolled up his jeans, and took off his socks and shoes.

"Now what are you doing?" I asked.

"Making the most out of this." He put his feet in the water. "Come on. Do something bad for a change. Not that it's really *that* bad. We aren't trashing this place or anything."

I hesitated, but the water was intoxicating, as though it too could wield compulsion. Settling down, I copied Adrian and dipped my bare feet into the water. Its coolness was startling—and wonderful—in this intense heat.

"I could get used to this," I admitted. "But what if the owners come home early?"

He shrugged. "I can talk us out of it, don't worry."

That wasn't exactly reassuring. I turned back to the gorgeous view and lush property. I wasn't always the most imaginative person, but I thought back to what I'd said about living another life. What would it be like to have a home like this? To stay in one place? To spend days by the pool, soaking in the sun, and not worrying about the fate of humanity? I fell into daydreams and was so caught up that I lost track of time.

"We have to get back to the shop," I exclaimed. Glancing over, I was astonished to see Adrian watching me, a look of contentment on his face. His eyes seemed to study my every feature. Seeing me notice him, he immediately looked away. His usual smirky expression replaced the dreamy one.

"The mechanic will wait," he said.

"Yeah, but I'm supposed to meet Brayden soon. I'll be—" That's when I got a good look at Adrian. "What have you done? Look at you! You shouldn't be out here."

"It's not that bad."

He was lying, and we both knew it. It was late afternoon, and the sun was merciless. I'd certainly felt it, though the coolness of the water had helped distract me. That, and I was human. Sure, sunstroke and sunburns were concerns, but I loved the sun and had a high tolerance for it. Vampires did not.

Sweat poured off Adrian, soaking his shirt and hair. Pink

blotches covered his face. They were familiar. I'd seen them on Jill back when she'd been forced to play outdoor sports in PE. Left unchecked, they'd turn into burns. I jumped to my feet.

"Come on, we have to get out of here before you get worse. What were you thinking?"

His expression was astonishingly nonchalant for someone who looked like he would pass out. "It was worth it. You looked . . . happy."

"That's crazy," I said.

"Not the craziest thing I've ever done." He smiled as he looked up at me. His eyes grew slightly unfocused, as though they were seeing more than just me. "What's a little crazy here and there? I'm supposed to be doing experiments . . . why not see which is brighter: your aura or the sun?"

The way he looked at me and spoke unnerved me, and I remembered what Jill had said, how spirit slowly drove its users insane. Adrian hardly seemed insane, but there was certainly something haunted about him, a definite shift from his usual sharp wit. It was as though something else had seized hold of him. I remembered that poem line, about dreaming and waking.

"Come on," I repeated. I held out my hand. "You shouldn't have used spirit. We need to get you out of here."

He took my hand and staggered to his feet. A rush of warmth and electricity went through me, just as it had the last time we touched, and our eyes held. For a moment, all I could think about were his earlier words: *You looked happy . . .*

I brushed such sentiments aside and quickly got him out of there, only to discover the mechanic hadn't finished. At least in his shop, we were able to get Adrian some water and air conditioning. As we waited I texted Brayden. *Running an hour late with family stuff. Sorry. Will be there as soon as I can.* My phone chimed back about thirty seconds later: *That only leaves an hour for the textile museum.*

"That's not nearly enough time," said Adrian deadpan. I hadn't realized he'd been reading over my shoulder. I moved the phone away and suggested to Brayden we just meet for an early dinner. He concurred.

"I'm a mess," I muttered, checking myself out in a mirror. The heat had definitely taken its toll, and I looked sweaty and worn.

"Don't worry about it," Adrian told me. "If he didn't notice how awesome you were in the red dress, he probably won't notice anything now." He hesitated. "Not that there's even anything to notice. You're as cute as usual."

I was about to snap at him for teasing me, but when I looked over, his face was deadly earnest. Whatever retort I might have managed died on my lips, and I quickly got up to check our status, in order to hide how flustered I felt.

The mechanic finally finished—no problems found—and Adrian and I headed downtown. I kept watching him anxiously, afraid he'd pass out.

"Stop worrying, Sage. I'm fine," he said. "Although . . . I'd be better with some ice cream or gelato. Even you have to admit that'd be good right now."

It would, actually, but I wouldn't give him the satisfaction. "What is it with you and frozen desserts? Why do you always want them?"

"Because we live in a desert."

I couldn't argue with that reasoning. We reached his place, and I swapped cars. Before he went inside, I inundated him with advice about getting water and resting. Then, I spoke the words that had been burning inside of me.

"Thank you for the poolside outing," I said. "Your near-sunstroke aside, that was pretty amazing."

He gave me a cocky smile. "Maybe you'll get used to vampire magic after all."

"No," I said automatically. "I'll *never* get used to that."

His smile immediately disappeared. "Of course not," he murmured. "See you around."

I finally made it to dinner. I'd chosen an Italian restaurant, filled with the scents of garlic and cheese. Brayden sat at a corner table, sipping water and earning glares from the waitress, who was probably impatient for him to order. I sat down opposite him, dropping my satchel beside me.

"I am *so* sorry," I told him. "I had to do this thing with my, uh, brother."

If Brayden was mad, he didn't show it. That was his way. He did, however, give me a scrutinizing look. "Was it something athletic? You look like you ran a marathon."

It wasn't an insult, not by any means, but it did take me aback—mostly because I was thinking of Adrian's comment. Brayden had had almost nothing to say about my Halloween costume, but he noticed this?

"We were out in Santa Sofia, getting his car looked at."

"Nice area. Keep going up the highway, and you can get to Joshua Tree National Park. Ever been there?"

"No. Just read about it."

"Iconic place. The geology's fascinating."

The waitress came by, and I gratefully ordered an iced latte. Brayden was more than happy to tell me about some of the park's geology, and we soon fell into our comfortable rhythm of intellectual discussion. I didn't know the park's specific makeup, but I knew more than enough about geology in general to keep up. In fact, I was able to talk on autopilot while my mind wandered back to Adrian. I recalled again what he'd said about the red dress. I also couldn't shake the comment about me being happy, and how that was worth his suffering.

"What do you think?"

"Hmm?" I realized I'd lost the thread of our conversation after all.

"I asked which type of desert you find more striking," Brayden explained. "The Mojave region gets all the hype, but I actually prefer the Colorado Desert."

"Ah." I slipped back into the flow. "Um, Mojave. I like the rock formations better."

This triggered a debate of the regions while we ate, and Brayden seemed happier and happier. He really did like having someone who could keep up with him, I realized. None of my books had said anything about the way to a man's heart being through academic debates. I didn't mind it, though. I liked the conversation, but it didn't exactly send thrills through me. I had to remind myself it was still early in our relationship—if I could even call it that. Surely the head over heels part would come soon.

We talked for a long time after the meal was over. The waitress brought us an unsolicited dessert menu when we finished, and I surprised myself by saying, "Wow . . . I can't believe how much I want gelato right now. That never happens." Maybe the sweat and heat had leached my nutrients . . . or maybe I still had Adrian on the brain.

"I've never heard you order dessert," said Brayden, sliding his menu away. "It's not too much sugar?"

It was another of those weird statements of his that could be interpreted a number of different ways. Was he judging me? Did he think I shouldn't have any sugar? I didn't know, but it was enough for me to close the menu and set it on top of his.

With no other scheduled forms of entertainment for the night, we decided to just go for a walk after dinner. The temperature was down to moderate levels, and it was still light enough out that I wasn't as concerned about the Warriors of Light jumping out from corners. That didn't mean I ignored Wolfe's teachings, however. I still kept an eye on my surroundings, watching for anything suspicious.

We reached a small park that only took up one city block and found a bench in the corner. We sat down on it, watching children play on the opposite side of the lawn while we continued a discussion on bird watching in the Mojave. Brayden put his arm around me as we talked, and eventually, we exhausted the topic and simply sat in comfortable silence.

"Sydney . . . "

I turned my gaze from the children, surprised at Brayden's uncertain tone, which was very different from the one he'd just been using to defend the superiority of the mountain bluebird over the western bluebird. There was softness in his eyes now as he looked at me. The evening light made his hazel eyes take on a little more gold than usual but completely hid the green. Too bad.

Before I could say anything, he leaned forward and kissed me. It was more intense than the last one, though still a long ways from the epic, all-consuming kisses I'd seen in movies. He did rest his hand on my shoulder this time, gently bringing me a little closer. The kiss also lasted longer than previous ones, and I again tried to let myself go and lose myself in the feel of someone else's lips.

He was the one who ended it, a bit more abruptly than I would've expected. "I—I'm sorry," he said, looking away. "I shouldn't have done that."

"Why not?" I asked. It wasn't so much that I'd been yearning for the kiss as it was that this seemed exactly like the kind of place you'd want to kiss: a romantic park at sunset.

"We're in public. It's kind of vulgar, I suppose." Vulgar? I wasn't even sure if we were really all that much in public, seeing as no one was next to us and we were in the shade of some trees. Brayden sighed with dismay. "I guess I just lost control. It won't happen again."

"It's okay," I said.

It hadn't seemed like that much of a loss of control, but what did I know? And I wondered if maybe a small loss of control wasn't such a bad thing. Wasn't that kind of the basis of passion? I didn't know that either. The only thing I knew for sure was that this kiss had been a lot like the last one. Nice, but it didn't blow me away. My heart sank. There was something wrong with me. Everyone was always going on about how socially inept I was. Did it extend to romance as well? Was I so cold that I'd spend my life never feeling anything?

I think Brayden misread my dismay and assumed I was upset with him. He stood up and held out his hand. "Hey, let's go walk to that tea shop one block over. They've got this local painter's art on display that I think you'll like. Besides, no calories in tea, right? Better than dessert."

"Right," I said. Thinking of the gelato didn't cheer me up any. The Italian place had had pomegranate, which kind of sounded like the best thing ever. As I stood up, my cell phone rang and startled both of us. "Hello?"

"Sage? It's me."

I had no reason to be mad at Adrian, not after what he'd done for me, but somehow I felt irritated by the interruption. I was trying to make the most of this night with Brayden, and Adrian unsettled everything.

"What's going on?" I asked.

"Are you still downtown? You need to come over right now."

"You know I'm out with Brayden," I said. This was pushy, even for Adrian. "I can't just drop everything and entertain you."

"It's not about me." It was then that I noticed how hard and serious his voice was. Something tightened in my chest. "It's about Sonya. She's missing."

CHAPTER 19

"SHE WAS LEAVING TOWN," I reminded him.

"Not until tomorrow."

He was right, I realized. When we'd spoken to Sonya last night, she'd said two days. "Are you sure she's really disappeared?" I asked. "Maybe she's just . . . out."

"Belikov's here, and he's freaked out. He says she never came home last night."

I nearly dropped the phone. Last night? Sonya had been gone that long? That was nearly twenty-four hours ago. "How did no one notice until now?" I demanded.

"I don't know," said Adrian. "Can you just come over? Please, Sydney?"

I was powerless when he used my first name. It always took everything to an extra level of seriousness—not that this situation needed any particular help. Sonya. Gone for twenty-four hours. For all we knew, she wasn't even alive if those sword-wielding freaks had caught her.

Brayden's face was a mix of incredulity and disappointment when I told him I had to leave. "But you just . . . I mean . . . " It was a rare moment of speechlessness for him.

"I'm sorry," I said earnestly. "Especially after being late and ruining the museum. But it's a family emergency."

"Your family has an awful lot of emergencies."

You have no idea, I thought. Instead of saying that, I simply apologized again. "I really am sorry. I . . . " I nearly said I'd make it up to him, but that was what I'd said when I left the Halloween dance early. Tonight was supposed to have been the makeup date. "I'm just sorry."

ADRIAN'S PLACE WAS CLOSE ENOUGH that I could've reasonably walked, but Brayden insisted on driving me, since dusk was falling. I had no problem accepting.

"Whoa," said Brayden, when we pulled up to the building. "Nice Mustang."

"Yeah. It's a 1967 C-code," I said automatically. "Great engine. My brother's. He's moved it again! I hope he wasn't out driving anywhere he wasn't supposed to—whoa. What's that?"

Brayden looked at where I was staring. "A Jaguar?"

"Obviously." The sleek, black car was parked just in front of Adrian's Mustang. "Where'd it come from?"

Brayden had no answer, of course. After more apologies and a promise to get in touch, I left him. There was no pretense of a kiss, not when he was so disappointed in the evening's outcome and I was too anxious about Sonya. In fact, I forgot all about Brayden as I walked up to the building. I had bigger concerns.

"It's Clarence's," said Adrian, as soon as he answered the door.

"Huh?" I asked.

"The Jag. I figured you'd want to know. He let Belikov drive it over since Sonya left with the rental." He stepped aside as I entered and shook his head in dismay. "Can you believe it was locked away in his garage the whole time I lived with him? He said he forgot he owned it! And there I was, stuck with the bus."

I would've laughed under almost any other circumstances. But when I saw Dimitri's face, all humor left me. He was pacing the living room like a trapped animal, radiating frustration and concern.

"I'm an idiot," he muttered. It was unclear if he was talking to himself or us. "I didn't realize she was gone last night, and then I spent half the day thinking she was out gardening!"

"Did you try calling her cell?" I knew it was a foolish question, but I had to begin logically.

"Yes," Dimitri said. "No answer. Then I double-checked to make sure her flight hadn't changed, and *then* I talked to Mikhail to see if he knew anything. He didn't. All I succeeded at doing there was making him worry."

"He should," I murmured, sitting on the edge of the couch. Nothing good could come of this. We knew the Warriors were obsessed with Sonya, and now she'd disappeared after going out alone.

"I only just found out she came to see you two," added Dimitri. He stopped pacing and glanced between us. "Did she say anything at all about where she was going?"

"No," I said. "Things didn't exactly . . . end well between us."

Dimitri nodded. "Adrian implied the same thing."

I looked up at Adrian and could tell he didn't want to get into it any more than I did. "We had an argument," he admitted. "She was trying to push Sydney into some experiments, and Sydney refused. I jumped in when Sonya kept pushing, and finally she just took off. Never said anything about where she was going."

Dimitri's face grew darker. "So, anything could've happened. She could've been taken right outside on the street. Or she could have gone somewhere and been abducted there."

Or she could be dead. Dimitri was speaking in terms of her still being alive, but I wasn't so sure. The hunters who had jumped us in the alley had seemed pretty intent on killing her then and there. If she hadn't come home last night, the odds seemed good they'd found her then. Twenty-four hours was an awfully long time to keep a "creature of darkness" alive. Studying Dimitri's face again, I knew he was well aware of all of this. He was simply operating on the hope that we had a chance to do something, that we weren't powerless.

Resolved, Dimitri strode for the door. "I have to go talk to the police."

"Missing person report?" asked Adrian.

"That, and more importantly, to get a search out on that car. If she was taken . . . " He hesitated, driving home the fear that lurked in all of us. "Well. If she's hidden away somewhere, she's going to be very difficult to locate. But it's a lot harder to hide a car than one woman. If the police can get its description out there, we might get a clue if it turns up." He started to open the door and then glanced back at us. "You're sure you don't remember anything else she said that could help?"

Adrian and I reiterated that we didn't. Dimitri left, giving us unnecessary instructions to alert him immediately if we thought of anything or—if by a miracle—Sonya showed up. I groaned once he was gone.

"This is my fault," I said.

Adrian looked at me in surprise. "Why on earth would you say that?"

"Sonya came here—left when she wasn't supposed to—because of *me*. Because of my blood. Who knows what would've happened if I hadn't refused? Maybe a few minutes difference, and the hunters wouldn't have been around. Or maybe if she hadn't been so upset, she would've been able to defend herself more." A million memories tumbled through my head. Sonya making the lily grow for me. Sonya talking to the queen on Adrian's behalf. Sonya showing me pictures of bridesmaid dresses. Sonya working diligently to stop Strigoi and redeem herself. All of that could be lost now.

"Maybe, maybe, maybe." Adrian sat down near me on the couch. "You can't think like that, and you sure as hell can't blame yourself for the actions of some crazy paranoid fringe group."

I knew he was right, but it didn't make me feel any better. "I should call the Alchemists. We've got ties to law enforcement too."

"Probably a good idea," he said, though his words were a little halfhearted. "I've just got a bad feeling about those guys. Even if . . . well, even if she's alive, I really don't know how we're going to find her. Short of some miraculous, magical solution."

I froze.

"Oh my God."

"What is it?" he asked, looking at me in concern. "Did you remember something?"

"Yes . . . but not what you're thinking." I closed my eyes and took a deep breath. *No, no, no.* The thought in my head was crazy. I had no business even considering it. Dimitri had the right idea. We needed to focus on normal, concrete methods of locating Sonya.

"Sage?" Adrian lightly touched my arm, and I jumped at the feel of his fingertips against my skin. "You okay?"

"I don't know," I said softly. "I just thought of something crazy."

"Welcome to my world."

I looked away, conflicted about the decision before me. What I was contemplating . . . well, some might argue it wasn't so different than what I'd done before. And yet, it all came down to the fine line between doing something by choice and doing something because I had to. There was no question here. This would be a choice. An exercising of free will.

"Adrian . . . what if I had a way to find Sonya, but it went against everything I believe in?"

He took several moments to answer. "Do you believe in getting Sonya back? If so, you wouldn't be going against everything you believe in."

It was odd logic, but it gave me the nudge I needed. I took out my cell phone and dialed a number I almost never called—though I certainly received texts and calls from it all the time. An answer came after two rings. "Ms. Terwilliger? This is Sydney."

"Miss Melbourne. What I can do for you?"

"I need to see you. It's kind of urg—no, no 'kind of' about it. It's urgent. Are you at the school?"

"No. As shocking as it is, I do go home on occasion." She paused for a moment. "However . . . you are certainly welcome to come to my house."

I don't know why that made me uneasy. After all, I spent

plenty of time at Clarence's. Surely a vampire's sprawling estate was much worse than a high school teacher's home. Of course, said teacher was also a witch, so I wasn't certain if I could expect a boring suburban flat or a house made of candy.

I swallowed. "Do you keep a lot of the same spell books at home that you do at school?" Adrian arched an eyebrow at the word *spell*.

Ms. Terwilliger hesitated for much longer this time. "Yes," she said. "And more."

She gave me her address, and before I could even hang up, Adrian said, "I'm coming with you."

"You don't even know where I'm going."

"True," he said. "But lack of information's never stopped me before. Besides, I know it has something to do with Sonya, which is good enough for me. That, and you looked scared to death. There's no way I can let you go alone."

I crossed my arms. "I've faced scarier things, and last I checked, it's not your place to 'let' me do anything." There was such concern in his face, however, that I knew I wouldn't be able to refuse . . . especially since I was kind of scared. "You have to promise not to tell anyone what we're going to do. Or talk about what you see."

"Damn. What's going on, Sage?" he asked. "Are we talking animal sacrifice or something?"

"Adrian," I said quietly.

He grew serious again. "I promise. Not a word, unless you say otherwise."

I didn't have to study him to know I could trust him. "Okay, then. But before we go, I need your hairbrush . . . "

Ms. Terwilliger lived in Vista Azul, the same suburb

Amberwood was in. To my surprise, the house really did look quite ordinary. It was small but otherwise blended in well to its older neighborhood. The sun had long since set when we arrived, and I was conscious of the school's approaching curfew. When she let us into her house, I found the interior a bit more in line with what I'd been expecting. Sure, there was a TV and modern furniture, but the décor also featured a lot of candles and statuary of various gods and goddesses. The scent of Nag Champa hung in the air. I counted at least three cats in the first five minutes and didn't doubt there were more.

"Miss Melbourne, welcome." Ms. Terwilliger took in Adrian with interest. "And welcome to your friend."

"My brother," I said pointedly. "Adrian."

Ms. Terwilliger—fully aware of the Moroi world—smiled. "Yes. Of course. You attend Carlton, correct?"

"Yeah," said Adrian. "You're the one who helped get me in, right? Thanks for that."

"Well," said Ms. Terwilliger, with a shrug, "I'm always happy to help star pupils—especially those who are so diligent about keeping me in coffee. Now then, what's this urgent matter that brings you out at night?"

My eyes were already on a large bookcase in her living room. The shelves were filled with old, leather-bound books—exactly the kind she always made me work on. "Do you . . . do you have a spell that would help locate someone?" I asked. Each word caused me pain. "I mean, I know they're out there. I've come across them in my work a couple of times. But I was wondering if there was maybe one that you'd recommend over another."

Ms. Terwilliger laughed softly, and I looked away. "Well, well. This is definitely worth a late-night visit." We were in her dining room, and she pulled out an ornate wooden chair to sit down. One of the cats brushed against her leg. "There are a number of location spells, certainly—though none are quite at your level. And by your level, I mean your constant refusal to practice or better yourself."

I scowled. "Is there one that you could do?"

She shook her head. "No. This is your problem. You're going to do it. You need to."

"Well, not if it's beyond me!" I protested. "Please. This is a matter of life and death." That, and I didn't want to taint myself with her magic. Bad enough I was encouraging her at all.

"Rest easy. I wouldn't make you do it if you couldn't handle it," she said. "To make it work, however, it's imperative we have something that can connect us to the person we're looking for. There are spells where that's not necessary—but those are definitely out of your league."

I produced Adrian's brush from my purse. "Something like a strand of hair?"

"Something exactly like that," she said, clearly impressed.

I'd remembered Adrian's complaint about Sonya using some of his personal items. Although he apparently cleaned the brush regularly (and really, I'd expect nothing less from someone who spent so much time on his hair), there were still a few lingering red strands. Carefully, I plucked the longest one from the bristles and held it up.

"What do I need to do?" I asked. I was trying to be strong, but my hands shook.

"Let's find out." She rose and walked into the living room, studying the shelves. Adrian turned to me.

"Is she for real?" He paused and reconsidered. "Are *you* for real? Spells? Magic? I mean, don't get me wrong. I drink blood and control people's minds. But I've never heard of anything like this."

"Neither had I until a month ago." I sighed. "And unfortunately, it *is* real. Worse, she thinks I have a knack for it. Do you remember at all when one of the Strigoi in your apartment caught on fire?"

"Vaguely, but yeah. It kind of all got brushed aside, and I never thought much about it." He frowned, troubled by the memory. "I was out of it from the bite."

"Well, it wasn't some freak accident. It was . . . magic." I gestured toward Ms. Terwilliger. "And I made it happen."

His eyes widened. "Are you some kind of mutant human? Like a fire user? And I use *mutant* as a compliment, you know. I wouldn't think less of you."

"It's not like vampire magic," I said. Some part of me supposed I should be pleased that Adrian would still be friendly with a "mutant." "It's not some internal connection to the elements. According to her, some humans can work magic by pulling it from the world. It sounds crazy, but . . . well. I *did* set a Strigoi on fire."

I could see Adrian taking all of this in as Ms. Terwilliger returned to us. She set down a book with a red leather cover and flipped through the pages before finding what she wanted. We all peered at it.

"That's not English," said Adrian helpfully.

"It's just Greek," I said, skimming the ingredient list. "It doesn't seem to require much."

"That's because a huge part of it is mental focus," explained

Ms. Terwilliger. "It's more complicated than it looks. It'll take you a few hours at least."

I took in the time on an ornate grandfather clock. "I don't have a few hours. Too close to curfew."

"Easily remedied," said Ms. Terwilliger. She picked up her cell phone from the table and dialed a number from memory. "Hello, Desiree? This is Jaclyn. Yes, fine. Thank you. I have Sydney Melrose out here right now, helping me on a very crucial project." I nearly rolled my eyes. She was perfectly aware of my last name when she needed to be, apparently. "I'm afraid she might be out past the dorm curfew, and I was wondering if you'd be kind enough to allow an extension. Yes . . . yes, I know. But it's very important for my work, and I think we can all agree that with her exemplary record, she's hardly the type we need to worry about abusing such privileges. She's certainly one of the most trustworthy students I know." That got a small smirk from Adrian.

Thirty more seconds, and I was free of curfew. "Who's Desiree?" I asked, once Ms. Terwilliger hung up.

"Your dorm matron. Weathers."

"Really?" I thought of stout, motherly Mrs. Weathers. I never would've guessed her first name was Desiree. It was the kind of name I would associate with someone sultry and seductive. Maybe she had some scandalous life outside of school we didn't know about. "So, do I have an all-night pass?"

"Not sure I'd push it that far," said Ms. Terwilliger. "But we certainly have enough time for this spell. I can't make it for you, but I can help you with the ingredients and supplies."

I tapped the book, forgetting about my fear as I scanned the lengthy list. Details like this put me back in my comfort zone. "You have all of these?"

"Of course."

Ms. Terwilliger led us down a hall that branched off from the kitchen, where I'd expect to find bedrooms. One room did indeed give us a glimpse of a bed as we walked by, but our eventual destination was something else altogether: a workshop. It was kind of what you'd get if you crossed a wizard's lair with a mad scientist's lab. Part of the room had very modern equipment: beakers, a sink, burners, etc. The rest was from a different era, vials of oils and dried herbs, along with scrolls and honest-to-goodness cauldrons. Plants and herbs lined the sill of a dark window. There were two more cats in here, and I was pretty sure they weren't the same ones I'd seen in the living room.

"It looks chaotic," said Ms. Terwilliger. "But I daresay it's organized enough, even for you."

Upon closer inspection, I saw she was right. All of the plants and little vials were labeled and in alphabetical order. All of the various tools were equally identified, enumerated by size and material. The room's center was a large, smooth stone table, and I set the book down on it, careful to stay on the page I needed.

"What now?" I asked.

"Now, you construct it," she said. "The more of it you do on your own, the stronger your connection will be to the spell. Certainly come and get me if you have trouble with the ingredients or the directions. Otherwise, the more of *your* focus and concentration that goes into this, the better."

"Where are you going to be?" I asked, startled. As much as I disliked the thought of working with her in a creepy, arcane lab, I disliked the thought of being alone here even more.

She gestured toward where we'd come from. "Oh, just out there. I'll entertain your 'brother' too since you really do need to do this alone."

My anxiety increased. I'd protested Adrian's original request to come here, but now I wanted him around. "Can I at least get some coffee?"

She chuckled. "Normally, I'd say yes—particularly if you were just doing grunt work to build an amulet or potion. Because you'll be using your mind, the magic will work much better if your thoughts are free and clear of any substances that affect your mental state."

"Boy, that sounds familiar," muttered Adrian.

"Okay, then," I said, resolving to be strong. "I need to get started. Sonya's waiting." Provided she was still alive to wait.

Ms. Terwilliger left, telling me to get her when I was on the spell's last stage. Adrian delayed a moment to speak with me. "You sure you're okay with all of this? I mean, from what I know about you and the Alchemists . . . well, it seems like you'd actually be pretty not-okay with this."

"I'm not," I agreed. "Like I said, this goes against everything I believe—against everything they've taught me. Which is why you can't tell anyone. You heard her passive aggressive remark about me not practicing? She's been on me for a while now to develop my so-called magical skills, and I keep refusing—because it's wrong. So, she has me research spell books for my independent study with her, in the hopes of me learning by osmosis."

"That's messed up," he said, shaking his head. "You don't have to do this. You don't have to do anything you don't want to."

I gave him a small smile. "Well, I want to find Sonya. So I do have to do this."

He gave me no smile in return. "Okay. But I'm just going to be out there—having a tea party with her cats or whatever it is she has in mind. You need me? You yell. You want to leave? We go. I'll get you out of here, no matter what."

Something clenched in my chest, and for a moment, the whole world narrowed down to the green of his eyes. "Thank you."

Adrian left, and I was alone. Well, almost. One of the cats had stuck around, a sleek black one with yellow eyes. It was lying on a high shelf, watching me curiously, like it wondered if I could really pull this off. That made two of us.

For a moment, I couldn't move. I was about to willingly work magic. All the protests and arguments I'd given Ms. Terwilliger were like ash in the wind now. I started trembling and felt short of breath. Then, I thought about Sonya. Kind, brave Sonya. She'd devoted so much energy and time to doing the right thing. How could I do any less?

As I'd noted to Ms. Terwilliger, the spell was deceptively simple. It didn't require half as many steps as the fire amulet. I had to keep water simmering in a copper cauldron and add different ingredients to it, most of which were clear oils that had to be measured with exacting care. The air soon grew heavy with the scent of bergamot, vanilla, and heliotrope. Some of the steps had the same ritual redundancy I'd done before. For example, I had to pluck thirteen fresh mint leaves off one of her plants, dropping each leaf in one at a time while counting them off in Greek. Then, when they had simmered for thirteen minutes, I had to remove each one with a rosewood spoon.

Before leaving, Ms. Terwilliger had told me to stay focused and think about both the steps of the spell and what I was ultimately hoping to accomplish. So, I turned my thoughts toward Sonya and finding her, praying that she was okay. When I finally finished these initial steps, I saw that almost an hour had gone by. I'd barely noticed it passing. I wiped a hand over my forehead, surprised at how much the steamy room had made me sweat. I went out to find Ms. Terwilliger and Adrian, uncertain what weird activity I'd find going on. Instead, things were pretty ordinary: they were watching TV. Both glanced up at my approach.

"Ready?" she asked.

I nodded.

"Smells like tea in here," said Adrian, as they followed me to the workroom.

Ms. Terwilliger examined the small cauldron and nodded her head in approval. "It looks excellent." I didn't know how she could tell at a glance but figured I'd take her word for it. "Now. The actual scrying involves a silver plate, correct?" She scanned her shelves of dishes and pointed at something. "There. Use that."

I pulled down a perfectly round plate about twelve inches across. It was smooth, with no ornamentation, and had been polished to such brilliance that it reflected almost as well as a mirror. I probably could've done without that part, though, seeing as my hair and makeup were showing the wear and tear of the day. Around anyone else, I would have felt self-conscious. I set the plate on the worktable and poured one cup of water from the cauldron onto the silvery surface. All non-liquid ingredients had been removed, and the water was perfectly clear. Once it stopped rippling, the mirror effect returned. Ms. Terwilliger handed me a tiny bowl of galbanum incense, which the book said should be burning during this last stage. I lit the resin with a candle, and a bitter, green smell wafted up, contrasting with the sweetness of the liquid.

"You still have the hair?" Ms. Terwilliger asked.

"Of course." I laid it across the water's smooth surface. Part of me wanted something to happen—sparks or smoke—but I'd read the directions and knew better. I pulled a stool up to the table and sat on it, allowing me to gaze down into the water. "Now I look?"

"Now you look," she confirmed. "Your mind needs to be both focused and spread out. You need to think about the components of the spell and the magic they hold, as well as your desire to find the spell's subject. At the same time, you need to maintain a perfect clarity of mind and stay fixed on your task with razor sharp focus."

I looked down at my reflection and tried to do all those things she'd just described. Nothing happened. "I don't see anything."

"Of course not," she said. "It's only been a minute. I told you this was an advanced spell. It may take a while for you to fully muster the strength and power you need. Stay on task. We'll be waiting."

The two of them left. I stared bleakly at the water, wondering how long "a while" was. I'd been excited when the spell seemed so simple originally. Now, I wished there were more ingredients to mix, more incantations to recite. This high-level

magic, relying on will and mental energy, was much more difficult—mainly because it was intangible. I liked the concrete. I
liked to know exactly what was needed to make something happen. Cause and effect.

But this? This was just me staring and staring, hoping I
was "staying fixed" and using "razor sharp focus." How would I
know if I was? Even if I achieved that state, it might still take a
while to manifest what I needed. I tried not to think of that yet.
Sonya. Sonya was all that mattered right now. All of my will and
energy had to go into saving her.

I kept telling myself that as the minutes ticked by. Each
time I was certain I should stop and ask Ms. Terwilliger what to
do, I would force myself to keep looking into the water. *Sonya,
Sonya. Think about Sonya.* And still, nothing happened. Finally,
when an ache in my back made sitting unbearable, I stood up to
stretch. The rest of my muscles were starting to cramp up too.
I walked back to the living room; almost an hour and a half had
passed since I'd last been out here.

"Anything?" asked Ms. Terwilliger.

"No," I said. "I must be doing something wrong."

"You're focusing your mind? Thinking about her? About
finding her?"

I was really tired of hearing the word *focus*. Frustration was
replacing my earlier anxiety about magic. "Yes, yes, and yes," I
said. "But it's still not working."

She shrugged. "And that's why we have a curfew extension.
Try again."

Adrian flashed me a sympathetic look and started to say
something—but then thought better of it. I nearly left but
paused as a troublesome thought nagged at me.

"What if she's not alive?" I asked. "Could that be why it's not working?"

Ms. Terwilliger shook her head. "No. You'd still see something if she wasn't. And . . . well, you'd know."

I returned to the workroom and tried again—with similar results. The next time I went to talk to Ms. Terwilliger, I saw that it hadn't been quite an hour. "I'm doing something wrong," I insisted. "Either that, or I messed up the initial spell. Or this really is beyond me."

"If I know you, the spell was flawless," she said. "And no, this isn't beyond you, but only you have the power to make it happen."

I was too tired to parse her esoteric philosophy nonsense. I turned without a word and trudged back to the workroom. When I reached it, I discovered I'd been followed. I looked up at Adrian and sighed.

"No distractions, remember?" I said.

"I won't stay," he said. "I just wanted to make sure you're okay."

"Yeah . . . I mean, I don't know. In as much as anyone can be with all of this." I nodded toward the silver plate. "Maybe I do need you to get me out of here."

He considered for a moment and then shook his head. "I don't think that's a good idea."

I stared up at him in disbelief. "What happened to me not having to do anything I didn't want to do? And you nobly defending me?"

One of his knowing little smiles played over his lips. "Well. That was back when you didn't want to do this because it challenged all your beliefs. Now that the line is crossed, your problem seems to be a little pessimism and not believing you can do this. And honestly, that's bullshit."

"A little pessimism?" I exclaimed. "Adrian, I've been staring at a bowl of water for over two hours! It's nearly one thirty. I'm exhausted, I want coffee, and every muscle in my body hurts. Oh, and I'm about ready to throw up from that incense."

"Those things all suck," he agreed. "But I seem to recall you giving all of us lectures recently about enduring hardships to do what's right. Are you saying you can't do that to help Sonya?"

"I would do anything to help her! Anything within my power, that is. And I don't think this is."

"I don't know," he speculated. "I've had a lot of time to talk to Jackie—she lets me call her that, you know—and I've learned all about this human magic stuff. There's a lot you can do with it."

"It's wrong," I grumbled.

"And yet here you are, with the ability to find Sonya." Adrian hesitated and then, reaching some decision, stepped toward me and rested his hands on my shoulders. "Jackie told me that you're one of the most naturally gifted people she's ever encountered for this kind of stuff. She said that with a little practice, a spell like this'll be cake for you, and she's certain you can pull it off now. And I believe her. Not because I have proof you're magically talented but because I've seen how you approach everything else. You won't fail at this. You don't fail at anything."

I was so exhausted I thought I might cry. I wanted to fall forward and have him carry me out of here, like he'd promised earlier. "That's the problem. I don't fail, but I'm afraid I will now. I don't know what it's like. And it terrifies me." *Especially because Sonya's life depends on me.*

Adrian reached out and traced the lily on my cheek. "You won't have to find out what it's like tonight because you aren't going to fail. You can do this. And I'll be here with you as long as it takes, okay?"

I took a deep breath and tried to calm myself. "Okay."

I returned to my stool after he left and tried to ignore the fatigue in my body and mind. I thought about what he'd said, about how I wouldn't fail. I thought about his faith in me. And most importantly, I thought about Sonya. I thought about how desperately I wanted to help her.

All these things churned within me as I stared at the water, crystal clear except for the hair floating in it. One red line against all that silver. It was like a spark of fire, a spark that grew brighter and brighter in my eyes until it took on a more definite shape, a circle with stylized lines radiating from it. A sun, I realized. Someone had painted an orange sun onto a piece of plywood and hung it on a chain-link fence. Even with the shoddy canvas, the artist had gone to a lot of care in painting the sun, stylizing the rays and making sure the lengths were consistent with each other. The fence itself was ugly and industrial, and I caught sight of what looked like an electrifying box hanging on it. The landscape was brown and barren, but mountains in the distance told me it was still the greater Palm Springs area. This was kind of like the area Wolfe lived in, outside of town and away from the pretty greenery. Through the fence, beyond the sign, I caught sight of a large, sprawling building—

"Ow!"

The vision vanished as my head hit the floor. I had fallen off the stool.

I managed to sit up, but that was all I could do. The world

was spinning, and my stomach felt queasy and empty. After what could have been three seconds or three hours, I heard voices and footsteps. Strong arms caught hold of me, and Adrian helped me to my feet. I clung to the table while he picked the stool up and helped me sit back down. Ms. Terwilliger pushed the silver plate aside and replaced it with an ordinary kitchen plate filled with cheese and crackers. A glass of orange juice soon joined it.

"Here," she said. "Eat these. You'll feel better."

I was so disoriented and weak that I didn't even hesitate. I ate and drank as though I hadn't eaten in a week while Adrian and Ms. Terwilliger waited patiently. It was only when I'd practically licked the plate clean that I realized what I'd just consumed.

"Havarti and orange juice?" I groaned. "That's too much fat and sugar for this time of night."

Adrian scoffed. "Glad to see there's no lasting damage."

"Get used to it if you're going to be using magic a lot," said Ms. Terwilliger. "Spells can deplete you. Not unusual at all to have your blood sugar drop afterward. Orange juice will become your best friend."

"I'll never get used to it, seeing as I'm not going to—" I gasped, as the images I'd seen in the silver plate came tumbling back to me. "Sonya! I think I saw where she's at." I described what I'd seen, though none of us had any clue about where or what this place might be.

"You're sure it was like a regular sun? With rays?" asked Adrian. "Because I thought the hunters used that old Alchemist one—the circle and dot."

"They do, but this was definitely—oh God." I looked up at Adrian. "We have to get back to Amberwood. Right now."

"Not after that," said Ms. Terwilliger. She was using her stern teacher voice. "That took more from you than I expected. Sleep here, and I'll make sure everything's cleared up with Desiree and the school tomorrow."

"No." I stood up and felt my legs start to buckle, but in the end, they held. Adrian put a supportive arm around me, clearly not believing in my body's recovery. "I have to get back there. I think I know how we can find out where this place is."

Adrian was right that the sun I'd just described wasn't the design that had been on the sword or brochure. Both of those had used the ancient symbol. The one in my vision was a more modern adaptation—and this wasn't the first time I'd seen it.

The sun in my vision was an exact match for Trey's tattoo.

CHAPTER 20

GETTING TO TREY was easier said than done. A girl getting into the guys' dorm at normal hours would've been difficult enough. But after curfew? In the middle of the night? Nearly impossible. I had to resort to creative options and called Eddie while I was driving Adrian home. One thing I never had to feel guilty about was calling Eddie at any hour. He kept his ringer on (much to Micah's delight, no doubt), and I suspected he slept with the phone next to his pillow.

"Yes?" Eddie's voice was alert and ready, as though he hadn't been asleep at all. That was just how he was.

"I need you to go see if you can wake up Trey," I told him. "Sonya's been kidnapped and is being held at some weird compound with a logo like Trey's tattoo. We need to find out what he knows."

This was the first time Eddie was hearing about Sonya's kidnapping, but he didn't ask for further information—or how I'd known her location. He knew she'd been in danger recently, and this quick message was enough to get him going. I didn't exactly know what would happen when Eddie did find Trey, seeing as there was no way I'd be able to talk to Trey myself until morning. Still, we had to start somewhere.

"Okay," said Eddie. "I'm on it. I'll call you back."

We disconnected, and I stifled a yawn. "Well, here goes nothing. Let's hope Eddie can find out something."

"Preferably without beating up Trey in the process," said Adrian. He snuggled against the passenger seat, the only sign that he too was feeling tired from our late night. He'd long since converted from a vampire's nocturnal schedule. "Since that might limit how much we can find out."

I made a face. "If Trey's somehow involved with this, I'm not sure I want to take it easy on him. And yet . . . I just can't believe he is."

"People fool each other all the time. Look at you. You think Trey knows you're part of a secret society helping to keep vampires hidden from the world?"

"Actually . . . yes." I stopped at a red light and thought back on some of Trey's weird behaviors. "He knows Jill's a Moroi, I'm almost certain of it. He didn't notice right away, but when he did, he kept telling me to keep her hidden. Then after Sonya was attacked, he told *me* to stay safe." A horrible realization was dawning on me. "He knew. He knew I was friends with Sonya. He probably knew about the attack and never said anything!"

"Not a surprise if his group's working counter to yours." Adrian's tone softened. "If it makes you feel better, it sounds like he was kind of conflicted if he was trying to warn you."

"I don't know that it does. Oh, Adrian." I pulled up in front of his building and saw the yellow Mustang illuminated in the streetlight. "You left the car out. You're lucky it didn't get towed."

"I'll move it," he said. "And don't look at me like that. It's within a half-mile radius. I'm not breaking your rules."

"Just be careful," I muttered.

He opened Latte's door and glanced back at me. "You sure you want to go back to the school? You'll be locked in until morning."

"Not much I can do until then anyway. I want to be there the instant I can get access to Trey. I'll trust in Eddie for now."

Adrian looked reluctant to leave me but finally nodded. "Call if you need anything. I'm going to keep trying to see if I can find Sonya in her dreams. Didn't have much luck earlier."

One of spirit's more disconcerting powers was the user's ability to intrude on the dreams of other people. "Is she just not asleep?"

"That, or drugged."

Neither option made me feel any better. He gave me one last, lingering look before leaving. I returned to Amberwood where a sleepy student aide waved me in without comment. Mrs. Weathers had long since gone home, and her overnight coverage didn't seem particularly concerned about my comings and goings. As I was walking up the stairs, my phone rang. Eddie.

"Well, it took forever, but I finally woke his roommate up," he told me.

"And?"

"He's not there. I guess he wasn't last night either. Some kind of family emergency."

"No word on when he'll be back?" I was beginning to think

all of Trey's "family stuff" might be more insidious than I'd guessed. I was also willing to bet he wasn't the only one with a sun tattoo.

"No."

I DRIFTED IN AND OUT of sleep that night. My body was exhausted from the magic, but I was too on edge about Sonya to fully give in to the fatigue. I keep waking up and checking my cell phone, afraid I'd missed some call—despite the fact that it was on its loudest setting. I finally gave up and got out of bed a couple of hours before the cafeteria's breakfast began. By the time I'd showered and dressed—and put my coffee maker into high gear—I was back into open hours on campus. Not that it did me much good.

I made two more calls after that, first to Spencer's to see if Trey was working. I didn't expect him to be, but it was a good excuse to see if he'd been there in the last couple of days. He hadn't been. My next call was to Stanton, reporting Sonya's disappearance. I told her we had a lead that connected one of my classmates to the vampire hunters and that Sonya was likely being held at a compound outside of town. I didn't elaborate on how I knew, and Stanton was distracted enough by the kidnapping in general to ask much more.

At breakfast, I found my "family" sitting with Micah over at West's cafeteria. Eddie, Angeline, and Jill's troubled faces told me they all knew about Sonya. Micah was cheerfully chatting about something, and I had a feeling his presence was preventing the others from discussing what they really wanted to. When Micah turned to ask Eddie something, I leaned over and murmured to Jill, "Get him out of here."

"Tell him to go?" she whispered back.

"If you need to. Or go with him."

"But I want to—"

She bit her lip as Micah's attention returned to her. She looked unhappy about what she had to do, but soon put on the resolved expression that recently I'd often seen her wear. She nodded toward Micah's plate. "Hey, are you about done? I need to check on something with Miss Yamani. Will you come with me?"

Micah brightened. "Of course."

Once the two of them were gone, I turned to Eddie and Angeline. "Any sign of Trey?" I asked.

"No," said Eddie. "I checked in again this morning. His roommate's starting to hate me. Can't say I blame him."

"This is driving me crazy!" I said, feeling like I could beat my head against the wall. "We're so close and yet helpless. Every minute that goes by is another that Sonya doesn't have."

He grimaced. "Are we sure she's alive?"

"She was last night," I said.

Both Eddie and Angeline looked at me in amazement. "How do you know?" she asked.

"Um, well, I—no way!" My jaw dropped as I stared past Eddie. "It's Trey!"

Sure enough, a bleary-eyed Trey had just entered the cafeteria. Damp hair indicated a recent shower, but there were bruises and scrapes all over him that I could no longer attribute to football.

Eddie was in motion before I could say another word, and Angeline and I were quick to follow. I half-expected Eddie to tackle Trey then and there. Instead, Eddie walked right in front

341

of Trey and blocked him from entering the food line. I was just in time to hear Eddie say, "No breakfast today. You're coming with us."

Trey started to protest and then saw Angeline and me. Jill suddenly appeared as well, having apparently lost Micah. A sad look crossed Trey's features—almost defeated—and he gave a weary nod. "Let's go outside."

As soon as we'd cleared the door, Eddie grabbed hold of Trey and shoved him against the building. "Where's Sonya Karp?" Eddie demanded. Trey looked understandably surprised. Eddie was lean and muscled, but most people underestimated just how strong he was.

"Eddie, back off!" I hissed, glancing around uneasily. I had the same urge, true, but our interrogation wouldn't get very far if a teacher came by and thought we were roughing up another student.

Eddie released Trey and stepped back, but there was still a dangerous glint in his eyes. "Where's the compound you're holding her at?"

That seemed to wake Trey out of his sluggish state. "How do you know about that?"

"We'll ask the questions," said Eddie. He didn't touch Trey again, but his proximity and posture left no question he would go to extremes if needed. "Is Sonya still alive?"

Trey hesitated, and I almost expected a denial of knowledge. "Y-yes. For now."

Eddie snapped again. He grabbed the front of Trey's shirt and jerked him close. "I swear, if you and your messed-up associates lay one hand on her—"

"Eddie," I warned.

For a moment, Eddie didn't move. Then, reluctantly, he released Trey's shirt, but stayed where he'd been standing. "Trey," I began, keeping the same reasonable tone I'd just used with Eddie—after all, Trey and I were friends, right? "You have to help us. Please help us find Sonya."

He shook his head. "I can't, Sydney. It's for your own good. She's evil. I don't know what trick she's played on you or how she's got this illusion going on that hides her true identity, but you can't trust her. She'll turn on you. Let us—let us do what we need to."

The words were all correct, right in line with the Warriors' propaganda. But, there was something in the way Trey spoke, something about his posture . . . I couldn't quite put my finger on what it was that made me question him. People teased me about my inability to pick up on social cues, but I was almost certain he wasn't entirely on board with whatever this group wanted him to do.

"This isn't you, Trey," I said. "I know you well enough to know. You wouldn't kill an innocent woman."

"She's not innocent." There it was again—that mix of emotions. Doubt. "She's a monster. You know about them. You know what they can do. Not ones like her." He nodded toward Jill. "But the others. The undead ones."

"Does Sonya look undead?" asked Eddie. "You see any red eyes?"

"No," Trey admitted. "But we have other reports. Witnesses who saw her in Kentucky. Reports of her victims."

It was hard to keep a calm face through that. I'd actually seen Sonya when she was Strigoi. She'd been terrifying, and given half a chance, she would have killed my companions and me. It was hard to accept that when one turned into a Strigoi, they weren't in control of their senses or soul. They lost touch with their humanity—or whatever Moroi had—and weren't the same as they'd once been. Sonya had done terrible, terrible things, but she was no longer that creature.

"Sonya changed," I said. "She's not one of them anymore."

Trey's eyes narrowed. "That's impossible. You're being deceived. There's some kind of . . . I don't know . . . dark magic going on."

"This isn't getting us anywhere," growled Eddie. "Call Dimitri. Between the two of us, we'll get him to tell us where this compound's at. I've broken into a prison. Getting into this place shouldn't be that much harder."

"Oh, you think so?" A humorless smile crossed Trey's features. "That place is surrounded with an electric fence and packed with armed men. Plus, she's heavily secured. You can't just walk in there."

"Why is she still alive?" asked Angeline. She seemed to realize how weird that sounded and was quick to elaborate. "That is . . . I mean, I'm glad she is. But if you think she's so evil, why didn't you finish her off?" She glanced at my friends and me. "Sorry."

"It's a good question," Eddie told her.

Trey took a long time in answering. I had a feeling he was torn between keeping the group's secrets and wanting to justify his actions to us. "Because we're all being tested," he said finally. "To see who's worthy of performing the kill."

"Oh my God," said Jill.

"Hence all your bruises recently," I said. My fears of

domestic abuse weren't far off, really. "You're competing to kill a woman who's done nothing to you."

"Stop saying that!" Trey cried, truly looking distraught. "She's not innocent."

"But you're not so sure," I said. "Are you? Your eyes aren't telling you what your hunter friends are."

He evaded the accusation. "My family expects this of me. We all have to try—especially after we messed up the alley attack. We lost our authorization to kill her then, which is why the council ordered these trials to redeem ourselves and prove we were up to it." Getting "authorization" to kill someone was sickening, but it was the rest of what he said that made me do a double take.

"You were there," I said in disbelief. "In the alley, and—and it was you! You're the one who grabbed me!" It came back to me now, my assailant's surprise and hesitation.

Trey's face confirmed as much. "I knew you were friends with them. I can tell by looking at all of you, although I didn't figure you two out right away." That was to Eddie and Angeline. Trey turned back to me. "I recognized your tattoo the first time we met. I just ignored it because I didn't think you were involved in anything that I was. I thought you only hung out with harmless vampires, so I didn't expect you to be there that night. I never wanted you to get hurt. I still don't, which is why you need to let this go."

"I'm tired of this," said Eddie. It was a wonder he'd been patient this long. "We need to bust down the doors of that place and—"

"Wait, wait." An idea was forming in my head—and it was

another crazy one. "Trey, you said Eddie couldn't just walk into that place. But could I?"

"What are you talking about?" asked Trey, a mix of suspicion and confusion on his face

"You know what I am. You know what I do." Trey nodded. "Our two groups used to be united. Those guys who stopped me on the street even said they thought we should all be working together. The Warriors want Alchemist resources."

"So, what . . . you want a trade?" asked Trey, frowning.

"No. I just want to talk to this council of yours. I want to explain why Sonya isn't . . . er, why she doesn't look the way she used to. There's a Moroi who uses a certain kind of magic who could even show you—"

"No," said Trey immediately. "None of *them* would be allowed inside. They're tolerated, but that's it. You hybrids wouldn't be allowed either." Again, he spoke to Eddie and Angeline. I'd never heard the term *hybrids* used, but the meaning was clear.

"Okay," I said. "Only humans. I'm human. Your group wants to work with my group. Let me go with you. Unarmed. I'll talk to your leaders and—"

"Sydney, no," protested Eddie. "You can't go there alone! They tried to decapitate Sonya, for God's sake. And remember what Clarence said about radicals stalking him?"

"We won't hurt humans," said Trey adamantly. "She'd be safe."

"I believe you," I told him. "And I know you wouldn't ever let anything happen to me either. Look, aren't you curious about why Sonya is the way she is? Can you take the chance your people are making a mistake? You said you tolerate Moroi. She's one of them. Let me explain. I'm not asking for anything else except a chance to speak."

"And a guarantee of safety," added Angeline, who looked almost as outraged as Eddie. He nodded at her words. "You guys are big on the honor stuff, right? You'd have to promise she'd be safe."

"Honor's what makes us do what we do," said Trey. "If we promise she'll be safe, she will be."

"Then ask them," I urged. "Please? Won't you do this for me? As my friend?"

A pained look crossed Trey's features at that. He'd hinted before that he owed me for helping end the illicit tattoo ring last month. That would obligate any friend, let alone one instilled with a rigid sense of honor. I knew then, too, that more than honor was on the line here. Trey and I were friends—with more in common than I'd ever realized. We both were part of groups that wanted to control our lives, often in ways we didn't like. We also had domineering fathers. If Trey and I didn't have such opposing goals, we might have laughed about all this.

"I'll ask," Trey said. Something told me he too was thinking of our similarities. "Because it's you. But I can't make any promises."

"Then ask now," growled Eddie. "We don't have time to waste. And I'm guessing Sonya doesn't either."

Trey didn't deny it. I hesitated, suddenly wondering if this was a smart choice. What would happen if we let Trey out of our sight? Would it be better if we really did drag him to Dimitri? And Sonya . . . how much time did she have left?

"Now," I reiterated to Trey. "You have to get in touch with them now. Don't go to class." It was probably the first and only time I'd say those words.

"I swear," said Trey. "I'll call them now."

The bell rang, ending our meeting. Although, if we'd had the chance to save Sonya at that moment, I knew each of my friends would have walked off campus then and there. We let Trey go, and he headed back toward his dorm, not toward our classes. Angeline—newly free from suspension—departed with Jill while Eddie and I walked to history.

"That was a mistake," he said, face grim as he stared at where Trey had gone. "For all we know, he's going to disappear, and we'll have lost any chance we had at getting Sonya back."

"I don't think he will," I said. "I know Trey. He's a good person, and I could tell that even if he thinks Strigoi need to be exterminated, he's not 100 percent sure of Sonya. He'll do what he can. I think he's feeling torn right now, caught between what they've told him his whole life and what he's starting to see with his own eyes."

Sound like anyone else you know? an inner voice asked.

I'd sort of hoped that Trey would give me an answer right away—say, by chemistry. But he wasn't there either or anywhere else at school the day. I supposed these things took time, and my patience and faith were rewarded at the end of the day with a text from him: *Still checking. Some are willing to talk. Others need convincing.*

Eddie didn't take Trey's message as concrete proof when I showed it to him, but I didn't think Trey would've said anything if he'd skipped town. Eddie wanted to get together with Dimitri and discuss strategy on this new development. So, we decided to take a group trip downtown. I sent the summons to our family to meet outside the East dorm in a half hour. Jill was the first one to arrive, and she came to a halt when she saw me.

"Wow, Sydney . . . your hair."

I glanced up from where I'd been answering a text from Brayden, telling him I couldn't hang out this weekend. "What about it?"

"The way those layers are styled. They perfectly complement your face."

She was looking at me in that weird way again. "Well, yeah," I said, hoping to change the subject. "It's a, um, good haircut. Sorry we had to get rid of Micah earlier."

It took her a few seconds, but my distraction snapped her out of the hair-induced trance. "Oh, no. It's okay. I mean, things are getting weirder between us anyway."

"Oh?" Micah had seemed as chipper as ever, the last time I saw him. "You guys are still having problems?"

"Well . . . I guess I am. I really like him. I love hanging out with him and his friends. But I just keep getting reminded of how nothing can happen with us. Like, this morning. There's a whole other world we have going that he can't be a part of. And I can't stand the thought of lying to him or keeping him out of my life. I might have to do it . . . for real. End things. I know I've kind of said that before, but now I mean it."

"We're here for you if you do," I said. I technically meant it, but if Jill came sobbing to me afterward, I wasn't entirely sure what I should say. Maybe I could find a book on appropriate breakup counseling techniques before she did the deed.

A wry smile crossed her face. "You know what's silly? I mean, I don't want to go jumping from one guy to another—and I do still care about Micah—but I'm starting to notice what a really good guy Eddie is."

"He's a *great* guy," I confirmed.

"Moroi and dhampirs being together are discouraged when they're older, but now . . . I mean, I knew some who got together at St. Vladimir's." She gave an embarrassed laugh. "I know, I know . . . I shouldn't even be thinking like that. One guy at a time. But still . . . the more I see Eddie—he's just so brave and so confident. He'd do anything for us, you know? He's like some storybook hero in real life. But he's so dedicated, he'd probably never be interested in someone like me. No time for dating."

"Actually," I said, "I think he'd be very interested in you."

Her eyes widened. "Really?"

I wanted to tell her everything. Instead, I chose my words carefully, unwilling to give away his secrets after he'd spoken to me before about letting him handle his own personal affairs. "He talks all the time about how smart and competent you are. I think he'd definitely be open to something." He also talked about how he wasn't worthy of her love, but that resolve might fade if Jill actively went after him.

She grew lost in thought, and no more was said on the topic when Eddie and Angeline came walking up. We drove into town, and I dropped Jill and the two dhampirs off at Adrian's while I ran a few errands. Waiting for Trey was agonizing, and I needed distraction. Plus, I was low on some Alchemist supplies and wanted to make sure I was up to full strength before any venture into the Warriors' camp.

My phone rang as we were wrapping up. It was Trey, and I stepped outside an herbal store to take the call.

"Okay," he said. "You're good to go. They'll meet with you tonight—just you."

Anxiety and excitement raced through me. Tonight. It seemed surprisingly soon, yet that was exactly what I wanted. We needed to get Sonya out of there.

"I'll take you there at seven," Trey continued. "And . . . well, I'm sorry . . . but you'll have to go blindfolded. And I'll be checking to make sure no one follows us. If they do, everything's off."

"I understand," I said, though a blindfold certainly made the venture scarier. "I'll be ready. Thank you, Trey."

"Also," he added, "we want the sword back."

I made arrangements for him to pick me up at Adrian's, since I had a feeling Dimitri and Eddie would have a lot to say to me beforehand. In fact, I called them as soon as I was off the phone with Trey, to give them a heads-up. I also called Stanton to give her an update. It occurred to me I should have checked with her sooner, but I'd wanted a definitive answer from Trey first.

"I don't like the idea of you going alone," she said. "But it does seem unlikely they'd hurt you. They really do seem to stay away from humans—us in particular. And if there's a chance to get Karp out of there . . . well. That would save us a lot of fallout with the Moroi." Stanton's tone told me, however, that even if she thought I'd be safe, she wasn't so optimistic about Sonya. "Be careful, Miss Sage."

Adrian's apartment was filled with tension when I arrived. Dimitri, Eddie, and Angeline were clearly agitated, probably because they were being left out of the action. Adrian, surprisingly, looked upset too, though I couldn't figure out why. Jill watched him with concern, and they kept staring at each other, unseen messages undoubtedly passing to her through the bond. At last, he averted his gaze, like he was ending a conversation. Jill sighed and walked toward the others in the kitchen.

I started to speak to Adrian, but Eddie beckoned me forward. "We're debating on whether to give you a weapon or not," he said.

"Well, the answer is 'not,'" I said immediately. "Come on, they're blindfolding me. Do you think they won't search me for weapons too?"

"There must be a way," said Dimitri. Since we were in air conditioning, he wore the duster. "I can't let you go in there defenseless."

"I'm not in danger," I said, feeling like I'd been repeating the same thing all day. "They might be crazy, but Trey says if they give their word, they'll stick to it."

"Sonya doesn't have those guarantees," Dimitri pointed out.

"No weapon is going to help me save her," I said. "Except for my reasoning. And I'm armed with that about as well as I can be."

The dhampirs still didn't seem happy. They went back to arguing amongst themselves, and I left them to find some water. Adrian called to me from the living room. "There's diet pop in there."

I opened the refrigerator. Sure enough, it was stocked with all kinds of pop. And, in fact, it had more food than I'd ever seen. Another benefit of Nathan Ivashkov's generosity. I grabbed a can of Diet Coke and joined Adrian on the couch.

"Thanks," I said, opening the can. "This is the next best thing you could have to gelato."

He raised an eyebrow. "Gelato? Sounds like dessert to me, Sage."

"It is," I admitted. The mundane topic was comforting amidst all the tension. "It's kind of your fault for bringing it up yesterday. Now I can't stop thinking about it. I wanted some at dinner last night, and Brayden talked me out of it—which is probably why I'm even more obsessed with it. Ever had that happen? Once you can't have something, you want it that much more."

"Yes," he said bitterly. "It happens all the time."

"Why are you so down? You think I should have a weapon, too?" With Adrian, it was really hard to guess where his moods would go.

"No, I get your point, and I think you're right," he said. "Not that I like the idea of you going there at all."

"I have to help Sonya," I said.

He studied me and smiled. "I know you do. I wish I could come with you."

"Oh yeah? You going to protect me and carry me out of there like you threatened to do last night?" I teased.

"Hey, if that's what it takes. You and Sonya. I'll toss one of you ever each shoulder. Pretty manly, huh?"

"Very," I said, happy to see him joking again.

His amusement faded, and he became serious again. "Let me ask you something. Which is scarier: walking into a den of crazy, murdering humans or being with safe—though kind of wacky—vampires and half vampires? I know the hang-up you Alchemists have with us, but is the loyalty to your own race so strong that . . . I don't know . . . that the people themselves don't matter?"

It was a surprisingly deep question for Adrian. It also echoed my trip to the Alchemist bunker to see Keith. I was reminded of how Keith's father hadn't cared about his son's moral character so long as it meant Keith wasn't on good terms with vampires. I also thought back to the alley and how obstinate the Warriors were about hearing any truth but their own. And finally, I looked over at the dhampirs arguing in the kitchen, continuing to brainstorm covert ways of keeping Sonya and me safe, no matter the risk.

I turned back to Adrian. "I'd take the vampires. Loyalty to one's kind can only go so far."

Something in Adrian's face transformed, but I hardly paid it any attention. I was too struck by the realization that the words I'd just uttered were akin to high treason in the Alchemists.

Eddie and Angeline left later to get us dinner, and I let them take my car, so long as Eddie drove. While they were gone, Dimitri tried to drill in some more self-defense techniques, but it was hard to learn very much in so short a time. I kept thinking of Wolfe warning us to avoid dangerous places. What would he say about me walking into a den of armed vampire hunters?

Eddie and Angeline were gone for a while and finally returned, angry at how long the restaurant had taken. "I didn't think we weren't going to be back in time," said Eddie. "I was afraid you wouldn't get food before your mission."

"I don't even know if I can eat," I admitted. Despite my earlier brave words, I was starting to grow nervous. "Oh, you can keep those in case you need the car."

He'd walked over to my purse with the keys and dropped them in anyway. "Are you sure?"

"Positive."

He shrugged and then fished the keys out again. Adrian, to

my surprise, watched him with narrowed eyes and seemed upset about something. I couldn't keep up with his moods today. He stood up and walked over to Eddie. After a few moments, they moved even farther away and seemed to be having a whispered argument, one that involved a few glances at me. Everyone else looked uncomfortable and suddenly jumped in with any conversation topics they could find. I could only stare back and forth, feeling like I had missed something important.

Trey called me at seven on the dot, saying he was waiting out front. I rose from my chair and picked up the sword, taking a deep breath. "Wish me luck."

"I'll walk you out," said Adrian.

"Adrian," warned Dimitri.

Adrian rolled his eyes. "I know, I know. Don't worry. I promised."

Promised what? Nobody elaborated. There wasn't far to walk since he lived on the ground floor, but when we stepped outside, he caught hold of me, his hands resting on my arms. A jolt went through me, both at the touch and the unexpected gesture. His only displays of tenderness were usually with Jill.

"Sage," he said. "For real. Be careful. Don't be a hero—we've got plenty of them back there. And . . . no matter what happens, I want you to know that I never doubted what you're going to do. It's smart, and it's brave."

"You sound like it's already happened and failed," I said.

"No, no. I just . . . well, I want you to know that *I* trust you."

"Okay," I said, feeling a little puzzled. I again had the feeling that I wasn't being told something. "Hopefully my plan will work."

I needed to walk away, out of Adrian's grasp, but couldn't

quite do it. I was hesitant to go, for some reason. There was safety and comfort there. Once I left, I really was walking into the lion's den. I lingered a few moments more, safe in the circle we made, and then reluctantly slipped away.

"Please be careful," he repeated. "Come back safe."

"I will." On impulse I took off my cross necklace and pressed it into his hand. "This time, keep it for real. Hold onto it until I return. If you get too worried, look at it and know that I'll *have* to come back for it. It goes really well with khakis and neutral colors."

I worried he would give it back, but he simply nodded and squeezed the cross tight. I walked away, feeling slightly vulnerable without it, but hoped it reassured him. My discomfort suddenly seemed like a small thing. I wanted Adrian to be okay.

I got into the passenger seat of Trey's car and immediately gave him the sword. He looked about as miserable as he had earlier. "You sure you want to go through with this?"

Why did everyone keep asking me that? "Yes. Absolutely."

"Let me see your cell phone."

I handed it over, and he turned it off. He gave it back, along with a blindfold. "I'll trust you to put this on yourself."

"Thanks."

I started to slip it on and then, on impulse, looked back toward the building one last time. Adrian was still standing there, hands in his pockets, face concerned. Seeing my gaze, he managed a small smile and raised one hand in . . . what? Farewell? A benediction? I didn't know, but it made me feel better. The last thing I saw was the flash of the cross in the sunlight, just before I covered my eyes with the blindfold.

I was plunged into darkness.

CHAPTER 21

I'D SEEN MOVIES where blindfolded people were able to tell where they were going, based on some innate talent to sense motion and direction. Not me. After a few turns, I couldn't have told you where in Palm Spring we were—especially since I suspected Trey was taking a slightly roundabout way in order to make sure there wasn't a tail. The only thing I was certain of was when we got on I-10, simply because of the feel of the freeway. I didn't know what direction we were headed and had no way to accurately time how long we traveled either.

Trey didn't offer much in the way of conversation, though he did give short answers whenever I asked questions. "When did you join the vampire hunters?"

"Warriors of Light," he corrected. "And I was born into it."

"That's why you're always talking about family pressure and why so much is expected of you, isn't it? It's why your dad is so concerned about your athletic performance."

I took Trey's silence as an affirmative and pushed on,

needing to get as much information as possible. "How often do you guys have your, um, meetings? Are you always having those brutal tests?" Until very recently, there had been nothing to suggest Trey's life was much different from any other high school athlete who kept up with his grades, a job, and an active social life. In fact, thinking of all the things Trey usually did, it was hard to imagine him having any time at all for the Warriors.

"We don't have regular meetings," he said. "Well, not someone at my level. We wait until we're called, usually because a hunt's under way. Or sometimes we conduct competitions, in order to test our strength. Our leaders travel around, and then Warriors gather from all different places in order to be ready."

"Ready for what?"

"The day when we can end the vampire scourge altogether."

"And you really believe this hunt is the way to do it? That it's the right thing to do?"

"Have you ever seen them?" he asked. "The evil, undead vampires?"

"I've seen quite a few of them."

"And you don't think they should be destroyed?"

"That's not what I've been trying to tell you. I don't have any love for Strigoi, believe me. My point is that Sonya's not one of them."

More silence.

Eventually, I felt us exit the freeway. We drove for a while longer until the car slowed again and turned, onto a gravel road. We soon came to a stop, and Trey rolled down the window.

"This is her?" asked an unknown man.

"Yes," said Trey.

"You turned off her cell phone?"

"Yes."

"Take her in then. They'll do the rest of the search."

I heard a squeaking gate open, and then we continued on the gravel road until turning onto what felt like packed dirt. Trey stopped the car and turned it off. He opened his door at the same time someone on the outside opened mine. A hand on my shoulder nudged me forward.

"Come on. Get out."

"Be careful with her," warned Trey.

I was led from the car into a building. It wasn't until I heard a door shut and latch that my blindfold was finally taken off. I was in a stark room with unfinished drywall and bare bulb lights in the ceiling. Four other people stood around Trey and me, three men and one woman. All of them looked to be in their twenties, and two were the guys who had stopped me at the café. Also, all of them were armed.

"Empty out your purse." It was Jeff, the guy with buzzed dark hair, wearing a gold earring of the antique sun symbol.

I complied, dumping my purse's contents onto a makeshift table composed of plywood set on top of some cinderblocks. While they sifted through it, the woman patted me down for wires. She had hair with a bad bleach job and a perennial snarl on her face, but at least her frisk was professional and efficient.

"What's this?" Blond Hair from the café held up a small plastic bag filled with dried herbs and flowers. "You don't look like the drug type."

"It's potpourri," I said promptly.

"You keep potpourri in your purse?" he asked disbelievingly.

I shrugged. "We keep all sorts of things around. I took out all the acids and chemicals before I came here, though."

He dismissed the potpourri as harmless and tossed it into a pile with other cleared items, like my wallet, hand sanitizer, and a plain wooden bracelet. I noticed then that the pile also included a pair of earrings. They were round gold discs, covered in intricate swirls and tiny gems. They were beautiful—but I'd never seen them before.

I certainly wasn't going to call attention to anything, however, particularly when the woman snatched up my cell phone. "We should destroy this."

"I turned it off," said Trey.

"She might turn it back on. It can be tracked."

"She wouldn't," argued Trey. "Besides, that's a little paranoid, isn't it? No one has that kind of technology in real life."

"You'd be surprised," she said.

He held out his hand. "Give it to me. I'll keep it safe. She's here on good faith."

The woman hesitated until Jeff nodded. Trey slipped the phone into his pocket, and I was grateful. There were a lot of saved numbers that would be a pain to replace. Once my purse was deemed safe, I was allowed to put it back together and take it with me.

"Okay," said Blond Hair. "Let's go to the arena."

Arena? I had a hard time picturing what that would entail in a place like this. My vision in the silver plate hadn't shown me much of the building, save that it was single-story and had a ratty, worn look to it. This room seemed to be keeping right along with that theme. If the antiquated brochures were further proof of the Warriors' sense of style, I expected this "arena" to be in someone's garage.

I was wrong.

Whatever the Warriors of Light had lacked in other areas of their operation, they'd sunk it into the arena—or, as I was told its official name was, The Arena of Divine Radiance of Holy Gold. The arena had been built upon a clearing surrounded by several buildings. I wouldn't go so far as to call it a courtyard. It was bigger, and the ground was more of that sandy packed dirt we'd driven in on. This setup was far from polished or high tech, yet as I took it all in, I couldn't help but think of Trey saying the Warriors had come to town this week.

Because for them to have put this together so quickly . . . well, it was kind of impressive. And frightening. Two sets of rickety wooden bleachers had been erected on opposite sides of the space. One set held about fifty spectators, mostly men, of varying ages. Their eyes, suspicious and even hostile, were on me as I was led in. I could practically feel their gazes boring into my tattoo. Did they all know about the Alchemists and our history? They were all dressed in ordinary clothing, but here and there, I caught glimmers of gold. Many of them wore some kind of ornament—a pin, an earring, etc.—with either an ancient or modern sun symbol.

The other bleachers were nearly empty. Three men—older, closer to my dad's age—sat side by side. They were dressed in yellow robes covered in golden embroidery that glittered in the orange light of the setting sun. Golden helmets covered their heads and were engraved with the old sun symbol, the circle with the dot. They watched me as well, and I kept my head high, hoping I could hide the shaking of my hands. I couldn't present a convincing case for Sonya if I seemed intimidated.

Around the arena, draped on poles, were banners of all shapes and sizes. They were made of rich, heavy fabric that reminded me of medieval tapestries. Obviously, these weren't that old, but they nonetheless gave the place a luxurious and ceremonial feel. The banners' designs varied considerably. Some really did look straight out of history, showing stylized knights fighting against vampires. Looking at those gave me chills. I really had stepped back in time, into the fold of a group with a history as old as the Alchemists'. Other banners were more abstract, portraying the ancient alchemical symbols. Still others looked modern, depicting the sun on Trey's back. I wondered if that newer sun interpretation was meant to appeal to today's youth.

All the while, I kept thinking, *less than a week. They put all this together in less than a week. They travel around with all of this, ready to put it up at a moment's notice in order to conduct these competitions or executions. Maybe they are primitive, but that doesn't make them any less dangerous.*

Although the large crowd of spectators had a rough-and-tumble look to them, like some sort of backwoods militia, it was a relief that they didn't appear to be armed. Only my escort was. A dozen guns were still too many for my tastes, but I'd take what I could get—and hope that they mostly kept the guns for show. We reached the bottom of the empty stands, and Trey came to stand beside me.

"This is the high council of the Warriors of Light," said Trey. He pointed to each of them in turn. "Master Jameson, Master Angeletti, and Master Ortega. This is Sydney Sage."

"You are very welcome here, little sister," said Master Angeletti in a grave voice. He had a long and messy beard. "The time for the healing of our two groups is long overdue. We will be much stronger once we put aside our differences and unite as one."

I gave him the politest smile I could and decided not to point out the Alchemists were unlikely to welcome gun-toting zealots into our ranks. "It's a pleasure to meet you, sirs. Thank you for allowing me to come. I'd like to talk to you about—"

Master Jameson held up a hand to stop me. His eyes looked too small for his face. "All in good time. First, we'd like to show you just how diligently we train our youth to fight in the great crusade. Just as you encourage excellence and discipline in the mind, so too do we encourage it in the body."

Through some unspoken cue, the door we'd just come through opened. A familiar face walked out to the center of the arena: Chris, Trey's cousin. He was wearing workout pants and no shirt, giving a clear view of the radiating sun tattooed on his back. He had a ferocious look on his face and came to stand in the clearing's center.

"I believe you've met Chris Juarez," said Master Jameson. "He's one of the finalists in this last round of combat. The other, of course, you also know. Quite the irony that cousins should be facing off, but also fitting since both failed in the initial attack on the fiend."

I turned to Trey, my jaw dropping. "You? You're one of the . . . contenders to kill Sonya?" I could barely get the words out. I turned back to the council in alarm. "I was told I'd have a chance to plead Sonya's case."

"You will," said Master Ortega, in a tone that implied it would be a wasted effort. "But first, we must determine our champion. Contenders, take your places."

I noticed now that Trey was also in sweatpants, looking as though he could be going off to football practice. He stripped off his shirt as well and, for lack of anything else to do with it, handed it to me. I took it and kept staring at him, still unable to believe what was happening. He met my gaze briefly but couldn't hold it. He walked off to join his cousin, and Master Jameson invited me to sit down.

Trey and Chris faced each other. I felt a little embarrassed to be studying two shirtless guys, but it wasn't like there was anything too sordid happening. My impressions of Chris since the first time I'd met him hadn't changed. Both he and Trey were in excellent physical shape, muscled and strong with the kinds of bodies that constantly worked and trained. The only advantage Chris had, if it was one, was his height—which I'd also noticed before. *His height.* With a jolt, memories of the alley attack came back to me. There'd been little of our attackers to see, but the one wielding the sword had been tall. Chris must have been the one originally assigned to kill Sonya.

Another robed man appeared from the door. His robes were cut slightly differently from the council's and somehow sported even more gold embroidery. Rather than a helmet, he wore a headdress more in line with what a priest might have. Indeed, that's what he seemed to be as Chris and Trey knelt before him. The priest marked their foreheads with oil and said some kind of blessing I couldn't hear. Then, to my shock, he made the sign against evil on his shoulder—the Alchemist sign against evil.

I think that, more so than any of the spiels about evil vampires or shared usage of ancient symbols, was what really drove home the fact that our two groups had once been related. The sign against evil was a small cross drawn on the shoulder with the right hand. It had survived among the Alchemists since ancient days. A chill ran through me. We really had been one and the same.

When the priest was finished, another man came forward and handed each of the cousins a short, blunt wooden club— kind of like what police sometimes used in crowd control. Trey and Chris turned toward each other, locked in aggressive poses, holding the clubs in striking positions. A buzz of excitement ran through the crowd, as it grew eager for violence. Evening breezes stirred up dust devils around the cousins, but neither of them flinched. I turned to the council incredulously.

"They're going to attack each other with those clubs?" I asked. "They could be killed!"

"Oh no," said Master Ortega, far too calmly. "We haven't had a death in these trials in years. They'll take injury, sure, but that just toughens our warriors. All of our young men are taught to endure pain and keep on fighting."

"Young men," I repeated. My gaze moved down to the bleach blonde girl who'd brought me in. She was standing near our bleachers, holding her gun at her side. "What about your women?"

"Our women are tough, too," said Master Ortega. "And certainly valued. But we'd never dream of letting them fight in the arenas or actively hunt vampires. Part of the reason we do what we do is to keep them safe. We're fighting this evil for their good and our future children."

The man who'd handed out the clubs also announced the rules in a loud, ringing voice that filled the arena. To my relief, the Juarez cousins wouldn't be beating each other senseless. There was a system to the combat they were about to enter into. They could only hit each other in certain places. Hitting elsewhere would result in penalties. A successful hit would yield a point. The first person to five points was the winner.

As soon as it started, however, it was clear this wasn't going to be as civilized as I'd hoped. Chris actually landed the first hit right away, nailing Trey so hard on the shoulder that I winced. Animalistic cheers and whoops rang out from the bloodthirsty crowd, echoed by hisses of dismay from Trey's supporters. Trey didn't even react and kept trying to hit Chris, but I could tell there'd be a nasty bruise there later. Both of them were pretty fast and alert, able to dodge a majority of the attempted blows. They danced around, trying to get through each other's guards. More dirt was kicked up, clinging to their sweaty skin. I found myself leaning forward, fists clenched in nervousness. My mouth felt dry, and I couldn't utter a sound.

In a remote way, I was reminded a little of the way Eddie and Angeline trained. Certainly, they walked away with injury too. In their situation, however, they were playing guardian and Strigoi. There was a difference between that and two guys striving to inflict the most damage on other. Watching Chris and Trey, I felt my stomach twist. I disliked violence, particularly this barbaric display. It was like I'd been transported back to the days of the gladiators.

The crowd's fervor continued to increase. It was on its feet cheering wildly and urging the cousins on. Their voices rang out in the desert night. Despite being struck first, Trey could clearly hold his own. I watched as he made hit after hit on Chris and wasn't sure which sickened me more: seeing my friend hurt or seeing him hurt someone else.

"This is terrible," I said, when I could finally find my voice.

"This is excellence in action," said Master Angeletti. "No surprise since their fathers are outstanding warriors as well. They sparred quite a bit in their youths, too. That's them, down in the front row."

I looked at where he indicated and saw two middle-aged men, side by side, with gleeful looks on their faces as they shouted encouragement at the cousins. I didn't even need Master Angeletti's guidance to guess that they were related. The Juarez family stamp was strong on these men and their sons. The fathers cheered just as avidly as the crowd, not even flinching when Trey or Chris got injured. It was just like my father and Keith's. Nothing mattered except family pride and playing by the group rules.

I'd lost track of the points until Master Jameson said, "Ah, this will be good. Next point determines the winner. It always makes me proud when the contenders are so evenly matched. Lets me know we've done the right thing."

There was nothing right about this. Tears stung my eyes, but whether it was from the dry, dusty air or simply my anxiety, I couldn't say. Sweat was pouring off Trey and Chris now, their chests rising and falling with the exertion of battle. Both were covered in scrapes and bruises, adding onto old ones from days past. The tension in the arena was palpable as everyone waited to see who would land the final hit. The cousins paused slightly, sizing up each other as they realized this was the moment of truth. This was the blow that had to count. Chris, face excited and alight, acted first, lunging forward to land a hit on the side of Trey's torso. I gasped, jumping to my feet in alarm with most of the crowd. The sound was deafening. It was clear from Chris's expression that he could taste victory, and I wondered if he was already imagining the strike that would kill Sonya. Sunset bathed his face in bloody light.

Maybe it was because I'd seen enough of Eddie to learn some of the basics, but I suddenly realized something. Chris's movement was too rash and sloppy. Sure enough, Trey was able to evade the strike, and I breathed a sigh of relief. I sank back down to my seat. Those who had been certain he was about to be taken out roared in outrage.

That left Trey with a beautiful opening to get in on Chris. My tension returned. Was this really any better? Trey "winning" the right to take a life? The point was moot. Trey didn't take the shot. I frowned as I watched. He didn't exactly fumble, but there was something that didn't seem right. There's a rhythm to fighting, where instinct and automatic responses take over. It was almost as though Trey had purposely fought against his next instinctive move, the one that said *strike now*! And in doing so, Trey left himself open. He took a hit from Chris, which knocked him to the ground. I rested a hand on my own chest, as though I'd also felt the blow.

The crowd went crazy. Even the decorous masters jumped up from their seats, screaming approval and dismay. I had to forcibly stay seated. Every part of me wanted to run down there and make sure Trey was okay, but I had a feeling one of the armed members of my escort would shoot me or knock me out before I took two steps. My worry faded a tiny bit when I saw Trey stagger to his feet. Chris clapped Trey good naturedly on the back, grinning from ear to ear as those assembled shouted his name.

Trey soon retreated to the crowded stands, yielding the victor's spot. His father met him with a look of disapproval but said nothing. The man who'd given out the clubs approached Chris with the sword I'd returned. Chris held it over his head, earning more applause. Near me, Master Jameson stood up and bellowed, "Bring out the creature!"

Creature was hardly how I'd describe Sonya Karp as four heavily armed Warriors dragged her out across the dusty arena. Her legs barely seemed to work, and even from this distance, I could tell she was drugged. That was why Adrian couldn't reach her in dreams. It also explained why she wouldn't have used any magic to attempt escape. Her hair was a mess, and she wore the same clothes I'd seen her in that last night at Adrian's. They were bedraggled, but otherwise, she didn't seem to have any signs of physical abuse on her.

This time, I couldn't stop myself from standing up. The blonde girl immediately put a hand on my shoulder, forcing me down. I stared at Sonya, wanting so desperately to help her, but knew I was powerless. Swallowing back fear and rage, I slowly sat back on the bleachers and turned toward the council.

"You told me I'd have a chance to talk." I remembered their sense of honor. "You gave your *word*. Doesn't that mean anything?"

"Our word means everything," said Master Ortega, looking offended. "You'll have your chance."

Behind Sonya's guard came two more men hauling a huge block of wood with arm constraints on it. It looked like it had come straight out of a medieval movie set, and my stomach twisted when I realized it was for: decapitation. The shadows had increased, forcing the men to bring out torches that cast sinister, flickering light around the arena. It was impossible to believe I was in twenty-first-century California. I felt like I'd been transported to some barbarian castle.

And really, these hunters were barbarians. One of Sonya's guards pushed her to her knees from behind, forcing her head against the block's surface while he bound her hands with the leather restraints. In her addled state, it didn't require nearly the level of force the guy put into it. I couldn't believe they could act so self-righteous when they were about to end the life of a woman who could offer no resistance, let alone even knew she was here. Everyone was screaming for her blood, and I felt like I was going to get sick.

Master Angeletti rose, and a hush fell over the arena. "We have gathered here from all parts of the country for a great thing. It is a rare and blessed day when we actually have a Strigoi in captivity." *Because she's not a Strigoi*, I thought angrily. They'd never be able to capture a live one. "They plague decent humans like ourselves, but today we shall dispatch one back to Hell—one who's particularly insidious because of her ability to hide her true nature and pretend to be one of the more benign fiends, the Moroi—whom we will deal with one day as well." Murmurs of approval ran through the crowd. "Before we commence, however, one of our Alchemist brethren would like to speak out on behalf of this creature."

The approval vanished, replaced by angry mutterings and glaring. I wondered uneasily if the guards who kept their guns pointed at me would turn on one of their associates if I was attacked. Master Angeletti held up his hands and silenced them.

"You will show our little sister respect," he said. "The Alchemists are kin, and once, we were one. It would be a momentous event if we could once again join forces."

With that, he sat down and gestured to me. Nothing else was offered, and I assumed this meant the floor was mine. I wasn't entirely sure how I was supposed to make my case or where. The council made the decisions, but this seemed like something everyone should hear. I stood up and waited for the girl with the gun to stop me from moving. She didn't. Slowly, carefully, I made my way down the bleachers and stood in the arena, mindful not to go near Sonya. I didn't think that would go over well.

I kept my body angled toward the council but turned my head in a way that would hopefully carry to others. I'd given reports and presentations before but always in a conference room. I'd never addressed an angry mob, let alone spoken to such a large group about vampire affairs. Most of the faces out there were swallowed by shadows, but I could picture all those mad, bloodthirsty eyes fixed on me. My mouth felt dry, and, in what was a very rare occurrence, my mind blanked. A moment later, I was able to push through my fear (though it certainly didn't go away), and remember what I'd wanted to say.

"You're making a mistake," I began. My voice was small, and I cleared my throat, forcing myself to project and sound stronger. "Sonya Karp is not a Strigoi."

"We have records of her in Kentucky," interrupted Master Jameson. "Eyewitnesses who saw her kill."

"That's because she was a Strigoi back then. But she isn't anymore." I kept thinking the tattoo would stop me from talking, but this group was already well aware of the vampiric world. "In the last year, the Alchemists have learned a lot about vampires. You must know that the Moroi—your so-called 'benign fiends'—practice elemental magic. We've recently found out there's a new, rare kind of magic out there, one that's tied to psychic powers and healing. That power has the ability to restore Strigoi back to their original form, be it human, dhampir, or Moroi."

A few angry denials quickly rose to a frenzy. Mob mentality

in action. It took Master Jameson to quiet them again. "That," he said simply, "is impossible."

"We have documented cases of three—no, four—people this has happened to. Three Moroi and a dhampir who once were Strigoi and are now in possession of their original selves and souls." Speaking about Lee in the present tense wasn't entirely accurate, but there was no need to clarify. Besides, describing a former Strigoi who wanted to become Strigoi again probably wouldn't help my case. "Look at her. Does she seem Strigoi? She's out in the sun." There wasn't much of it left, but even these fleeting rays of sunset would kill a Strigoi. With the way I was sweating from fear, I might as well have been out under a blazing mid-afternoon sun. "You keep saying this is the work of some twisted magic, but have you ever, even once, seen her in Strigoi form here in Palm Springs?"

No one acknowledged that right away. Finally, Master Angeletti said, "She defeated our forces in the street. Obviously, she turned back into her true form."

I scoffed. "She didn't do that. Dimitri Belikov did—one of the greatest dhampir warriors out there. No offense, but despite all the training, your soldiers were hopelessly outclassed." I was met with more aggressive gazes. I realized that probably wasn't the best thing I could've said.

"You've been deceived," said Master Angeletti. "No surprise since your people have long since become enmeshed behind the scenes with the Moroi. You aren't like us, down in the trenches. You don't come face-to-face with the Strigoi. They're evil, bloodthirsty creatures who must be destroyed."

"I agree with that. But Sonya's not one of them. Look at her." I was gaining courage, my voice growing stronger and clearer in the desert night. "You keep bragging about capturing some terrible monster, but all I see is a drugged, restrained woman. Nice work. Truly a worthy enemy."

None of the council looked nearly as tolerant of me as they had before. "We simply subdued her," said Master Ortega. "It's a sign of our prowess that we were able to do so."

"You've subdued an innocent and defenseless woman." I didn't know if driving home that point would help, but I figured it couldn't hurt if they had twisted, chivalrous views of women. "And I know you've made mistakes before. I know about Santa Cruz." I had no idea if this had been the same group whose men had gone after Clarence, but I was gambling the council at least knew about it. "Some of your more zealous members went after an innocent Moroi. You saw the errors of your way then when Marcus Finch told you the truth. It's not too late to correct this mistake either."

To my astonishment, Master Ortega actually smiled. "Marcus Finch? You're holding him up as some kind of hero?"

Not exactly, no. I didn't even know the guy. But if he was a human that talked these crazy people down, then he must have some kind of integrity.

"Why wouldn't I?" I asked. "He was able to see right from wrong."

Even Master Angeletti chuckled now. "I would never have expected an Alchemist to praise his sense of 'right and wrong.' I thought your own views of that were immovable."

"What are you talking about?" I didn't mean to get derailed, but these comments were too puzzling.

"Marcus Finch betrayed the Alchemists," explained Master Angeletti. "You didn't know? I assumed a rogue Alchemist is the last person you'd use to make your case."

I was momentarily speechless. Was he saying . . . was he saying that Marcus Finch used to be an Alchemist? No. He couldn't be. If he had been, then Stanton would have known who he was. *Unless she lied about not having any record of him,* a voice in my head warned.

Master Jameson had apparently heard enough from me. "We appreciate you coming out here and respect your attempt to stand up for what you believe is true. We're also glad you were able to see just how strong we've become. I hope you'll take this news back to your order. If anything, your attempts here have demonstrated what we've long known: our groups need each other. Clearly, the Alchemists have gleaned a lot of knowledge over the years that could be very useful to us—just as our strength could be useful to you. Nonetheless," he glanced over toward Sonya and scowled, "the point remains now that whatever your intentions, you truly have been deceived. Even if there's some tiny impossible chance that you're right, that she truly is a Moroi . . . we can't take the chance that she's still been corrupted. Even if she believes she's been restored, she may still have been subconsciously influenced."

Again, I was speechless—but not because I appeared to have lost my case. Master Jameson's words were nearly identical to what Keith's father had said, when he'd told me Keith would be taken back to Re-education. Mr. Darnell had echoed the sentiment, that they couldn't take the risk of even a subtle bit of influence affecting Keith. Extreme actions had been required. *We're the same,* I thought. *The Alchemists and the Warriors. Years have divided us, but we came from the same place—in both our goals and blind attitudes.*

And then Master Jameson said the most shocking thing of

all. "Even if she is just a Moroi, it's no great loss. We'll come for them eventually anyway, once we've defeated the Strigoi."

I froze at those words. The blonde girl came forward and again forced me to sit down on the first row of the bleachers. I offered no resistance, too shocked at what I'd just heard. What did they mean they'd come for the Moroi? Sonya could just be the beginning, then the rest of my friends, and then Adrian . . .

Master Angeletti snapped me back to the present. He made a grand gesture toward Chris as he spoke. "By the divine power we have been granted to bring light and purity into this world, you are authorized to destroy this creature. Commence."

Chris raised the sword, a fanatical gleam in his eyes. A happy gleam, even. He wanted to do this. He wanted to kill. Dimitri and Rose had killed many, many times, but both had told me there was no joy in it. They were glad to do what was right and defend others, but they didn't take pleasure in bringing death. I'd been taught the existence of vampires was wrong and twisted, but what I was about to witness was the true atrocity. These were the monsters.

I wanted to scream or cry or throw myself in front of Sonya. We were a heartbeat away from the death of a bright, caring person. Then, without warning, the silence of the arena was pierced with gunfire. Chris paused and lifted his head in surprise. I flinched and looked immediately toward the armed escort, wondering if they'd take it upon themselves to become a firing squad. They looked just as surprised as me—well, most of them. Two of them didn't show much emotion at all—because they were crumpled on the ground.

And that was when Dimitri and Eddie burst into the arena.

CHAPTER 22

SHOTS RANG OUT across the arena, taking down several more armed Warriors. I realized that Dimitri and Eddie weren't alone—because neither was holding a gun. The shots were coming from the roofs of the compound buildings that surrounded the arena. Chaos broke out as the gathered spectators jumped to their feet to join in the fray. My breath caught as I realized that many of them had their own weapons too. I was shocked to notice that the fallen Warrior on the ground next to me wasn't bleeding. A small dart hung from his shoulder. The sharpshooters' "bullets" must have been tranquilizers. Who were they?

I looked back toward the entrance and saw that a few others with the look of guardians had entered the arena and were fighting with some of the Warriors, including Chris. This provided cover for Dimitri and Eddie to free Sonya. A flash of strawberry blonde hair caught my eye near them, and I recognized Angeline's lithe figure. Dimitri efficiently cut Sonya's straps then helped lift her toward Eddie. A zealous Warrior came at them, and Angeline quickly knocked him out—as though he were a motivational speaker.

Beside me, one of the masters shouted, "Get the Alchemist girl! Hold her hostage! They'll negotiate for her!"

The Alchemist girl. Right. That would be me.

In the roar of fighting, hardly anyone heard him—save one. The bleach blonde girl had managed to evade being tranquilized. She leapt toward me. My adrenaline kicked in, and I was suddenly no longer afraid. With reflexes I didn't know I had, I reached into my purse and pulled out the so-called "potpourri." I ripped it open and flung it out around me, shouting a Latin incantation that translated roughly to "see no more." Compared to the scrying spell, this one was astonishingly easy. It required will on my part, certainly, but most of the magic was tied into the physical components and didn't need the hours of concentration that the other one had. The power surged through me almost instantly, filling me with a thrill I hadn't expected.

The girl screamed and dropped her gun, clawing at her eyes. Cries of dismay from the masters sitting by me showed they too had been affected. I'd cast a blindness spell, one that would affect those near me for about thirty seconds. Some part of me knew that wielding magic was wrong, but the rest of me felt triumphant at stopping some of these trigger-happy fanatics, if only temporarily. I didn't waste any of that precious time. I jumped up from where I was sitting and ran across the arena, away from the fighting near the entrance.

"Sydney!"

I don't know how I managed to hear my name above all that noise. Glancing behind me, I saw Eddie and Angeline carrying Sonya out through the door. They paused, and a pained look crossed Eddie's face as he glanced around, assessing the situation. I could guess his thoughts. He wanted me to come with them. Most of the gathered Warriors had raced to the center of the arena, trying to stop Sonya's rescue. They outmatched me by a long shot, creating a wall between my friends and me. Even if I didn't have to actually fight anyone, it seemed impossible I'd slip by unnoticed—especially since several people were still shouting about "that Alchemist girl."

Shaking my head adamantly, I motioned for Eddie to go on without me. Indecision warred on his face, and I hoped he wouldn't attempt to break through the throng to get to me. I pointed at the door, again urging him to go. Sonya was the incapacitated one. I would find my own way out. Not waiting to see what he'd do, I turned and continued the way I'd been going. There was a lot of open space for me to cover, but fewer Warriors to stop me.

Several buildings ringed the arena, some with doors and windows. I moved toward them, though I had nothing to break the glass. Two of the doors had padlocks. That left two without. The first one I tried turned out to have some unseen lock and wouldn't open. Frantic, I ran to the second and heard a shout behind me. The bleach blonde girl had regained her sight and was coming after me. Desperately, I turned the doorknob. Nothing happened. Reaching into my purse, I pulled out what the Warriors had mistaken for hand sanitizer. I dumped it out, spilling acid over the metal knob. It melted before my eyes. I hoped that would kill the lock. I threw my shoulder into the door, and it gave. Then I dared a peek behind me. My pursuer was lying on the ground, another victim of the tranquilizers.

I breathed a sigh of relief and pushed through the door.

I'd expected to enter another garage like the one I'd first been taken to, but instead I found myself in some sort of residential building. The empty hallways turned this way and that, and I felt disoriented. Everyone was at the free-for-all in the arena. I passed makeshift bedrooms, filled with cots and partially unpacked suitcases and backpacks. When I noticed what looked like an office, I hesitated in the doorway. Papers covered large foldout tables inside, and I wondered if any contained useful information about the Warriors.

I wanted so badly to go in and investigate. These Warriors were a mystery to the Alchemists. Who knew what intel these papers contained? What if there was information that could protect the Moroi? I hesitated for the space of a few heartbeats then reluctantly kept going. The guardians were using tranquilizers, but the Warriors had real guns—guns they wouldn't be afraid to use on me. Better to get out of here with the information I already had than not get out alive.

I reached the far side of the building at last and peered out a bedroom window. It was so dark outside now that I could hardly see anything. I didn't have the benefit of torches anymore. The only thing I could tell for sure was that I was no longer adjacent to the arena. That was good enough for me, though it would've been better if there was a door leading outside. I'd have to make my own. Grabbing a chair, I swung it into the window and was completely astonished when the glass broke easily. A few shards hit me, but nothing large enough to cause injury. Standing on the chair, I managed to climb out the window without injuring my hands.

I was met by a warm, dark night. No electric lights were visible ahead, just open black land. I took this to mean I was on the opposite side of the compound where Trey had brought me. There were no roads, no sound from the highway we had traveled. There was also no sign of life anywhere, which I took as a good sign. Hopefully all the Warrior guards who normally paroled the grounds were off fighting guardians. If Sonya was out now, my hope was that the guardians would begin retreating—and grab me along the way. Even if they didn't, I wasn't above walking back to I-10 and hitchhiking.

The compound was sprawling and confusing, and as I walked around it and still saw no sign of the highway, I began to grow uneasy. How turned around had I gotten? I only had a limited amount of time to get off Warrior property. They could be hunting me right now. There was also the disconcerting problem that once I made it to the periphery, I'd have to deal with the electric fence. Still, it might be best to forget looking for the freeway and simply make for the edge of the Warriors' camp so that I could—

A hand grabbed my shoulder, and I screamed.

"Easy there, Sage. I'm no gun-toting crazy guy. Crazy, yes. But not the rest."

I stared in disbelief, not that I could really make out much of the tall, dark figure standing over me. "Adrian?" The height was right, as was the build. As I stared, I became more and more certain. His hands steadied my shaking. I was so glad to see a friendly face—to see *him*—that I nearly sank into his arms in relief. "It *is* you. How'd you find me?"

"You're the only human out here with a yellow and purple aura," he said. "Makes you easy to spot."

"No, I mean, how'd you find me here? At the compound?"

"I followed the others. They told me not to, but . . . well."

In the faint moonlight I could barely see his shrug. "I don't follow directions well. When Castile came out with Sonya and started babbling about how you'd gone out some random door, I thought I'd take a quick walk around. I don't think I was supposed to do that either, but the guardians were kind of busy."

"You *are* crazy," I snapped, despite how happy I was to know I hadn't been abandoned in this miserable place. "The Warriors are so mad that they'd probably kill a Moroi on sight if they saw you."

He tugged my hand forward. Even through his banter, there'd been a hard tone to his words. He was fully aware of the danger we faced. "Then we'd better get out of here."

Adrian led me back in the direction I'd come, then went around the opposite side of the building. I didn't see the freeway lights yet, but he soon turned and began running toward the property's far edge, away from the building. I ran alongside him, still holding his hand.

"Where are we going?" I asked.

"The guardians assembled near the back side of the compound, so they wouldn't be spotted. That part of the fence has been deactivated—if you can climb it."

"Of course I can climb it. I'm practically a prodigy in PE," I pointed out. "The question is, can you, Mr. Smoker?"

The fence began to come into focus as we approached, mostly because its shape blocked some of the stars. "That's the section. Behind the scraggly bush," Adrian said. I couldn't see any bush but trusted in his eyes. "Go a little ways past that, and there's this country highway that the guardians used as a staging point. I'm parked there."

We came to a halt in front of the fence, both of us a little breathless. I peered upward. "You're sure it's still off?"

"It was when we came in," said Adrian, but I could hear a little uncertainty in his voice. "You think those guys would have gotten their act together enough to fix it already?"

"No," I admitted. "But I'd still like to know for sure. I mean, most commercial electric fences won't significantly hurt someone, but we should know."

He glanced around. "Can we throw a stick at it?"

"Wood doesn't conduct." I rifled through my purse and found what I wanted: a metal pen with a foam grip. "Hopefully, the foam on this will block the worst of it if the fence really is hot." Trying not to grimace, I reached out and touched the pen's barrel to the fence, half-expecting some intense charge to send me flying backward. Nothing happened. I slowly ran the pen along the fence, since most electric ones had an intermittent pulse. Sustained contact would be needed. "Looks clean," I said, exhaling in relief and turning to Adrian. "I guess we're good to—ahh!"

A bright light shone in my eyes, blinding me and killing whatever night vision I'd gained out here. I heard Adrian cry out in surprise as well.

"It's the girl!" a male voice exclaimed. "And . . . and one of *them*!"

The flashlight was moved out of my face, and although spots still danced in my vision, I could make out two hulking figures rapidly approaching. Were they armed? My mind raced. Whether they were or not, they were still an obvious threat since Warriors apparently liked to practice bashing each other in their free time, and Adrian and I didn't.

"Don't move," said one of them. A blade shone in the gleam

of the lowered flashlight. Not as bad as a gun, but not great either. "You're both coming with us, back inside."

"Slowly," added the other. "Don't try any tricks."

Unfortunately for them, I still had a few up my sleeve. Quickly I put the pen back in my purse and grabbed another souvenir from Ms. Terwilliger's homework: a thin, round wooden bracelet. Before either Warrior could do anything, I snapped the wooden circle into four pieces and tossed them on the ground, calling out another Latin incantation. Again, I felt the rush of power and its exultation. The men cried out—I'd cast a disorientation spell, one that messed with equilibrium and made vision blurry and surreal. It worked a lot like the blindness spell, affecting those around me.

I lunged forward and pushed one of our assailants down. He fell easily, too incapacitated by the spell to resist. The other guy was so distraught that he'd dropped the flashlight and was practically on the ground already as his attempts at balance failed. Nonetheless, I gave him a good kick to the chest to make sure he stayed down and grabbed his flashlight in the process. I didn't necessarily need it with Adrian's night vision, but these two would now be helpless in the dark when the spell wore off.

"Sage! What the hell did you do to me?"

Turning, I saw Adrian clinging to the fence, using it to hold himself up. In my eagerness to stop the Warriors, I'd forgotten the spell affected *everyone* near me.

"Oh," I said. "Sorry."

"Sorry? My legs don't work!"

"It's your inner ear, actually. Come on. Grab the fence and climb. One hand in front of the other."

I caught hold as well and urged him up. It wasn't the most difficult fence to climb—it wasn't electrified or barbed—and having it for support negated some of Adrian's disorientation. Nonetheless, it was still slow going as we made it toward the top. This spell lasted a little longer than the blindness one, but I was painfully aware that as soon as Adrian was free from it, the Warriors would be too.

Against all odds, we made it to the top of the fence. Getting over to the other side was much more difficult, and I had to do a fair amount of acrobatics to help Adrian make the transition while keeping myself steady. Finally, I wrangled him into the correct position to climb down.

"Good," I said. "Now just reverse what you did before, one hand down in front of the—"

Something slipped, either his hand or foot, and Adrian plummeted to the ground. It wasn't that long of a drop, and his height helped a little—not that he was in any shape to actually use his legs and land on his feet. I winced.

"Or you can just take the short way down," I said.

I quickly scaled down after him and helped him stand. Aside from the spell's debilitation, he didn't seem to have suffered any damage. Slipping an arm around him and letting him lean his weight on me, I attempted to run toward the road he'd mentioned, which was now slightly visible. "Running" was difficult, however. It was hard work keeping Adrian up and I kept stumbling. Still, we made our way slowly from the compound, which was about as much as we could hope for. Adrian's state made him clumsy and heavy, and his height was a real inconvenience.

Then, without warning, the spell wore off, and Adrian

instantly recovered. His legs strengthened and his unwieldy gait straightened out. Suddenly, it was as though he were carrying me, and we practically tripped over each other trying to adjust.

"You okay?" I asked, letting go.

"I am now. What the hell was that?"

"It's not important. What is important is that those guys have recovered too. Maybe I knocked them down hard enough to slow them down." That seemed kind of unlikely. "But run anyway."

We ran, and even if he undoubtedly had the respiratory system of a chain smoker, his long legs made up for it. He could easily outdistance me but slowed so that we stayed together. Whenever he started to get ahead, he'd grab my hand again. Shouts sounded behind us, and I turned off the flashlight to make us harder to spot.

"There," said Adrian. "See the cars?"

Slowly, out of the darkness, two SUVs materialized, along with a much more conspicuous yellow Mustang.

"Very covert," I muttered.

"Most of the guardians have gotten away," said Adrian. "But not everyone."

Before I could respond, someone grabbed me from behind. In a maneuver that would have made Wolfe proud, I managed the backward kick that he'd tried so hard to teach us. It caught my attacker by surprise, and he released me, only for his companion to shove me to the ground.

Three figures ran toward us from the cars and hurled themselves at our attackers. Thanks to his signature duster, I knew Dimitri led the group.

"Get out of here," he called to Adrian and me. "You know where to meet. We'll cover you. Drive fast—they'll probably be on the road soon."

Adrian helped me up, and once again we ran together. I'd hurt my ankle in the fall, so I moved slowly, but Adrian helped me along and let me lean on him. All the while, my heart was threatening to pound out of my chest, even when we reached the safety of the Mustang. He guided me to the passenger side. "Can you get in okay?"

"I'm fine," I said, sliding in and unwilling to admit the pain was growing. I prayed I hadn't slowed us too much. I couldn't stand the thought of being the one responsible for Adrian's capture.

Satisfied, Adrian raced over to the driver's side and started the car. The engine roared to life, and he followed Dimitri's orders to the letter, peeling out at a speed I was envious of. Out on this country highway, however, it seemed unlikely there were any cops. I glanced behind us a few times, but by the time we made it to I-10, it was obvious no one had followed us. I sighed gratefully and leaned my head against the seat, though I was still a long way from being calm. I couldn't assume we were safe yet.

"Okay," I said. "How on earth did you guys find me?"

Adrian didn't answer right away. When he did, I could tell it was with great reluctance. "Eddie put a tracking device in your purse, back at my place."

"What? He couldn't have! They searched me."

"Well, I'm sure it didn't look like one. I don't know what he ended up getting. He got it from your people, actually. As soon as Trey confirmed the meeting tonight, Belikov was on the phone with every guardian in a two-hour radius, trying to recruit backup. He called the Alchemists too and convinced them to share some tech."

There were so many crazy things about what he'd just said, I didn't know where to begin parsing it. All sorts of wheeling and dealing had gone on without me realizing it. And even when it had been settled, no one had told me about it. Plus, the Alchemists had been involved? Helping the guardians to track me?

"The earrings," I said. "That's where they came from. The tracker must be in one of them. I never would have guessed."

"I'm not surprised, knowing the way you guys work."

The rest of tonight's reality began to sink in. The last of my fear subsided—only to be replaced by anger. "You lied to me! All of you! You should have told me what you were doing—that you were tracking me and planning a raid! How could you keep that from me?"

He sighed. "I didn't want to, believe me. I told them over and over they needed to get you in the loop. But everyone was afraid you'd refuse to take the device if you knew about it. Or that you'd somehow slip up and give away the plan to those nuts. I didn't believe that, though."

"And yet, you didn't bother telling me yourself," I snapped, still outraged.

"I couldn't! They made me promise not to."

Somehow, his betrayal hurt worse than all the others. I had come to trust him implicitly. How could he do this to me? "No one believed I'd be able to talk the Warriors down, so everyone just made contingency plans without me." Never mind that I *hadn't* been able to talk them down. "Someone should have told me. *You* should have told me."

There was legitimate pain and regret in his voice. "I'm telling you, I wanted to. But I was trapped. You of all people should know what it's like being caught between groups, Sage. Besides, don't you remember what I said just before you got in the car with Trey?"

I did, actually. Almost word for word. *No matter what happens, I want you to know that I never doubted what you're going to do. It's smart, and it's brave.*

I slouched further into my seat and felt like I was on the verge of tears. Adrian was right. I did know what it was like to have your loyalty stretched between different groups. I understood the position he'd been in. It was just, some selfish part of me wished that I'd been the one his loyalty had been strongest to. *He tried,* an inner voice said. *He tried to tell you.*

The meeting spot that Dimitri had told Adrian to go to turned out to be Clarence's house. The place was crawling with guardians, some of whom were patching up each other's injuries. No one had been killed on either side, something the guardians had been very cautious about. The Warriors of Light already thought vampires were twisted and corrupt. They didn't need more fuel added to the fire.

Not that tonight's raid was probably going to help matters. I had no clue how the Warriors would react or if there might be some lethal retaliation in store. I supposed the guardians and Alchemists had taken that into consideration. I wondered bitterly if any of them would share their opinions on it with me.

"I know better than to offer to heal you," Adrian told me, as we squeezed past a group of guardians. "Grab a seat in the living room, and I'll get you some ice."

I started to say I could get my own, but my ankle was

growing increasingly painful. With a nod, I left him and made my way to the living room. A couple of unknown guardians were there, along with a beaming Clarence. To my surprise, Eddie and Angeline were also in there, sitting side by side—and *holding hands*?

"Sydney!" he exclaimed. He immediately released Angeline's hand and hurried over to me, astonishing me with a hug. "Thank God you're okay. I hated having to leave you there. That wasn't part of the plan. I was supposed to have gotten you out with Sonya."

"Yeah, well, maybe next time, someone can fill me in on the plan," I said pointedly.

Eddie grimaced. "I'm sorry about that. I really am. We just . . . "

"I know, I know. Didn't think I'd go along with it, were afraid something would go wrong, etc., etc."

"I'm sorry."

I didn't entirely forgive him, but I was too tired to push the matter much further. "Just tell me this," I said, lowering my voice. "Were you just holding hands with Angeline?"

He blushed, which seemed ludicrous after the fierceness I'd seen him pull off back at the compound. "Er, yeah. We were just . . . talking. I mean, that is . . . I think we might go out sometime. Not at school, of course, since everyone thinks we're related. And probably not anything serious. I mean, she's still a little out there, but she's not as bad as I used to think. And she was really great in that battle. I feel like maybe I should get my head out of the fantasy with Jill and try some normal dating. If you'll let me borrow your car."

I had to pick my jaw up off the floor. "Sure," I said. "Far

be it for me to stop a budding romance." Should I tell him Jill might not be such a fantasy after all? I didn't want to meddle. Eddie deserved to be happy, but I couldn't help but feel a little bad that I'd told Jill he might be interested. I hope I hadn't made things more complicated.

Adrian returned with a bag of ice. I sat down in an armchair, and he helped position the ice on my ankle after I propped it up on a footstool. I relaxed as the ice began numbing the pain and hoped I hadn't broken anything.

"Isn't this exciting?" Clarence asked me. "Finally, you were able to see the vampire hunters for yourselves!"

I wasn't sure I'd describe the night with that much enthusiasm, but I did have to concede a point to him. "You were right," I said. "I'm sorry for not believing you sooner."

He gave me a kind smile. "It's all right, my dear. I probably wouldn't have believed a crazy old man either."

I smiled in return and then thought of something from earlier. "Mr. Donahue . . . you said when you encountered the hunters before that a human named Marcus Finch intervened on your behalf."

Clarence nodded eagerly. "Yes, yes. Nice young man, that Marcus. Certainly hope I run into him again someday."

"Was he an Alchemist?" I asked. Seeing Clarence's puzzled look, I tapped my cheek. "Did he have a tattoo like mine?"

"Like yours? No, no. It was different. Hard to explain."

I leaned forward. "But he did have a tattoo on his cheek?"

"Yes. Didn't you see in the picture?"

"What picture?"

Clarence's gaze turned inward. "I could've sworn I showed

you some of my old pictures, back when Lee and Tamara were young . . . ah, such good days those were."

I worked hard to stay patient. Clarence's moments of coherence were sometimes hard to get a hold of. "And Marcus? You have a picture of him too?"

"Of course. A lovely one of the two of us. I'll find it one day and show you."

I wanted to ask him if he'd show it to me now, but with his place so crowded, it didn't seem like the right time.

Dimitri arrived shortly thereafter, along with the last of the guardians who'd been at the compound. Dimitri immediately asked about Sonya, who I'd learned was resting in her bedroom. Adrian had offered to heal her, but Sonya had had enough clarity of mind to refuse him, saying she simply wanted blood and rest and a chance for the drugs to wear off naturally.

Once Dimitri got this report and could rest easy about Sonya, he came straight to me, looking down from his lofty height at where I sat with my ice. "I'm sorry," he said. "I know you must have heard by now what happened."

"That I was sent into a dangerous situation with only half the information I needed?" I asked. "Yeah, I heard all about that."

"I'm not a fan of lies and half truths," he said. "I wished there'd been another way. We had so little time, and this just seemed like the best option. No one doubted your ability to reason and make a compelling case. It was the Warriors' ability to listen and see reason that we didn't believe in."

"I can see why you guys didn't trust me with the plan." Near me, I saw Adrian flinch at the way I said "you guys." I hadn't intentionally meant anything by it but realized now that it sounded very condescending and Alchemist—so Us versus Them. "But I still can't believe the Alchemists went along with that—that they condoned keeping me out of the loop."

There were no free chairs left, so Dimitri simply sat down cross-legged. "There's not much I can tell you about that. Like I said, it was all short notice, and when I spoke with Donna Stanton, she felt it would be safer all around if you didn't know what was coming. If it makes you feel better, she was very adamant about us keeping you safe once we were there."

"Maybe," I said. "It'd be better still if she'd thought about how I might feel when I found out I wasn't trusted with vital information."

"She did think about it," said Dimitri, looking slightly uncomfortable. "She said you wouldn't mind because you understand the importance of not questioning your superiors' decisions and that you know what they do is for the best. She said you're an exemplary Alchemist."

Don't question. They know what's best. We can't take any chances.

"Of course she did," I said. *I never question anything.*

CHAPTER 23

IT TOOK SONYA a few days to recover, thus delaying her return to Pennsylvania. When she was ready to go to the airport, I offered to drive her. The rental car had been found, but Dimitri was using it to clean up after the mission. Within twenty-four hours, the Warriors had vacated their compound, which had turned out to be a rental facility generally used for retreats. They'd left almost no trace of their presence behind, but that hadn't stopped the guardians from scouring every inch of the abandoned compound.

"Thanks again," Sonya told me. "I know how busy you must be."

"It's no problem. It's the weekend, and anyway this is what I'm here for—to help you guys."

She laughed softly to herself. Her recovery in the last couple of days had been remarkable, and she now looked as pretty and bright as usual. She wore her auburn hair down today, letting it fall in fiery waves around the delicate lines of her face.

"True, but it seems like you keep having to go above and beyond your job description."

"I'm just glad you're okay," I said earnestly. I'd grown close to Sonya and was sad to see her go. "Back in that arena . . . well, it was kind of terrifying."

Some of her amusement faded. "It was. I was out of it most of the time and not really able to process what was going on around me. But I do remember your words. You were pretty amazing, not to mention brave, to face down that crowd and defend me. I know how hard it must have been to be in opposition with your own kind."

"Those people are *not* my kind," I said adamantly. Some part of me wondered exactly who my kind were. "What's going to happen to your research now?"

"Oh, it'll continue back East. Dimitri will be returning soon too, and there are other researchers who can help us at Court. Having an objective spirit user like Adrian was extremely useful, and we've got plenty of data to keep us busy now, thanks to the blood samples and aura observations. We'll let Adrian continue with his art and get in touch later if we need him again."

I still couldn't shake the guilt over how my refusal to give more blood had indirectly resulted in Sonya's kidnapping. "Sonya, about my blood—"

"Don't worry about it," she interrupted. "You were right about me being pushy and also that we need to focus on Dimitri first. Besides, we might be making some headway with getting Alchemist help."

"Really?" Stanton had seemed pretty against it when we spoke. "They said yes?"

"No, but they said they'd get back to us."

I laughed. "With them, that's a pretty positive answer."

I fell silent for a moment, wondering if this meant everyone would forget about my blood. Between the Warriors and the potential of Alchemist aid, surely my blood was no longer important. After all, initial study had found nothing special. No one had any reason to worry about my blood anymore. Except, the thing was . . . I was kind of worried. Because no matter how much I dreaded being experimented on, that nagging question wouldn't leave me alone: Why hadn't the Strigoi been able to drink my blood?

Sonya's earlier mention of auras reminded me of another burning question. "Sonya, what does purple mean in someone's aura? Adrian says he saw it in mine but won't tell me what it is."

"Typical," she said with a chuckle. "Purple . . . well, let's see. From what I've observed, it's a complex color. It's a spiritual but passionate color, tied to those who love deeply and also seek a higher calling. It's interesting in that it has such depth. White and true gold tend to be the colors associated with higher powers and metaphysics, just as red and orange are linked to love and baser instincts. Purple kind of has the best of all of those. I wish I could explain it more clearly."

"No, that makes sense," I said, pulling into the airport's circle driveway. "Kind of. It doesn't exactly sound like me, though."

"Well, it's hardly an exact science. And he's right—it's there in you. The thing is . . . " We'd stopped at the curb, and I saw her studying me carefully. "I've never noticed it before. I mean, I'm sure it's always been there, but whenever I looked at you, I just saw the yellow of most intellects. Adrian isn't as adept at reading auras as I am, so I'm surprised he noticed what I missed."

She wasn't the only one. Spiritual, passionate . . . was I really those things? Did Adrian believe I was those things? The thought made me feel warm all over. Elated . . . and confused.

Sonya seemed like she was about to say more on the matter and then changed her mind. She cleared her throat. "Well, then. Here we are. Thank you again for the ride."

"No problem," I said, my mind still swimming with visions of purple. "Have a safe trip."

She opened the car door and then paused. "Oh, I have something for you. Clarence asked me to give it to you."

"Clarence?"

Sonya rustled through her purse and found an envelope. "Here you are. He was pretty adamant you get it—you know how he is when he gets worked up about something."

"I do. Thanks."

Sonya left with her luggage, and curiosity made me open the envelope before I drove away. Inside was a photograph, showing Clarence and a young guy, close to my age, who looked human. The two of them had their arms around each other and were smiling at the camera. The unknown guy had straight blond hair that just barely brushed his chin and stunning blue eyes that stood out against suntanned features. He was extremely handsome, and although his eyes mirrored his smile, I thought there was a little sadness too.

I was so caught up in his good looks that I didn't notice his tattoo right away. It was on his left cheek, an abstract design made of clustered crescents of various sizes and orientations, lying together so that they almost looked like a vine. It was exotic and beautiful; the rich indigo ink a near match for his eyes. Studying the design more closely, I noticed something familiar about its shape and swore I could see a faint glimmer of gold edging the blue lines. I nearly dropped the picture in shock. The crescents had been tattooed over an Alchemist lily. I flipped the picture over. One word was scrawled on it: *Marcus*.

Marcus Finch, whom the Warriors had claimed was an ex-Alchemist. Marcus Finch, whom the Alchemists had claimed didn't exist. The crazy thing was, unless someone locked away like Keith counted, there were no "ex-Alchemists." You were in it for life. You couldn't walk away. Yet, that obscured lily spoke for itself. Unless Marcus had had a name change that somehow eluded the Alchemists, Stanton and the others were lying to me about knowing who he was. But why? Had there been some rift? A week ago, I would have said it was impossible that Stanton wouldn't tell me the truth about him, but now, knowing how carefully information was parceled out—or not—I had to wonder.

I stared at the picture a few more moments, caught up in those haunting blue eyes. Then, I tucked it away and returned to Amberwood, resolved to keep the photograph a secret. If the Alchemists wanted to deny Marcus Finch's existence to me, I would let them continue until I figured out why. That meant my only lead was Clarence and the absent Warriors. Still, it was a start.

Somehow, sometime, I was going to find Marcus Finch and get my answers.

I was surprised to see Jill sitting outside our dorm when I walked in. She was in the shade, of course, still able to enjoy the nice weather without the sun's full force. We'd finally moved into a sort of autumn around here, not that eighty was what I usually associated with brisk fall weather. Jill's face was pensive, but she brightened a little when she saw me.

"Hey, Sydney. I was hoping to catch you. Can't find you anymore without your phone."

I made a face. "Yeah, I need to replace that. It's been a huge pain."

She nodded in commiseration. "Did you drop Sonya off?"

"She's on her way back to Court and Mikhail—and hopefully a much more peaceful life."

"That's good," said Jill. She glanced away and bit her lower lip.

I knew her well enough by now to recognize the signs of when she was bracing to tell me something. I also knew better than to push the matter, so I waited patiently.

"I did it," she said at last. "I told Micah it's over . . . really over."

Relief flooded me. One less thing to worry about. "I'm sorry," I said. "I know that must have been hard."

She brushed curly hair away from her face as she considered. "Yes. And no. I like him. And I'd like to keep hanging out with him—as friends—if he wants to. I don't know, though. He took it kind of hard . . . and our mutual friends? Well . . . they're not very happy with me right now." I tried not to groan. Jill had made such headway with her status here, and now it could be shattered. "But it's for the best. Micah and I live in different worlds, and there'd be no real future with a human anyway. Besides, I've been thinking a lot about love . . . like, epic love . . . " She looked up at me for a moment, her gaze softening. "And that wasn't what we had. Seems like if I'm with someone, that's what I should feel."

I thought epic love was kind of a stretch for someone her age but didn't say so. "Are you going to be okay?"

She snapped back to reality. "Yeah, I think so." A small smile played over her lips. "And once this has passed, maybe Eddie will want to go out sometime—away from campus, of course. Seeing as we're 'related.'"

Her words were almost a repeat of what I'd heard the other night at Clarence's, and I stared in surprise as realization dawned on me. "You don't know . . . I thought you would since Angeline's your roommate . . . "

Jill frowned. "What are you talking about? What don't I know?"

Oh God. Why, oh why, did I have to be the one to deliver this news? Why couldn't I be locked away in my room or the library doing something enjoyable, like homework?

"Eddie's, um, asked Angeline out. I don't know when it's going to happen, but he decided to give her a chance." He hadn't borrowed my car, so presumably there'd been no date yet.

Jill looked stricken. "W-what? Eddie and Angeline? But . . . he can't stand her . . . "

"Something changed," I said lamely. "I'm not sure what. It's not like, er, epic love, but they've gotten closer these last few weeks. I'm sorry." Jill seemed more devastated by this than breaking up with Micah.

She looked away and blinked back tears. "It's okay. I mean, I never encouraged him. He probably still thinks I'm dating

Micah. Why should he have waited around? He should have someone."

"Jill—"

"It's okay. I'll be okay." She looked so sad and then, amazingly, her face grew even darker. "Oh, Sydney. You're going to be so mad at me."

I was still thinking of Micah and felt totally confused at the topic change. "Why?"

She reached into her backpack and pulled out a glossy magazine. It was some kind of southern California tourism one, with articles and ads highlighting the area. One of the pages was marked, and I turned to it. It was a full-page advertisement for Lia DiStefano, a collage of pictures of her various designs.

And one of the photos was of Jill.

It took me a moment to catch it. The picture was a profile shot, with Jill in sunglasses and a fedora—as well as that peacock-colored scarf Lia had given her. Jill's curly hair streamed out behind her, and the angles of her face looked beautiful. If I hadn't known Jill so well, I would never have identified her as this chic model—though it would certainly be obvious that she was a Moroi to anyone who knew what to look for.

"How?" I demanded. "How did this happen?"

Jill took a deep breath, ready to accept her blame. "When she dropped off the costumes and gave me the scarf, she asked if I'd let her take a picture to see how the colors photographed. She had some of the other accessories in the car, and I put those on too. She wanted to prove to me that with the right coverage, she could hide my identity. But I never thought . . . I mean, she didn't say she'd use it. God, I feel so stupid."

Maybe not stupid, but certainly naïve. I nearly crumpled

up the magazine. I was furious at Lia. Part of me wanted to sue for using a picture of a minor without permission, but we had much bigger problems. How wide was this magazine's circulation? If Lia had only put Jill's photo on display in California, maybe no one would recognize her. Still, a Moroi model could raise eyebrows. *Who knows what kind of trouble this was going to cause for us now?*

"Sydney, I'm sorry," said Jill. "What can I do to fix this?"

"Nothing," I said. "Except to stay away from Lia." I felt ill. "I'll take care of this." I really didn't know how, though. I could only pray no one noticed the picture.

"I'll do whatever you need if you think of something. I—oh." Her eyes lifted to something behind me. "Maybe we should talk later."

I glanced back. Trey was walking toward us. Another problem to deal with.

"Probably a good idea," I said. Jill's heartache and publicity would have to go on the back burner. She left as Trey came to stand beside me.

"Melbourne," he said, attempting one of his old smiles. It faltered a little.

"I didn't know you were still around," I said. "I thought you'd left with the others." The Warriors had scattered to the wind. Trey had said before that they traveled for their "hunts," and Master Angeletti had also mentioned gathering from various places of the country. Presumably, they had all returned to where they'd come from. I'd thought Trey would simply disappear as well.

"Nope," he said. "This is where I go to school, where my dad wants me to stay. Besides, the other Warriors never had a

permanent base here in Palm Springs. They'll move on to wherever . . . "

He couldn't finish, so I did. "Wherever you get a tip-off
about monsters you can brutally execute?"

"It wasn't like that," he said. "We thought she was one of
the Strigoi. We still do."

I scrutinized his face, this guy I'd thought was my friend.
I was pretty sure he still was. "Not you. That's why you threw
the fight."

"I didn't," he protested.

"You did. I saw you hesitate when you could have taken
out Chris. You didn't want to win. You didn't want to kill Sonya
because you weren't sure she really was Strigoi."

He didn't deny it. "I still think they should all be destroyed."

"So do I." I reconsidered. "Well, unless there's a way to save
them all, but that's unclear." Despite how much I'd said while
advocating for Sonya, I wasn't quite comfortable letting him
on the secrets and experiments. "If the Warriors travel around,
what'll happen the next time they're in this area? Or even L.A.?
Will you join them again? Will you travel to the next hunt?"

"No." The answer was hard. Blunt, even.

Hope surged in me. "You've decided to split off from them?"

The emotions on Trey's face were hard to read, but they
didn't look like happy ones. "No. They decided to cut us off—
me and my dad. We've been outcast."

I stared for a few moments, at a loss for words. I didn't like
the Warriors or Trey's involvement, but this wasn't quite what
I'd been trying to achieve. "Because of me?"

"No. Yes. I don't know." He shrugged. "Indirectly, I guess.
They don't blame you personally or even the Alchemists. Hell,

they still want to team up with the Alchemists. They figure you just behaved in your typically misguided way. But me? I'm the one who pushed to let you in, who swore everything would be fine. So, they blame me for the lapse of judgment and fall-out that came from it. Others are taking the blame too—the council for agreeing, security for not stopping the raid—but that doesn't make me feel better. Dad and I were the only ones exiled."

"I . . . I'm sorry. I never thought anything like that would happen."

"Wasn't your place to," he said pragmatically, though his tone was still miserable. "To a certain extent, they're right. I was the one that got you in. It is my fault, and they're punishing my dad for what I did. That's the worst part of all." Trey was trying to play it cool, but I could see the truth. He'd worked so hard to impress his father and ended up causing the ultimate humilia-tion. Trey's next words confirmed as much. "The Warriors have been my dad's whole life. To be kicked out like that . . . well, he's taking it pretty badly. I have to find a way to get back in— for him. I don't suppose you know where any easy-to-kill Strigoi are, do you?"

"No," I said. "Especially since none of them are easy kills." I hesitated, unsure how to proceed. "Trey, what's this mean for us? I understand if we can't be friends anymore . . . seeing as how I, uh, ruined your life's work."

A hint of his old smile returned. "Nothing's ruined for good. I told you, I'll get back in. And if it's not by killing Strigoi, who knows? Maybe if I learn more about you guys, I can bridge the gap between our groups and get us to all work together. That would score me some points."

"You're welcome to try," I said diplomatically. I really didn't think that would happen, and he could tell.

"Well, I'll figure something out then, some big move to get the Warriors' attention and get my dad and me back in with them. I *have* to." His face started to fall again, but then there was a brief return of the phantom smile—though it was tinged with sadness. "You know what else sucks? Now I can't ask Angeline out. Hanging out with you is one thing, but even if I'm an outcast, I can't risk being friendly with Moroi or dhampirs. I especially can't date one. I mean, I'd figured she was one a while ago, but I could have played dumb. That attack in the arena kind of killed any chance of that. The Warriors really don't like them either, you know. Dhampirs or Moroi. They'd love to see them brought down too—they just think it's too hard and less of a priority right now."

Something about those words made me shiver, particularly since I recalled the offhand Warrior comment about eventually taking out Moroi. The Alchemists certainly had no love for dhampirs and Moroi, but that was a far cry from wanting to bring them down.

"I gotta get going." Trey reached into his pocket and handed over something that I was grateful to see. My phone. "Figured you were missing this."

"Yes!" I took it eagerly and turned it on. I hadn't known if I'd get it back and had been on the verge of buying a new one. This one was three months old and practically out-of-date anyway. "Thanks for saving it. Oh. Wow." I read the display. "There are like a million messages from Brayden." We hadn't spoken since the night of Sonya's disappearance.

The mischievous look I liked so well on Trey returned. "Better get on that then. True love waits for no one."

"True love, huh?" I shook my head in exasperation. "So nice to have you back."

That earned me an outright grin. "See you around."

As soon as I was alone, I texted Brayden: *Sorry for the radio silence. Lost my phone for three days.* His response was almost immediate: *I'm at work, due for a break soon. Come by?* I thought about it. Seeing as I had no life-saving tasks right now, this was as good a time as any. I texted back that I'd leave Amberwood right away.

Brayden had my favorite latte ready for me when I got to Spencer's. "Based on when you were leaving, I calculated when I would need to make it in order for it to be hot when you arrived."

"Thanks," I said, taking it. I felt a little guilt that I had a greater emotional reaction to seeing the coffee than him.

He told the other barista he was going on break and then led me over to a remote table. "This won't take long," Brayden said. "I know you probably have a lot of things to do this weekend."

"Things are actually starting to lighten up," I said.

He took a deep breath, showing that same resolve and anxiety he'd had when asking me for future dates. "Sydney," he said, voice formal, "I don't think we should see each other anymore."

I stopped mid-sip. "Wait . . . what?"

"I know how devastating this probably is for you," he added. "And I admit, it's hard for me too. But in light of recent events, it's become clear you just aren't ready for a relationship yet."

"Recent events?"

He nodded solemnly. "Your family. You've broken off a number of our social engagements to be with them. While that kind of familial devotion is admirable, I just can't be in that kind of volatile relationship."

"Volatile?" I just kept repeating his key words and finally forced myself to get a grip. "So . . . let me get this straight. You're breaking up with me."

He thought about it. "Yes. Yes, I am."

I waited for some internal reaction. An outpouring of grief. The sense of my heart breaking. Any emotion, really. But mostly, all I felt was kind of a puzzled surprise.

"Huh," I said.

That was apparently enough of a distraught reaction for Brayden. "Please don't make this harder than it is. I admire you a lot. You're absolutely the smartest girl I've ever met. But I just can't be involved with someone as irresponsible as you."

I stared. "Irresponsible."

Brayden nodded again. "Yes."

I'm not sure where it started, somewhere in my stomach or chest, maybe. But all of a sudden, I was consumed by uncontrollable laughter. I couldn't stop. I had to set down my coffee, lest I spill it. Even then, I had to bury my face in my hands to wipe away tears.

"Sydney?" asked Brayden cautiously. "Is this some kind of hysterical-grief reaction?"

It took me almost another minute to calm myself enough to answer him. "Oh, Brayden. You've made my day. You've given me something I never thought I'd get. Thank you." I reached for the coffee and stood up. He looked completely lost.

"Um, you're welcome?"

I left the coffee shop, still laughing like a fool. For the last month or so, everyone in my life had gone on and on about how responsible I was, how diligent, how exemplary. I'd been called a lot of things. But never, ever, had I been called irresponsible.

And I kind of liked it.

CHAPTER 24

BECAUSE THIS DAY couldn't get any weirder, I decided to stop by Adrian's. There was something I was dying to know but hadn't had a chance to ask.

He opened the door when I knocked, a paintbrush in hand. "Oh," he said. "Unexpected."

"Am I interrupting anything?"

"Just homework." He stepped aside to let me in. "Don't worry. It's not the crisis for me that it would be for you."

I entered the living room and was happy to see it filled with canvases and easels once again. "You've got your art studio back."

"Yup." He set the brush down and wiped his hands on a rag. "Now that this place is no longer research central, I can return it to its normal artistic state."

He leaned against the back of the plaid sofa and watched me as I strolled from canvas to canvas. One of them gave me pause. "What's this? It looks like a lily."

"It is," he said. "No offense, but this lily is kind of more badass than yours. If the Alchemists want to buy the rights to this and start using it, I'm willing to negotiate."

"Noted," I said. I was still smiling from Brayden's breakup, and this only added to my good mood. Although, admittedly, the painting kind of lost me a little—as the abstract nature of his art often did. The lily, despite being more stylized and "badass" than the prim one on my cheek, was still clearly identifiable. It was even done in gold paint. Splashes of free-form scarlet paint surrounded it, and around the red was an almost crystalline pattern in ice blue. It was striking, but if there was some deeper meaning, it was beyond me.

"You're in an awfully good mood," he observed. "Was there a sale at Khakis-R-Us?"

I gave up on my artistic interpretation and turned to him. "Nope. Brayden broke up with me."

Adrian's smirk faded. "Oh. Shit. I'm sorry. Are you . . . I mean, do you need a drink? Do you need to, uh, cry or anything?"

I laughed. "No. Weirdly, I'm fine. It really doesn't bother me at all. But it should, right? Maybe there's something wrong with me."

Adrian's green eyes weighed me. "I don't think so. Not every breakup is a tragedy. Still . . . you might be due for some kind of comfort."

He straightened and walked over to the kitchen. Puzzled, I watched as he pulled something from the freezer and rifled through his silverware drawer. He returned to the living room and presented me with a pint of pomegranate gelato and a spoon.

"What's this for?" I asked, accepting the offering out of shock alone.

"For you, obviously. You wanted pomegranate, right?"

I thought back to the night at the Italian restaurant. "Well, yeah . . . but you didn't need to do this . . . "

"Well, you wanted it," he said reasonably. "That, and a deal's a deal."

"What deal?"

"Remember when you said you'd drink a regular can of pop if I didn't smoke for a day? Well, I calculated the calories, and that's the same as a serving of this. If you can believe there are four servings in that tiny thing."

I nearly dropped the gelato. "You . . . you went a day without smoking?"

"Almost a week, actually," he said. "So you can eat the whole thing if you want."

"Why on earth would you do that?" I asked.

He shrugged. "Hey, you laid out the challenge. Besides, smoking's an unhealthy habit, right?"

"Right . . . " I was still stunned.

"Eat up. It's going to melt."

I handed the gelato back. "I can't. Not with you watching. It's too weird. Can I eat it later?"

"Sure," he said, returning it to the freezer. "If you'll really eat it. I know how you are."

I crossed my arms as he stood opposite me. "Oh?"

He fixed me with a disconcertingly hard look. "Maybe everyone else thinks your aversion to food is cute—but not me. I've watched you watch Jill. Here's some tough love: you will never, ever have her body. Ever. It's impossible. She's Moroi. You're human. That's biology. You have a great one, one that most humans would kill for—and you'd look even better if you put on a little weight. Five pounds would be a good start. Hide the ribs. Get a bigger bra size."

"Adrian!" I was aghast. "You . . . are you out of your mind? You have no right to tell me that! None at all."

He scoffed. "I have every right, Sage. I'm your friend, and no one else is going to do it. Besides, I'm the king of unhealthy habits. Do you think I don't know one when I see it? I don't know where this came from—your family, too many Moroi, or just your own OCD nature—but I'm telling you, you don't have to do it."

"So this is some kind of intervention."

"This is the truth," he said simply. "From someone who cares and wants your body to be as healthy and amazing as your mind."

"I'm not listening to this," I said, turning away. A mix of emotions churned in me. Anger. Outrage. And weirdly, a little relief. "I'm going. I never should have come by."

His hand on my shoulder stopped me. "Wait . . . listen to me." Reluctantly, I turned. His expression was still stern, but his voice had softened. "I'm not trying to be mean. You're the last person I want to hurt . . . but I don't want you hurting yourself either. You can ignore everything I just said, but I had to get it out, okay? I won't mention it again. You're the one in control of your life."

I looked away and blinked back tears. "Thanks," I said. I should have been happy he was going to back off. Instead, there was an ache inside me, like he'd torn something open that I was trying to ignore and keep shut away. An ugly truth I didn't want to admit to myself, which I knew was hypocritical for someone who claimed to deal in facts and data. And whether I wanted to agree with him or not, I knew without a doubt he was right about one thing: no one else would've told me what he just had.

"Why did you come by anyway?" he asked. "You sure you don't want to make my awesome painting the new Alchemist logo?"

I couldn't help a small laugh. I looked back up at him, willing to help him with the abrupt change in subject. "No. Something much more serious."

He looked relieved at my smile and gave me one of his smirky ones in return. "Must be *really* serious."

"That night at the compound. How did you know how to drive the Mustang?"

His smile vanished.

"Because you *did*," I said. "You drove it without any hesitation. As good as I could have. I started to wonder if maybe someone else had been showing you how to do it. But even if you'd had lessons every day since you got the car, you couldn't have driven like that. You shifted like you've been driving manual your whole life."

Adrian turned abruptly away and walked to the opposite side of the living room. "Maybe I'm a natural," he said, not looking at me.

It was funny how quickly the tables had turned. One minute he had me backed into a corner, forcing me to face issues I didn't want. Now it was my turn. I followed him over to the window and made him meet my gaze.

"I'm right, aren't I?" I pushed. "You've been driving one your whole life!"

"Not even Moroi give licenses to infants, Sage," he said wryly.

"Don't dodge this. You know what I mean. You've known how to drive stick for years."

His silence answered for him, telling me I was right, even if his face was hard to read.

"Why?" I demanded. Now I was nearly pleading. Everyone said I was so exceptionally smart, I could string random things together and make remarkable conclusions. But this was beyond me, and I couldn't handle something that made so little sense. "Why would you do that? Why would you act like you didn't know how to drive?"

A million thoughts seemed to cross his mind, none of which he wanted to share. At last, he shook his head in exasperation. "Isn't it obvious, Sage? No, of course it isn't. I did it so I'd have a reason to be around you—one I knew you couldn't refuse."

I was more confused than ever. "But . . . why? Why would you want to do that?"

"Why?" he asked. "Because it was the closest I could get to doing this."

He reached out and pulled me to him, one hand on my waist and the other behind my neck. He tipped my head up and lowered his lips to mine. I closed my eyes and melted as my whole body was consumed in that kiss. I was nothing. I was everything. Chills ran over my skin, and fire burned inside me. His body pressed closer to mine, and I wrapped my arms around his neck. His lips were warmer and softer than anything I could have ever imagined, yet fierce and powerful at the same time. Mine responded hungrily, and I tightened my hold on him. His fingers slid down the back of my neck, tracing its shape, and every place they touched was electric.

But perhaps the best part of all was that I, Sydney Katherine

Sage, guilty of constantly analyzing the world around me, well, I stopped thinking.

And it was glorious.

At least, it was until I started thinking again.

My mind and all its worries and considerations suddenly took over. I pulled away from Adrian, despite my body's protests. I backed up from him, knowing my eyes were terrified and wide. "What . . . what are you doing?"

"I don't know," he said with a grin. He took a step toward me. "But I'm pretty sure you were doing it too."

"No. *No*. Don't get any closer! You can't do that again. Do you understand? We can't ever . . . we shouldn't have . . . oh my God. No. Never again. That was wrong." I put my fingers to my lips, as though I would wipe away what had just happened, but mostly I was reminded again of the sweetness and heat of his mouth against mine. I promptly dropped my hand.

"Wrong? I don't know, Sage. Honestly, that was the most right thing that's happened to me in a while." Nonetheless, he kept his distance.

I shook my head frantically. "How can you say that? You know how it is! There's no . . . well, you know. Humans and vampires can't . . . no. There can't be anything between them. Between us."

"Well, there had to have been at one point," he said, attempting a reasonable tone. "Or there wouldn't be dhampirs today. Besides, what about the Keepers?"

"The Keepers?" I nearly laughed, but no part of this was funny. "The Keepers live in caves and wage campfire battles over possum stew. If you want to go live that life, you're more than welcome to. If you want to live in the civilized world with the rest of us, then *do not* touch me again. And what about Rose? Aren't you madly in love with her?"

Adrian looked way too calm for this situation. "Maybe I was once. But it's been . . . what, nearly three months? And honestly, I haven't thought much about her in a while. Yeah, I'm still hurt and feel kind of used, but . . . really, she's not the one I'm always thinking about anymore. I don't see her face when I go to sleep. I don't wonder about—"

"No!" I backed up even further. "I don't want to hear this. I'm not going to listen to any more."

With a few swift steps, Adrian stood in front of me again. The wall was only a couple inches behind me, and I had nowhere to go. He made no threatening moves, but he did clasp my hands and hold them to his chest while leaning down to me.

"No, you *will* listen. For once, you're going to hear something that doesn't fit into your neat, compartmentalized world of order and logic and reason. Because this isn't reasonable. If you're terrified, believe me—this scares the hell out of me, too. You asked about Rose? I tried to be a better person for her— but it was to impress her, to get her to want me. But when I'm around you, I want to be better because . . . well, because it feels right. Because *I* want to. You make me want to become something greater than myself. I want to excel. You inspire me in every act, every word, every glance. I look at you, and you're like . . . like light made into flesh. I said it on Halloween and meant every word: you are the most beautiful creature I have ever seen walking this earth. And you don't even know it. You have no clue how beautiful you are or how brightly you shine."

I knew I needed to break away, to jerk my hands from his. But I couldn't. Not yet. "Adrian—"

"And I know, Sage," he continued, his eyes filled with fire. "I know how you guys feel about us. I'm not stupid, and believe me, I've tried to get you out of my head. But there isn't enough liquor or art or any other distraction in the world to do it. I had to stop going to Wolfe's because it was too hard being that close to you, even if it was all just pretend fighting. I couldn't stand the touching. It was agonizing because it meant something to me—and I knew it meant nothing to you. I kept telling myself to stay away altogether, and then I'd find excuses . . . like the car . . . anything to be around you again. Hayden was an ass-hole, but at least as long as you were involved with him, I had a reason to keep my distance."

Adrian was still holding my hands, his face eager and pan-icked and desperate as he spilled his heart before me. My own heart was beating uncontrollably, and any number of emotions could have been to blame. He had that distracted, enraptured look . . . the one that he held when spirit seized him and made him ramble. I prayed that's what this was, some spirit-induced fit of insanity. It had to be. Right?

"His name is Brayden," I said at last. Slowly, I was able to quiet my anxiety and gain some control. "And even without him, you have a *million* reasons to keep your distance. You say you know how we feel. But do you? Do you really?" I pulled my hands from his and pointed at my cheek. "Do you know what the golden lily truly means? It's a promise, a vow to a lifestyle and a belief system. You can't throw something like that away. *This* won't let me, even if I wanted to. And truthfully, I don't want to! I believe in what we do."

Adrian regarded me levelly. He didn't try to take my hands again, but he didn't back away either. My hands felt painfully empty without his. "This 'lifestyle' and 'belief system' you're defending have used you and keep using you. They treat you like a piece in a machine, one that's not allowed to think—and you're better than that."

"Some parts of the system are flawed," I admitted. "But the principles are sound, and I believe in them. There's a divide between humans and vampires—between you and me—that can never be breached. We're too different. We're not meant to be . . . like this. Like anything."

"None of us are meant to be or do anything," he said. "We *decide* what we're going to be. You told me once that there are no victims here, that we all have the power to choose what we want."

"Don't try to use my own words against me," I warned.

"Why?" he asked, a slight smile on his lips. "They were damned good ones. You're not a victim. You're not a captive to that lily. You can be what you want. You can choose what you want."

"You're right." I slipped away, finding no resistance from him at all. "And I *don't* choose you. That's what you're missing in all of this."

Adrian stilled. His smile dropped. "I don't believe you."

I scoffed. "Let me guess. Because I kissed you back?" That kiss had made me feel more alive than I had in weeks, and I had a feeling he knew that.

He shook his head. "No. Because there's no one else out there who understands you like I do."

I waited for more. "That's it? You're not going to elaborate on what that means?"

Those green eyes held me. "I don't think I need to."

I had to look away, though I was unsure why. "If you know me so well, then you'll understand why I'm leaving."

"Sydney—"

I moved quickly toward the door. "Goodbye, Adrian."

I hurried toward the door, half-afraid he'd try to hold me again. If he did, I wasn't sure I could leave. But no touch came. No effort at all was made to stop me. It wasn't until I was half-way out on the lawn in front of his building that I dared a peek back. Adrian stood there leaning against the doorframe, watching me with his heart in his eyes. In my chest, my own heart was breaking. On my cheek, the lily reminded me who I was.

I turned from him and walked away, refusing to look back.